PRAISE FOR KIRA BRADY

"Dazzling...thrilling...irresistible..."

— PUBLISHERS WEEKLY STARRED
REVIEW OF HEARTS OF DARKNESS

"If you enjoy uplifting, character-driven romances with mature protagonists, emotional depth and a touch of sport, I'd absolutely recommend this one. It's the perfect feel-good read for anyone who loves stories about second chances and self-discovery."

— BECKA, NETGALLEY REVIEW OF LOVE
AND PICKLEBALL

"Beautifully rendered prose and multidimensional characters who capture readers' hearts."

— PUBLISHERS WEEKLY REVIEW OF
HEARTS OF CHAOS

LOVE AND PICKLEBALL

A SALMON BAY NOVEL

KIRA BRADY

Editing by Susan Barnes

Book Cover Illustration by Kira Brady

Crossword Puzzles by Scott Graham

 Formatted with Vellum

For those who Labour
You are not alone

AUTHOR'S NOTE

Dearest Reader,

Thank you for visiting Salmon Bay, the small town settled by Scandinavians on the shores of Puget Sound, inspired by my hometown. I hope you fall in love with Celeste, Hayden, and their wonderful community as much as I have!

My friend Scott made all the crossword puzzles for Love and Pickleball. The answer keys are available at the end of this book and also on my website, kirabrady.com/crosswords. On each crossword puzzle in the book is a QR code that will allow you to work on the puzzle online.

I love to hear from my readers! Please subscribe to my newsletter for bonus content, deleted scenes, serialized novellas, and updates on the Salmon Bay series. Links to my socials can be found at kirabrady.com/links.

Tack så mycket!

~ Kira

1

CELESTE

The sense of deja vu sours my gut as my eyes lock with the groom's across the crowded church. I'm loath to admit it, but he looks good. Almost as good as he did at his first wedding, and I hate how kind the years have been to him. Strong, broad shoulders, square jaw, and a full head of close-cropped hair threaded with grey—his new bride is getting a handsome silver fox to hang on her arm, and I'm counting my lucky stars that he's her problem now. A pretty package that hides a poisoned core. Good luck to her, and good riddance.

"He's still obsessed with you," Marissa whispers in my ear.

"He's only mad his little doormat escaped. Has to lick his own boots now," I whisper back as I motion to the ruffle-bedecked church and the more than five hundred folks packed into the pews for the wedding of the season. "He replaced me quick enough." The retired marine getting a second chance at love with the younger, beautiful daughter of a local real estate mogul—my ex-mother-in-law keeps telling anyone who will listen that Hallmark is going to come knocking for the inside scoop any day now.

Vomit.

"Only half these people have tried to murder you with their

eyes," Marissa whispers. "Maybe they're softening toward you. Maybe this olive branch wasn't the worst idea."

"Kill 'em with kindness. I just want the gossip to die down so it doesn't affect Ryder and Brody anymore."

Marissa snorts. "They're grown-ups. They can handle it."

"They're college boys."

"Man-children."

"Whatever. They'll always be my babies, and I don't want to embarrass them by being called the 'crazy ex'."

"You have to put yourself first sometimes, girl. Haters gonna hate."

I wish I had her confidence. Marissa has been the peanut butter to my jelly since I moved here with my ex-husband and our teen boys. We settled in the small town of Salmon Bay on the shores of Puget Sound, just across the water from Seattle, when Brett was stationed at the nearby naval base four years ago.

I slouch farther down in the pew, hiding my face behind the ceremony program, where I've hidden this week's crossword from my favorite bagel shop. Crosswords have gotten me through some hard times. There's no room to ruminate when you're solving a nine-letter word for "Hot takes?" or a seven-letter word for "High beams".

(SEXSCENES and RAFTERS, if you were curious.)

The anonymous creator, writing as Lord Lexicon, has gone a little naughty with this week's theme, maybe as a nod to today's event. It isn't every day that we get to witness a whirlwind, rebound, age-gap, gala of epic ostentatiousness.

I like that word. Sixteen letters. How would Lord Lexicon clue it? *Splashy, flashy, Over-The-Top?*

The string quartet that Lander hired for her big day starts playing a classical version of *You Belong with Me* by Taylor Swift, and I wince, because *awkward*. She is welcome to him. Be my guest.

The officiant motions for everyone to stand for the

processional. Marissa and I are in the very last row of chairs, so I get the first peek at the bride as she swans around the corner on her daddy's arm. Her wedding dress is a bold virginal white with lace sleeves that cover her arms to the wrist, but the neckline plunges to almost her bellybutton. With her brunette curls and heart shaped face, Lander is a younger, prettier, peppier version of me.

I'm the one who left. I'm the one who should have ridden into the sunset in my chic divorcee Cadillac; instead, I'm still paralyzed, like one of those zoo animals that can't survive in the wild.

Shake it off, Celeste. Crowd out those memories with *17-Across: What a mailman has?* Ten letters. Words I associate with mailmen: Envelopes. Letters. Shorts in the snow, wind, and hail. The love of dogs? A love-hate relationship with dogs?

Maybe I should come back to this one.

16-Across: Greek god of love. Four letters, and easy, even if being shot by Eros' arrows is sometimes very hard. Just because you fall in lust at first sight doesn't mean personality-wise you're a good fit. Eros should conduct interviews before he starts shooting people.

The bride glides past us, stopping every few steps to pose for another camera. Like a veteran paparazzi, her maid of honor is filming the whole thing for social media.

"I heard everything was donated for promotional placement," Marissa says. "Brett's getting a steal."

"For the low, low price of exposing all your personal business in the gossip column." God, what an awful thought. This last year of having everyone dissect the *Why* of leaving Brett and the *How could I* of leaving Brett has been torture. Former friends speculating on our sex life or lack thereof. Family throwing around accusations with no clue as to what went on behind closed doors. Neighbors and acquaintances suggesting counseling or a vacation together or ginseng as if anything could erase twenty years of slow suffocation.

I watch the procession with the Honorazzi clicking away while Marissa keeps up her whispered commentary on everyone in the audience. She's trying to distract me, and I love her for it.

"Check out Dr. Tanaka's outfit," she whispers. "Do you think she looks more like a grape or an eggplant?"

"I'd say Dr. Plum, in the conservatory, with the wrench."

Marissa snorts.

The dentist is a sweetheart and smart as a whip, but she's married to Brett's BFF, and since I'm due for a cleaning, I need to find a practitioner that doesn't think I deserve a root canal. For twenty years, I sent a Christmas card that showed the perfect family, and everyone bought it, hook, line and sinker. I am a victim of my own success.

Brett always waited until no one was looking to make one of his thousand little cuts.

My ex is managing to keep his eyes firmly on his bride this time, a soft look in his eyes. Nostalgia makes my temple throb. Before kids, before the years isolated overseas, before he started spending more time drinking with his friends than paying attention to me, we'd had something sweet. He was my first love. My first everything. Back then, I'd thought that it would last forever.

Back then, I didn't know the words BOUNDARY, GASLIGHT, and RED FLAG.

The ceremony drags on. Great aunt Charlotte performs a particularly vigorous rendition of *My Heart Will Go On*. Even Lander winces.

I tune back into the program when my boys take the mic to read a poem together. I start to get a little teary-eyed listening to their deep voices talk about love and commitment. At eighteen and twenty, they've grown into the tall, muscled frames they inherited from their dad. I miss them. Not just because they moved to Seattle for college, but I miss their child-selves: their high shrieks of laughter; their little squishy bodies small enough to tuck under my chin; their smiles blinding as they run to show me their latest treasure: a worm on a fall leaf, the perfect Lego ship, a basketball sunk from a foot farther away than last week.

My marriage might have fallen apart, but I would never give up the gift of Ryder and Brody in my life.

Soon it's time to exchange rings and say the vows beneath an arch heavy with bright orange dahlias and soft green leaves. The Honorazzi nudges the officiant out of the way so she can capture the perfect shot to share the pretty promises on social media.

Officiating is the dubious honor of the long-standing principal of Salmon Bay High, Lars Larsson. He's as much town royalty as the mayor, the chief of police, the head judge, and Lander's daddy—all officers in the Sea Lion Lodge, a social club founded by the city's first male citizens that still operates as the city's unofficial political back room—and he's officiated so many weddings that he jokes he should retire from education and make it a full time job.

Principal Larsson clears his throat. I don't think he likes being shooed out of the way by the Honorazzi. "Didn't realize Harry and Catherine were getting royally hitched today. I would have worn my bedazzled tie." Cue appreciative chuckles. He beams, having the attention back his way. "Seriously, though, this is the Salmon Bay love story that many of us have been waiting for since little Miss Lander Lindström came toddling into the world with a pen in one hand and a tiara in the other. For the past twenty-eight years, she's been slaying hearts and splashing her story across the page, and there's no one more deserving of a happily ever after than our own Miss Salmon Bay. And though some of us put money on the head of our student paper marrying our high school quarterback"—I can see Brett's ears flush from my seat in the far back—"we are all pleased that she found such charming and upstanding new blood in our very own Captain America, Captain Brett Knowles."

I grit my teeth at the comparison. If only I'd been married to the sweetest, most steadfast Avenger, Steve Rogers; I'd still be married.

I study the crossword as if it holds the answers to all my problems while the bride starts reciting her vows, which borrow heavily from Taylor Swift. Brett, as expected, reads something bland and scripted. I swear it must be my imagination, but when he gets to "till death do us part", half the attendees turn around in their seats to glare at me.

"Is it me, or is there a chill in the air?" Marissa asks, tongue in cheek.

I duck my head from the judgment. If only they knew—but no, I refuse to make my kids pawns in a cold war between me and Brett. They deserve better. I would endure any discomfort to spare my kids the same childhood I had. Brett demanded I attend this wedding—for appearances, of course—and after half a lifetime of trying to please him, I'm still doing it.

Marissa bites her lip as she studies me, seeing too much. "You want to leave?"

"Not until I get my piece of cake."

"Okay, good. You can do this. Hold your head up high."

I'd love to tell them all to fuck off, but my reputation in this town affects my ability to get clients. I need these rumors about me to fade asap—and for everyone to see that I'm a reliable, mature, trustworthy adult. You'd hire me to sell your aging mother's house and help her find a retirement home that fits her, right?

Marissa leans in and whispers in my ear. "Maybe tug your neckline down a bit and flaunt what you got. Don't look now, but Harrison is checking you out."

We both cast glances across the aisle at the sleek haired, middle-aged man who's Marissa's main competition in Salmon Bay real estate. He smirks as he gives us both a once over. He's been too happy to smear my name with potential clients, as he's a golfing friend of Brett's and heard a lot of insider shit from Brett's perspective. None of it true.

"See?" Marissa whispers. "Harrison is here picking up clients. We should too. Work waits for no woman." I elbow her in the side, and she laughs. I love Marissa, but she's pushy when she's got an idea.

"Are you sure he's here for the clients and not Lander's single friends?"

"Two birds, one stone."

"Gross."

"Pig," Marissa agrees.

"Drew wouldn't approve."

"Drew would punch him in the face if he knew he was looking this direction."

"Shoot me now," I murmur to Marissa. "There are twelve-thousand other people in Salmon Bay. Do we really need to care what these five-hundred think of me?"

"Are you kidding? Where's the popcorn?"

Marissa's not heartless, but she's been cooped up with her sick toddler twins for the last week, and she's enjoying getting out of the house far too much. Her husband Drew caught their radioactive preschool germs. He's home with them watching back-to-back Bluey episodes and mainlining juice. He keeps texting her for updates, because she's right, this is the event to see and be seen and will fuel the small-town gossip mill until Salmon Bay SummerFest in August.

I like Drew; he's madly in love with Marissa and he's an involved dad. He treats her like a queen, which is exactly what she deserves.

Don't I deserve that too?

The principal finally announces Mr. and Mrs. Brett Knowles, and they dance back down the aisle to Taytay's *Lover* as the bridesmaids wrapped in burnt orange taffeta release nets full of orange butterflies.

Marissa and I escape before the bugs get tangled in our hair, and we make our way over to the reception hall next door—a beautiful boat yard turned event space right on the bay. On one side of the building, decks flare off at different levels like fungi growing from a nurse log. The large picture windows and elegant French doors catch the fading sunlight from behind the mountains. The sky is clear, the sea lions are barking, and I can't wait to eat my cake and get the hell out of here.

Mature Professions
by Lord Lexicon

 **Miel Bagels** - *Sweeten your day the Montréal way*

ACROSS

1 What a baker has?
10 Singer-songwriter Bareilles
14 Bulletins
16 Greek god of love
17 What a mailman has?
18 Gremlins and Hornets of automotive history
19 Really old letters?
20 In jeopardy
22 Wise old goat in "Animal Farm"

DOWN

1 Jibber-jabber
2 Dictator Amin portrayed by Forest Whitaker
3 Mean number: Abbr.
4 Spoonful
5 LAX carry-on container
6 Bowling in Bergamo
7 "Family Matters" nerd
8 "The Marvels" director DaCosta
9 Sonic creator

ACROSS

25 Words before "coming" or "so good"
26 Egret cousin
27 What a grocer has?
30 Website where you'll see stars
31 Style
32 Many crossword clues... and a hint to 1-,17-,27-,41-,54-, and 63-Across
39 Billionaire with a book club
40 Duchamp's art movement
41 What a diver has?
45 Piquant
46 Novel
47 Dr. Jekyll's counterpart
49 Traditional handmade toy
52 Lingus beginning
53 Stick in the mud, say
54 What a farmer has?
60 Member
61 "Why didn't I think of that?!"
62 Mexican dough?
63 What a butcher has?

DOWN

10 Northwest airport named for two nearby cities
11 Fleet of warships
12 "Dick Clark's New Year's ___ Eve"
13 Strengths
15 Stand-up routine
21 Soft luster
22 It's out of office
23 Pakistan's official language
24 Stark in "Game of Thrones"
26 Tucked away
27 Grannies
28 Narrow strip of land: Abbr.
29 Brain disease for many ex-NFL players: Abbr.
31 Word
33 "Ha ha, yeah right", in a text
34 Clean Air Act govt. org.
35 Critical WWII event
36 Shoe part above the sole
37 Barely triumph over
38 "So, here's a thought..."
41 Stretch
42 "Seinfeld" role
43 River in the Middle East
44 Give up ownership of
45 Beat the wheat, in a way
47 First lady before Jackie
48 Romulus' twin
50 "Come on!" in online shorthand
51 Shakespearean "happily"
55 Vacay, initially
56 DMV-provided ID
57 Vehicular prefix to meter
58 IBM competitor
59 Hefty Cinch ending

2

CELESTE

Marissa and I find the quietest, darkest nook we can in the back where we can hide from Harrison and the mob of Knowles family members who still haven't given me a piece of their mind. The servers make their rounds, eventually reaching us. Guests wander in and out, looking for empty bistro tables. Marissa points out everyone she knows from a safe distance as we stuff our faces on goat cheese canapés and avocado bruschetta.

"Quick!" Marissa says, stepping to the left to block my view. "Drop your head and look busy."

I don't bother checking which relative is hunting me down; I hide my face behind the crossword sheet, as if being busy ever stopped anyone from interrupting me. I can barely make out the letters with only the dim fairy lights twinkling overhead.

25-Across: Words before 'coming' or 'so good'. Five letters, and it sounds dirty, so now I need brain bleach to recover from imagining the newlyweds *in flagrante delicto.*

Thanks bunches, Lord Lexicon.

"Phew, she's gone." Marissa's shoulders relax. "Didn't realize this date was bodyguard duty."

"Who was it?"

"Your evil ex-mother-in-law."

I shudder. "You're a lifesaver."

"I am, aren't I?" She swipes another glass of prosecco from a passing waiter and taps my plastic flute of sparkling apple juice that I stole from the kids' table. "*Skål!*" She downs half the glass. "You know what you need?"

"What?"

"To get back out there. Get on Tinder or iEros or whatever the kids are using these days."

I roll my eyes. "I'm so far from a kid that's laughable. What would I do with a younger guy?"

"Anything you want." She winks lasciviously. "Seriously though, men are losing stamina right as women are coming into their sexual empowerment. You should find a guy who can keep up with you."

I snort. "Right. Keep up? I've only ever been with Brett."

"And that's exactly why you should play the field, Ceecee. You need to practice. Lots and lots of practice."

"Sounds exhausting." My cheeks heat. If I was an extrovert like Marissa, maybe I'd be able to play the field, live a little, but I'm not. I'm painfully, awkwardly, shy.

"I'm not saying jump back into matrimony; hell, no. Dating around teaches you more about what you like and what you don't like than sticking with one dick for twenty years. And it will give you some self-confidence. You put yourself out there, and you'll see what a catch you really are. Not every guy is like Brett—he's a special breed."

I keep my eyes glued to the crossword as Marissa goes on with her motivational speech.

"'What a baker has?'" I read. "'What a grocer has?' Diver... Farmer...Butcher...?" They're the themed clues, now what am I missing? Something that makes them not safe for work, maybe, given the spiciness of the other clues.

Marissa ignores me like I'm ignoring her well-meaning, but insane, advice. "Give me your phone."

I hand it over like the gullible friend I am, and Marissa unlocks it with my face before navigating to the app store. "What are you doing?"

"I'm helping you, honey."

I scoff. "I don't need to date. I have two hands and extra batteries."

"Get it, girl, but you still need a warm body every once in a while. Your little fledglings have flown the nest; your cage door is open; be free."

"Easy for you to say." It's not that I don't want to get out there; I don't know where to start. I'm free of Brett, but even more constrained by society. Forty is over the hill, and I'm not getting any younger. And what if I end up in the same situation? What if I fall for another charmer who turns critical, demanding, and demeaning as soon as he's got me ensnared in his web? Can I even trust myself to recognize the liars and cheats?

"Don't you have a decent headshot somewhere?" Marissa holds up my phone and snaps a photo of me that probably looks like the police took it.

"Give me that!" I try to grab the phone, but she swings out of my reach.

"You'll thank me for this. I'm doing all the boring work of setting up profiles for you. You're welcome." She smiles down at the picture she took. Thank God I let her do my hair and makeup for this thing. "When Drew and I met, you know I wasn't looking to settle down. I'd been on dating apps for a few years, and I learned a lot about myself from all the duds before I found him. You have to start somewhere. Make a list of the things you love to do. Or the things you remember loving before Brett. Didn't you play a sport in high school?"

"Tennis," I say glumly.

"Good! You and I are going to make a date to go play tennis."

"I'm not sure I even remember how."

"Thou doth protest too much." She keeps typing but won't let me see what's she's filling out for the "looking for" category. "Anyway, I'm sure you'll kick my ass. It's time to clear out those cobwebs. Climb back in the saddle and ride that cowboy into the sunset."

A tall man walking behind her overhears part of our conversation on his way to the empty bistro table next to us. His snort is loud, startling her out of her enthusiastic, but embarrassing speech. Now I know how my boys feel when I start preaching, "wrap it before you tap it".

"What do we have here?" Marissa asks, drumming her long blue nails on the table as she gives our eavesdropper a skeptical once-over.

He's alone. He pulls out a high back stool at the bistro table and throws the jacket of his powder blue tuxedo over the back. He's either in disguise or he walked off the set of a 70s porno: giant mustache, sideburns, a shaggy mop of mahogany hair, and aviator sunglasses that hide his eyes. The ruffles down the front of his white dress shirt distract from his wide shoulders and tall, lean frame. His sleeves are rolled up, revealing muscular forearms lightly dusted with hair. He manages to look both hot and ridiculous.

Ridiculously hot?

No, I can barely see his face.

I will die if he reports back my sexcapades, or lack thereof, to Brett.

"You're killing me, Rissa," I whisper-hiss. "Let's pretend you didn't say anything, and he didn't hear anything, before I die of shame." I hide behind my crossword sheet as soon as he looks over at us.

"Wasn't he sitting on the bride's side during the ceremony?" Marissa says. "I don't recognize him. That thing on his upper lip is wild. You don't think that'll catch on, do you? Drew is always threatening to grow a mustache for Movember. But the

thought of him going down on me with a caterpillar on his lip
—no. Just no."

I glance at 'Stache Guy again, feeling my cheeks burn. "Not
so loud, Rissa."

"Girl, if people are trying that hard to listen in, they deserve
to hear what I think about them."

I rub the growing ache between my eyebrows. Marissa is
having fun with the bubbly. Sometimes I miss that feeling of
losing my inhibitions for an hour or two, never more so than
here at my ex's wedding. My sobriety was one of the things that
annoyed Brett most; he felt like my choice was a direct criticism
of how much he drank.

"Don't you wish Drew was here to ask you to dance?" I ask,
trying to distract her.

"That's a great idea, Ceecee."

"What do you—"

"Hey, Tom Selleck! I've got a proposition for you!"

"Shush you!" I hiss, but it's too late. Mr. 'Stache looks
around to see who she's talking to, but there's no one else
hiding in the back of the event space. He points to his chest and
raises one thick eyebrow. How can he see anything with those
aviators on? It's so dark.

"Yeah, you," Marissa confirms. Dragging me behind her, she
marches right up to him. "You single?"

He clears his throat, his mustache trembling. It's big. More
David Crosby than Tom Selleck. "Why?" His voice is a
pleasantly deep bass that vibrates through me.

"My hot, very single friend and I need a third opinion."

I tug on my arm, but Marissa refuses to let go.

He smirks, and even though I can only see half his face, I
feel a ghost of appreciation flutter in my belly. *Oh, no.* I'm going
to put laxatives in her coffee. Or crayons in her dryer. Maybe I'll
gift a giant carton of glitter to her toddlers and tell them to go
nuts all over her designer-decorated white-on-white house.

Glitter is the herpes of craft supplies: easy to catch, impossible to get rid of.

Marissa leans in. "What's sexier—an innocent young woman or an experienced older femme fatale?"

"Rissa!" I hiss and this time succeed in jerking myself free. I cross my arms over my chest like I can protect myself from this train wreck. Did I say she was my best friend? Ex-best friend.

'Stache guy raises his aviators, exposing rich hazel eyes framed with unfairly long lashes. He slowly drags his gaze from my high heels, up my bare legs and over the navy shift dress that is far too tight on my curves, to the curls slipping out of my half updo. I feel every inch of his gaze like a phantom touch. His slow wicked smile puts everything he's not saying into words, and I shiver. When he drops his aviators back down, I take my first real breath.

"I like a woman who knows what she wants," he says. "Who can ask for it."

Welp. That's not me; I wish it was.

"You should ask her to dance," Marissa tells the guy.

I'm going to strangle her. "What happened to the dating apps?" I hiss desperately.

"This is better," Marissa said. "Just like my toddlers' swim class—we're throwing you in the deep end and you'll magically learn to float. Exposure therapy or some shit. Relax. It's just a dance."

'Stache guy glances between the two of us before straightening and holding out his hand to me. His fingers are long with square nails. "I'll take that bet."

"You don't have to—"

"*Mais, oui*," he murmurs in that exaggerated, growly voice. "*Voulez-vous danser avec moi ce soir*?" He waggles his eyebrows, and I can't help but laugh.

"You're enjoying this, aren't you?" I ask.

"It was dull until this moment, *ma petite chou*." He leads

me away from a smirking Marissa toward the dance floor on the main level.

My palms sweat with the feeling like everyone is watching me, but as I look around, most people are busy chatting and ignoring their kids running amuck. "What did you call me?"

"Little cabbage." He winks at me as we weave between tables.

I duck my head as we pass tables full of Brett's friends. They used to be ours, but somehow Brett got them in the divorce. Dr. Tanaka is there with her husband. She gives me a half smile. I swallow and nod back.

My luck runs out before we make it to the dance floor.

"Celeste. You have some nerve showing your face here." My former mother-in-law steps out of the shadows like a dark villain. She's short and likes to dress only in black and white, which she claims is thinning. I think it makes her look like the Penguin, but what do I know? Her thick glasses and the hoity-toity angle of her nose don't help. She's not mean, per se, but she thinks her darling boy walks on water. Never once did she side with me, even though she got a front row seat to the wreckage on occasion. We agree on one thing—Brody and Ryder are awesome.

I owe it to my boys to maintain a civil relationship with their father and his family. I am responsible for my own actions; I will not tell her to fuck off. I will maintain my emotional balance; I will not tell her to fuck off. I take a deep breath. "Deb, you're looking lovely this evening."

There. Good job, self. That was almost believable. Nailed it.

Her shoulders relax a hair, but she's still got that bulldog expression I know so well. "You left the best thing to ever happen to you. You'd be nothing without my son. You think anyone else will put up with your lazy ass?"

I will not tell her to fuck off. I take another deep breath through my nose and squeeze my fingers together.

"Deb," I say with a calm I don't feel, "Brett asked me to

come to support the boys. He wanted the boys to be able to build a healthy relationship with his new wife without feeling like they're betraying their mom, which is totally healthy." If completely out of character for Brett. He wanted me to come to make himself look good to everyone else. He doesn't know how to feel inside without me to push around. I just have to remember that his feelings are not my burden anymore, unless he uses his relationship with our sons to bully me into doing what he wants.

We both know I would do anything for Ryder and Brody, even stay in a loveless marriage for years to give my boys a stable home.

Deb puffs herself up like a hen fluffing her feathers. "You were never good enough for him—"

My hands start to shake. I blink back the burn at the corners of my eyes. "I know you're disappointed how it turned out, but Brett and I parted amicably and are committed to supporting Brody and Ryder without any rancor. I hope, as their grandmother, that you'll do the same."

Deb winds up, but Mustachio the Magnificent cuts her off. "*Madam, vous êtes une garce du plus haut niveau. Veuillez vous faire foutre.*"

Deb's eyebrows pinch together, like she knows she was just insulted even if neither of us speaks French. He doesn't give her time to recover, before he's pulling me away and down a level to the packed dance floor, where we escape into the crowd.

"What did you say to her?" I ask him.

"I told her to fuck off. Pardon my French."

I can't hold in my giggle as he pulls me against his firm chest. "No one has ever told her to shut up before."

He leans down so he can speak in my ear over the music. "I don't know why not."

"She's going to find something on you now," I warn him. "That woman holds grudges until the grave."

He tosses his hair back from his face and strikes a superman pose with one fist resting on his trim hip. "Saving the world, one Momzilla at a time."

I grin at his foolishness. It's hard to spiral when he's cracking jokes. His strength is different than I'm used to—protective instead of domineering. His body is hard planes and a narrow waist, square jaw and an Adam's apple that is strangely appealing. There's something about him that makes me feel lighter. He doesn't care what people think of him in this 70's tux. He doesn't have a problem telling the mother-of-the-groom to fuck off.

Get ahold of yourself, woman. I can't just throw myself at the first guy who shows me a modicum of kindness.

"So how do you know Lander?" I shout over the music.

"You really want to talk about the bride?"

"I want to make sure you're not related to her or anything."

He chuckles and leads me in circles, making sure to dodge toddlers chasing the light images projected on the checkered tiles. Little girls in giant puffy taffeta skirts are twirling beneath the flashing strobes until they fall. "Fortunately, no. Not even on the guest list."

"You snuck in?"

"A late addition—a plus one. My sister is off schmoozing with work colleagues. Merci for rescuing me from ennui by filling my dance card." The edge of his mouth kicks up.

Ennui—that's a good word. He's not just a hot body; he's smart too.

My shoulders tense as he pulls me into his embrace. He's at least a head taller than me, and I have to crane my neck and look up at that ridiculous mustache to talk to him, straining to be heard over the music. He's still hiding behind the aviators, even though it's dark. He might be anybody, but as long as he's not buddy-buddy with the bride or groom, he'll do. Right?

God. How pathetic do I sound? I haven't flirted with a boy since sophomore year of high school. "I can't remember the last time I did this."

"What, dance?" He pulls one of my hands to his back and holds the other up and to the side like we're going to waltz. "'The tango is a vertical expression of a horizontal desire.'"

"Fred Astaire?"

"Jennifer Lopez."

I snort-laugh, and he grins down at me. Slowly my body relaxes as he leads me in circles around the dance floor, dodging older couples shimmying awkwardly. His feet move like magic and following him is easy. "How did you learn to dance?"

"Sisters."

"Really?"

"Yup. If they needed a partner, a fall guy, a guinea pig, a crash-test dummy, you name it—they had me."

"Do you still talk to them? Or have you cut them off and sent them the therapy bill?"

He chuckles. "I talk to them every day." He lifts my left hand and twirls me under his arm. I'm not sure how we're ballroom dancing to a modern pop song, but somehow, he's making it work. I'd probably be more self-conscious if we were shuffling foot to foot in a slow circle around some of the other couples. Somehow, he's making this fun. He moves smoothly, like an athlete, and I can feel the muscles of his back contract beneath my hand. He's slimmer than my ex, but taller. Brett's definition of leading was yanking my arm and dragging me after him, and his rhythm resembled a walrus on land trying to Gangnam Style.

Damn it. When will I stop comparing every guy to my ex-husband? I don't want him back. I wish he and Lander the best, truly I do, because he needs someone to take care of him, and I'm glad it isn't me anymore.

"Do you have siblings?" 'Stache Guy asks.

I shake my head. "Only child."

"Lucky you."

"Not really. Family is what you make it."

Off to the side I catch sight of the two people I love most in the world, Brody and Ryder, standing with their heads together watching us. They've got their arms crossed and identical scowls on their faces. I hope they're not going to cause a scene. But what if they do? Am I embarrassing them? I should go sit back down.

'Stache Guy leans down to speak directly in my ear, and his minty breath is warm on the sensitive skin of my neck. I shiver. "Something wrong?"

"No. No, just—you want to go somewhere more...?"

"Private?"

"Yeah, I feel like a goldfish with everyone watching me like this."

"*Mais, non*, my little Angelfish. You are too fin-tastic to be a common goldfish."

I roll my eyes, but my cheeks are warm. His joking banter is so over-the-top it jars me out of my self-conscious spiral. He's not angry that I suggested we do something else. He's not taking it personally or scowling down at me, squeezing the bones of my hands in a silent show of displeasure.

"Too much?" He leads me off the floor right past my sons, and I give them stern mom eyes, hoping they behave. The last thing I need is a scene. Brett will claim I'm seeking attention.

Ryder gives me a thumbs up, but Brody reserves judgement, as usual. He's the older brother, serious as a brick wall. We're still figuring out this adult dynamic. Some things were easier to navigate when they were children and thought I hung the moon. I think Brody is worried about me living alone. He doesn't realize how much easier it is for me—I only have to clean up after myself. No dirty dishes, potato chip wrappers, or abandoned laundry that I'm expected to whisk away like a damn house elf. I'm not constantly on edge as I wait for the emotional twister to sweep through my home, decimating my heart in its wake.

"Come, *ma chère mademoiselle*." 'Stache Guy chuckles that

cliché *hon-hon-hon* like Maurice Chevalier, and I can't help but laugh.

Brett used to tell me to shush-up and look pretty, that I was bad at peopling so I should let him handle it. He could charm the panties off a nun, but he was only sincere when he was correcting my faults.

I'm not sold on the powder blue tux or facial hair, but the way 'Stache Guy is carefully drawing me out, like he knows I'm feeling vulnerable in this place, pulls me toward him. My gut feels light, like champagne bubbles are rising in my core.

Taking the leap, I adopt an even worse French accent and tell him, "Oh, Lumiere, you are so dramatic!" and he grins like I handed him a Golden Ticket. I could get used to the mustache if it came with that look.

Winding our way through the crowd, we finally make our way to the back of the event space where the crowd thins out. The music is muted back here, the hallway lights dimmed to set the mood. A red velvet chaise hides behind a couple of giant potted palms. He takes a moment to appreciate the plants; the red crown shaft sets off the full green leaves. "Lipstick Palm. Excellent."

I don't know plants, but I appreciate them as a screen to hide from the constant filming and photographing that every guest in attendance is posting online. The hashtag #Brander is already trending on the town's social media.

It's exhausting to always be on display, and though Marissa pretends everything is positive marketing for her real estate business, my skin is thin as the ice that covers Lake Dibble in the winter.

He pulls me to the chaise, but before we can sit, my luck runs out. I catch sight of Deb pushing through the crowd toward us like an angry rhino, and I know we won't escape as easily this time.

My erstwhile protector spots her too and immediately pulls me farther down the hallway toward a door marked, "Staff

Only." He opens the door to find another hallway lit with ugly fluorescent lights.

"Where are we going?" I whisper as he helps me through it with a warm, guiding hand on my lower back.

"A linen closet, but of course, Plumette." He turns to give me a wink as he guides me gently down the hall. My dress separates his skin from mine, but the heat of his palm soaks to my sacrum, waking up long neglected nerve endings.

Sneaking around makes me feel like a teenager again. Daring and irresponsible. It's not me—but I like it.

"Are you a rebel, Mustachio?" I whisper.

"For a good cause." He raises one thick eyebrow at me with a mischievous smirk beneath that ridiculous mustache, and I'm caught up in the play. Dopamine is surging through my brain, and I feel buoyant and awake like I haven't felt in years. Fireflies spark in my belly. I let him lead me down the dim hallway, opening doors at random until he finds what he's looking for.

He gives me a dramatic flourish. "Here it is, Mademoiselle. Welcome."

"Will I find the library of my dreams behind this door?"

"I don't gift libraries until the second date."

My smile feels so natural. "But of course," I say in my best French accent.

"*Mais, oui!*" He follows me into the broom cupboard and shuts the door, shutting out the light.

My breathing hitches. The only light filters in from beneath the door.

"If I only had a candlestick," he mutters. His big body takes up most of the space, caging me against the shelves of toilet paper and cleaning products, but he doesn't make a move.

"Are you okay?"

"I didn't, ah, plot farther than this." His deep voice holds an edge of vulnerability that makes me relax. He's not seducing women in closets regularly. He's as out of his element as I am.

It makes me bold. I lick my lips. "Kiss me?"

He clears his throat and settles, as if my request helped him over whatever hurdles his brain had thrown up. Maybe it's all part of the act, but I don't think so. We fumble in the dark until his big hands find my face and hold me still. I clutch the back of his shirt. His breath is minty, and in this small space I catch the scent of his cologne—something dark and herbal. A flash of pleasure strikes across my lower belly, and I have to squeeze my thighs together against the ache. His body is warm and solid against mine. We're two lost souls reaching for each other in the dark.

When was the last time I felt this alive? Young and dumb and so very carefree? Pushing boundaries just because we can.

He lowers his head and his lips touch mine, teasing gently at the creases of my smile, peppering light caresses across the seam, before his teeth bite oh so softly on my lower lip and my mouth falls open in surprise. A shiver rolls down my spine and I let out a soft moan. That's all the permission he needs to surge forward in the kiss to end all kisses. His fingers tangle in my hair. His tongue explores my mouth. His body presses me against the shelf, and he's surprisingly muscular beneath the suit.

Untucking his dress shirt from his slacks, I slip my fingers beneath the hem and find smooth, hard skin. His body radiates heat, and I lean into it, wanting him to light all the dusty corners of my soul.

I wish I could see his expression, but the energy feels illicit in the dark, safer, somehow. What if he doesn't like what he sees? The dark folds around us, hiding my soft curves from view. He can't see how much his touch sets me on fire.

I trace his spine with one hand, while my other sinks lower to cup his muscular ass, and he moans, as if he's as turned on as I am. I pull his hips forward, giving him permission to grind into me, and we both pant as his hardness meets the softness of my belly. He lifts me easily and, dress shucked up around my waist, he settles into the V of my thighs, fitting perfectly against me. His touch, his taste, his smell—it's too much, too searing on my sensitive skin.

His mustache tickles. I laugh and pull away.

"What?"

"It's so..."

"Amazing? Sexy? Scintillating?"

I laugh again and pull myself up by his shoulders to kiss him again. I don't like the mustache, but it keeps things light. What am I even doing here? This isn't me. But maybe it could be. I want it to be. I like this version of myself—wild and carefree.

He trails kisses over my cheekbone to my ear, then breathes on the sensitive skin of my neck, where his mustache sweeps like a prickly broom.

"Maybe you should be the feather duster," I say.

His chuckle vibrates against my nipples, and I can feel them pebble against the thin fabric of my bodice. "Oh, Lumiere!" he says in falsetto, and I laugh at his antics. "What a big candlestick you have!"

"The better to light you up with, *ma chérie*," I respond in as deep a voice as I can, which sounds so dumb, but I can feel his grin against my neck. His teeth close lightly over my pulse. Quickly the playfulness turns to something hotter, and I can't help grinding my pelvis against his, chasing that flame.

3

HAYDEN

My Plumette moans, and I bite my own lip to keep myself focused. I'm unwrapping her reservations, one by one. Stripping her of society's expectations. I can tell she feels safe in the dark. We've got that in common.

I run my hands over her voluptuous ass and squeeze. She likes that, so I do it again, grinding her against my erection until I have to bite my tongue to keep from coming.

Think of line edits. Think of feeding Seymour those nasty flies. Don't come yet. Don't ruin this.

When she rubs her hand against the front of my suit pants, all my self-control goes out the window. I lower her to her feet and drop to my knees. There's no ego booster like making a woman come on my tongue.

"What...?" she whispers, but I put her bunched up skirt in her hands and squeeze gently to tell her to hold on tight, and then I bury my face between her legs. She's wearing a full pair of panties that squeeze everything from her bellybutton down to the lower crease of her ass cheeks. Practical. Some might call them granny panties, but I prefer to think about them like a present that I take my time slowly unwrapping.

I bite the waistband and tug them down with my teeth. It's

less smooth than it sounds like it's going to be when I read about it in books. Actually, it's hella awkward.

She giggles as I give up and have to use my fingers to get the other leg off. Finally, the frustrating things reach her ankles, and I help her step out of them. Her wedges have two-inch heels, and I remember noticing her toenails are painted black. I like it. A little rebellion when everything else about her outfit is bland as wallpaper. Suitable for hiding in plain sight but not worthy of her pretty face.

I wonder how kinky she is under that shyness. I'd love to learn what makes her tick. Maybe tie her up and call her my bad girl. Or hand her a feathered flogger and ask her to call me a good boy. See how wet she gets. For science.

"Hold still," I admonish her as her thighs shake. Nerves, or excitement? Having met her ex, I bet he's not the sort of guy to care much about her pleasure.

Her curls are trimmed neatly, and she smells divine, feminine musk and coconut body wash. I dig the natural look —a mature woman has hair down there.

"You don't have to—"

"Baby, I've been dreaming of this. Don't take it away from me." I part her folds with my tongue and lick her taint to clit. Her knees bend, but I catch her beneath the ass and push her against the wall. Her soft moans and shaky limbs make me feel like a king. This woman deserves to be worshiped.

I start counting how many little breathy moans she makes. The writer part of my brain is trying to take notes to distract certain parts of me from turning this from a romcom into a tragedy. I'm enjoying her taste too much. Enjoying the power of making her feel good. I want to record her little sounds to listen to while I jack off or write love scenes. She's exquisite. Thick thighs and juicy hips. I wish there was enough light in here to watch her face when she comes.

But not today. I have to be satisfied with her audible pleasure. Her muscles wind tighter, and I keep up a steady pressure until she shatters. Her legs give out, and she falls sideways, knocking over brooms and mops. A handle whacks me in the head before toppling a stack of toilet paper. I can't decide if making-out-in-the-supply-closet is hot because it's forbidden or awkward because there's no room to move. But it's funny, and I'm not bored anymore. Far from it.

I'm ready to see where the rest of this unexpected night takes us, when Plumette slams her elbow into a shelf and swears. I chuckle against her soft belly and hold her hips steady. The dark covers some of the awkwardness, but we're still like two teenagers fumbling in the dark. "Definitely smoother in the movies."

She hums something that sounds like agreement as she pulls her hands from my shoulders.

I run my thumbs down the crease between her pelvis and thigh. I don't want to stop touching her. Her skin is soft and warm, and she smells like musk and sin. All my blood has rushed to my groin, leaving me lightheaded. "Let's find somewhere with more light."

I plant a teasing kiss on her bellybutton, just as she shoves my shoulders.

"I have to go," she squeaks out. "S-sorry!" She pushes past me so fast, I get whiplash, and she struggles to find the doorknob in the dark. A little whimper leaves her throat. What is going on? Did I totally misread this situation?

Fuck.

My boner immediately deflates, and I give her as much space as I can in between the cleaning supplies.

The door opens, and she falls out. I can see her illuminated in the dim hallway lighting—her hair a mess, her lips plump, her dress wrinkled. She glances back at me with eyes so wide she looks like a frightened doe.

"Sorry," she breathes out, and the door slams behind her.

What the hell just happened? Was it the outfit? The mustache?

Fuck. What went wrong?

I screw my eyelids closed and try to preserve every moment in my mind. How she tasted. How she smelled. Her moans. Her luscious curves. Fuck me. I need to write this down—the wedding was a bust for plot help, but eating out this girl in a closet was right out of my darkest fantasies.

Two strangers at a ball, one night of passion, finding out they're on opposite sides of the war...I can see it now, the passion that was missing from my manuscript. Susan has been hounding me for months to turn it in, but it was missing the spark.

Hook up with some girls, she said, like it's that simple. In a small town, it's not easy to find a one-night-stand who doesn't remember when the high school football team filled your locker with fish guts.

I stand on shaky legs and grab onto a broom to catch my balance, feeling wrecked.

Just when I thought things were going well, she bolted. I brush it off. I'm not going to let it bother me. I'm not. Her loss.

But, wow.

I better tell my sister that I'm bailing on this circus, because I need to get home and put this shit down on paper while it's still fresh. Cinderella doesn't want to see where this chemistry could go? I'm not going to waste time begging someone to stay.

I rub my hands down my face and wish I could have a do-over.

All I can smell and taste is her—and that last sight of her dilated pupils and kiss-swollen lips is going to haunt my dreams.

4

CELESTE

So POWERFUL, I FREAK OUT. So out of character, I run. I can't breathe with the adrenaline coursing through me. Can't think with the languid post-sex haze fogging up my brain.

Who is this woman who gets off with strange men in closets?

Not me.

I don't even say goodbye or thank you, like my mama taught me. I stumble out of the closet, panty-less and disheveled, and haul ass down the hallway, back to the party. Slipping out of the "Staff Only" door, I bump into the last person on earth I want to see: Captain Brett Knowles in the flesh.

"Celeste?" His disapproving eyes sear me head to toe and back up again, like a full-body scanner at the airport, and I swear he can see everything. The post-coital hair. The wetness dripping down my thighs. The staccato of my heart and heavy breathing like I've just sprinted a mile. His lips pull back from his teeth, and I cringe back against the door.

None of the therapy skills I've learned can prepare me for facing my ex with my muscles still shaking and my nerve endings lit up like the fourth of July.

"Celeste," he repeats. Lower. Angrier. "Are you drunk? You're a mess."

My body freezes like a deer in the headlights—well trained bitch that she is. I'm almost hyperventilating. This is bad. So bad. How will he lash out when we're surrounded by witnesses?

The thought cuts some of strings holding me still, and I peel myself away from the door. I don't answer to him anymore. I don't have to explain myself. My nervous system is slow to upload this realization and bring it online, and still my reactions are so ingrained, it takes everything I have to lift my chin and look Brett in the eyes. "Congratulations, Brett. I wish you and Lander the best."

And then I tear my gaze away and hurry past him like he might be capable of shooting laser beams out of his eyes and into my retreating back.

"Oh, my god," I mutter to myself, caught in a panic spiral. "Oh my god!"

The party is a mad whirl as I struggle to get back to Marissa and our table, where I left my purse. I grab it and my phone, tell Marissa my plan, and head to the coat check. Goddess that she is, she offers to grab me a piece of cake to go, and then we meet at my car. Night blankets the town, and everything smells like salt brine and seaweed. We peel out of the parking lot like Bonnie and Clyde.

"Honey," Marissa coos with a devious smirk to her lips. "Bribery time—spill the goods. No gossip, no cake."

"You wouldn't." I don't want to tell her about the closet. It feels too fragile to put into words. My body is still shaking. I'm like a helium balloon that's escaped its anchor to float to the stratosphere—far beyond the worries of the real world. If I could, I'd stay there stretched across the milky way and never come back down.

Which is terrifying.

I have a job. Responsibilities. Kids...or young adults, but

they still need me on occasion. I can't throw caution to the wind and chase my pleasure on the morning tide.

Who even is this person? Who makes out at her ex-husband's wedding, while her ex-mother-in-law and probably kids watched her sneak away with some stranger in a powder blue tux and porn stache? Not me. What was I thinking?

But I liked it. I liked it a lot. I wish I could be this person—reckless and giving no fucks. But I can't find my way free of this respectable, boring, middle-aged lady that everyone out there expects me to be. Even before Brett made me afraid to speak my mind, my parents trained me to be on my best behavior. I'm a, *yessir*, people pleaser through and through.

But God. How I wish I could be that woman. I wish I could be vibrantly alive.

Mustachio broke me out of my shell, but I couldn't possibly face him in the light. My whole body is still flushed. I'm still dripping. I want to scream it to the rooftops and also hide away forever. Right now, the memory is perfect and precious and all mine.

If I expose it to the light of day, it'll tarnish. I can't tell Marissa.

"I can see that look in your eye, missy. I'm happy eating two cakes. Greta makes a mean lemon chiffon."

"Just give me a minute, okay?" I'm still breathing fast as I pull onto the main road along the canal. My orgasm high is fading in the harsh reality that I might have set off the gossip train for good. If Brett finds out, he'll retaliate. He still has the power to make my life difficult. "What did I do? Marissa—what if somebody finds out? I'm so screwed."

"I don't know. What did you do? Did you get screwed? OMG don't leave me in suspense!"

"You were right."

"Wait! Wait. Hold that thought." She digs in her purse for her phone, pulls it out, and opens voice memo. "Okay, go. Say that again."

"You. Were. Right."

"Yes!" she crows. "Yes! Okay, details. About what?"

I glance over at Marissa, and she looks so earnest, I can't lie to her. She's been my ride or die since we met. She was the one I called when I finally drummed up the courage to leave. She helped me sneak out of Brett's house and serve him divorce papers a year ago. Marissa had thought of everything. She'd taken me in, no judgment, and helped me get back on my feet. She's full on invested in my journey to wholeness, and I couldn't ask for a better sister-of-my-heart.

"You were right," I tell her honestly. "I needed that boost of self-confidence. Needed a push to get out of my comfort zone—"

"Whooop! How was he? Tell me it was amazing! Tell me he had a big dick to back up all that rizz. Tell me he's got enough game to make up for that ginormous mustache."

I laugh in spite of nerves. "Better not let Drew hear you drooling over my conquests. He'll think you're jealous."

"I wouldn't give up my baby daddy or his fun stick for anything, and he knows it."

I splutter. "I'm not calling it that."

"But I can hear all the drama through you like my real life Fifty Shades of Grey—"

"Nope. Not into that emotionally stunted Peter Pan nonsense. Been there, done that."

"Right, girl." Marissa pats my arm. "Let's take notes for your dating profile—looking for, man, not a boy—"

"Right."

"—with a big dick—"

"Rissa!"

"—and a healthy, regular sized ego, who likes..." she pauses the dictation and chews on her lower lip as she studies me. "What did you love to do before Brett?"

I try to remember. That was a lifetime ago. The sleepy little town passes by, little craftsman bungalows and spartan modern walk ups clustered around the main high school, where a giant sign proclaiming, "Go Sockeye!" is lit up like a marquee in Times Square. People take their local athletics seriously here. I spent the last four years volunteering in that brick building— copying worksheets for teachers, shelving books at the library, selling raffle tickets to raise money for the music program.

My hobbies were actually my boys' hobbies. I still see the echoes of their childhood as I drive by and myself cheering them on from the sidelines. There's the field where they spent hours throwing the frisbee. There's the greenhouse where they learned enough botany to help me in the garden at home. It was a relief when Brody's trumpet career gave up the ghost, but I miss Ryder practicing his Vocal Jazz parts in the shower.

I stop at a red light next to the tennis courts. Before Brett, that's where I spent my time. I used to love it. I used to dream of a college scholarship to play. Maybe if I'd been a little better, I might have ended up far away from Brett and his pretty little prison. But then I wouldn't have my boys. I wouldn't give them up for anything, not even my own happiness.

"Let's see, before Brett, I liked to listen to the Backstreet Boys? Um, watch Buffy the Vampire Slayer? Pretty sure none of the things I did as a teenager are going to light me up like they used to. I went to school and tried to stay out of my parents' way. I spent a lot of time at my friends' houses, but I don't talk to any of them anymore." I try to remember what I was passionate about back then. "Maybe you could put tennis in my dating profile."

"Great idea," Marissa says. "Let's find you a tennis player with big quads and a penchant to smack it. You and I need to set a date to play so you can brush up. I'll let you kick my ass as long as you promise to give me the details. All the details."

"It's been so long—"

"Exactly like getting back on a horse."

"I think you mean bicycle."

"Wasn't making out with Mustachalicious as easy as getting

back in the saddle? Between the sun-Gs and the hair, I couldn't see his face, but his body was F-I-N-E."

I blush and shake my head, unable to deny it. My thighs squeeze together with remembered pleasure.

"I see that look, hun. You can't fool me."

"It was good," I admit.

She dog-whistles and shimmies a piece of cake next to me. "Details for deliciousness."

"He defended me from Deb."

"Swoon! He's a white knight. What did the old dragon do this time?"

"'Bout what you'd expect."

"And you told her to shut her judgmental pie hole, right?"

"I said Brett and I were working to coparent amicably, and if she wanted to have a relationship with Brody and Ryder, she better get on board."

"Yes!" she gasps.

"Well, something like that," I mutter. That's what I wanted to say at least. I've been swallowing down my words for so long, it's going to take some work to let them flow freely again. What do I have to lose? There's no one to get angry with me if I step out of line anymore. No one to throw things or storm off. No one to give me the silent treatment for perceived offenses. I get to go home to my peaceful tiny apartment and be safe from other people's emotional tantrums.

"So, then what happened? He had his sword out already and decided to show you it could be used for more than slaying dragons?"

"You're so dirty. What would our clients say?"

"Old people are kinky as fuck. Don't be a prude. Come on, Celeste, get to the good stuff."

I turn down her street, where streetlights illuminate the pink cherry blossoms scattered over cars and sidewalks. Most of the little fishing cabins in this neighborhood have been taken down and replaced with modern townhomes, but Marissa lives in a century old farmhouse built by one of the original settlers of Salmon Bay. The adjoining orchard is now a city park and notorious pea patch, where community members fight over plots and potatoes. The only source of news more scandalous is the Sea Lion Lodge. Gotta love small towns.

Marissa takes a big bite of my cake and gives a porn-worthy moan. "End of the line: too bad you haven't finished oversharing yet."

I pull in front of the beautiful house that Marissa and Drew have lovingly restored. I'm jealous of what they have, of course, but if any person deserves a happily-ever-after, it's my BFF.

"If it was so good, why did you rush out of there before tasting this orgasmic goodness?" She takes a big bite of cake and moans around the plastic fork.

"I got scared. It was...I just got scared, okay? My kids were in the main room. What would they think?"

"They'd think, good job mom! Get it!"

I cough. "No."

"Come on. Brody and Ryder are adults. They want you to be happy. Don't use them as your excuse."

"Pretty sure they don't want to think about their mom getting some in a broom closet at their dad's wedding."

"Get it, girl!" Marissa laughs. She takes another bite of cake. "You know I love you." Marissa drops her usual teasing to tell it to me straight, punctuating her seriousness by handing me the second cake. "I support you one hundred percent. You did the right thing leaving Brett. You did the right thing protecting your boys from the stress of your marriage—of not parentifying them like your parents did to you. You should be proud of yourself and proud of the emotionally mature young men you raised. But they want you to be happy—you can move on and be yourself."

"I know, I —it's hard. I've been so focused on them for the past twenty years, I don't even know who I am."

"Don't keep living in the dark because you're afraid of other people's judgement. You can find who you used to be, or you can reinvent who you want to be. Just know that you have people who love you and will be here for you every step of the way. You have to love yourself before you can truly love another person."

"And you have to kiss a lot of frogs before you can find a prince?"

"Damn straight." She gives me a big hug, careful not to squish the cake between us. "And when you're ready to talk, I'm here to listen."

"Thanks, Rissa. I love you too."

"Good. Now, plan time. We're going to brainstorm your profile and get this ball rolling."

"Speaking of balls, let's play tennis. I promise I'll go easy on you."

"Yes! Next weekend? Parks and Rec has a ton of courts. I'll make reservations. You still have a racket?"

"No." All that stuff had been ditched back when the military moved us the first time. We only kept essentials. A few baby mementoes. Some photo albums. No point keeping my racket when I didn't have time for hobbies once I became a mom. At least that's what Brett said, and back then, I didn't have enough backbone to stand up to him.

"No worries. We can stop by Salmon Bay Sporting Goods on our way to the courts. I'll pick you up. Saturday? Ten am?"

"Perfect."

Marissa climbs out of the car and saunters up the steps to the wide wrap-around front porch outfitted with two wicker rocking chairs and two mini toddler-sized ones. My heart gives a squeeze, but I know better than most how easy it is to project the image of the perfect family. Still, I know Marissa wouldn't stand for having a partner be as uninvolved and neglectful as Brett. She found a good one. I see the living room curtain flutter, and there's Drew with a big dopy smile for his wife. Their dog watches through the window beside him, and I swear

I can see the hearts in both their eyes as Marissa comes through the front door, the queen returning to her castle.

Returning home to my small second floor walkup apartment at Svensk Hamn, I unlock the door and brace for the conflicting emotions that waft out like baking bread with an undercurrent of mold. The sink leaks and the walls are paper thin, but it's cozy and mine. I don't have to share it with anyone. I'm safe here. Emotionally, at least.

Physically, the sixties-style building is, like me, in need of a little TLC. The grumpy landlord won't fix anything if he can get away with it. Thank the good lord for home repair videos on YouTube. For now, the rent is what I can afford.

It was my only option when I moved out of the house I shared with Brett, and that screwed me over in the divorce. My settlement was much less than if I had stayed in our house, and now I'm stuck here until I get our old house fixed up and sold.

Brett doesn't waste an opportunity to tell me I can't do it. For our whole marriage, he controlled the finances. He made the money; he chose how to spend it. Any questions I had about budgeting, saving, or purchases was met with anger. "My" money was spent on groceries and the kids. "His" money was spent on sports and beer and outings with friends. Restricting my access to finances, withholding assets, and threatening to sue to restructure our divorce settlement is playbook economic abuse—and I only know that after six months of post-divorce therapy.

The lawyer Marissa helped me find worked the home sale into our settlement. I have eighteen months to fix it up, stage it, and sell it, then split the profits with Brett. I'm so close, and I can't let anything distract me.

Inside, I dump my purse and kick off my wedges, sighing at the feel of the red and orange shag carpet between my toes. The lime green refrigerator buzzes happily. If I were a more fanciful person, I might imagine it's welcoming me home.

I should get a dog.

I'm not alone—I'm independent. This is the first home I've had that's all mine.

I text Brody and Ryder to let me know when they get home safely so I won't worry, and Ryder sends me a thumbs up while Brody sends me a selfie from the photo booth of himself and all the bridesmaids. They're all wearing props—feather boas, tiaras, and mustaches.

My belly swoops with memory. I'm going to have to rethink my stance on mustaches. I'm sure I'll never see Mustachio the Magnificent again—no matter how much my lady bits are desperate for a repeat—my heart is too battered to trust again. Once is enough. It has to be.

5

HAYDEN

AFTER A TWENTY-FOUR HOUR writing marathon where I opened a vein and wrung every millisecond of my closet escapades onto the blank page, and an exhausted slumber where I dreamed about brooms, I arrived bright and early to the pickleball courts at Lake Dibble. The city park encompasses the three-mile lake and a couple acres of forest where my nephews' cross country team practices. Tennis courts built in several spots have all been taken over by pickleball. It's the official sport of Washington State and the unofficial sport of Salmon Bay, even more popular than unicycling, which every third grader learns in gym class and never abandons.

I slam the ball down, and it makes a satisfying crack as it hits right at Russell's feet. He's an old family friend of my parents, and after my dad split, he stayed. He visits my mom every week and checks in with us kids. He's one of the best people. Reliable. Non-judgmental. Doesn't insist on filling silences with small talk. Doesn't scare off easily.

No matter the weather, he wears a white polo shirt, khaki pants with a braided leather belt that his kid made in Home Ec a billion years ago, and red court shoes that look like something from Ronald McDonald's closet. He keeps his hair shaved close to his head now that the frosted curls are thinning and there's a stoop to his wide shoulders that didn't used to be there, but he's still fast when he wants to be. If I let down my guard, he'll pickle me eleven to zero with no remorse.

He misses the return and gives me a wary side eye. "You're feeling extra energetic this morning, youngster. Got something to share?"

I chuckle and drop my gaze to the ground. The pickleball courts are crisscrossed with fading tennis lines. The lines for pickleball are taped in some places, some of which survived the winter; whoever got to the court early this morning drew in the missing lines with chalk. I should follow up with Dr. Fisher about repainting, before some yahoo gets it into their head to do it themselves. Like me.

The courts are busy like they are any day it isn't raining, and one of the players waiting on the sideline for their turn collects the pickleball and throws it back to Russell. He tosses the ball to me, and I return to the serve line.

"Sorry, Russ." I serve more gently this time, and he returns it to my partner, who swings and misses.

My partner for this game, Harold, is closer to my own age than most of the retirees who play during the workday—but he still has about twenty-five years on me. He's a thin guy who usually wears a sweater vest and newsboy cap, especially when he's busking with his accordion in front of the supermarket on the weekends, but for pickleball he carefully switches into a yellow bucket hat and safety glasses.

All his buddies in the Sea Lion Lodge All-Star Band play pickleball here on Tuesdays and Fridays, and most also volunteer as Vikings for the annual Salmon Bay SummerFest that raises funds for the children's hospital. Harold's role is "cabin boy" which means he mostly hangs out in the rigging, flexing the bellows, and serenading onlookers with the *Immigrant Song* by Led Zeppelin. Not sure real Vikings ever played the accordion, but our marauders march to the beat of their own reindeer rawhides.

Harold misses the ball again and looks sheepish. "Not enough coffee, I guess. Sorry Hayden."

"No worries," I tell him. "You're doing fine." And he is. Not everyone has a flexible schedule and can play five times a week. Anyone can learn to play, from eight to eighty, and since the pickle gods are fickle, newbies have a fighting chance against experienced old timers. That's what makes it fun—the unpredictability and camaraderie with complete strangers.

"Hayden?" Russell asks after I collect and toss him the ball. "How's the block?"

Russ is the only one who knows I'm a writer. It's something I've kept close to the chest ever since gramps told me to my face that when he finds "those dirty books" at the church rummage sale, he throws them right in the trash.

My breakout novel had just won Best Historical Romance of the year.

And then I made the mistake of telling my girlfriend Jordyn about my hobby-turned-career, and...well...that went up shit creek. People get weird when they find out you write "bodice rippers" under a female pen name. Weird and judgy. In middle school well-meaning adults would tell me that it gets better; turns out, bullies come in all ages.

Took me a long time to start writing again after being doxed online. New pen name, and my new fans have no idea that it's really a dude penning their epic love stories. It has to stay that way. The town gossip has mostly died out. They see me as that marginally employed, former fat kid who still lives with his mother, but I know the truth. My family and best friend know the truth. Everyone else can go fuck themselves.

Russell is basically family. He's my biggest fan.

"Pretty good, actually," I tell Russell. "Found that spark that was missing."

He waggles his eyebrows. "Inspired by real life?"

"Maybe," I say with a grin as I tap the ball over the net—a perfect dink that lands right in the kitchen, the no-volley zone on either side of the net. Tennis players are all about slamming the ball, but pickleball requires a softer hand. Accuracy and patience matter more than brute strength. The first team to earn eleven points wins, but you have to win by at least two points.

Our game is progressing quickly, and when Russell's partner lobs the ball my way, I jump and smack it down for a satisfying point. We usually give ourselves a handicap when facing less skilled opponents, so I'm using my non-dominant hand for this game.

"'Bout time!" Russell grins.

Celeste, Celeste, a rose by any other name....

After observing the ex-mother-in-law attack my beautiful mystery woman, it was pretty easy to figure out Cinderella is the ex of the groom and her name is Celeste Knowles. The experience is tattooed on the inside my brain. Her taste. Her smell. The little noises she made as she came undone. It was the hottest experience of my life, but it crashed and burned so fast, I had whiplash and a decidedly uncomfortable deja-vu.

Did I do something wrong? She came so hard, but she didn't stick around to find out anything about me after the orgasmic high. I feel almost used.

I've been there before; women dig the athletic bod—thanks, Coach!—but the real me is a nerd, not a billionaire, alphahole, football star. For fun on Friday nights, I sometimes flip through the dictionary for good words while I binge BBC dramas and talk to my pet pitcher plant like he's a real person. Cinderella never got a chance to see that super-cool side of me.

Maybe she actually hated the mustache?

Not sure why I thought my mystery woman would be different. My gut was...wrong. Again. Better I found out upfront than after I've let my sensitive squishy heart get *ideas*.

Russell and I take turns hitting gentle but tricky shots to

each other, sometimes going for a good drop shot or a lob barely out of reach. When hitting to the greener player, I try for extra accurate shots that increase my difficulty level while still being playable by my opponent. I save my spin shots for Russell. No one likes to be pickled—losing a game zero to eleven—and I don't find it fun to grind a weaker opponent into the dust. I want them to feel welcomed, like I did when I first started.

For this game, my brain is giving me an extra handicap by replaying Cinderella's taste on my tongue. I miss the ball more often than I should.

Harold steps in to save me from a short ball that rolls along the top of the net before falling over to my side. He manages to dink it back out of the kitchen to score.

"Great save!" I tell him, coming across as a patronizing nut job because I forgot for a moment that I was playing with adults and not coaching my nephews' track practice.

Russell laughs at me like he always does when I use my coaching voice. "Earth to Hayden," he jokes before returning the ball with a spin shot to me, which I miss.

As we finish off the match, my team barely scraping by with a win, Russell motions me over to the sideline where paddles are arranged in neat little piles of four by ability—beginner to expert—which is indicated by the handle orientation. There are three stacks in line before us, and the line moves quickly at this time of day. We'll get an open court soon.

It's a public court, but Russell can't help himself but make upgrades to it. He built the court sweeper—kind of like a Zamboni for leaves—and the hangers on the fence for jackets and bags. His background in carpentry has come in handy. He takes advantage of my grandpa's woodshop in the garage beneath my apartment and always stops by the main house to visit with mom.

"So," he begins. "Who is she?"

I lean against the cyclone fence and cross my arms over my chest. "Someone I'll never see again."

"Why not?"

"She's a beautiful woman who's way out of my league, and she ran from me like Cinderella at the stroke of midnight."

"Leaving a shoe?"

"Heh. No, leaving without giving me her name or number." I put a hand dramatically on my chest. "Leaving my ego in tatters."

"Ah. Bummer."

"What's wrong, Holstrom? You striking out with the ladies?" Warren, the self-appointed king of the court, sidles up and sticks his and his partner's paddles in my stack, bringing our number to four. He's a beefy, retired guy who used to be in sales and still likes the thrill of getting people to listen to him talk. His stiff gait could benefit from some yoga, but he can slam the ball with the best of them. He's been instrumental in getting amateur tournaments up and running, even though he's mostly an idea guy. I think his wife does all the paperwork. "Maybe you need some advice on how to snag a doll like my Fran." He pulls his wife to his side, and she clucks her tongue at him in exasperation.

"He needs a woman's opinion if he's trying to catch a lady," Francesca says, "not a big lug like you, Tonito."

"Aw, you love me."

"You know I do." Francesca is a small-boned woman with a serious love of chartreuse—yellow-green track suit, yellow-green fanny pack, yellow-green nails and eyeshadow. Her grey hair holds a large skunk stripe in chartreuse that perfectly matches her glasses. She looks like a stiff wind might blow her over, but she hits one mean topspin. "Now, Querido, tell Tia all your troubles."

She's not actually related to any of us, but we all call her Auntie. You forgot your paddle? Tia Francesca's got a spare for you. Hungry? Tia brought biscochitos she made fresh this morning. Ran out of water? Tia stuffed her trunk with La

Croix from Costco. She'll get you one. Must stay hydrated, niños.

"Nothing's wrong, Tia. Actually, everything's great." I'd give my favorite pickleball paddle for another chance with Celeste, but she already rejected me once. I gave up begging to be liked a long time ago. Silver lining—I wrote through the night pouring all my disappointment and unfulfilled yearning into my current manuscript, and it's the best stuff I've written in months. I'm almost ready to send my book back to my editor —this time she can't return it for lack of sexual tension.

"You've got her name, right?" Russell cuts into my woolgathering. "You can Google her."

"Sure, but what's the point?"

"Her loss."

"Exactly." Rejection hurts, but this isn't my first rodeo. I run my hands over my clean-shaven face and appreciate finally ridding myself of that itchy facial hair. My friends gave me a lot of shit for it, but I'd lost Sam's bet, fair and square. At least now I can breathe again. I couldn't help but notice Celeste's reaction to the 'Stache. It's kind of funny in hindsight, but if I could have made a better first impression, maybe she wouldn't have been so hot to run off?

"Maybe you came on too strong?" Warren suggests with a smirk. "Try asking her out for coffee. Or have kids these days forgotten how to have basic conversations?"

"Be nice!" Tia scolds. "Hayden, you are so handsome. You'll make some lucky girl very happy one day." She pats my cheek like my grandma used to do, and I give her a wink. Addy says the older ladies on the court are going to give me a big head, and she's not wrong.

"We're up," Russell points out. We all grab our paddles out of the stack and find the open court. Outdoor play is invigorating—fresh air, but also faster paced. During the nine months it rains in the Pacific Northwest, we take over the indoor basketball courts at the community center with our pickle-mania. The indoor ball is slightly softer, with fewer and bigger holes allowing for more control on the wood floor.

The courts aren't too busy mid-morning like this, but after work they get packed. In the summer, making reservations for the courts is essential. Warren takes up a collection to reserve all tennis courts for drop-in pickleball, and when the weather is nice, sometimes fifty people are playing or waiting on the sidelines, watching the action. Dogs sleep under the benches and someone usually brings a portable speaker to counterpoint the loud off-beat rhythm of the balls.

Russell and I are playing doubles against Warren and Francesca. It's an evenly matched game, and I use my dominant hand to hit a soft topspin drop shot to Warren's backhand foot, which he misses. Russell serves again, and Tia Fran returns it with a brutal slice that sneaks down the alley between me and Russ. We give each other flat looks, both slightly embarrassed.

Serve moves to me, as the second server, and I hit it low and hard to Tia. She returns it to my far corner, and I let it bounce as required before I backhand it back down the middle. Warren returns the ball lightly to the far edge of our kitchen, forcing Russell to hustle to save the ball before it goes out of bounds. He manages to return the ball over the net, but his whole side is open.

I'm supposed to cover for him. I know that. But my head is not in the game. I'm watching it play out while my brain is back in that broom closet, and Tia takes advantage of my distraction to spin the ball right into the wide-open space between me and Russell. I'm caught with my metaphorical pants down, and Russell shoots me a flat look that says I should go sit on the sidelines if I'm just going to watch the ball fly past me.

The serve moves to their team, Warren first.

"You gotta get out more," Russell tells me as we wait for Warren to get in position. "Get out in the world and out of your own head. You ever tried online dating? Even Bob found his lady on iEros."

"What am I going to say, Russ? 'Lives over mom's garage with his carnivorous plant collection. Enjoys talking to himself and staring at the wall. Messy, drama-prone people need not apply'?"

Russell gives me a wry look and then the ball is in play—our conversation paused while we dink and drive—until the ball goes out of bounds and we have a moment to catch our breath while a grumbling Warren trots to fetch it. "If you need help workshopping that idea, I might know a writer."

"Funny."

Serve moves to Tia, and we're all concentrating too hard to talk for a while. She's got a fast serve and pushes the tempo of the game. It's not leisurely—I'm sweating.

Next time there's a pause in game, Tia motions to me with her paddle. "That reminds me, niño, I brought you a snake plant. A neighbor put it out with the trash—can you imagine? Don't worry, Tia rescued it for you. I knew you'd like it."

"Thanks, Tia," I say as Russell snorts softly. Somehow, I became known as the Plant Doctor. In a world of brown thumbs, my reputation precedes me, and I've been the chagrined recipient of hundreds of houseplants, some abandoned, some gifted, some that need a little TLC before they join that great rain forest in the sky. I've also been forced to dedicate space to what is affectionately called the Lothlórien Spa and Resort, where plants go when their owners are on vacation.

Not that I asked for that role, mind you. I can't seem to say no.

"My neighbor, she is very pretty. Single. Maybe you want her number to ask her about her plant?"

I shake my head but grin. I have so many people trying to set me up; I could have a whole harem by now. But after getting burned a few dozen times, I'm a lot pickier about who I take home. Dating someone's niece or sweetheart neighbor sounds good until things go south, and I'm stuck facing down the disappointment of whichever do-gooder set me up. Addy likes to tease me that I think plants are better than people. They're not much for cuddling, but they never tell me to leave D&D to the kids. Noelle, my Christmas cactus, doesn't get jealous about the flies Seymour, my pitcher plant, gulps down for his monthly meal. She's happy with her sunny spot on the windowsill and a soak of water every other Tuesday.

"Maybe instead of a girlfriend, you should start small, like get a fish," Warren suggests.

"A beta fish," Russell says.

My wry grin softens as I remember my beautiful little angelfish from the wedding. She was nervous, but so responsive. Maybe Warren is right—I came on too strong, too fast. It's a small town, and there are plenty of places to "accidentally" run into Celeste. Do I want to try again? A do-over? Slow it down...*way* down?

Having her reject me a second time would really set me on my heels, but I've built up thick skin and the tenacity of a blackberry vine since Jordyn and the internet trolls flayed me alive. It won't kill me.

She just seemed so perfect—beautiful, smart, witty, sweet. Could I live with myself if she's the one and I let her get away? I didn't let Jordyn kill my writing dream. I shouldn't let one setback keep me from being with the woman of my dreams, not when I believe whole-heartedly in HAPPILY EVER AFTER.

I've got one trick up my sleeve—Celeste likes crosswords. I might know a guy who could put in a good word for me. I just need a second chance.

6

CELESTE

The little craftsman bungalow where my newest client lives has seen better days. The grey paint is peeling, and the windows are the original single panes that let wind and rain right through the cracks. The bones are good, as Marissa would say. She's the real estate agent who will list this baby as soon as the owner finds a suitable retirement home to move to. My job is playing tour guide.

I park on the street and approach the cracked front stairs that are bookended by large blue ceramic planters overflowing with spring flowers. Someone loves to garden. Flashy purple irises lord over trailing white lobelia. I'd kill to have a bit of space to plant tomatoes and basil—it's what I've missed most after moving out of Brett's house—but at the moment all I have is a single Chinese juniper in a planter next to the door of my little apartment.

"You here to work?" a scratchy voice with a thick Swedish accent takes me by surprise. "Oh, don't stop on my account. I'm not in any hurry."

"Frida!" another voice hisses.

I adjust my neutral mask and come up the stairs, to the front yard where I can see two women sitting in willow rocking chairs on the front porch. The older one is wearing a baby blue midriff top and cutoff jean short, even though she's closer to eighty than eighteen. Her cloud of white curls is cut into a cute bob. An unlit cigarette hangs from long nails that sparkle with gold glitter polish, garish against the white cancer stick.

The other woman is younger, around my age. Her blond hair is pulled tightly back against her scalp, and her smile is brittle. "Celeste Knowles?" she asks.

"That's me," I say, thinking I should change my last name back now that there's a new Mrs. Knowles. But what do you call yourself when you've had your husband's last name for half your life? Maybe I should pick something completely new. Celeste...Saratoga, or something fanciful like that.

"I'm Emme, Frida's daughter-in-law."

"Nice to meet you." I shake her hand and turn to the older woman. "Frida Bergstrom? Your flowers are beautiful."

"*Tack*," Frida thanks me in Swedish. She mouths her cig as she studies me for a long moment. I try not to fidget—I'm used to being found lacking—but then she grins. "You garden?"

"I used to. I just put my name down for a plot at the pea patch actually," I tell her. "I live in an apartment, so..." I shrug. "No dirt to dig in."

"I thought real estate agents were loaded," Emme murmurs.

"The housing boom has been good to everyone in the industry," I say politely, "but I'm relatively new here. I'm studying for my Real Estate license while I apprentice under Marissa."

"*Ja*. Dat's why you got stuck with de old lady," Frida says. "Da bad job."

I scoff. "I'm the Queen of the Carpool, actually. This is the easy job—I help people find the right spot for the next phase of their life. I get to listen to good stories and eat a lot of dessert. What's not to love?"

"*Ja*, Carpool Queen." Frida stands and tucks her cigarette into her breast pocket. "Let's get dis over with then."

"Frida, you promised to take this seriously." Emme tucks her hands under her armpits. Her jaw is tight.

"Get de old witch in the home. You get rich off dis place, eh?"

My stomach sinks. I guess this assignment is going to be a tough one. Marissa's boutique firm specializes in helping older people with their real estate investments. She hired me to tour retirement centers with her clients who are putting their homes up for sale because they need the next level of care. The hard assignments are the ones where I'm driving around someone who isn't ready for that next phase. Sometimes they had a bad fall or medical scare that means they can't live alone anymore. Sometimes their adult children are forcing them to move.

It's heart breaking to hear these stories, and I always call up Brody or Ryder afterwards and make sure they know how much I love them. I can only hope I set enough money aside to cover me through retirement, especially after Brett tried to take it all in the divorce. I don't want to rely on the kindness of strangers or put my boys in the no-win position of taking care of me. I can't rely on anyone but myself.

"Frida—" Emme starts.

"Oh, *tyst*, girl. You're getting what you're after."

Emme puts her hands on her hips and shakes her head. She addresses me, searching my face to see if I'm going to take her side. "How does this work? Frida promised to give this a chance. She can't take care of this house anymore, and she can't be trusted to manage her finances on her own."

Frida scoffs.

I need to step in before these two start yelling at each other. Frida doesn't want my chauffeur services. Noted. "No worries! We're only going to take a look at three and see if anything looks interesting. Usually, my clients like to get a tour and try the dining hall. The food is the biggest sell."

"How much does dis cost?" Frida asks.

"You pay nothing," I assure her. "I'll keep driving you

around until you find something you like. No pressure. We won't see more than three per day. If you find something that interests you, we can take all the time you need to make sure it's a good fit."

Emme exchanges a long look with Frida, her eyebrow raised.

"*Ja*, fine. I go for dessert."

"Of course," I say. "Cheesecake is usually a favorite at these places. You like cheesecake?"

"Am I alive? *Ja, visst*."

I take a deep breath. I can work with that. The retirement home pays me a finder's fee when a new resident decides on their establishment, and I'm also salaried with Marissa.

I help Frida into the passenger seat of my car. Emme gives Frida an awkward pat on the shoulder before shutting the door, and we're off. Frida smells like Chanel no 9. She stares out the window at her retreating home. I don't think she's one of the ones who chose to move.

"How long have you lived in Salmon Bay?" I ask to fill the silence.

"You care?"

"I wouldn't ask if I didn't. I want to get to know you so I can help you find the best fit."

She glances back at me. "I moved when I was twenty from Sweden, to be with my brother and his family. Town was too small den. People too backwater. I wanted de lights, you know? I was young."

"So, you left?"

She grins then. "Hopped a train east and left the church ladies praying for my immortal soul."

"Wow. Oh, to be a fly on the wall for that adventure."

She settles into the seat with a big smile on her face, and I know I've found an in with her. Everyone wants someone to listen. Everyone has stories to tell. She watches the houses pass by and points out the most memorable places. Every few blocks we pass another Lutheran church, because the Nordic immigrants who settled Salmon Bay each wanted to worship in their own language— Swedish, Norwegian, Danish, Finnish, and Icelandic. The feuds of the original residents shaped the urban fabric of the town, even though few immigrant Scandinavians are left now. She's one of the old guard, and she doesn't have any interest in sunsetting her flag. Her son is making her.

I can relate to the feeling like I've been sidelined in my own life, and my heart hurts for her. I think that's why this job calls to me, even though it's not exactly what I dreamed of doing. Whatever place they're in, they deserve to be active participants. They deserve someone who will listen to them and help them find the best fit.

"How long did you stay away?" I ask her.

"Not long enough. Came back for my brother's funeral. Cancer."

"I'm sorry to hear that."

"Pfft. Long time ago. Met his friend at the funeral and decided to stay. Handsome and strong. He was a fisherman, *ja*? I wasn't going to be a fishwife. Not in my worst dreams."

I turn onto the main street through Salmon Bay, lined with bakeries and a three-screen movie theater. The ice cream parlor is full of pinball machines. The old Carnegie library building is slowly being reclaimed by the earth, but at one time it was a beautiful temple of books. "And did something happen with this handsome and strong stranger?"

Frida cuts me a sly look. "You tell me something, Carpool Queen. Tell me something no one else knows."

I laugh awkwardly. "Like?"

She stares me down until I crumble. I've got a crazy story— maybe only one, but it was a doozy.

"Okay," I say and take a deep breath. "I-I went to my ex-husband's wedding last weekend and made out with a stranger in a storage closet."

Her smile widens. "Now dat's something, little one. How was it?"

"Embarrassing. Awkward."

"No good. No. You have a hot stranger in a broom closet—you cannot leave it like dat. What did you do? Did he fuck all da starch out of you?"

I splutter as my hands tighten on the wheel. "No!"

"No." She sighs. "No good."

I huff out a laugh. "Sorry to disappoint. It was the raciest thing I've ever done."

"When I was your age, I was a secretary in New York. It was de eighties." Frida shrugs. "Big shoulder pads and big hair. Drinks after work, flowing booze. I loved it. My boss called me into his office during lunch and bent me over his big desk—"

"Frida!" I clear my throat. "You don't have to finish that sentence."

"But I want to. Part of your job, *ja*? You need to listen to my talk." She bends in and clutches my arm, a spark in her eye. "I'm old now but used to be full of piss and vinegar. I don't want to die in an old home surrounded by strangers. But dese young people? Pfft. I know my boy resents me. He tinks I abandoned him."

"Did you?"

"*Ja*. Maybe. But I said I was sorry, *ja*? I can't change de past, and I'm not dead yet. It's not too late for him to forgive me. It's not."

"Frida, I'm not qualified for family therapy, but you're right, I can listen. If you don't want to do this, we can talk to Marissa—"

"No! No good. My boy and dat troll won dis round." She stares out the window as we approach Hygge House, the first stop on our tour.

"Let's give this a chance," I say. "Maybe the cheesecake will be worth it."

"Better be *some cheesecake*."

I pull up in front of Hygge House and park. The blue-grey siding on the older building is weather worn, but the plantings along the sidewalk are tidy. Frida eyes it skeptically as we approach. It probably wouldn't matter if it was the Fairmont Hotel, she'd find fault in something. Who can blame her? This isn't her choice.

By the time we've finished our cheesecake, Frida and I have become fast friends. She's managed to coax out more stories of my marriage than I ever thought I'd share with a complete stranger, like how this is my first real job outside the home. Brett never wanted me to work—which only meant I worked full time inside the home with no paycheck, no vacation, and no appreciation. I found it hard to rejoin the workforce when I first set out on my own. Brett tied up the money as long as he could, because that's how he'd always controlled me. He made the money; he made the decisions for our family. I felt like I was sleepwalking through life. My boys were everything, but my own needs were simply ignored.

Frida tells me she's glad she never married exactly for that reason—my story is utterly common. Her own path was unconventional and hard in its own way, but at least it was hers. I wish I had even a fraction of her chutzpah.

"I need a smoke," she tells me after we finish touring the second retirement center. This one is across the street from Lake Dibble, which locals refer to as Lake Dribble for its modest start as a swampy pond, even though landscapers have terraformed and dammed the outlet to turn it into our most appealing urban park. Spring paints the park in a multitude of greens and blossom pink. Runners circumnavigate the lake on the paved trail, dodging dogs on leashes and little kids running from their strollers. A small group of bird watchers coo delightedly as they watch the resident bald eagle nesting pair perch at the top of a giant cedar tree on the bank.

I follow Frida to a bench where we can people watch both the path and the tennis courts. The courts are crowded with pickleball players and noisy with the thwack of plastic balls off wooden paddles. So much louder than tennis.

"You play dis sport?" she asks as she shakes her box of cigarettes and pulls one out.

"Maybe once or twice in gym class. I used to play tennis."

"You miss it?"

"Yeah, I do." I don't see any tennis players on the courts right now. Pickleball has taken over like an ant infestation, and there's a line of players waiting for their turn.

"Dis is the hot young ting," she says. "You should play."

"I don't know how—"

"Pfft. Be brave, little one. You don't get unlimited chances to find someting—or someone—to love." She lights her cigarette and takes a drag. "You should be with dese young people, not old ladies like me. It is good, this ting. Many people play. You find a new story for yourself. Don't waste more time on dat patetic ex of yours."

I want to tell her I'm trying, but is it enough? Am I doing enough to break ties with my past? Am I taking risks and saying yes and being open to opportunities the universe is sending my way? Or am I still running scared?

Mustachio can answer that one. Being vulnerable is terrifying.

"My sister in Florida says all the hot young men are playing dis, but it started here. Bainbridge Island. You just show up. Say yes."

I let out a breath of amusement. She's so pushy, but in an endearing way. At least she seems like she means well when she's trying to manipulate me to do what she wants. "I was going to try tennis again. I used to love it, before..."

"No." Frida lets out a slow exhale and studies me with sparkling blue eyes the color of the winter sky.

"No?"

"I see vat you want to do. De old Celeste is dead; do not

resurrect her. Who is da new Celeste? Who is she really? Not who some man told her to be."

I have to bite my tongue, because Frida is my client. She feels pushed into a box, and I can't help but feel like she's shoving that on me. "I've never been as wild as you."

"But you can: just say 'Yes' more. *Ja*? Make some big mistakes. That will teach you who you are faster than anyting." She waggles her eyebrows and nods her head to some male pickleball players who are aggressively hitting the ball.

"I'm too old for that," I laugh. "I'm a mom."

"And single. Live a little, den come back and tell Frida about it. Humor an old lady? You are never too old to learn new tricks," she says, and then she spends the next half hour telling me about all the sex tips she learned after she got her second wind at forty. I'm beet red by the time we get back in the car to drive to the last retirement home, and that tickles Frida to no end. She's a troublemaker, that one. "What do da kids say? Be a freak between de sheets, *ja*?"

I cover my face with a groan. "Please tell me you like one of these places we saw today, because I don't think I can survive another day with you." It's been endlessly entertaining, but I'm going to die of mortification if I have to drive her around again.

"No worries, little one, dere is still time for Mama Frida to tell you all she knows."

"That's what I'm afraid of."

7

HAYDEN

Saturday morning, I'm leaning against the cyclone fencing of the pickleball court while I wait for my turn, trying to soak up more warm rays of sun. The air has a crisp bite to it, but after an hour of play, I'm as warm as I'm gonna get. Around me, the weekend crowd is buzzing. Some of the regulars, like Russell and Warren, are still here, but we've been joined by the tech jocks and jills who commute into Seattle during the week. We don't get too many assholes who need to dominate on the court rather than have fun. Whenever I see a guy like that, I take pleasure in showing them exactly how it feels to be picked on.

My T-shirt is plastered to my back with sweat, and I lift the bottom hem to wipe my brow. When I drop it, my eyes land on a familiar face. My Cinderella is walking through the gate with a tennis racket under her arm and a metal basket of tennis balls. My heart catches in my throat. She looks hot in a short black tennis dress and white court shoes. Her brown curly hair is pulled up in a high ponytail, and she wears a white visor to keep the sun out of her eyes. Sporty Spice, I want to call her. Her wide caramel eyes take in the crowd, and a little frown forms between her thin brows.

I jog toward her like I'm in a tractor beam. I can't believe she's here. Will she run if she sees me? Will she give me another chance?

I'm right in front of her when she notices me, and it's gratifying to watch her check out my abs first. Her gaze drifts down my body and back up, her eyes widening, until she reaches my face. I suck in a breath, watching for the beat of recognition, and give her a little finger wave.

Her cheeks flush as she turns quickly away.

Is that blush because she remembers me? Or just embarrassed that I caught her checking me out? I rub my hand down my smooth jaw, calculating my odds. With a haircut and smooth shave, I'm less recognizable. That could be good—I'd get another chance to make a better first impression. Or it could be bad—I'd have to start all over with the awkward small talk phase, which I hate. I only vaguely register that her wing woman is by her side.

Catching up to me, Russell groans in annoyance. "Tennis players, incoming."

"I see them."

"The courts are packed."

"Uh-huh."

I wait another beat for Cinderella to look my way, but she doesn't. *See me*, I want to beg. She tucks a stray wisp of hair behind her ear and lets her friend stomp past her with that boss bitch attitude. Wing Woman gives the players on court one a blinding smile and they stop play, confused. The audience of waiting players is starting to take notice. We don't usually have a problem reserving the courts for drop-in pickleball.

I shake myself out of my stupor, because this hot girl could have every court if she'd only turn that shy smile on me one more time. Damn it. Where are the sparks? Where is that attraction that electrified the space between us at the wedding? Can she not recognize me without the mustache? Or is she ashamed of our hookup? I can't really ask in front of an audience without shooting myself in the foot.

Wing Woman is starting to shoo people off the court, and the picklers are getting antsy.

"Warren?" I call to the far courts, where Warren is busy getting clobbered by Lane and Lin, a mother-son duo who slay at pickleball. "You got your reservation info?"

Warren has been responsible for reserving the courts whenever the weather is moderately adaptable to the game. He looks up as Lin slams the ball toward him, and it clocks him in the foot.

"Damn it! Hold on a minute." Shaking his head, he weaves through players to reach Celeste and her friend. I hurry to catch up, just in case. Warren's chest is puffed up and his face is red, like they're swindling him personally. I don't want to have to hold the guy back, but I will. He comes in like a wrecking ball when he's wound up.

"We reserved the court for the next two hours," Wing Woman is explaining to the confused picklers. "See?" She shows them the confirmation email from the Salmon Bay Parks and Rec.

"Now see here," Warren blusters. "We've got thirty to forty players waiting for their turn. Good turn out with this weather. You can't just tell them to screw off."

Wing Woman—who really needs a better nickname because she's obviously calling the shots—levels her steely gaze in his direction. "Bless your little heart. This reservation says I can."

My Cinderella is looking around at all the pickleball players and twirling her tennis racket nervously. She's shifting her weight from side to side. Her cheeks are pink. Attention must make her nervous, or is it confrontation? I remember her mother-in-law cornering her at the wedding reception. I'd probably be wary of conflict too if I had family who treated me like that. The thing is people usually don't corner men like that. Warren's doing it now, leaning forward to get in her assertive friend's space.

Wing Woman doesn't budge, even though she's a good foot

shorter than Warren. Celeste, however, wraps her arms around her torso. She bites her plump bottom lip between her teeth. I want to gently pull it out and soothe the thin bruised flesh.

"Can I see your paperwork?" Wing Woman asks. She's polite, but direct.

Warren grumbles but pulls out his phone and starts searching through his messages. We wait. I can't keep my eyes off Celeste. She's beautiful even without any make up. It felt good to slay a dragon for her, even if she'd done most of the fighting successfully herself before I stepped in. I want to rub that tension out of her shoulders and run my fingers through her curls. I want to cook for her, maybe feed her pastry from my fingers and have her lick the crumbs from her full lips.

My head is so full of fantasies, Russell has to nudge me to get my attention. "Earth to Hayden. Come in Hayden. What about the donation box?" he asks.

"Huh?"

"Jesus, what's gotten into you? The donation box. It's full. We could get more to buy them off." He motions to the coffee can where Warren accepts money to pay for the court reservations. It's only ten dollars a day per court, but there are eight courts, and we play for hours, until the lights shut off at ten.

Warren can't find his reservation confirmation, and he gets increasingly frustrated while everyone looks on. He eventually calls his wife over to check with her. They confer in low hurried voices, and my gut starts to cramp with a bad feeling.

"So, I'm going to start playing while you look for that, hun," Wing Woman says. She motions for the pickleballers currently on the court to move their nets. The tennis nets are stationery and act as a boundary between the two pickleball courts that occupy that space. The pickleball nets are either on wheels or are lighter weight aluminum, easy to pick up and move.

"Wait!" Warren calls as a few players and I line up to lift the nets. "Just wait a sec here. What about we play for the court? Winner gets it."

Wing Woman pops a hip and looks him up and down. "Now why would I do that, when I paid twenty bucks for a two-hour session? This is my court."

"Er, right." Warren stands straighter. "Usually, I reserve all the courts for pickleball, but I guess I forgot this time. Look at all the people who will be put out by you kicking us off the court."

"Gee, that's a tough one. Better luck next time." Wing Woman looks at her nails and then back up at Warren. She doesn't spare a glance for all the players nervously watching to see how this plays out.

Celeste does, though. Her struggle is painted all over her face, the need to please all these people wanting to play pickleball versus her own desires to play tennis. I want to step in and help her, but she doesn't recognize me. Besides, I'm on the bad side—pickleball versus tennis is a notorious rivalry. Tennis has long been the king of racket sports, requiring more time and athleticism to master. The problem is that Salmon Bay, like other local governments, have simply painted over existing tennis courts instead of building new courts exclusively for pickleball. As the sport has grown in popularity, communities have only been too happy to repurpose tennis courts to gain favor with voters.

"Marissa," Celeste murmurs to her friend, and I'm relieved I finally have a name other than *Wing Woman*. "We can't piss off all these people."

"Girlfriend, I thought we talked about this. You're going to seize the day. No backing out now."

"But your clients—"

"Admire an agent who will go to bat for them. No buts, unless they're sexy butts. Come on, let's hit some balls."

I resist the urge to cover mine. Celeste looks nervously at Warren, who is fuming.

The veins in his temples throb. "How much?" he demands. "I'll pay you back your twenty dollars."

"Pssht," Marissa scoffs. "Nuh-uh, friend. My time and my money and my pleasure are worth far more than twenty. Get outta my way so my girl and I can start banging."

I need to smooth this over, if only to get that panicked look off Celeste's face. I run over to the benches and grab the coffee canister. Taking the top off, I start passing it around for cash. Everyone chips in something, and it was pretty full before. "How about this?" I ask. "Way more than twenty. You can go out for a nice dinner and reserve a court for a month. Just not this court."

Marissa looks me up and down. "Do I know you?"

Celeste doesn't give me a second glance as she pulls on Marissa's sleeve. "The Boat House probably has walk ins. We could catch a bite and watch the sunset. Talk about our approval ratings."

Marissa frowns at her friend. "What happened to standing up for yourself? You're really gonna let this game ice you out?"

Celeste looks down at her feet. "I'm fine. Come-on. Let's take the money and go. We can try again another time."

Conflicting feelings churn in my gut. Part of me hates that she's giving in so easily, but another part of me breathes a sigh of relief. I don't want to be her enemy—but she'd surely see me that way if she thought I was bullying her out of her reservation, right? I want another chance with her. The pickleball players crowding the sidelines start to cheer, sending pink flushing through Celeste's skin.

"Hey," I tell her. "Can I talk to you for a minute?" But Celeste clutches her wire ball basket and racket to her chest like it can protect her from all the attention, and high tails it back out of the gate.

She looks good in her tennis dress, her long curvy legs bare, the skirt barely covering her round ass. I know there's gotta be shorts underneath, but my imagination runs wild. I already know how she tastes. How easily could I flip that little skirt up and take a second helping?

Cool it, dude. I adjust my shorts.

Marissa glares at me, and I feel like making a joke to deflect the tension. That's my go-to, but I don't think she's an appreciative audience at the moment. I've got four sisters; I know sometimes you have to let a person be mad.

As Marissa hurries after her friend, I run to catch up. "Wait!" I call. I can't let her escape without...something. Her number? A date? A second chance? What if this is the universe putting her in my path a second time, and I let her walk away? This feels like fate, and who am I to displease the fates? I follow them out through the gate. "Hey, wait!"

Celeste and her friend make it all the way past the community center before they take pity on me and stop. The lake blooms, verdant with spring. Celeste looks like a shy dryad stepping out from her tree as she turns back to me. "Yeah?"

I clear my throat. "There's a tournament."

They both blink at me.

"A pickleball tournament in two months. It's...I know it's hard to find a court for tennis these days."

Marissa crosses her arms. "I found one. I was strong-armed out of keeping it."

"Right, well." I run my hand over my mouth, forgetting for a minute that I no longer have a big hairy 'stache to smooth down when I'm nervous. Celeste didn't like it, but I kind of enjoyed the disguise. Another barrier between these hard conversations and my real feelings. "The tournament kicks off Salmon Bay SummerFest. It raises money for the Children's Hospital and to build a new court in the parking lot of the Sea Lion Lodge. The winner gets exclusive use of the court for the first year. No need for reservations. You could use it for tennis, if you want. It would give you a dedicated place to play."

"A pickleball tournament." Marissa raises her eyebrows. "Against a bunch of experienced players?"

"That's the great thing about pickleball—it's easy to pick up and get good in a short amount of time, especially for players who know another racket sport. You already know tennis, so...I could teach you a couple tricks, if you want." I offer before Marissa can shut me down like I can see she wants to. "I'd be happy to."

My offer is for Celeste, but she's watching her friend for approval. I recognize the signs of fawning from watching my mom and sisters. Kirsten is a couple's therapist, never hesitating to point out our unhealthy coping mechanisms, and Molly went through a lot of therapy after her jerk face baby-daddy.

Marissa gives me a once over again. Her gaze turns speculative, and I get an eerie shiver down my spine. Good thing about having sisters—I know a plot hatching when I see one. Her eyes dart to Celeste and back to me. Does she recognize me despite the smooth face and athletic gear? Does she remember how badly she wants her friend to date?

Celeste already gave me a chance, and even though she ran away after, I know she enjoyed our closet shenanigans. Her body sways closer to me, chemistry pulling us together. She can feel it too—that buzzing beneath the skin, the curiosity drawing our eyes to each other. The flush of her cheeks brings out her freckles.

I want to beg, "Trust me. Give me a chance," but they're not likely to take my word for it. I want to crack a joke to dispel this anxious silence, but I don't. I hunch my shoulders, so I don't look so intimidating. "Also, because it's for charity, the tournament doubles teams have to have one experienced player and one novice." I give Celeste a friendly smile that hopefully doesn't show the need driving me to wrap her in my arms again. "I'm looking for a partner. A newbie."

Celeste and Marissa exchange a weighted glance.

"I guess if you can't beat them, join them?" Celeste tells her friend, and the tension in my gut relaxes. That's not a no.

"I like beating them," Marissa retorts. "Tell me more about this tournament."

"It's mixed doubles with restrictions to try to even the playing field. The point is to build community and raise money, so the combined age of the team can't be less than sixty-five or over a hundred."

"So, no young jocks can sweep in and sweep up?" Marissa asks.

I nod. "But you might be surprised how cutthroat some of the retirees I play with are. You also can't get two old sharks together to beat out all the newbies."

"You'd teach us both to play?" Celeste motions between herself and her friend.

"Sure thing." I'd rather she plays on my team, but this is at least a step toward that goal. I want the chance to spend more time with her. "I'm Hayden, by the way. Hayden Holstrom. I've coached a lot of new picklers. We have drop-in play here every day when it's not pouring rain, and when it is raining, the gym in the community center has three pickleball courts open."

"We'll think about it." Marissa tucks Celeste's hand under her arm, ready to drag her away.

"Why would you help us?" Celeste asks hesitatingly. "What's in it for you?"

"I'm just your friendly neighborhood pickleballer," I say. "We didn't get off on the right foot, and I just want another chance to show you how good it can be."

"How good pickleball can be?" Marissa asks with a calculating gleam in her eye. "You mean, you're not all overbearing court hogs?"

"No," I laugh weakly. "Not always. We're good people." I think we're talking about the same thing, aren't we?

"Give me your number," Marissa says. "We'll let you know."

Eternally grateful to this wing woman, I eagerly pull out my phone and exchange contact info: Celeste Knowles and Marissa Yang. Now that I have more to go on, I can do some info gathering before my next campaign. Celeste gives a little goodbye wave and her lips lift in a shy smile that makes me want to dance. Is Marissa on Team Second Chance? I hope she's planning to help and not screw me over. I need her.

"Let's go, hun," she tells Celeste, "And eat our weight in oysters."

Celeste glances at me one last time before following her friend back to the parking lot. I've served my shot. I just hope she returns it.

8

CELESTE

THE HOLE IN THE WALL beneath the windows of my midcentury split level is big enough to crawl through and transport me to another world. Maybe I'd find an alternate universe where my ex-husband said yes to all the home repairs we needed to do. Maybe instead of complaining about the money and the hassle, he would put his whole day on hold to meet with electricians, plumbers or carpenters. Maybe in this alternate reality, he'd help find solutions instead of always pointing out problems.

He was never the one to meet the tradesmen or make that kind of mystical male small talk that let them connect. I was the little lady, talked down to about every repair. The house was straight out of the 1950s and so were their attitudes. They overcharged, which made Brett livid. Why didn't I know how much of a racket fixing each crack and leak would be? he demanded. Did I like wasting our money by flushing it down the broken toilet?

No, but Brett never got up to fix things, and there's only so much a girl can learn on YouTube to DIY a burst pipe or replace the knob and tube.

But now the house is mine to fix up—alone—and I don't

get any settlement from the divorce until it's sold. Most of our assets are tied up in the house, just another way for Brett to drag his feet setting me free. This hole in the wall is like our marriage: the seal on the window leaked, and every time it rained, water came through the wall and broke down the wood, bloated the plaster. I could put my hand there and feel the water swelling beneath the surface like a boil needing to be lanced. Eventually there was nothing left to do but take a hammer to the damaged wall and break on through to the fresh air and freedom on the other side.

I've replaced the windows with double-paned glass and caulked the shit out of the seals. The drywall repairs are next, but I can't help wondering when Brett and I stopped trying to dam the leak and let the water suffocate our relationship. I don't want Brett back. I want to know how I can see the signs, so I don't stumble into a dysfunctional trap again. Marissa is right —I should try dating, but I'm so afraid of being caught up in the charm that I can't see the red flags.

Can I trust my own instincts when they failed me so spectacularly before?

Some days I feel like fixing up this house to sell is my penance. Other days, I enjoy the process of renewal, like I'm giving the old house and my life a new chance to shine.

It's nice being in charge for once. I can do what I think makes the most sense for the resale within my budget. I don't have to ask Brett's permission. Not for anything. And it's looking good, except this hole that's a little too big to patch with a quick plaster bandage. I stand up to see if the patch I have will fit the other hole on my list today.

I move across the dining room to the avocado green wall next to the kitchen and gently take down the framed photo of our family. In it, we're all smiling. There's not a hair out of place, perfect coordinating sweaters, perfect teeth, but our smiles don't reach our eyes. Placing the frame on the table, I take a deep breath and turn back to the wall, to the crack made by Brett's fist. He never hit me, but he had a temper, and I learned to be still and silent to not upset him. Dinner was on the table exactly as he walked in the door. The house was tidy, his laundry washed and folded with military precision. Making the bed first thing in the morning was a pillar of his day, some motivational speech by a general he admired, but he was never the one responsible for it. I was, of course, and if the sheet wasn't pressed into crisp hospital corners, his mood would sour.

When Brett's mood soured, I wanted nothing more than to escape. But it had taken me twenty years to work up the courage. My boys came first, and I was convinced they needed their father.

I might have been wrong.

Nina Simone is playing on the speaker when my ringtone suddenly shuts off the music. I turn from the ugly memories and check the caller ID. It's Brett, and I let it go to voice mail. I don't have any time to waste on my day off to get this place sale ready. It's already going to be a stretch. I need more hands.

The next thing I know, someone is banging on the front door, and my stomach sinks into my shoes. I know that sound, the impatience shaking the drywall and causing little snowy bits to fall off and onto the floor.

"Coming!" I can't ignore him. It's not allowed. He can ignore me, give me the silent treatment for days, and then expect me to "get over it" as soon as he feels like he's done punishing me. "You can stop banging, Brett, I'm—"

My ex-husband doesn't wait for me to answer the front door. Why would he? His time is valuable, and I'm ...here. Like a part of the wallpaper, waiting for him to honor me with his presence. Eternally optimistic that this will be the day he decides to act like a friend, a rational polite human being, and ask how I am, how my day went, anything, really, to indicate interest in me as a person.

But no, this is the Brett show. He opens the door and strides right in like he still owns the place. He doesn't. He called it a dump and agreed to let me sell it as my first solo real estate listing once I get my license. He thought it was worthless, not seeing that all the old girl needs is a bit of time and patience. Years of deferred maintenance can't be fixed overnight, but I can do enough that a buyer with a dream and a little sweat equity could make it shine.

Bits of mud fall off Brett's shoes onto the scuffed oak floor as he plants himself in the entryway and casts a critical eye at the changes I've made. Nothing is ever good enough for him, myself included, and I breathe in through my nose and out through my mouth in an effort to stop the old anxiety from welling up. He doesn't control me anymore. He can't hurt me.

That's a pretty lie, like the coat of paint on the walls and the new light fixtures I found at Salmon Bay Consignment that give the place a little midcentury modern cool. Beneath the new clothes, I'm still the woman who Brett trained to cater to his every whim. I'm still the girl so desperate for love that I was willing to take scraps. Don't get me wrong—I'm a tough mother; I survived—but I'm no longer willing to settle for "fine".

I want to *thrive*.

I lift my chin and force myself to hold my hands neutrally at my sides instead of crossing my arms. Brett turns his inspection to me, to my threadbare corduroy overalls covered in paint, paste, and bits of drywall. To my chipped nails. To my messy bun and lack of concealer on the dark circles under my eyes.

"You look rough," he says. "What, are you trying to do all this work yourself? That's crazy."

"Why are you here?" I ask. There's so much resentment burning a hole in my chest. I blow out a slow breath and imagine that pain leaving me too. It's only hurting me. I don't need to suffer to punish myself for my mistakes. I need to give myself permission to let go and spread my wings and fly.

"You don't answer my calls."

"I don't answer calls when I'm in the middle of something else, but I always call back when I have time."

He frowns, carving deeper grooves in his handsome face. "You always used to pick up when I called."

Because we were married! Go bother your new wife. But I bite my tongue and put on the mask I've perfected. "And now that you're here..." I struggle to remember not to offer to do something for him at the outset. Appeasing him is so ingrained, it's my automatic response to hearing his voice. He's in my space, so much bigger than me, leaning in with that unconscious need to intimidate, and my whole body tenses.

Boundaries! Marissa would be hissing at me if she were here too. But I'm alone in the house that used to be ours. Brody and Ryder are both back at college, and it's only me and Brett and his needs and his opinions.

I don't want to give ground, but I need fresh air. Giving him my back, I walk into the dining room and pick up the plaster patch.

He follows me, inspecting everything. "You've really cleaned up this place."

"Yup."

"Would have been nice if it could have looked like this when we were married."

I will not rise to the bait. I will not rise to the bait. "Mmm-hmmm."

"Lander and I drove past yesterday."

Yes, please tell me about your new wife and what she thought of our old house. Not. What could have been so important that he had to drop in to tell me? Or to convince my mother to get involved? Mom sided with Brett in the divorce and told me I was making the biggest mistake of my life in leaving him, and it still hurts. You're not supposed to remove the sharp object from a stab wound or you'll bleed out, right? But I can't decide which is worse—walking through life with a knife in my back or giving up on that relationship entirely.

I can't let my pain ruin Brody and Ryder's relationship with their grandmother.

So many of my choices have been about doing what's best for my babies, and I wouldn't change that, but when will they be old enough that I can protect myself without worrying that I'm negatively impacting them? I'm so tired of being the peaceful, patient, reasonable, responsible one.

When can I be like Frida—grab life by the horns and ride the mechanical bull at eighty?

He's still talking. "Celeste? This is important. Are you even listening?"

Honestly? No. My therapist gave me permission not to.

"I'm busy, Brett, and I need to get back to it if I'm going to get this place ready to put on the market in a few weeks."

"Don't be so ungrateful. I was offering you a deal."

"For?"

"Lander and I are still looking for a house."

"And?"

"And you could give me a friends and family discount. Besides, you'll be desperate for new clients. Not many people would take a chance on an untried agent. We'd be doing you a favor."

I turn to him slowly. Blood is rushing to my face. "I'm sure Lander can find another real estate agent that she'll enjoy working with. I'm not the right person for the job."

Do men see a doormat when they look at me? Because I'm starting to feel like I need a whole bad-ass bitch makeover. The plumber I called showed up four hours late and wanted to charge me an arm and a leg to replace the sump pump, which I paid, only to have him forget to plug it in. Toilet overflow flooded the water access closet, and he refused to come back and clean it up. The electrician insisted I was wrong about the type of voltage I needed to install the new washer/dryer combo in the upstairs linen closet and tried to make it out to be my "miscommunication" when I called him on it. Everyone in the construction trades seems to be male, and they all talk down to me like I'm some naïve little girl, even though I'm the homeowner paying for the work.

Now Brett's demanding my time and attention at a discount, like he deserves one iota of my appreciation.

"Wait a second," Brett puts out his hands. "I allowed you to sell this house for us and we would split the profits, but you're not planning to take real estate fees out of the sale price, are you?"

"Yes, Brett. The profit is the sale minus the fees, which, after all this work to fix up the place, include an inspection, staging, title, and the agent fee—"

"But that's you. You're selling it, so it shouldn't come out of—"

"I'm doing the work," I say between clenched teeth. "I deserve equal pay for equal work. Just because I did all the physical and emotional labor for the family for the last twenty years for free doesn't mean that I'm going to keep doing it! That's why we got divorced!"

Brett snarls, and I pull back. God, what was I thinking? This is a guy with a temper tantrum and I'm alone in the house with him. He's already got a new wife to cater to his needs. Why won't he leave me alone? But I should know better than to poke the beast. I should know better than to escalate.

Brett stops himself from lunging forward and putting another hole in my wall. He shuts his eyes and takes a deep breath, nostrils flaring and muscle ticking in his jaw. "You've turned into a real ball buster, huh? Glad I got out when I did." He spins on his heel and strides out, slamming the front door behind him so hard that the picture frames rattle against the walls. One falls off and shatters on the floor, revealing another bruise behind it.

For so long I told myself that I had it good. My husband had a good job. My two kids were healthy. How could I give that up for the unknown? Brett never hit me or the kids. No physical bruises. No broken bones. But the emotional toll of being married to a man-child weighed me down until I couldn't hold my breath beneath the water any longer.

I get the broom like the mature, responsible adult I've been for decades and clean up his mess.

When is it my turn to set down my worries and be free? When was the last time I was really happy?

The memory of letting go in that supply closet slams into me, and I clutch the broom as my heartbeat picks up. Like a brain freeze after drinking a slushy too fast—delicious satisfaction followed by, oh, no, what have I done?? Shamefaced at my vulnerability, I ran.

I should have gotten 'Stache Guy's number. I wish I could have a redo. Fear still has its claws sunk in my gut, and I deserve better. Even if Brett wasn't still harassing me about the house, *I'm* holding myself back. *I* ran. *I* let fear win. Don't I deserve whatever goodness the Universe aims my way? Yes. Yes, I do.

My phone dings from the dining room table, like an announcement from on high, and I make my way over to check it with anticipation tingling down my spine.

Marissa is texting about a tennis do-over. Can I face the confrontation and rejection of the pickleball players who feel like they own the courts now? Could I actually beat them at their own game? It seems unlikely, but that cute guy—Hayden —said he could teach me. Is it really easy to pick up as a newbie?

I bite my lip as I consider taking the leap of faith. Why did I stand down and let them have the court when we had a reservation? Why do I bend myself to please everyone else?

For a moment I imagine what winning would look like. My therapist said imagining good things happening, instead of always picturing and preparing for the worst, can go a long way towards improving my mental health. My stomach clenches like I'm calling down fate to smite me, but I stay strong and imagine holding the pickleball trophy aloft with Hayden-hot-abs by my side, and Marissa cheering. I imagine training hard, working hard, just like I've been putting my all into this house. I imagine the sold sign outside on the post. The big check padding my lean bank account. The satisfaction of showing Brett that my ideas are worthwhile. Of showing all those dismissive picklers that I belong here too. I deserve space to breathe. Space for joy.

Maybe. I shiver, half excited, half terrified. If I can win that tournament, I could win myself a tennis court for the summer, fair and square. I'd be one step closer to carving out a space for myself. To rediscovering the joy of doing something for the fun of it. For the thrill of it. For me.

Maybe I should take a page from Frida's book and say *Ja*. Believe it, you manifest it, right? *Ja*.

I pull up my contact list, find Hayden BigDill, and open up a new chat.

9

HAYDEN

"Coach, I got one for you," Bear says, his scrawny eleven-year-old muscles easing him up this hill like he ate Wheaties for breakfast. Getting these kids to run isn't so much about technique or energy levels as it is about keeping their brains engaged. I love kids, especially my nieces and nephews, for their crazy, off-the-wall ideas and their complete lack of self-awareness. If they've got a story and a snack, they can run for miles.

Bear is one of the kids who lives to tell me the thoughts buzzing around in his head as we run through Vidland Park. I coach the eleven- and twelve-year-old boys so I can spend time with Elias and Ethan, Molly's Irish twins. With their dad out of the picture—good riddance—I'm the closest adult male role model they've got.

For better or worse. They're under the impression that I sit at home all day and play video games. *#lifegoals*.

"What you got?" I ask Bear as we crest the hill. Practice is almost over, and I breathe a sigh of relief. Usually I'm dragging by this time, but today I get to see Celeste right after practice. Inside I'm singing and dancing around street lamps.

Bear is happy to go on a long winding tale while I zone in

and out, thinking of a curvy girl with big eyes. My stories today are flat. Usually I'm the one entertaining the kids—the instant gratification of my audience and the heightened brain state of running make spinning weird-ass, awesome tales all the more fun, fart jokes included.

Today, my brain is elsewhere. I'm bouncing on my toes, smelling myself to make sure I can get away with a quasi-date after practice like this, as I wait for the kids to get picked up. Elias and Ethan are both muddy from their toes to their ears, and I laugh when I see my sister's resigned expression.

"Good practice today," I tell them, ruffling their hair.

"Thanks, Uncle Hay-Hay."

Not going to share that nickname with any of my pickle friends anytime soon, but a certain movie came out when the nephews were toddlers, and it stuck. Even my sisters call me it, especially when they're goading me into a bad bet. *Hay-Hay— you chicken? Booowk!*

Yeah, sisters can be the worst.

"You boys have a good practice?" Molly asks them.

"Yeah, mom. Uncle Hay-Hay told us a story about a superhero who had poisonous gas belches that knocked the bad guys out."

"Oh, did he now?" My sister shakes her head at me, but she's grinning. She thinks I should write books for children, but there's something too intimidating about that. Children's literature has an outsized impact on young minds—the books that shaped the person I am today are still my favorite. Books got me through the hard, confusing days when I came home from school with bruised knuckles and detention, only to see dad's rare nod of approval for standing up for myself with my fists. Books got me through the taunts of being too much, too sensitive. Books opened my eyes to a more diverse, caring, magical world than the one my father pictured for me.

Children's book authors change lives, and as a great

philosopher once said, "with great power comes great responsibility."

Spidey's a braver man than I am. I'll stick to entertaining adults. Maybe throw in a splash of actual history to appease Mr. Tower, my favorite history teacher (may he rest in peace). Always finish with a happily-ever-after, because I want to believe, as much as my readers do, that true love conquers all.

I don't want to be responsible for warping the minds of the next generation.

"Don't forget the barbecue on Sunday," Molly says. "What are you bringing?"

"Triple chocolate threat!" Ethan yells.

"Five cookie surprise!" Elias shouts over him.

"Uh, you heard my little dudes. Sign me up for what they said."

Molly pats my head like I'm still twelve myself and don't tower over her. "You're a good man, Hayden Holstrom. I hope you find someone who appreciates you."

I grin back and flex a bit in my sweaty tee-shirt, showing off. Girls have paid attention to me since I grew a foot and got swole at the end of my senior year of high school, but inside I'm the same nerdy dork. The same guy who doesn't mind prancing around in a princess dress and drinking pretend tea with his sisters and nieces. I make a really good Anna, if I do say so myself. Awkward social skills and all.

Dad's words come back to me; *Boys don't wear dresses. When are you going to toughen up?* But Ethan gazes up at me with impressed, wide eyes, and I know I've got to model a healthier masculinity than was presented to me.

Elias pretends to vomit into his hands at the mention of romance; Dad would probably be proud.

"Don't do it, Uncle Hay-Hay. It's a trap!"

"Where would you even put a girl? Your house is already full of plants!"

"Good points, little dudes. But maybe this is a convo we can fill in when you're older."

"Say goodbye to Uncle Hotcakes," Molly says.

That kind of nickname is exactly why I tell my family almost nothing. Did I mention four sisters? The more they try to dig into my love life, the less I tell them. At this point, their imaginations are almost as crazy as the boys'.

Saying goodbye to the last kid, I shoulder my backpack and jog off through the lazy Spring evening along the path that circumnavigates the lake. Pedestrians block the trail as they stop to watch the baby ducklings swimming like fat, fluffy Peeps in a row. Purple and white irises wave merrily along the path. Tree branches droop with pink and white cherry blossoms. It's my favorite time of year—the earth is fecund with hope and possibility.

My father would be rolling in his grave with how much I love flowers and fluffy ducks, but that's my truth. This "sissy" is bucking his stereotypes, and there's not a damn thing he can do to stop me.

As I near the courts, I hear the distinctive *thwop* of a pickleball, and my heartbeat picks up. I wipe my sweaty hands on my running shorts and make my way to the fence. There she is—Celeste. I half worried she'd get cold feet and run again. Her short baby blue tennis skirt barely covers her round ass. Her thighs are thick and toned. Her ponytail swishes as she moves.

Fuck. Me.

She doesn't notice me at first, and I take a moment to get my shit together as my eyes graze the sweet curve of her chin and her full chest. My dick perks up with the memories, and I take another moment to squash any thoughts of a repeat right here. Do not be a creeper!

I watch her bouncing the pickleball on her paddle, and energy floods my body, like I haven't been racing preteens for hours up and down hills. She's trying pickleball, and I love pickleball...so, a match made in heaven? Maybe that's a step too far, but a guy can hope. My heart is thumping in my chest and my palms are sweaty.

She swears and tucks a loose curl behind her ear. I watch her move to the serve line with a bucket of outdoor balls and place them by her feet. She throws one in the air and serves like it's a tennis ball—way too hard. The plastic ball sails clear across the court and thwacks against the wire fence on the opposite side. She's strong.

I hover for a few minutes and watch her work to master the ball. I can work with this. We have a shot at winning if she can invest the time to train with me. I'll take every moment I can get.

A couple of younger guys in their mid-twenties enter the court and ask if they can play on the side of the court she's not using. She tells them to go ahead, then checks her surroundings, and her eyes land on me. Busted. I cover my chagrin with an awkward wave.

Way to play it cool, asshole.

To my surprise, her tense shoulders lessen a fraction. She approaches the fence with a hesitant smile. "Hey, Pickleball Guy."

"I am the pickleball guy," I agree. I'm so off balance I'd probably agree to being Sasquatch right now. My fingers are laced through the wire of the fence, and I clench my hands in anticipation. It's not like asking a girl out on a date, but somehow it feels more momentous.

See me, I want to say to her. *Give me a chance.*

"Hey." She wipes her palms on her skirt. Pink flushes her cheeks. "I...I guess I said that already. Sorry."

"No, don't apologize. I'm Hayden."

"Celeste."

"I was just finishing up coaching my nephew's track practice. You ready to dink?"

"Yeah?" She looks me up and down quickly, then bites her lips and looks away.

She's so nervous. It's cute. I can see why her friend had to step in for her, but it also makes me want to write a nasty character and name it after her ex.

"So, looks like you've already started giving pickleball a chance. Your form looks good. You've got good hand-eye coordination."

She smiles shyly at me and nods. "Trying to. I used to love hitting a ball around outside. It made me feel...I dunno...alive I guess."

"Nature, exercise, teamwork—that's a lot of dopamine right there. Pretty much the perfect activity if you ask me."

A rosy glow spread across her cheeks, and she looks up at me through her lashes with a naughty twinkle in her eye. "Perfect, huh?"

I clear my throat. Does she remember our *other* doubles activity? That twinkle makes me think she does. I crack a half smile. She's shy. If she can play it cool, I can too. Right? "Maybe second best activity."

She laughs, and it is the loveliest sound I've ever heard. I'm going to make it my mission to make her laugh again.

I clear my throat. "I'm glad you texted. I'm happy to share what I know, and if you need a partner—"

"I have Marissa."

"Sure. No problem. I love pickleball and I love to share my love of pickleball with new people."

"If you're sure it's not an imposition."

I almost sprint to the gate in my haste to get in the court before she changes her mind. "No, ma'am. Ambassador Dill, at your service."

She laughs again, that light sound that makes all my nerve endings stand on end. I need to write that into the scene I wrote inspired by our closet escapade. There's no way I can turn that scene into my editor now that I know Celeste in real life, but I reserve the right to keep it for my spank bank—personal use only.

"Okay, Celeste, your swing looks good, but tennis players like you tend to be bangers when you need a soft hand." Celeste bursts out laughing, and I realize how that sounded. "Right." I rub the back of my neck, feeling a flush rise. "There's more where that came from, ladies and gentlemen."

She snorts. "With a name like Pickleball, innuendos are expected."

"Yeah. That." I really want to kiss her. Her lower lip is full and pink. Her upper lip, a soft bow. *Go slow, go slow.*

"Got it. I need to be gentler," she says easily, completely ignorant of my inner turmoil.

"Mm-hmm. Here, let me demonstrate a couple different ways to serve, and then you can decide what works best for you."

She raises an eyebrow. "You're not going to tell me how you do it and claim it's the only way?"

"I've got four older sisters and a healthy dose of self-preservation."

"Fair enough." She returns to her place by her almost empty bucket of balls, and I take the other side of the court.

Pulling the hem of my shirt up and out to use as a basket, I run around collecting her strays, and when I turn around, I catch her checking out my abs. *Yeah, babe. Look all you want. You couldn't see this rock-solid eight pack in the dark closet.* I'm going to keep flashing my assets until she begs me for another chance. She catches me catching her and quickly looks away. I smile to myself. Our chemistry is still red hot out of the closet. I need her to be curious enough to take another look, to give the nerdy guy inside a chance too.

"You have any siblings?"

"No. Only child. My parents never wanted kids."

"Harsh. They told you that?" My parents were far from perfect, but at least I knew they loved me.

"All the time." She scrunches up her pert nose. "So, gently."

"Be one with the ball."

"If you try to make me wax your car, you're going to be disappointed."

I laugh. "No, but there are some posts closer to the lake we could stand on to practice our balance. Balance is important. Be the heron. Are those court shoes?"

She looks down at the trainers on her feet and shakes her head. "I haven't bought them yet."

"That should be your first order of business. No twisted ankles on my watch."

"Yessir."

It trips off her tongue so easily; I shouldn't like it so much. Shouldn't want to wrap her ponytail around my hand as I do dirty things to her.

I know she's older than me, probably closer to Molly's age, and maybe there's some dark shit Kirsten might unpack about me bossing around older women, but I don't care. She's got that black cat energy—vulnerable but with teeth. It's only her that makes me think of dark fantasies, of having her say, *Yes, Sir*, as she's on her knees. A mature woman who knows her own mind and knows what she wants, choosing to submit her body to me because she knows I can make her feel good? *Yes, please.*

I turn my back to her as I make a little pile of balls next to the serving line on my side. I stuff my pockets with a couple more, and hope that the weird shape of pockets full of pickleballs will draw attention away from another pickle trying to attract notice.

Damn it, I'm like a pre-teen with a crush.

I think about all my least favorite things as I will my dick to go down. People who use the last of the toilet paper but don't replace the roll. People who leave dog shit in the piles of leaves the kids like to run through at the park. People who talk during movies. People who confuse *there, their,* and *they're*. Most people, if I'm being honest.

"I bought a paddle online. It had five stars. Is that okay?"

I get in position to serve and check out her paddle from

across the court. The vulnerability in her question gives me a weird feeling. "Of course. People get crazy with their opinions on paddles. Did you know the family that invented pickleball used ping pong paddles that they had lying about?"

"Yeah, I read up on the origin story. But did they name the game after the dog or the boat?"

My heart trips in my chest as she drops *origin story* like it ain't no thing. "How much time do you have?"

She chuckles. "I forgot I was talking to Ambassador Dill."

"Maybe I can regale you over drinks?"

Her eyes dart to the side. "Maybe."

Not tonight then. She's skittish.

"No worries. Let's dink some balls."

The next hour goes by in a blink. As predicted, she's able to pick up the gist of the game very quickly, which is one of the best parts about the sport. Her tennis skills come in handy; she already knows about positioning, reading people to anticipate the ball, and the mechanics of certain shots. Volley, top spin, slice, and drop shots are similar enough with both sports. I only have to remind her a dozen times not to bang it but to tap it gently. It is a genuine pleasure to draw out her laugh. Word play zings back and forth, and my nerdy little heart is falling fast.

"Atta girl. Balance and footwork are key," I tell her as we take a break and hydrate. The sun disappeared a while ago, leaving only the court lights to keep us company. The young guys were loud and liked to razz each other, but they're packing up now. Celeste watches them warily. "A lotta people skip practicing the quick movement part of it. You don't have to run as far or as hard as tennis, but you do have to pivot and not hurt yourself."

"Are you calling me old?" she asks dryly.

"Never," I backpedal. "Everyone should be practicing agility drills. Everyone. My sister is a personal trainer at Magnus Fitness, and she specializes in weight training for women. Do you ever lift?"

She's shaking her head and looking at the ground. "My ex didn't think women belonged in the weight room. He thought yoga and spin class were for girls. Martial arts and weightlifting were for boys."

"Your ex sounds like a dick."

She raises her chin and looks right at me, eyes wide like she can't believe I'd disagree with him just because I'm a man. "He is a dick, isn't he?"

"So, what are you gonna do about it?"

"Do?"

"You're not going to let his backward opinions keep you from weightlifting and doing what's best for you, right?"

"No. No, I'm not."

"Attagirl, Ladybird." I grin as a blush flares across her cheeks.

"I'm a member of Magnus Fitness. What's your sister's name? Maybe I know her."

"Samantha Stowell. She also teaches self-defense and women's power lifting."

"Brown hair, about yay tall—" she holds up her hand to indicate my shortest sister's height.

"That's right. Short and feisty, like a little French bulldog."

The smile that breaks over her face could keep me warm for a week. "Does your sister know you call her that?"

"Of course. She calls me the Greyhound. Better than the Doberman, which is what she calls our oldest sister Molly."

"You guys must love dogs. How many do you have?"

"None, unfortunately."

"Me either," she says wistfully. "I'm in a little apartment at the moment. No space for a pet. But someday I'll get a small cottage and grow an English garden. I'd love a dog then."

"What breed?"

"Depends on what I find at the shelter. I'm going to take home the one that looks like it needs love the most."

I consider the gravity of her words, the beauty of not caring what something looks like, and the depth of pain revealed in that statement. I'm pretty sure if I could shapeshift into a dog and wait for her at that shelter, I'd do anything to convince her to pick me. "That's lovely."

She crosses her arms. "I'm going to do it. I'm going to live alone with my dog and my garden and finally be happy."

"I was being honest. I love that plan."

Her shoulders relax.

I recognize that defensiveness from Molly, and it hurts my heart. I'm not a violent guy, but her ex needs a take down. Sam knows jujitsu. I should drag her along to give him a taste of his own medicine—having a little French bulldog take you down is a real ego killer. My style is less confrontational, but I'd make an exception for the guy who put that pain in Celeste's eyes.

10

CELESTE

THE PICKLEBALL AMBASSADOR—HAYDEN—IS a big goof. A fine, *fine* specimen of a man, but he puts me at ease in a way that most men do not. I catch the pity lurking in his eyes when I blabbed about getting the saddest dog from the pound. God, how pathetic. Forty years old, and still desperate for love. Well, I'm familiar with cages, and I'm going to rescue one soul to be my woman's-best-friend. We'll save each other.

Besides, I'll be safer living alone and walking outside and hiking alone if I have a dog.

It still makes my stomach churn as I wait for Hayden to say something about my slip up. In my experience, people hate talking about real emotions. They'll change the subject or push on through like I didn't just admit that everything isn't picture perfect. *Real* makes people uncomfortable. But I'm real and messy and uncomfortable, and I'm done making myself small for other people's comfort.

I reach down to start loading up my bucket of balls, sure that Hayden is about to make his excuses and rush off, but he stops me with a hand on my arm.

"I'm sorry someone hurt you." His voice is steady, sincere, and his big hazel eyes are fixed on mine, like he's holding my pain with me, witnessing this burden and standing with me in the rain. "I'm sorry someone ever made you feel like you weren't enough. Not loved enough. Not wanted enough. Those other people—your parents, your ex, your landlord, whoever—were assholes. You are beautiful inside and out."

"You hardly know me."

"But I see you, Celeste, and I don't see a single part of you that isn't worthy of love."

I swallow and drop my gaze to break the connection. When was the last time someone told me they loved me? Besides Marissa. Besides Ryder and Brody, of course. I know my kids love me. I love them with my whole heart and soul, and I never understood how I couldn't be enough for my parents.

Now this guy I barely know is telling me sweet, dream-guy things, and I don't know what to believe. Who talks like that? Who is this guy? Is this some elaborate hoax Brett dreamed up to torment me, and he and his buddies are waiting to jump in and laugh at how gullible I was to believe it?

I twist my ponytail around my hand. "Thank you, Hayden."

"Let's practice dinking," he says when I take a break to get some water. "That's not a thing in tennis, but it's hugely important in this game. We're going to toe the line here at the kitchen."—He points to the box on either side of the net.—"Stay out of the kitchen if you're going to hit a volley. You can step inside only if you let the ball bounce before you hit it. And remember soft, slow, and steady."

"First time a guy has told me to stay out of the kitchen," I quip before I can catch myself. My face blazes. For a moment there, I was so comfortable I forgot I'm not with Marissa.

Hayden's eyes soften. "You've just been with the wrong guys."

Isn't that the truth? I shake it off and move forward, taking my feelings out on the ball. At first, my muscle memory blasts through the ball, and I end up popping it up or hitting it into the net. I can't keep it in bounds.

Hayden keeps making jokes until I relax enough to feel the dance of the dink game. "Remember, tennis girl, we're not banging it out—dinking is a gentle seduction."

Of course, I get flustered and end up lobbing the return. He shows me how hard he can bang it when he slaps the ball back to my side of the court, and it lands right between my feet.

"That's gentle for you?" I ask.

I swear I feel his low chuckle in my core, and my face heats.

"Just wanted to show you what happens when you lob it right to your opponent." He pulls another ball out of his pocket. "Here, I'll toss you a few up high, and you can show me how you smash it."

I can't help my snort. His answering grin feels easy, like we've known each other forever and not only exchanged a bit of small talk on the court. He hits me some pop-ups and I practice jumping to bring them down. This is what I love about tennis —channeling all my anger and resolve into the physical release of walloping the ball. My teenage self exorcized a lot of demons on the court. There wasn't another outlet available to me.

Anything but cheerful obedience made my family and Brett uncomfortable, and I learned to swallow down any rage I felt. *Be a good girl. Be a nice girl. Be a pretty girl.*

My next hit cracks the pickleball. My stomach turns over, because I broke Hayden's ball. I pull my shoulders in and bite my lip to head off the thunderstorm about to descend. "I'm so sorry! I can pay you back for that. I didn't mean to hit it so hard. I—"

Hayden raises his eyebrows. He ignores the busted ball. But as he watches my reaction, I see it—the tightening of his jaw. The muscle twitch under his eye.

"I'm sorry," I repeat. I know this is fawning. I can't help it.

He walks slowly to the net, and I brace for anger even as I hear my therapist's voice in my head telling me to calm down.

I'm a grown woman. No one should yell at me. I don't have to let anyone treat me that way anymore. With utmost care, he raises his hands in the universal gesture of "I come in peace," keeping his eyes locked on mine the whole time.

"Celeste—balls break all the time. It's no big deal."

I hiccup.

"You didn't do anything wrong. Things can be replaced. People can't. Breathe, sweetheart. Just breathe."

A traitorous drop overflows, and I angrily wipe it away. I'm not even crying about the stupid ball, but I can't stop my body's trained reaction. So much for keeping it all together. After a whole year, I wanted to be the smooth mountain lake, not the storm-tossed sea. "I didn't mean to hit it so hard. I should have kept my emotions in check," I whisper.

He steps over the net with his long legs, still moving carefully like he's approaching a skittish animal. "Can I give you a hug?"

I don't know what I expected, but in that moment a hug is all I've ever wanted. I nod, and he wraps his arms around me, pulling me into his chest and resting his chin on the top of my head. "You're safe here. You're safe with me."

His chest is hard muscle, and he smells like clean sweat and Old Spice. He doesn't badger me with questions. He doesn't demand I stop crying or tell me I'm being too sensitive. He just holds me against his shirt and breathes with me, deep inhales and long, slow exhales, until my breathing slows and my heart rate steadies. His hands are still against my back—he doesn't move them one inch, as if he's afraid I'll think he's copping a feel or taking advantage if he expands his touch.

He's so sweet, and it's dangerous to my fragile heart. I hope my sons can grow into dangerous men like this one—men who aren't afraid to show emotion or express comfort. Men who don't feel threatened by a woman's tears. Maybe it was the four older sisters Hayden's mentioned, or maybe he had a great male role model growing up. This guy seems too good to be true. He's got to have skeletons somewhere in his closet.

Am I so screwed up that I have to imagine the worst of everyone?

I wipe my eyes one last time and pull away from the warmth of his embrace. I'm a grown woman. I need to stand on my own two feet.

He studies me, seeing far too much. "You better?"

"Yeah—yes."

"Atta girl." He nods and lets me have my pride. Some people would have overruled me even when I said I'm fine. Hayden takes my words at face value. He's letting me lead, and I'm so grateful.

"I'd love to practice more another day. I've got to get home. Work tomorrow, you know?"

"Sure. No problem." He bends to help me gather the balls. "Can I walk you to your car? It's dark, and my mama would kick my ass if I didn't."

He's obviously pretty close with his family, and that makes me trust him a little more. Family is important to me. We seem to have that in common. He's younger, but I can't tell by how much. I thought Brett was crazy to marry someone ten years his junior, but maybe I was jealous that she's still got the hips and breasts of someone who has never borne children.

I want to be strong. Maybe I should look into personal training with Samantha. I like the idea of doing something good for myself. Brett not approving is icing on the cake. If I can get faster and stronger, spend time outside and meet new people with similar interests, why wouldn't I prioritize that?

The life I want is right in front of me, I just have to be brave enough to reach out and grab it.

"Hayden." I clear my throat.

"Yeah?"

"Is that offer of a drink still on the table?"

"Absolutely."

I breathe out. Butterflies dance beneath my sternum. He's very handsome. Tall and fit. How old is he anyway? Before I can second guess myself, I think my new mantra: What would Frida do? She might push him down on the bench where people wait their turn for a court and have her wicked way with him. The thought has merit. It's so outlandish to think I could ever do something like that, I laugh.

"It's a date then." Hayden flashes me his boyish grin that has my insides swooping like a pimple-faced teenager.

I haven't been on a date in years.

I swallow, my mouth dry, and nod. He takes my hand and weaves our fingers together. His skin is warm and calloused. I like it far too much. He smells like sweat, but a little spicy, a little woodsy, and I take a surreptitious sniff of my own armpit. We've been exercising pretty hard. Should we take a rain check on drinks so we can shower?

Hayden's low chuckle rumbles through our connection. "Don't overthink it, Ladybird. I like the smell of good, clean sweat. We can smell pretty, together."

If he's not going to mind, I guess I won't either.

11

HAYDEN

I'M HOLDING IN MY GLEE by the skin of my teeth as I gently guide Celeste into the Fire Station no 18 Brewery across from the library and movie theater. The 1911 brick building was Salmon Bay's first fire station, and like most of Salmon Bay's historic buildings, the station was built in a Germanic style with stepped gables and wide overhanging eaves. The brick chimney tower currently displays BREWERY vertically in neon lights. The bright yellow bay doors that used to let horses and fire carriages out are open to the warm breeze, and small round tables dot the courtyard. All the tables are full as citizens of Salmon Bay enjoy the dry and sunny evening in late spring.

There are always patrons at the town's best loved brew joint. Inside are exposed beams and artfully preserved brick. A carved wooden bar lines one wall. Red leather booths with brass rivets fill the rest of the space, and I spot all the usual pickleballers and old friends from high school.

Why didn't I take her to a less crowded place? Now I have to share her.

Damn it.

"Hey Priest," I greet the head brewer, Stellan "Priest" Sorenson. He's a broad-shouldered guy with a big beard and long blond hair pulled back in a man bun. He was a year or two above me at school and has a reputation for being a taciturn, growly son-of-a-bitch.

"Holstrom."

If you want a friendly bartender, you have to go somewhere else. The Copper Gate, maybe, where the redheaded Madam K dishes out hard knocks to the Roller Derby team. Or the Schooner Tavern, manned by Salty Smitty and inhabited mostly by old fishermen and young hipsters.

"What would you like, Celeste?" I lean awkwardly against the bar, struggling to look suave, and failing.

Priest rolls his eyes like he can see my inner golden retriever panting to know everything about her. What's her favorite drink? Her favorite book? Her favorite movie based on a book? I'm being a very good boy though. I haven't bombarded her with personal questions. Yet.

"I-I don't drink alcohol," she says and bites her lip like she's expecting me to be mad or something.

"No worries," I tell her. "Two ginger beers? Liv makes it."

Her shoulders drop away from her ears and she nods. "Thanks."

"It's good. I like a ginger beer. Who doesn't like a ginger b —" I'm thumped on the back, which breaks me out of my nervous slide into drivel. "Whit! What are you doing here?"

"Hayden. Just in town to resupply." My good friend from high school, Whittaker Boone, gives me a half smile-half grimace. When he's in town we get together for brews and pickleball. He nods at Celeste, and my inner caveman wants to cover her eyes so she can't see the rich fucker who looks like the Swedish royal prince. I scramble to think of reasons he's not a catch—prefers spending time in the wilderness where there are no flush toilets being the obvious moral failure—when I suddenly remember he's not available. "Where's Shelby?"

The farther away, the better, in my humble opinion. His influencer girlfriend never stops filming—herself, her food, and any hapless mortal with the bad luck to be caught in the shot. After everything went down online with my first book, I deleted all my social media and avoid anyone with a smart phone like the plague. One benefit of hanging out with the retiree crowd—they're a lot more focused on in-person interactions than building an online following.

Whit's eyes dart to the back of the brewery, and I follow his gaze to find his thin, blond girlfriend filming herself on her phone in one of the booths in back. Shocker.

"The hustle is real, huh?"

"She doesn't even notice I left," he says morosely. He turns back to Celeste and introduces himself. "What are you doing with this clown?" he jokes.

I'm holding my breath and cursing small town life to blazes, until Celeste grins at me and playfully squeezes my bicep. I have to swallow as a wave of her coconut shampoo overwhelms me. I wish she smelled bad after exercising; it'd give my brain a little dose of reality. But, no. My brain thinks the girl I like smells good. Psych 101 was right.

"Hayden is teaching me how to play pickleball," she tells him.

"No shit?" Whit looks between us as he flags down Priest to order a FisherFolk IPA and a fruity cocktail for Shelby. "Good for you. He's a great coach. Taught me to play too. Never took me out for a drink after though." He raises his eyebrow at me.

"You're not pretty enough," I deadpan.

He smirks. "Checks out. Take me up on that offer to use the cabin, yeah? If you want some privacy in a beautiful place, that is. It's usually free." He nods his head at Celeste again, and he couldn't be clearer if he shouted.

Whit's family cabin is one of a handful grandfathered into Olympic National Park. It's got a gorgeous view of the Pacific Ocean—grey whales and seals frolic in the waves as bald eagles dive for fish. I would, yes, like to take this woman far away from the noisy crowd, especially if that noisy crowd is the family I live with, but our relationship isn't there yet. Maybe after we win the tournament we could escape for a long weekend together. August is really nice on the Olympic Peninsula.

We do the bro fist bump and Whit squares his shoulders to return to Shelby.

"His girlfriend looks familiar," Celeste says as she sips her drink.

"Doesn't everybody in a small town?"

"It's not so small. I've lived in smaller."

"Yeah?" I put a hand on her lower back and usher her away from the bar. Immediately, people I know are calling me over to join them.

"Just your friendly, neighborhood pickleballer, yeah?" She laughs at my long face. "So sad for you to be so popular."

"It is! It's a burden to be *really, really, ridiculously good-looking.*" I strike a Zoolander pose with the duck lips, and she laughs again. I love it. I love that sound. I love her smile. I'm halfway to dropping down on one knee, and thank God, she doesn't have telepathy, because that thought would definitely send her running for the hills.

She smiles, but her eyes are sad as she studies the room. "No worries. Thanks for teaching me some pickleball moves. I should really get going. I'll leave you to your adoring fans."

"But—"

She places a hand on my arm again. "Really, it's fine. I've got work to do. But this has been great. Maybe we can meet up again sometime?"

"Absolutely." I take a deep breath. "I'd love to train you. What time works for you?"

"What do you charge for your coaching services?"

"Nothing. I just like pickleball."

She gives me a look that says she smells something fishy, and I have to laugh. I hold my hands up to show her I mean no harm. The last thing I want is to scare her off. "Okay, you win. I get to spend more time doing something I love with a beautiful woman who makes me laugh. Is that okay?"

She squirms at the compliment.

"I swear my intentions are good, because if they weren't—"

"Your sisters would kick your ass. Got it."

"That's right, they would. Absolute Amazons, the lot of them. But go ahead and ask Sam. She'll vouch for me. Or we could video chat Molly right now."

She lifts her eyes to peek at me through her lashes. I wish she could see what I see right now—full, kissable lips, soft curves I want to fall into, smile sweet as cotton candy. "That, okay," she agrees. "I trust you."

Three words have never felt so dear.

12

CELESTE

On Saturday, Marissa and I meet bright and early at the courts to start our new attempt at beating the competition at their own game. We place our paddles in a stack on the side of the court with our handles in the direction indicating advanced beginner. There are a few other stacks of advanced and expert players, but it shouldn't be too long of a wait.

I glance around the courts to see if I see anyone I know, and my eyes land on a familiar face. Hayden is focusing so hard I feel at ease drinking him up with my eyes. His hair falls across his forehead. He hasn't shaved today, and his beard is starting to come in, giving him a rakish look. His baby-blue tee-shirt clings tightly to his fit torso and shoulders, and every quick jump to get to the ball shows off his sculpted leg muscles to perfection.

I tear my eyes away and force myself to focus on other matches before Marissa catches me ogling him. He's much too young for me.

No luck. "Ceecee, isn't that the guy who offered to help us out?" Marissa points to my very off-limits, newly acquired, pickle-coach.

"Who?" I try to play it off. "Oh, yeah...I think you're right."

"He's good. You should ask him to play us."

"What, right now?"

"No, when he's done with his match. What's wrong with you? You need more coffee this morning?"

"Probably." I can't bring myself to tell her that I stopped making a pot of coffee for myself in the morning—part of breaking out of my old, ingrained routine. Brett always expected his coffee to be waiting when he rose. Some parts of living alone I love—no one criticizing me, no one expecting me to clean up after their mess. There are other parts I hate—no one noticing when I'm gone or if I've come back. Brett sure noticed if I didn't have dinner on the table exactly at six pm; I don't miss that.

But even without the stress of sharing a living space with someone, sometimes I feel like there's an emptiness in my life. No one to share my day with. No one to cuddle up and watch tv with.

Since Marissa is watching Hayden's game, I let myself drift after her and watch too. He's quite good. His partner is in a wheelchair—he gets two bounces to hit the ball, but otherwise the same rules seem to apply. The handle of his paddle ends in a suction cup to pick the ball up off the ground. Hayden anticipates the shots that will be too difficult for his partner to get to, but he doesn't try to take over the court. He's focused on playing as a team.

He catches us watching him when they're only two points away from winning. A brief flash of surprise passes over his face before his grin widens like a Cheshire cat. I swear my retired ovaries release an egg on the spot.

Marissa nudges me. "Girly, you seem to be holding out on me. What's that all about? Have you seen him since last weekend?"

"You want to win this tournament, don't you? I'm not about to turn down offers to help."

"Have you asked him to help you out with anything else?"

I give her a flat look as I feel my cheeks burn.

"Did he offer? Come on, dish!"

"He gave me some tips, that's all." And a drink. I leave that part out. It was a friendly drink—not a date.

"Court!" Someone yells from the sidelines to tell everyone that the next players are up. I check if it's our stack of paddles, but we're still two short.

Hayden struts off the court and over to our stack, where he quickly sets his paddle down on top of mine. The edge of his mouth lifts, and he winks at me.

"You're not beginner," I tell him, feeling that wink like I've been splashed in a dunk tank. "You're going to squash us."

"Wrong game," he deadpans. "Let's do this. Or are you chicken?"

Marissa elbows me in the ribs.

"What, is this is a test?" I ask.

His smile could light up the whole court after dark. "That's right. Let's see what you got, pretty girl."

Marissa's glee is visceral. I give her a surreptitious swat, and my laser eyes telegraph a death threat if she embarrasses me.

When another free court is announced—we're up. As Marissa and I get in position on one side of the court, she dogs my steps and hisses in my ear about holding out on her.

"There's nothing to share!" I whisper back. "I ran into him the other day and we hit some balls. That's it. There's nothing going on!"

"You are delusional, Ceecee. Completely dill-lusional."

I bat her away and tell her to get on her side of the line.

Hayden teams up with a snowbird named Rose who says she's visiting from Florida. Hayden shakes her hand, greeting her warmly, and grabs the ball from where it was balanced on the post.

"Who serves first?" I ask. Scoring and serving are different in tennis.

"Whoever is closest to Bainbridge Island, where the game was invented."

"That's...really?"

Hayden shrugs. "That's how it's done here. Don't know about Florida." He glances at his partner, who agrees. "You know how to score in double? We start with the points, zero-zero, and the server, either one or two. The first serve of the game always starts with the second player. After my serve, it will go to your team. Marissa will give the score, then say one for the first server. Celeste, you'll go next. Give the score, then say two. Then the play passes back to me, then my friend Rose here." He switches his paddle to his left hand and salutes me with it. "Ready?"

I'm confused already, but I'm sure he'll call it out and help us get the hang of scoring. "So right now it's love-love-two?"

"Nope. Unlike tennis, there is no love in pickleball." He winks at me before he bounces the ball once and smacks it across the net, right between Marissa and me, where it hits just inside Marissa's side of the court before going out.

Damn it.

"One-zero," Hayden announces.

Marissa runs to get the ball, and I can tell she's done messing around with me. She's like a bulldog when she sets her mind to something, and she wants to win.

Hayden switches places with Rose for his second serve. I get to the ball in time to return it, and Rose volleys it back straight down the line between Marissa and me. We both defer and miss it entirely.

"I guess we should call those," I tell Marissa.

"Too busy imagining his pickle, eh?"

"Shush." I slap my hand over her mouth and quickly glance at Hayden, who is talking to his teammate. I can't tell if he heard.

She giggles.

"Keep it together. Are we going to win this thing?"

"I can't help it," Marissa snorts. "All the bad puns are brining in my brain."

"You're hopeless. Did the twins keep you up last night?"

"Nope." She flashes me a shit-eating grin. "Drew did."

"Lucky you. Can we get back to kicking ass and taking names now?"

"You got it. Hey, we need a team name. What do you think about Gherkin Girls? Super Smash Sisters? Paddle....Mamas?"

I snort. "Us? The Paddle Mamas? I'm not...no, but you do you."

"Two-zero-two," Hayden calls, and sends an easy serve over the net, which I manage to return. Even though he's not using his dominant hand, his shots are good enough to make this a tough game. I'm trying to pull back on slamming the ball, but my muscle memory still thinks we're playing tennis.

"Sorry. Sorry!" I tell Marissa after I hit the ball sailing over Hayden's head.

"Easy there, slugger," Hayden grins at me. "Soft hands, remember?"

My stomach flutters. He's distracting—not just the smooth way he moves, making it look easy, but the energy coming off him. This is not going to help me get better at the game. I need to focus. I motion for Marissa to join me for a tete-a-tete.

"What's up?" Marissa asks, wiping the sweat from her brow.

"Strategy talk. If it's down the middle, you get it because it'll be your forehand. We're supposed to play up by the kitchen line. We can do this."

"You got it, teammate." We high five and go back to our places.

Hayden serves the ball, and this time I pull back and return it with more of a love tap—it kisses the top of the net and rolls over, dropping into the kitchen in a shot impossible to return.

Marissa and I squeal and clutch each other like we're kids again. The pleasure in making a good shot lights me up, and I remember how much fun I had playing tennis. This feeling is what I've been missing for so long. Play—the joy that fires my synapses. I can feel the dopamine and serotonin flooding my brain.

When was the last time I did something for the fun of it?

"Good play," Hayden compliments me, and the butterflies in my belly take off. I have to turn around to give myself a moment to wipe the goofy grin off my face.

After that, Marissa and I settle into a rhythm. We lose the match, but it's close. Turns out the rules of pickleball are nothing like tennis, but I know that once I get my brain on board with the new program, this is going to be a sport that I actually have a shot at. Hayden was right—it is easy to pick up, especially with a background in a racket sport. There are a ton of players of all ages waiting to play, and we give up our court to the next teams in line.

Hayden follows me back to the sideline. When Marissa adds our paddles to a stack of two, completing the people who will face off for that match, his face falls, but he smoothly moves his to the more advanced stack next to it. We take up positions on the sidelines, and he points out shots that the players are making and the hits I should watch out for. He's surprisingly easy to talk to.

Marissa waggles her eyebrows at me and mouths, "You go, girl!" behind him, before making up some excuse to give us some space.

I feel conflicted. What happens when Hayden realizes that I'm a middle-aged college drop out with grown kids and almost nothing to show for myself? I'm not running my own firm like Marissa or semi-retired like Brett. I don't even like the sales side of real estate. I can't shut up my ex-husband's voice in my head when he tells me all the things wrong with me. All the reasons I'm going to be alone forever if I leave him. All the reasons I'm past my prime, washed up, biologically useless now that I'm forty.

The other part of me wants to punch that ghostly voice in

the larynx and do exactly the opposite of everything he ever told me not to do.

"Have you signed up for the tournament yet?" Hayden asks, breaking me out of my downward spiral.

"I think Marissa went off to do that." I search the busy courts to try to find my missing teammate.

Hayden runs a hand through his hair, and it flops back over his eyes, boyishly cute. I want to ask him how old he is, but that'd be rude.

"How long have you played?" I ask instead.

"Couple years."

"Wow. How often do you play? You're really good."

He smirks at me, and I shiver. I need to get hold of myself before I do something embarrassing.

"Four or five times a week," he says. "I think your court's up."

Flustered, I find a stranger holding up the four paddles and looking for Marissa and me. I hurry over to join them. I glance back at Hayden, and he gives me a two fingered salute like he's wishing me luck. I barely know him, but having someone rooting for me feels good. Really good.

"Someone's got an admirer," Marissa singsongs.

"Shut up." I give her angry mom eyes and she laughs.

"You are too funny. Let's kick some ass so you can show your boy how much of a baller you are."

"Used to be," I say. "And, not my boy."

"Still got it, babe."

I hope so. The swing of my paddle, the shuffle of my feet, the high pitched thwap-thwop—so different from tennis, a cacophony that's strangely appealing the longer I'm in the thick of it. Marissa and I get better at calling the ball, letting only one or two slip between us. We win, eleven to eight. I needed a win.

"I think I like this game," I confess to Marissa as we make our way back to the line. Hayden is playing a fast-paced match against two older gentlemen who seem slower to move position around the court but drive killer shots across the net. Hayden is moving like an octopus to compensate for his less-experienced partner. His muscles flex like a jungle cat as he jumps up and smacks down the ball, winning a point.

"Yeah? You like something all right," Marissa teases me.

"I'm divorced, not dead."

"Babe, I've been trying to tell you that all year. Your best years are ahead of you. Go get it, girlfriend. Don't let that asshole keep controlling you from the sidelines. Have some agency in your own life."

I sigh. "That's what Frida told me, too."

"The feisty client?"

"Yeah. She doesn't want to move. I think we're going to drive to California before she finds a place she'll deign to give a second glance to."

Marissa nods. "That happens. Kids making her move?"

"Yeah. Her son got power of attorney after she fell in love with the wrong guy. Swindler."

"So sad. That can happen to anyone. She didn't let that stop her from living though, did it?"

I shake my head.

"And neither should you. One bad apple shouldn't ruin the whole crop."

"Eve ate the apple and doomed all of humanity to exile and pain."

"If Adam had eaten the apple, we'd have proclaimed it International Day of Knowledge or some shit. It's a sin only because a woman did it."

"True."

Marissa turns to me and puts a hand on my shoulder. "I just want you to be happy. With a partner or without one, it doesn't matter as long as you're not letting fear make the choice for you."

"Thanks, Rissa. I'm so lucky to have you." I give her a big hug and she squeezes me extra tight. I don't know how I would have gotten through the last few years without her. Maybe I would have worked up the courage to leave Brett years ago if I had met her sooner.

"Back at you, babe. Okay, enough blubbering. Let's sign up for this tournament and kick some ass. Tennis, pickleball, whatever you want. That court will be ours."

13

HAYDEN

I MISS ANOTHER SHOT because I'm too busy stealing glances at Celeste. She's cute in another short tennis dress and new shiny white court shoes that should help her not twist an ankle. Pickleball isn't fashionable like tennis yet—it's still too new, too much of an upstart rebel to tennis's worldly sophistication. But it'll get there. I know I'm not the only person to fall in love with the scrappy game. I'm not much into athletic-leisure or fashion, but I am self-aware enough to admit that Celeste's little tennis skirts are a welcome distraction on the court.

I let another ball fly by me, and Russell taps me lightly with his paddle. "Earth to Hayden. Come in, Hayden. You plotting again, or what?"

"Sorry, dude." I shrug self-consciously. Here I am ogling a woman instead of being a good teammate, but can you blame me? She's hot and I love the way she sneaks a peek at me when she thinks I'm not looking. Every thought flashes across her face like dappled sunlight through the trees, even though she only lets the polite words fly free. How I'd like to unbind her from those ropes of anxiety that hold her back and hear what she actually thinks.

"Are you thinking about signing up for the tournament?"

Russell asks, following my line of sight to where Celeste and her friend are studying the tournament poster and signing up on the website with their phones.

Maybe just turned into yes, but I'd really like to get in Celeste's good graces and earn more time with her. Maybe she'll let me train her. She's got good instincts, but you can tell she's a tennis player. I think she can get in fighting shape with some dedicated one-on-one time. I would love to give her that. Would love to have another shot learning her body and making her moan.

I just have to find an in.

Russell and I pull out the stops to finish the game with a narrow win, and Russell walks off shaking his head at my lack of attention. I almost trip over my own feet trying to get to the paddle stacks to see if there's room in Celeste's match. Hallelujah, the fates favor me today. I snag the last spot and stand up with a grin.

"You a beginner?" Marissa comes waltzing up with a smirk on her face.

"You know it," I say.

She hums noncommittally. I might be nervous if I didn't know she approves of Celeste dating. Marissa has been a good wingman so far. *Don't fail me now.*

"We're in the tournament," she says. "Looks like there's an age limit and experience limit."

"Right. So experienced players have to pair with newbies to keep it fair."

"What's stopping you from pretending to be a newbie to win?"

"My ego."

She laughs. "Of course. How many people typically show up for these tournaments?"

I scratch my jaw. "It's the first one the league has held since we convinced Dr. Fisher to learn to play."

"The athletic director?"

"He's the superintendent of Parks and Rec in Salmon Bay. King of kings around the court."

Celeste has joined us and my whole body turns to include her in the conversation, even though she stands a step behind her more extraverted friend. I try not to tower over her. My sisters are always knocking me for that, but I can't help being a beanpole. I don't mean to glower down at the peons; I'm just a bit awkward still, a bit uncomfortable talking to someone new. Someone I want to impress.

"Fisher is the one who's been repainting all the tennis courts with pickleball lines instead of making new dedicated pickleball courts?" Celeste asks.

I wince. "That'd be him."

"Has he ever asked the tennis players how they feel about giving up their courts?" Marissa asks.

"I don't know. Russell's friends with him though. I'll hit him up, see what he's got."

Celeste gives me a sad smile, and I wish I had a court to wrap in a pretty bow and gift her. Maybe I can ask Russell what he thinks. Maybe Dr. Fisher would consider dedicating certain courts for only tennis? It seems cruel to cater to one group at the expense of another.

I make a note to look into that, but I don't want to get Celeste's hopes up. One tennis court can serve a lot more pickleball players for a couple hours of fun and exercise than it can tennis players, and I know it's in his job description to get the population of Salmon Bay outside and exercising.

When our court is called, I find myself partnered with Warren. We size each other up skeptically. I want to ask him what he thinks he's doing in a beginner match, but he could just as easily turn that around to me. I can't exactly admit I'm here to hit on a pretty girl.

"You want to serve first or last?" he asks.

"First."

The ladies take their places. Celeste is worrying her lower lip between her teeth. She holds her paddle in a tennis grip, but I don't want to correct her here in front of everyone. Even I know that'd be a dick move.

Warren isn't playing to lose. Marissa pops a lob, and he slams it down the line in a move too fast for a beginner court. The ladies exchange a worried look, then Celeste runs to get the ball.

"Keep hitting them right there," Warren tells Marissa. "It's perfect."

I give Warren a flat look. "What's your deal?"

"Aw, bud. Did you forget your Big Boy paddle?"

I take a deep breath through my nose and let it out sharply through my mouth. Warren isn't a bad guy, but he doesn't always let kindness rule over competition. The pickleball rulebook is thick as an old phonebook, but there are certain rules that remain understood but unwritten—no head shots, no hitting people with your paddle, no being a dick. The general feeling is that this is a game, make it fun for everyone. But as it's gotten more popular, I've noticed more jerky behavior on the courts.

"Are you standing there for moral support?" he asks Celeste after she misses a ball.

She's not going to want to play if she thinks harassment is typical court behavior.

I've never heard Warren shit talk so much. He's not usually a dick.

After Warren fires the shots down the line and brings our score to seven-nothing, I start to get mad. Are we trying to scare new people away from the sport, or welcoming everyone? There's nothing like crushing some newbies to make them never want to come back.

I hit some easy balls to Celeste, and she drives them back toward my feet like I showed her. *Atta girl.*

"Soft serve," Warren chides, "You craving some ice cream?"

Then the worst happens: Marissa hits a forehand ball across

the net, and Warren returns it to her backhand. She twists to reach it, over rotates, and falls. Her ankle twists beneath her. Everyone watching inhales sharply in collective pain. Marissa's wail stops play on all courts. She's on the ground, clutching her foot.

Fear hits my gut like an iceberg.

"Is there a doctor on the court?" I call, running around the net to kneel by the fallen woman. "Is it broken? I saw a guy tear his Achilles like that once—"

"Please stop talking." She glares at me. "I don't want to hear worst case scenarios. Celeste, can you please call my husband?"

"Do you want me to call an ambulance?" I ask. "I could drive you to the ER."

She shakes her head. "Help me off the ground and onto a bench."

Warren is slower to come around to see his victim. It's not like he meant to injure her, but he wasn't playing very friendly either. "You good?" he asks gruffly.

Celeste glares at him, and I have to agree. "She's not, man. Here," I help her up by lifting her under the armpits and knees in a bridal carry. It's more comfortable than the fireman, less embarrassing for the injured too.

"Wow," Marissa says as I carry her to the benches and the whole audience cheers. "If I didn't know better, I'd say you set this all up just to look good in front of my girl."

I snort. "Pretty sure injuring her BFF would make me the least likely person she'd go out with, so no."

"But it wasn't your fault."

"That's right. It was Warren's." I grimace. Was he trying to sabotage a team right after they signed up for the tournament? She embarrassed him in front of his pickle kingdom—not on purpose, but guess it doesn't matter to him? Is his ego really that fragile that he had to lash out? My sisters are always talking about viewing the world through their shoes and seeing how many dangerous situations they face every day. What if I'm missing the dark side of the court because I'm a dude? I'm fairly likable, and I'm not easily intimidated, not after tangling with my dad.

Warren would never dare a cheap shot like that at me.

An emotion I haven't let myself feel in a long time bubbles up, thick and molten. He didn't hurt me, but I'm taking it personally because he's brought an ick factor into my safe space. He put a target on someone I like and hurt—accidentally on purpose—someone who is important to someone I care about.

The king needs a humpty-dumpty moment.

People clear the bench for me to put Marissa down on. Someone's waiting nearby and introduces themselves as a medical resident. They start probing Marissa's ankle and announce that it seems like a sprain, not a break, but she should get an x-ray.

Celeste is kneading her hands together as she watches her friend.

Marissa looks up at her. "Don't you dare."

"What? You got injured because—"

"If you say because of you, I'll climb off this bench and hide all your crosswords."

Celeste lets out a choked laugh that sounds suspiciously like she's trying not to cry. I want to hold her. I jam my hands in my pockets so I don't do something stupid, like reach out and tuck her beneath my chin. I feel like this is my fault. I shouldn't have put my paddle in a beginner game. I should have stopped Warren from joining too.

Another part of my brain latches onto our shared love of crosswords. How can I use that as another in with her?

"Doesn't matter, Rissa," Celeste tells her. "I just want you to be okay."

"You have to win the tournament for the two of us, Ceecee. Show that bully he can't pick on the little guy."

"But how can I play without you?"

"I'm sure you can find someone to fill in for me." Marissa

turns her laser eyes my way, and I stumble forward, ready to volunteer as tribute.

Me! Please pick me. I suddenly feel like I'm the fat kid back in middle school hoping I make it onto someone's team. "Marissa is right—you can't let him win. Team up with me. We can beat Warren. We can practice together and win that court for you and revenge for Marissa. Everyone loves an underdog story."

Celeste bites her lip, and again, I want to kiss it better. She's got an adorable crease between her brows. I try to look nonthreatening and guileless.

"I accept." Marissa holds out her hand to shake on it like I'm a knight pledging my loyalty to the queen, and I'll just bet she isn't as hurt as she's making out to be. I'll take it though. I'll take whatever help she's willing to throw my way so that I can get another chance with my Plumette.

Celeste gives her friend a flat look. Marissa smiles like a cat in cream. I could kiss her.

14

CELESTE

THE SKY IS PARTLY CLOUDY, mirroring my mixed feelings about meeting Hayden on the court to practice. On one hand, yeah, I'm tired of letting people push me around, and Marissa getting hurt ignited the tinder of rage that's been stacking up in my gut. It's time to let it burn. Time to make a stand. On the other hand, I've already started crushing on my pseudo coach. Am I strong enough, brave enough, to put myself out there again?

He's way too young for me, isn't he? What would people say?

Marissa told me to chill in no uncertain terms this morning when I called her with cold feet. She's resting on the couch, and Drew is managing the toddlers and bringing her ice and hot tea. He's pushed his meetings off so he can take care of his wife. I don't know how she got so lucky to have a guy who thinks she hung the moon and takes care of her when she's sick. I want that.

When I had little kids and was sick—even if I desperately needed a nap—asking for help always came back to bite me in the ass. Brett might give in grudgingly to watch the baby, but it was always followed by the rumble of his displeasure through the house, a storm cloud that never dissipated, no matter how pleasant and agreeable I tried to be. It was better to power through and not risk his wrath.

I shake my head out of my dark memories and pinch the skin between my thumb and pointer finger, using pain to ground me. I'm safe. Spring is busting out all over; irises stretch their purple blooms to the periwinkle sky. Pretty white clouds drift lazily across. I'm alive. I'm free. I don't have to be on guard against someone's constant anger anymore.

"You ready?" Hayden bounces a pickleball on his paddle, warming up his hand-eye coordination. Today he's in grey joggers that show off his muscled backside and a tight grey tee shirt that reads, "I'm dill-ightful!". The early morning sunlight gleams off his mahogany hair, bringing out strands of auburn and russet.

He is hard to look directly at without my heart rate picking up and a fluttery feeling squirming in my belly. I haven't felt this way since Mustachalicious ate me out in a broom closet and ignited my long-dead libido.

But Hayden is young and hot and charming—he could have his pick of the pretty girls jogging around Lake Dibble at this overachieving hour. I busy myself getting my bag hung up and my court shoes tied so he can't see the turmoil written all over my face. "Yeah, I guess."

"Naw, I want to hear—Hell, yeah! As I tell my kids, attitude is everything."

That brings my head up. "You have kids?"

He rubs the back of his neck. "Er, the kids I coach. My nephews and nieces."

"Oh, right. And how do they take your motivational pep talks? Do they think you're dill-ightful too?"

His eyes twinkle. "Don't matter what the critics say. I think I'm dill-ightful. That's all that matters. How's Marissa feeling today? Have you talked to her?"

Maybe my bar is low, but I'm tickled that he remembers her

name and checks up on her. "Yeah, she said we have to win it for her. She'll accept nothing less than total domination."

"I like that attitude. Let's warm up." Hayden is less attractive when he makes me jog with him around the lake. He's full of pep, while I'm dragging. My muscles burn with lactic acid, but even though it's uncomfortable, I know I should build this into my routine.

"Good job, Ladybird. 'Aight. Let's get hitting." He fills his pockets with pickleballs and takes his place at the serve line. The quick grin he gives me makes my heart trip in my chest. "Always serve with a smile; it's a dill breaker."

I laugh through the stitch in my side. "Your dad-joke game is strong."

"Coaching secret sauce: If they're laughing, they're not complaining." He bounces the ball once, then locks eyes with me. "Ready?"

"Yes, coach."

He smirks and drops his gaze to the ball. I feel hot suddenly.

"Score is zero-zero." He's very patient and encouraging, and I can just imagine him with the kids, running with them through the rain and mud of cross country. Not going to lie, it's hot. I'm telling myself to chill out as I watch his muscles flex beneath the soft cotton of his tee, but my body feels tingly in a way that makes me feel alive.

I fumble more easy shots. My embarrassment makes my playing even worse.

"We're going to work our way up and win our qualifying match," Hayden tells me. "I know we can do it, and Warren's ego is so big, he won't know we're coming until he gets pickled in his own vinegar. That work for you?"

"I want to win for Marissa. I'm committed, if you think we have a shot."

"More than a shot. We got this." He pats my shoulder, and I feel tingles all the way down my arm. "I hate bullies. Taking one down is going to be fun."

There's no point arguing. I'm going to practice and get better. No more bobbing along in the sea, letting my little boat be pushed around by outside forces. I'm going to loft my own sail and make the wind be my bitch to take me where I set out to go.

His eyes are deep green with brown striations, and a little gold. The more I get the know him, the more attractive his face becomes. Is it fair that he's both easy to look at and easy to be with? My poor heart doesn't stand a chance.

We move to the courts for drop-in pickleball and put our paddles in the intermediate stack, with the handles facing right. The courts are starting to fill up with an older crowd this early, but our first match turns out to be with a thirty-something couple who greets Hayden by name. He knows everyone here.

Ginny has a short purple pixie cut and full sleeve tattoos, and she's playing with a short stocky guy named Adam who has a septum piercing and a modern mullet. She touches his elbow playfully and gives him a smile that conveys more than a passing familiarity. We dink back and forth to warm up.

"Are they together?" I whisper to Hayden.

He studies them for a beat, then shakes his head. "You see that buff guy over there who looks like he eats small children for breakfast? That's her ex-husband, Max." I follow his subtle nod and see the guy who could be a strong man for a circus, complete with handlebar mustache, black curls to his nape, and a tight white tank top that shows off some impressive guns. His tongue is down the throat of a shorter, skinny dude.

"Who's the other guy?"

"Armando. Max fell in love, left Ginny, and moved into a camper van he parked in Mando's front yard. The three of them still play pickleball Monday, Wednesday, and Friday."

"What happens when they play each other? Or do they avoid putting their paddles in the same stack?"

"Oh, no. They've got something to prove, and they play

dirty. Pretty much everyone else pauses to watch. Better than Days of Our Lives."

"You watch Days of Our Lives?"

"With my mom. Don't judge."

"I'd never." I snort. Hayden looks like he got caught with his hand in the cookie jar and he's not mad about it.

Ginny and Adam start off strong, but they're so busy flirting with each other, I'm managing to hold my own. When Max isn't sucking face with Armando, he's watching Ginny flirt with Adam, and she plays it up any chance she can get. I'm not sure if Adam realizes he's just a prop or if he's fine with that.

Hayden and I are still trying to find our groove working as a team. He's still playing with his left hand to make the game more challenging for him and to give less experienced players a better chance at winning. I admire that. The only problem is that we're either clashing paddles in the middle, or we've got an open alley between the two of us.

"When we play in the tournament, you'll use your dominant hand, right?"

"Of course. Wouldn't want to give Warren an unfair advantage."

"Why not use it now so we can get accustomed to working together?"

"That's a good call." He switches his paddle to his right hand. His casual term of endearment has me fumbling the next shot.

Ginny serves next. Hayden lets the serve bounce in his corner and returns it to the far right. Adam lets it bounce and then dinks it back over the net into our kitchen. I rush forward and manage to hit the ball before it bounces a second time on our side. The next few minutes are slow, methodically placed dinks, and I wish I could slam a few to let this anxiety out.

Hayden spins the ball over the net, and it bounces at an unexpected angle. Ginny misses, and we earn a point. The evidence of progress soothes some of my anxiety, even if I didn't earn the point myself. I can do this. I know I can.

I serve low and fast, an inch above the net, and hear Hayden say, "Beautiful!" in his low, confident drawl. His praise is like a soothing hand over my head and down my nape, petting me, protecting me. I eat it up. His smile is a lighthouse in the endless night, and I need that light turned on me again and again, until I forget what it feels like to live in the dark.

I have it bad.

Ginny drives a ball down the middle. Hayden and I both go for it and run into each other. The shot goes out.

"You okay?" Hayden helps me off the ground, and I brush off my tennis skirt.

"Bruised my ego. No biggie."

"Let's work on our communication. Call it if you think you're set up best to hit it."

"Sorry."

He shakes his head again. "I'm going to have to institute a sorry jar policy."

"Is that like a swear jar?"

"That's right. Every time you say sorry, you have to add a dollar to the jar. When it's full, you buy me a drink."

"Is that so?"

"Yes, ma'am. No over apologizing."

"Did your sisters make that up?"

"You know it." He stretches, and the hem of his tee shirt rides up, displaying toned abs and a trail of dark hair leading down.

I yank my eyes away. My skin feels thin as a butterfly's wing. "Do they play pickleball too?"

"Sometimes. They've got real jobs too."

"What is it that you do?"

"I'm a writer."

"Really? That's cool. What do you write?"

"A little of this, a little of that," he says noncommittally, his eyes on something else across the court.

I wonder at his sudden cageyness.

"Like copy for marketing companies? Ghostwriting? Journalism?"

"I've done all of the above. Sometimes I write articles for the Salmon Bay Tribune with my sister Molly, who's a staff photographer."

"How—" I pause. "How old are you?"

His nose wrinkles as Ginny shouts out the answer, "Twenty-nine!"

"Oh, wow."

"Yeah, and he still lives with his mom," Ginny supplies with a wide grin. It seems like gentle teasing, but my stomach turns over. He's so young.

"Age is just a number, Celeste," Hayden tells me.

I don't get to dwell on his response, because our opponents serve. Twenty-nine? No wonder he's fit and agile. Have I totally misjudged his attention? Maybe charming and flirtatious is just his default setting? And he lives with his mom? Is he like Frida's ex and is hanging out with the retirees looking for his next sugar mama?

The ball wizzes past me and hits right inside the line. Hayden studies me, eyebrows drawn together. I should have gotten to that. I—God, my brain is whizzing at a hundred miles an hour as it goes over every interaction we've had. Have I been reading him wrong the whole time?

Before I know it, Hayden has called a time out and he gathers me into his arms.

I try to step back before people get the wrong idea about us. "What are you doing?"

"Celeste." He holds my arms very gently. I could get out if I wanted to, but his chest is hard and warm and...I like this, being held. I'll give it one more minute before I pull away. "Get your head in the game. Remember how Warren trash-talked you the last time you played him? He's going to do that again. And again. And you've got to let it slide off you like water over waxed canvas."

"You're really young."

The edge of his smile lifts on one side. "You're really beautiful."

My mouth opens and closes like a fish, but nothing comes out.

He leans down to whisper in my ear, and I smell his cotton and laundry detergent scent, the coconut of his sunscreen. His fingers stretch as he widens his grip across my back and pulls me more firmly against his chest. Maybe I haven't misjudged his attention at all. "Get your head in the game, Ladybird. Keep your eyes on the goal—payback for Warren and every other asshole who tried to hold you back."

"O-okay. Sorry."

"Another dollar. I think you owe me a drink after this."

I duck my head and chuff out a laugh. It's so ingrained, I don't even realize I'm apologizing.

"Are we playing, or what?" Adam calls from the other side. He scratches the back of his neck beneath his mullet with his paddle.

Hayden ignores him. "You good?" he asks me.

"Yeah. I'm good."

"Atta girl."

Our next match is against a mother-son duo who doesn't smile or talk. They're insanely competitive, and I have to double down on my mental game just to keep up.

"I like the way you dink it," Hayden murmurs in a low, flirty tone as we tap paddles and switch sides of the court, as we do every serve when we win the point.

"You can't say it like that," I tell him.

"Like what?"

I bite my lip, and the edge of his mouth quirks up. He knows exactly like what. I *like* him, and that makes me vulnerable to his sweet, silver tongue. If he's canvasing the court for his next sugar mama, he should look elsewhere—I've got nothing to offer. My money is tied up in the house. My baggage would require a jumbo jet.

But my hesitant, bruised heart won't listen to my practical, cynical brain.

My brain says Brett was charming too, to everyone else. Will Hayden start telling me to act a certain way around his friends? Look a certain way? Criticize me later when we're alone for tiny, imagined slights?

My heart says to give him the benefit of the doubt. Trust him until he breaks that trust. When people show you who they really are, believe them. I can't let Brett keep getting in my way of making a new life for myself, new friends, new...something more.

I take a deep breath and let it out in a long exhale.

"You good?" Hayden brushes his hand across my shoulder, and I let go of the tension I've been holding there.

"I'm fine."

He snorts. "Sisters, remember? Fine doesn't cut it."

"Sorry. I got lost in my head for a moment. I'm having fun playing. Really."

His fingers squeeze gently. "You let me know if that changes. We can take a break whenever."

I *have* been having fun, despite the worry simmering beneath the surface. I manage to last three more matches before I exhaust myself. By the last game, I'm missing balls left and right.

"You did well," Hayden says, sending a pleasant shiver down my arms. I'm dragging, but he's still got bounce in his step, ready to keep cracking.

"How do you have so much energy?" I gripe.

Hayden spreads his arms wide to encompass all the players huddled on the sidelines waiting for their turn. "Don't give me that excuse. You're a spring chicken compared to most of these energetic folks. You've just got to up your cardio. Add in some foot work and kettle bell. Have you connected with Sam yet?"

I look down at my feet and shake my head.

"None of that." He lifts my chin with two fingers, and the way he looks at me makes me feel like an onion—he's peeling back all my layers, all my shields. What if he sees all the tears I'm hiding?

"I've been busy."

"What could possibly be more important than your health?"

"Work. I'm trying to rehab my house to sell it."

"By yourself?"

I nod.

Hayden rubs his hand across the scruff of his jaw and looks around us like he's trying to decide something. "Alright, teammate. You wanna grab some lunch?"

"With you?"

"You still owe me that drink." His eyes twinkle, and my stomach swoops. "I know I'm hungry after running around. You must be. This is like our second date, right? You buy me that sorry-jar drink, and I'll feed you."

A whole herd of wildebeest starts a stampede in my chest. Guess this attraction isn't one sided? Winning the pickleball tournament seems easy in comparison to eating together, just the two of us. Some place casual. Some place familiar. "How does Miel Bagels sound? I like to get their crossword once a week."

Something flashes in his eyes. "You don't say?"

"Guilty." I shrug and look away. "I'm a nerd."

"You say that like it's a bad thing, Ladybird. Lead the way—"

15

HAYDEN

I'm on a date with a beautiful woman, and I'm trying to play it cool, but I know exactly what we're walking in to. I didn't mean to be there when she finished the crossword this week. My hands feel a little clammy, and I wipe them on my shorts before I place one on her lower back to guide her away from the court.

I hope Henrí isn't working today. He can't keep a secret for shit.

Celeste is glistening with sweat and make-up free. Tendrils of brown curls stick to her forehead. I imagine reaching out to smooth them back but force my left hand into my pocket instead. *Go slow, go slow.* She's like a Calathea, a house plant that provides beautiful foliage in striking patterns but needs a little extra love, a careful hand.

Miel Bagels is a small wood-fired bagel shop that makes amazing, traditional breads. The coffee is the best in the town, though some people might say those are fighting words. Scandinavians and Seattleites are religious about their coffee. I want to ask Celeste how she takes her coffee at home. I want to know everything about her, but she's skittish. I'm holding the interrogation back.

I hold the door open for her, and she takes a deep breath in of the warm, yeast-scented air. Her eyes roll back in her head, and she moans. My body reacts, and I have to distract myself by thinking of gross stuff, like toddlers with winter snot, health insurance lifetime limits, and viral TikTok books with bad writing and no plot.

Inside, Jorge is rolling out a strip of dough with a quick back and forth before pulling the ends together to make a ring. Montreal bagels are better than New York bagels in my humble opinion—they're smaller, thinner, denser, and always handmade. Sweeter too, as Jorge bathes the dough in honeyed water before giving them to Mama Leah to bake in the wood burning oven's fiery depths.

My stomach sinks when I see the grizzly of a man in a pink polo shirt and brown apron at the till. When Henrí sees me walking in with my hand proprietarily on a beautiful woman, his eyes light up. I make a slashing motion with my left hand down low, hoping Celeste won't see it, hoping Henrí will behave and play along. He lifts one eyebrow but turns to my girl without his usual bear hug.

"How can I help you, Celeste?" Henrí asks. "You want a bagel to go with your crossword today?"

I didn't realize he knows her by name, but I should have guessed, given she's a regular and Henrí's parents, Jorge and Leah Bellemare, own Miel Bagels. Salmon Bay is small, but not small enough that I know everyone. Our circles overlap, but we've never crossed paths. I would have remembered. My esophagus feels a little sour knowing Henrí met her first.

"Yes, please," Celeste tells him. "A baker's dozen."

"Good choice," Henrí says. His eyes flick to me, humor crinkling the edges where his lids kiss. He's a big dude, terse and intimidating, but inside he's a teddy bear.

"I'll take the rainbow bagels," Celeste says.

"Those are gluten free."

"And *rainbow*."

"A woman of discerning taste." Henrí rings her up, and she asks for the crossword.

Please be cool. Please be cool. I give Henrí my best glare as he reaches behind the counter to grab this week's printed crossword for her. Then he smirks and decides to mess with me.

"Hot off the press." He leans on the counter, closer to Celeste, a move that draws attention to his dinner-plate biceps. "Puzzle fan?"

"Crosswords," she says. She's not paying any attention to the former Salmon Bay High linebacker. He flexes again as she taps her phone to ring up her order, but her focus is one hundred percent on my latest creation. "Oh, look at this title— Love is a game for two." She laughs to herself, and I get a swoop of excitement low in my abdomen. "Frida will love this."

"Who's Frida?" Henrí asks. "Another woman of discerning taste?"

"More like debauched, lascivious, and wanton."

"Oh, a word nerd. I like this one." Henrí's eyes find me, and he smirks. I shake my head hard and motion with my hands to communicate the pain and torment I will inflict if he outs me.

Celeste finishes paying and moves to a table, still immersed in my latest creation.

Henrí stays leaning lazily on the counter. He rests his chin on one fist and bats his eyelashes comically. "Hey."

"Hey." I search the bagel case, but my mind is anywhere else. It's not like I want to lie to Celeste—not by omission—but I don't want her to stop treating me as a regular person. I don't want to take away the joy of the art by knowing the flesh and blood, imperfect, fallible human behind the curtain. *Never meet your heroes* might as well be tattooed across my clavicle.

"So this is the girl, huh?"

"Friend from pickleball," I say. I definitely told Henrí all about my wedding hookup, not because I wanted to gossip but because I wanted his perspective on whether I'd done something wrong to make her run. My shy girl would die of shame if she knew I spilled our intimate details. She doesn't even want to acknowledge it happened.

"Hmmm." He studies me for a beat longer, before standing up and pulling together my usual—salt bagel sandwich with tomato and cheese. I always get the same thing. "She's your biggest fan, Clark Kent. Is there a reason you're hiding your true identity?"

"Not hiding. But people like the mystique. If I show her behind the curtain, it'll take away some of the magic for her."

"You sure, dude?"

I frown down at the bagels, debating. She doesn't seem to have a problem glossing over our broom closet tryst. "She likes uncovering things for herself, and I don't want to make it weird. I laid the first clue. Don't take away the joy of discovery for her."

"I won't say anything." Henrí rings me up, then comps the meal with his employee discount. "I bet you—"

"No."

"—that you can't get her to go on a real date by the end of this meal."

This doesn't count? "No."

"I bet I could. I could tell her I know a guy who—"

"No! No, and if you do, I'm telling Molly that you're being a jerk."

Henrí fakes a gasp and clutches his imaginary pearls. "Hot Mama will never believe you."

I shrug and grab my sandwich. "You wanna risk that? I'm her favorite little brother."

"You're cutthroat, that's what you are," Henrí calls after me.

I'm usually the easy going one, but yeah, I can fang-up when I'm defending my territory. I fill two glasses of water and sit down across from Celeste. She's got a cute little wrinkle to her nose as she focuses on the crossword, her bagel forgotten by her elbow. "You do any other word puzzles? Wordle? Spelling Bee?"

She glances up at me through her lashes. "I've tried them, but I always come back to crosswords. Brett didn't like to subscribe to the New York Times, even for the puzzles."

"How long have you been divorced?"

She colors slightly. "Almost a year. Some habits are hard to break though, you know? He was controlling with the finances, and now that I'm on my own, I still have to count my pennies." She glances up at me again and back down.

Is she trying to tell me she's financially insecure? It feels like her comment is leading somewhere, but she doesn't elaborate. "I'm frugal too," I admit. "Nature, nurture, who knows? It's a way to stay in control of my own destiny."

"Mostly I'm saving for the house. I'm fixing it up on my own. Everything I have is going into getting it ready to sell. It will be my first big solo project once I get my real estate license. I've been apprenticing to Marissa."

She doesn't strike me as a person who'd enjoy sales. She's shy and introverted. A shell closed up tight against the raging tide. "You enjoy it?"

She bites her lower lip again. "It kind of fell into my lap. Marissa was doing it already, and she needed someone to help drive her clients around to look at retirement homes so she could sell their houses. I was experienced at driving carpool. The job gave me flexibility to still be there for my kids while they were in high school." Her hair falls over her face as she studies the puzzle. "Made Brett mad." She fills in the answer to a clue and crosses 14-Across off the list.

"He didn't like you making your own money?"

"He wanted me cooking and cleaning and waiting on him. The perfect little tradwife."

"Got it." Sounds like an asshole. I can't believe she went to his wedding. I can't believe I went to his wedding, but I didn't know the guy then, and I'm so glad I did go. I got to sweep this sweet woman who is far too good for him off her feet. When she looks at me, does she see *me*, or does she still see the man with too much hair and polyester? Despite how ridiculous I looked —ridiculously awesome—did she find the costume less intimidating than she finds me now?

"What's the crossword this week?" I use the opportunity to lean closer to her so that I can see the paper and smell her shampoo. I'm shameless. I know.

She puts the end of the pencil between her teeth. It shouldn't look so sexy, but my blood runs south. "It's a heart," she points out. "A love theme. Oh! 60-Across is 'words to end a tennis match'! Fifteen letters."

"Cute." I tap my fingers on my thighs, antsy as fuck to be right here when she untangles my clever clues.

"I know: GAME SET AND MATCH." Her light laugh is the tinkling of fairy bells, and I'm such a hopeless case now, I might as well melt into the floor like a puddle of goo.

Should I grab a pencil and paper from Henrí so I can take notes on this feeling? It's uncomfortable. I don't think I've ever read a book that nails this tightness in my chest, this need to move. I feel like I need to slather my skin in calamine lotion. Am I breaking into hives—or is this love?

Can't put that in my novel. My editor will send me back another lemon emoji.

But maybe my readers would understand—at least those who've recently been afflicted with a growing crush. It's so much less ravished and wind swept than I remember. This vulnerability is not a warm glow, but maybe that will change if she gives me some indication that she feels the same way.

"What are you grinning about?" Celeste's cheeks are pink, her chocolate eyes wide and hypnotizing.

"Am I?"

"Are you what?"

"Grinning. Am I making you nervous?"

"People don't usually grin and stare crazily at me."

I chuckle and wave at her puzzle. "Just enjoying the show."

"I'm not doing anything—oh! I'm sorry. Am I ignoring you?" Her eyebrows kiss in cute little frown.

"Nah. I don't mind. I'm not someone who needs to fill the silence. Keep on. I just like to watch you light up while you puzzle it out."

She tucks a curl behind her ear. So cute. "We could chat while I work. Or you could help me answer—"

"I wouldn't dream of depriving you of the discovery. Tell me about your house projects. Are you working with a contractor?"

She grimaces. "I'm doing most of it myself. Lots of little patches and sprucing to be done. Lots of deferred maintenance."

"Let me guess, your ex didn't want to spend the money on it when you guys lived there?"

"Nope. I got really good with duct tape."

"Industrious."

"Desperate times call for desperate measures." She shrugs like it's no big deal and not super impressive that she's persevering through adversity. "Since then, I've learned a lot on YouTube. It's satisfying working with my hands, you know? It's validating to find a problem and fix it myself."

"Hella impressive." *As clever as you are beautiful*, I want to tell her, but it's too soon. It's always too soon. I'm always too much. The women I've dated in the past were never ready for the real me. Is Celeste going to be the same? I should test the waters.

"Not really. I wish I knew how to do more. The community college has home repair classes for women, and maybe once this house is sold, I'd have the money to take a class or two. Right now, I have to hire professionals for the electrical and more complicated plumbing projects but working with them is... difficult."

"Let me guess, a bunch of burly guys talking down to the little woman?"

"Yeah." Her shoulders relax. "You wouldn't believe how difficult it is to get them to listen to me. They always ask to talk to my husband first, even though I'm the one who hired them. Then they tell me the problem is not what I've told them it is, or that it isn't a problem, or they make a mistake and turn it around so it's somehow *my* mistake." She scoffs. "I wish there was a team of tradeswomen who I could hire. No mansplaining. No gaslighting."

"I get it. My mom and Molly sometimes ask me to come over and stand next to them while they describe their problem to the contractor. I'm embarrassed on behalf of my gender."

Her small smile draws an answering one of my own. "I never tried that, but I bet I could ask Brody to run interference for me. It's the principle of the thing, you know? It's the 21st century. It should be better than this."

"I'm happy to provide my manly moral support anytime you need." I take a bite of bagel so I can't offer to slay all her dragons for her—she doesn't want that or need that. "I'm happy to be a shoulder to lean on or a friendly ear."

"Thanks." She takes a big bite of bagel too and gets a bit of cream cheese stuck to her lip. I reach across and brush it off for her. "So why are you single?"

I start laughing, and after a moment of surprise, she joins me.

"Sorry! Sorry. That just came out. I mean, you seem emotionally available and good looking, so…"

"Thanks." I grin at the adorable reddening of her cheeks and the way she clutches the napkin to her mouth like she can stop herself from saying anything else embarrassing. "My mom asks the same question."

"She must be a strong woman."

"She is. So are you."

She clears her throat and picks up her pencil again. "Not really."

"You survived what sounds like a difficult marriage with a difficult man, raised two sons, had the ovaries to leave the life that was making you miserable, to start over and reinvent yourself. If that's not strong, I don't know what is."

"I guess I always hoped I'd have more to show for myself at forty."

"That's kind of the human condition, isn't it? To never be satisfied and always be striving?"

Her nose wrinkles again. "I'm not like that."

"What? Unsatisfied?"

She chews her bottom lip, and I know she's picking up on the innuendo that I'm laying down. Her eyes flick up to me and hold my gaze. "Like I said, I'm good with my hands."

Fuck me. The blood rushes from my brain to my balls, and I have to readjust myself.

Henrí, my *former* friend, decides that's a good moment to pop in and check on our table. "Can I get you fine folks anything else?"

Celeste uses her napkin to hide her smile.

"Nope," I bite out. "We're good here."

"Are you sure? Because I could get you some more waters. Hey, you need any help with that crossword?" With that, Henrí, the dead man, plops himself down on the bench next to Celeste and starts reading over her shoulder. He was a big guy in high school, but he got even more ridiculous in his early twenties, and now he towers over Celeste. I watch her body freeze like a rabbit beneath the eyes of a wolf. Her knuckles are white where they grip the pencil. I want to take that pencil and write a blistering review on her ex-husband's Linked-in.

I guess you type those, but...whatever. That asshat isn't worth the ink.

Henrí is an observant dude, and he scoots the hell away from her before I can even get a word out. "You're crushing that crossword. You didn't even need help, did you? Most folks ask me for a hint or two."

"I guess I find it fun?" I hate the tremor in her voice, because I recognize that fear that you'll be judged for the things that make you happy. Like you aren't worthy of joy. Like what you want and who you are doesn't matter.

"You're smarter than me," Henrí says as he scratches the back of his thick neck. We became friends sophomore year when I had to tutor him in math so he could get his grades up and play football. Our friendship took a short break after graduation when he admitted he was crushing on my sister.

I learned pretty quickly that good guys like Henrí are much preferable to assholes like Molly's ex. If only she'd see him as a grown man with a heart of gold and not her little brother's friend.

"Do you play pickleball?" she asks tentatively when Henrí doesn't leave.

He grins. "*Mais oui.*"

I watch her face pale and her eyes flicker over Henrí's body before coming back to his face. Henrí is from Montreal. He taught me French in high school—but only enough dirty talk to woo the ladies. Does she replay our closet escapades like I do? I enjoyed murmuring sweet ridiculousness in her ear as my hands molded her curves to mine almost as much as she loved hearing it.

It's been on my tongue multiple times to bring it up. Only her reluctance to address it stops me. I don't want to make her uncomfortable. I want to repeat it, asap, but I can be patient. She's worth this itch in my skin, this strain in my lungs when she's near.

I need to think of a better way to word this feeling of being stretched thin between hope and fear. "So, Celeste, read any good books lately?"

Not my smoothest conversational lob, but it'll do.

"I've been listening to an audiobook: Wild by Cheryl Strayed."

"I love audiobooks." Henrí pulls up a chair from a nearby table and makes himself at home.

I try not to grimace. "How is it?"

"Fine. I'm reading a bunch of big life change literature written by women. Oprah's book club stuff. Go ahead, laugh."

"Why would we laugh?" I ask, hating her ex again.

"Ah, no reason." She bites her lip. "Mommy porn and bra-burning books aren't real literature?"

Fuck. Is she repeating something she heard, or does she believe that? I'm afraid to find out.

"Actually," Henrí says solemnly, "I love historical romance audiobooks. Sweeping, epic awesomeness. Have you ever read Tru—"

I cut him off. "Try Outlander. Everyone's heard of that. Lots of guys like it. That author is laughing all the way to the bank. You read it?"

She shakes her head. "Brett wouldn't...I guess I could. If it's good. Have you?"

"I stole it off my sister Molly's bookshelf when I was thirteen, and my whole world shifted. That story swept me away from the trials of being a teen and the creeping reality of my mom's declining health. Violent, passionate men who wear skirts—such a different model than my dad gave me for being a man."

Celeste is gaping at me. My leg is bouncing underneath the table, but I can't cut off my train of thought. Is this too much? It's only our second date.

Henrí comes to the rescue. "I loved it too."

"You?" Celeste's focus turns to my best friend, and I have the sudden urge to throw my bagel at him.

"The narrator for the audiobooks does a killer job on the accent," Henrí says. "Sexy as fuck."

"Huh." Celeste turns back to her crossword and studies the next clue. "Guess it wouldn't be so popular if it wasn't good."

"Another book I really like—" Henrí tries again.

"Look, dude. We should really be off. Celeste is going to buy me a drink." I stand and pick up my plate.

"I..am?" She follows my lead and stands. "Right, I am. Uh, Station 18 again?"

"Sounds good. See ya, Henrí"

The answer to this quandary has to wait until later; I can't bear to see her face if she finds out right now. It's too soon. I'll tell her when we're farther along. When she's gotten comfortable with me. When I've had more of a chance.

Dad always told me to suck it up and be strong, but books gave me a safe place to *feel*. I was hooked after that first one, and I used to help Gramps out with the church rummage bins just to get my hands on more used Harlequins that all the grandmas donated. Having to hide that part of me was ingrained from the get-go, and even though Gramps and Dad are long gone, I still have their voices stuck in my head.

The one time I tried to share my passion with my girlfriend, she had a problem with it. Jordyn took to social media to talk about her boyfriend using a female pen name to write books about falling in love, and the internet took up their pitchforks. She quickly decided we should be just *friends*.

Celeste hasn't built enough trust for me to spill my guts yet. I'm enjoying her company and hoping for more, but there's a lot of ground to cover before we go sharing our darkest secrets. Henrí just has to keep his big yap shut and let me woo her a little longer. Let me make it through this pickleball tournament, then I'll tell her. If she hasn't fallen for me by then, there's no point dragging this out. Either she likes me for me, or she doesn't.

I just hope she chooses door number one.

Love Is a Game for Two

by Lord Lexicon

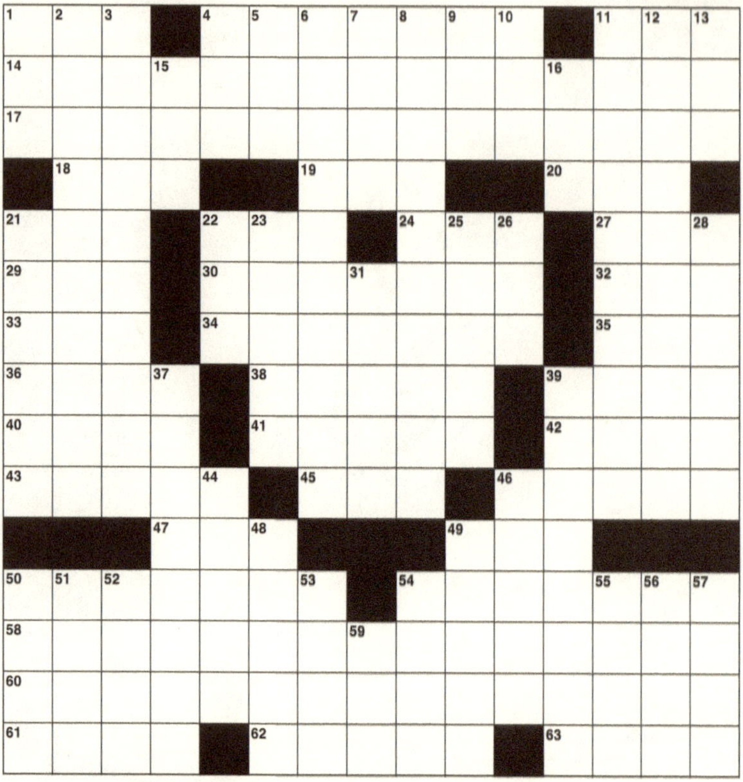

1	2	3		4	5	6	7	8	9	10		11	12	13
14			15								16			
17														

(grid continues)

Miel Bagels - *Sweeten your day the Montréal way*

ACROSS		DOWN	
1	Def predecessor	1	Inedible type of candy
4	Winding	2	Enterprise entrance
11	One millionth of a gram: Abbr.	3	Baker's mixture
14	Words before a fresh start	4	"ttyl" response
17	Words for bending the rules	5	Confess, with up
18	"Smol" yowl	6	"Yeah, there's a noise"
19	Trouble	7	LPGA golfer Thompson
20	Objects once burned for loved ones, briefly	8	Affirmative additions
21	Big hotel waiter?	9	Bill devoted to science
		10	Lincoln's party, in brief
		11	Robin Hood's lady love

ACROSS

22 49-Across skill
24 Actress Thurman
27 Brand with a butterfly logo
29 Legal org. founded in 1878
30 "Let's settle this!"
32 Bedazzle
33 Nip
34 Concisely
35 Dorm supervisors: Abbr.
36 Senior worries, briefly
38 Happy-hour seat
39 Bed buildup
40 First class, briefly?
41 Lustful
42 Cut
43 TV spot seller
45 Post-WWII treaty grp.
46 Stark in "Game of Thrones"
47 Like one just out of the shower
49 22-Across expert
50 Time for a booty call?
54 Roman magistrate
58 Words to start a relationship
60 Words to end a tennis match
61 Parched
62 Savvy
63 "How Do I Love Thee?", for example

DOWN

12 Pedestrian paths
13 Lead-in to X, Y, or Z
15 Morning moisture
16 Global time standard: Abbr.
21 Himalayan retreat?
22 One on a beat
23 Scam with a fake email
25 Ecstasy, slangily
26 Even one
28 Arizona competitor
31 Actress Birch of "Ghost World"
37 Sharply criticized
39 Atlas page for the United States
44 Sly looks
46 Blarney
48 Yarns
49 Weather away
50 Rapper in the press for dating Kylie Jenner
51 Feathery type of frost
52 Widely read Persian poet
53 Love of one's life
54 Inks
55 Latin jazz bandleader Puente
56 One time only
57 Former NPR host Diane
59 Loo

16

CELESTE

WHEN I PICK UP FRIDA the next morning, I'm eager for her perspective. I couldn't stop thinking about Hayden, and I'm pretty sure you could pack leftover cheesecake in the bags under my eyes. He's young. He's hot. He's ridiculously good at pickleball. Why would he be interested in me in *that* way? Am I reading too much into it? Or am I being needlessly self-sabotaging?

Today Frida is wearing an orange velour track suit over another midriff top and giant gold hoop earrings. Her curls are plump, her bangs pulled back in a diamond clip. Her wooden clogs have two-inch heels and cute rhinestone-encrusted buckles. Her fingernails are long and orange and glued with matching sparkly stones.

"Vat do you have for me today?" she asks when she settles into the car, and I hand her the drip coffee and apple Kringle slice I picked up at the bakery for her. As usual, the morning line snaked out the door, even though the coffee is strong enough to stand up a spoon. "I hope it is better dan de last place."

"I hope so too," I tell her honestly. "But I'm enjoying driving you around until you find a place that suits you. I think you'll like the community feel once you get settled. Maybe you'll find people with similar interests or—"

"Hot Silver Daddies."

"Excuse me?"

She takes a drink and gives me a judgy look over the top of her cup. "Did you tink us old people don't get it on? Pfft. Dose homes are full of disease. Too many randy dicks and not enough good sense."

I put the car in gear and pull away from the curb. "I see...so you're looking for love? Or not?"

She snorts. "You blush at the littlest tings. You are entering the prime of your life."

"Middle age is hardly—"

"Your prime as a woman," she says. "You are empowered. Go get what you want, and don't let anyone get in your way."

"How about you? Or did I get the wrong idea about whose idea it was to sell your house and find a retirement community?" I immediately feel bad about being snarky. I squeeze my fingers on the steering wheel as I glance over at Frida to see if she's going to fire me.

Frida scowls and turns toward the window. "Make one mistake, and they want to lock me up and trow away the key. You can still fight. You must fight for what you want." She reaches her hands forward and squeezes her fists like she's grabbing hold of something.

It's powerful, the way she talks. I want to believe her. I know I birthed and raised two amazing young men. I know I did it alone, far from friends and family. I know I survived twenty years married to a narcissist. But Frida's right—I'm no longer content with survival—I want to *thrive*.

"When I vas your age, I traveled and met a younger man on the beach in Spain. He was much younger, and we spoke almost none of the same language. He took me to the movies, and he fucked me in the women's bathroom in the middle of the show. But he only had one condom. No boy scout, that one."

I take a drink of my latte partly to cover my chagrin. I can't even imagine hooking up with a stranger in a public bathroom.

On the other hand...is a storage closet any different?

I guess I do have a little crazy in me. Stache Guy stoked an ember deep inside, and it's still burning, waiting for more passion to consume me. I wish I had stayed to see what he would do next.

"And once the condom came off inside me, we had to stop to pull it out, but didn't have a spare one. He wanted to keep going and put it in the back door!"

I choke and spray latte all down my shirt.

"I know, *ja*? What was he tinking? Not in the restroom of the movie theater with no condom and no lube. He is not getting a second chance with me, *nej*."

"So, you ...walked out?"

"No, of course not. We went back to watch the movie, *ja*?"

"With...okay." I shake my head and rummage in the door pocket for the wet wipes I keep on hand for emergencies like this. I find them and manage to blot my shirt while still driving in a straight line. "Was the movie...good?"

Frida laughs her deep rasp and examines her nails. "Don't remember a ting about it. He fingered me in the seats when we sat back down. Poor planner, but good at improvising."

I shift in my seat, remembering my mustachio fling in the broom cupboard. Improvising is good.

We drive up the ridge to Dane Hejm, a newer grey-on-grey building with killer views of Salmon Bay, both the little town and the body of water it's named for. The ship canal slithers through the industrial neighborhoods, cement trucks and seafood packaging plants competing for space along the waterfront. Past the bridge, Fishermen's Terminal bustles with working boats getting ready for their next stretch at sea. In the distance, white ferry boats carry passengers to and fro across a sparkling Puget Sound. The iconic railroad bridge across Salmon Bay is lit by the morning sun, and, with the jaw dropping backdrop of the snow-capped Olympic Mountain range, it looks like the most glorious postcard brought to life.

"You could have this view every day if you lived here," I tell Frida, almost wishing I was over fifty-five and qualified for residency. Even Frida lets out a low whistle. Sometimes I forget how beautiful this town is. It's right in front of me, every day, and I take it for granted until the clouds part and I'm hit right in the face. I'm lucky to be here.

"This one is promising," I tell her, "Even though it's called the Dane and you're a Swede—"

Frida flicks her hand through the air to cut me off. "I had a Dane once. Dis is more promising for the Hot Silver Daddies."

"Right." I park in front of the building and run around to her door to help her out.

"You're blushing again."

"Sorry."

"*För i helvete*,"—Frida exhales in exasperation—"stop apologizing."

I'll get right on that. Blinking against the sudden tightness in my eyes, I guide her to the welcome desk, and we start our tour, ending with dessert, of course. The Dane is more expensive than the places we toured the first day, but the residents seem happy, and the views are amazing. Frida sniffs at the dessert, lemon custard, but manages to eat both her serving and mine.

She studies me from across the table. The dining hall is decked out in lavish crystal chandeliers and a big modern gas fireplace that gives it a cozy ambiance. Even if Frida couldn't afford one of the nice apartments looking west toward the water, she could enjoy this view from the dining hall every day. This place has a huge number of social clubs, from gin rummy to pickleball to silver screen cinema. I think Frida could thrive here.

I hope I can afford a place like this when I'm eighty.

Sometimes I feel like I started so late at making and saving my own money, I'll never catch up.

"You look like a girl who needs some dessert in your life."

I look up from my notepad as I gather my thoughts.

"Your eyes," Frida says, pointing at me with her spoon, "dey are sad."

"I'm...in transition," I say diplomatically. "We share that."

Her smile curls like a cheshire cat. "*Ja*, we have lots in common. You read?"

"Yeah, when I have time."

"But romance. You read romance? You know, bare-chested men on covers, swooning ladies? Fabio?"

Brett never wanted me to read romance. I think he worried I would get *ideas*. Porn for women, he called it. I shake my head. "My ex was intimidated by it."

"He's an ex for reasons, *ja*?" Frida leans forward and drops her volume. "I have never met someone who needs a good dicking as much as you."

I cover my face with my hands as my cheeks blaze. What is it with everyone telling me I need to get some? Everyone is desperate for drama, as if I should provide them a front row seat to the reality TV show that is my life. Honestly, the thought of meeting strangers on the internet, suffering through small talk of a first date, and working up the courage to take someone home sounds like hell on earth. I'm not outgoing. I wasn't before Brett, and I'm certainly not after him.

Frida digs in her purse and pulls out a trade paperback with the image of a couple dressed in vaguely 1940s clothes watching the sunset together. It's got a vintage postcard feel, but modern typography. "Here. You read dis and tell me what you tink next time we meet. I have more for you. You like vampires? Mafioso? Billionaire playboys?"

"None of the above?"

"How do you know until you try?"

I take the book. Besides, I don't live with Brett anymore. I should probably start doing exactly all the things I've been curious about that he told me not to. I read the cover. "Captive Hearts by Trudy Belle?"

"She is good. Dis one won many awards. You will like it." Frida waggles her eyebrows at me. "On fire too." She pretends to touch a flame and jerks her hand back like she got burned. "Ow!"

My laugh bubbles up. "Sure. I'll give it a go."

"Good. Now let us get out of dis house of sin. I need fresh air and a smoke."

I tuck the book under my arm and let her lead the way back to my car. We stop at the same park as before on our way back home. Frida picks the same bench so she can heckle the pickleballers while she mouths her unlit cancer stick. She points out which men are in good shape for their age, and which younger guys I should go talk to. As if. She tells me what she would do if she had my young, spry body—and it wouldn't be playing pickleball. I blush, but I'm more relaxed today than I was before at her antics.

"Have you ever tried pickleball?" I ask her.

"In the seventies, *ja*. It was a fun little game. Look at it now —all grown up and looking *good*." She motions to the fit guys playing an aggressive game on the far court. "If I had known it would be such a good view, I would have kept at it. How is your game? Is your coach getting you fit and physical?"

I give an awkward laugh and feel heat race across my skin, which Frida picks up on immediately. She starts to laugh, and it turns into a hacking cough. She thwacks her chest until it subsides, and she can get a lungful of air.

Instead of begging her to stop smoking, I tell her about the tournament and Hayden, leaving out the juicier details even when she presses hard. Unsurprisingly, she spends the next twenty minutes telling me how to seduce my new pickleball coach. I am inordinately glad that Hayden is not at the court right now listening to this. He would be rolling on the ground laughing. I'm beet red and my eyes are starting to water from holding in my laughter by the time she gives up.

Unfortunately, the players closest us can hear Frida's loud suggestions just fine; I can tell because their play slows, the loud thwop of the ball quieting to the plink-plunk of dinks into the kitchen. I catch them sneaking looks our way with curious side eyes. I recognize Max and Amalie, who are practicing drills. Looks like the experienced Max is coaching the greener Amalie on how to win the tournament. I give them a bashful wave before pulling the crossword out of my bag so I can hide my face behind it. I make appropriate noises of interest as Frida goes on about her past escapades and how I should do everything she did but worse.

"Look at that serve," Frida declares, "dat one would be a god in the bedroom."

I blow out an amused breath. Marissa would love this woman.

"What do you tink?"

"I think a six-letter word for patron of the arts is—"

She whacks me on the arm. "You are not listening to my sage advice."

"I'm listening! That guy is much too young for—"

"And you are in love wit your pickle coach."

"And I'm—no! I'm not in love. I *like* him. I like him more than I should. He's very attractive and charming and too young for me, so there's no future for us—"

"Bah! You listen here, *lille en*, society will never embrace *gumma* like us until we start embracing ourselves. You are powerful. You are beautiful. And, *fan också*, you deserve to be worshiped like the goddess you are."

"Someone hears you talk like that, they'll come with the pitchforks."

"*Ja*, they burn us; still we rise. My son says I have no filter. I say, if an old woman can't speak her mind, who can?"

"Sorry, I have a lot of things on my mind." She prods and

pries until I tell her all about my struggles fixing up the house to sell, studying for the real estate exam, and mom-life supporting Ryder and Brody from an approachable—but not smothering —distance. Running through the mental load helps clarify what I actually need to do, versus what would be nice to do. "Maybe you should send me a therapy bill," I joke.

"Life coach," she says. "Young people never tink to ask, but we have years of experience to draw on."

"You should organize," I say. "Rent-a-Granny for Sage Advice."

There's a moment when our eyes meet, and I can almost see the lightbulb turning on reflected in her face.

"Celeste," she says slowly, calling me by name for the first time since we met, "you might have a verra *gud* idea there."

"Frida," I tell her. "You might be right."

17

HAYDEN

FOR THE NEXT THREE WEEKS, I meet Celeste on the pickleball court for an hour before dark to practice for the upcoming qualifier. It's never as much time as I want to spend with her, and most of that time is spent talking about pickleball, but she's unfurling slowly like the spiral buds of a moonflower vine, bright white petals against the dusk. I look forward to this hour like every one might be my last. Careful, ethereal, elegant. She's warming up to me. Building trust and teamwork as we dink and drop shots.

Sunday, I plan something different for our agenda. I pick Celeste up from the house she's working on. It's a nineteen fifties split level in a sea of similar homes—obviously built at the same time by a single developer for the baby boom after the war. I can't believe she's doing all the work herself. It must be a labor of love; her pride at her accomplishments shines through. She shows me the native landscaping that she's replaced the yard with—azaleas and rhododendrons, Salal and cascade strawberries. Kinnikinnick lines the river rock dry creek bed that helps the rainwater drain naturally away from the house.

Needs a paint touch up. Her face tightens when I mention that.

"The painter took off," she says miserably. "Said he finished the job, but even you can see the mess he made of the trim, right? I don't even think the south wall is the same color as the rest of it, and he got paint on the brick."

"You called him on that, didn't you?"

"Of course. He told me I was wrong. We argued." She holds up her hands in a helpless gesture. "Maybe if I were a man he wouldn't have dared take off and leave me with this mess."

"So what are you going to do about it?"

"The only thing I can do is not pay him the last part of the invoice, but he said he'd sue me if I fail to pay."

"Take pictures of his mess ups and then find someone else."

"No one else has room in their schedule to do this in the next month. I have to do it myself."

I raise an eyebrow at her, but she's too busy cataloging the work stacked up for her to see. Ask for help, I want to say to her, but I bite my tongue. She'd say no without hesitation. "Have you ever thought of starting your own woman-owned and operated construction firm? You could have your own painters, plumbers, carpenters, and electricians."

"Me?" she laughs. "Who'd hire me with my YouTube DIY education?"

"You'd be surprised at what people will pay you to do if you're passionate about your job."

She hums noncommittally, but the crease in between her eyebrows tells me she's thinking about it.

"I bet you could reach out to some local trade schools and connect with recent female graduates. You're good at organizing things, right? You could be like the creative director. The boss."

I'm not sure what I'm expecting with my unasked-for advice, but she tucks her hands in the crook of my elbow and leads me back toward my car. My heartbeat skips along, merrily excited at this not-quite-date. We're not going anywhere fancy, but showing her where I live and maybe meeting my mom is a big step. Is it too soon?

"We could turn around and stay in," I tell her. "I could help you with a project."

"You know anything about plumbing?"

"No, but I know how to google."

She snorts. "Don't tempt me with a good time." She takes one last look at the house before shaking her head. "Another time. Let's go play. I'm ready for a break."

I open her door and help her in. With one hand braced on the top of the car and the other on the door, I cage her in. She doesn't seem to mind me lording over her anymore. Her body trusts me, even if her mind shies away.

"So where are we going?" Her eyes are wide pools of caramel, and her thick lashes shadow her cheekbones. I want to touch the smooth skin of her cheek and trace the curve of her jaw. I want to brush her curls behind her shoulder so I can reach her neck with my lips and tongue. "You're being so cagey."

"Good things come to those who wait." I take a big step back and gently close the door. My writer's brain was hijacking the show there—I need to remember that this isn't only partly a date, and we won't have any privacy once we leave here. I send one more longing glance to her house. We could stay and make new, better memories in every room. Really reconsecrate it with positive energy. Chase the ghosts from the halls with the sounds of our lovemaking.

Celeste knocks on the window and gives me a "WTF?" look. Henrí would have a field day with this. I was always getting called out by teachers for not paying attention in class.

Climbing in the driver's side, I start up the car and point us toward the water. "We're going to my mom's childhood home," I tell her. "My grandma left it to me when she died, but I didn't need all that space. I told Molly to move in there after she split from her ex."

"You live with your mom, right?"

"I live in the carriage house. It's been converted into a sweet little one-bedroom apartment. Molly's got two kids that needed room to run around. My mom lives in the big house too and watches them after school so Molly can work. I help out whenever they need me."

"Wow, that's...amazing."

"That's what families do." I get the feeling Celeste didn't have much of a support structure. My dad might have been old school in some of his beliefs, but he was there for me if I needed him. I turn down the next arterial and toward the water. The sun beats down overhead. It's looking like a beautiful day for outside sports.

When I pull up in front of the historic landmark that is my grandparent's house, there are far too many cars parked along the street. I recognize every one of them, and my stomach sinks. I hurry around to the passenger side and offer Celeste my hand to step out of the car.

She draws in a sharp inhale when she catches sight of the house. "Wow. You live here?"

"I promise, it looks best from outside," I tell her. "Only three beds, one bathroom. Barely modernized."

"It looks like a haunted house," she says, but her eyes crinkle in the corners as she smiles. She's not scared of a few ghosts.

"Slander." I straighten an imaginary tie and point toward the gingerbread cupola topped with a weathervane like I'm giving an architectural tour. "This Swiss Chalet Revival style historic home might come with its own cemetery, but the rumors of ghostly inhabitants are entirely unsubstantiated. Yes, the kitchen hearth is big enough to roast half a cow, but we have no evidence that Brunhilda Norgard lured neighborhood children with cookies and baked them into her blue-ribbon winning meat pies."

Celeste gasps in mock horror.

I hold my hand up like a boy scout. "No lie. Besides, the main building has all the ghosts. I live in the carriage house." I point out the smaller building tucked beneath a towering arthritic Big Leaf Maple. The former garage matches the color and gingerbread of the big house. My little enclave over the wood workshop is a roomy one-bedroom apartment. "That's me."

"It's beautiful, Hayden."

My chest swells with fizzy bubbles of pleasure from her approval. I like the way my name sounds on her lips.

Just then, the squeal of little demons splits our sweet little bubble of quiet perfection. I grit my teeth. "You know how I said my mom has a court in her backyard?"

"Yeah?"

"Well, I might have mentioned that we're stopping by to use it."

"And? You're making me nervous."

Another squeal splits the air, followed by the high donkey bray of a tween-age boy. "I told them so that they'd stay away, but they obviously have too much time on their hands. Looks like we'll have company. They're a lot, but they mean well."

"I'm sure they're lovely," she soothes.

Ha! If only she knew. "Steel yourself, woman. We're going in."

"Is your family that bad?"

"Unruly, the lot of 'em. Whatever you do, don't let them trick you into any wagers. Pretend you're in fairyland here."

"Me?" She runs her hands down the front of her pink pleated tennis skirt. Her breasts push up on the white cotton of her polo, and my devious mind wanders to bribing the kids to bring out the water balloons. Accidents happen.

I hear giggling from the side yard as we mount the front steps to the iron rail fence that gives the place a cemetery vibe. Little heads peek out from behind the rhododendrons and duck back when they catch us looking.

"My lady," I say with an exaggerated deep voice, "I believe the gremlins have escaped. We must be quick before they take over the castle!"

The shriek of little girls and stomp of elephant feet can be heard throughout the neighborhood as my nieces run off. I grin and turn back to Celeste, who is giving me a funny look. "What? My nieces love to play pretend."

"It's not that," she says softly. "You ..." Her tongue darts out to lick her lips. "You reminded me of someone. Never mind." She shakes her head and turns back to the house. "How many nieces and nephews do you have?"

"Two of each. Molly's got the two runners—Elias and Ethan, eleven and twelve. Sam and Aaron have the two gremlins —Hattie and Vera, who are three and five. Kirsten and her wife Lara don't have any yet. Addy has a ferret named Billie-Jean."

"Are they all here?"

"Yeah. Don't worry though. They're not serial killers or anything. Perfectly normal weirdos." I can feel Celeste's fingers digging into my arm, but her face is a mask of calm. I wince knowing that my family might screw this up. This should have been a date, but meeting the fam is a big jump ahead in our relationship. Is she going to run?

"I heard that!" Kirsten calls before I see her round the side of the house with gremlin number one in her arms.

"Unca Hay-Hay!" Hattie squeals and holds out her arms to me.

Celeste releases my arms, and Hattie jumps at me. I pretend to stumble like she weighs a ton, groaning about how much candy she must have eaten since I last saw her—last night at dinner. Her laughter bubbles up like rainbows and unicorns and pink bubblegum bubble bath.

Kirsten introduces herself and guides Celeste back down the pathway to the backyard, where the family has gotten an early start on the BBQ.

"Make yourselves right at home, why don't you?" I say dryly. The family has a BBQ once a month at least, and I never bring anyone but Henrí to these things. He always follows Molly around like a lovesick puppy. It'd be embarrassing if she even noticed.

"We will, thanks," Kirsten grins. I widen my eyes at her, projecting *what the hell are you all doing??* and she just rolls hers.

Mom rises from her chair on shaking legs, and Addy tries to make her sit back down. "Nonsense. I want to greet our guest." She holds out quaking hands toward Celeste, and I release a tense breath when Celeste takes my mom's illness in stride, walks right up to her, and clasps her hands like she's perfectly healthy. My mom is as sharp and sweet as she's always been, but her body is falling to pieces around her. Before Molly and the kids moved in, it was just mom and me in a big empty house. I know mom appreciates the kids being loud and boisterous—it takes attention away from her illness in a positive way. She doesn't like to dwell on things she can't change.

"Thank you for having me to your lovely home," Celeste says. "You have a very sweet son."

"I know, dear." Mom's eyes flick to mine and she winks. "He's a keeper."

I clear my throat. This is why I've never brought someone around, because I've never found a woman who didn't get scared away by a big, over-the-top family. Do they have to say out loud every thought that comes to mind? Family is important to me. Women never understand why a grown-ass man would want to live with his mom and sister, even if it's a separate building. Why her son should take care of her when she's got four daughters. Why I'm not living it up, partying, like other guys my age. Why I don't feel the need to have my own kids, like the nieces and nephews I have are somehow lesser deserving of my love and attention than my own biological spawn would be.

Aaron sidles up to me, holding gremlin number two upside down. She's giggling as he tickles her belly. "Did you order a side of potatoes? Here you go!" and passes me his daughter, to her accompanying laughter.

I like Aaron. He's a good dad, and he makes Sam happy.

That's pretty much all you need to know to judge a guy's moral character. Aaron gets an A plus.

"What do we have here?" Celeste tilts her head so that she's upside down too. "Is this gremlin activated by water?"

"Unicorn farts," I say. I swing her back and forth until she asks to get down, and then I do so immediately. Active play is important but so is instilling the expectation that their words will be heard and responded to the first time they ask. Vera runs off clucking like a demented chicken.

"Hay-Hay, huh?" Celeste nudges me with her shoulder. "Chicken?"

"Not me. I'm brave," I tell her.

"You seem to like kids."

"What's not to like? I get to rediscover the awesomeness of the universe through their eyes. They're slowly healing my jaded, wounded heart."

Celeste laughs, and I can't help grinning like a bespelled fool. I mentally ask Henrí for forgiveness for giving him shit all these years for the way he smiles at my sister.

Eventually Celeste asks to see the bathroom, and we make our way into the big house, where the evidence of my nerdy childhood self is displayed on every wall. I try to keep my body between her and the family photos, but it's impossible when there are enough to wallpaper my entire apartment.

She gasps and pushes me out of the way. "Is that you?"

"No," I say with all seriousness. "That was my twin brother, Hayduke, who ate some gum he found on the sidewalk and turned into a giant blueberry. It was sad. Very sad. We had to roll him away and—"

She covers my mouth with her hand. "You are so full of it! That's you. You and your sisters, right? Wow."

"Yeah, wow." I stare at the photo. I'm in middle school and hadn't hit my growth spurt yet. My body was storing up fat for the endless winter.

"Look at your cute little face! And that cute little bowtie."

"Cute?" I glance at her to see if she's mocking me, but she genuinely looks like she's ogling babies or small furry creatures. "Huh. The kids called me a lot of things, but cute wasn't one of them."

"Teenagers can be cruel." We slowly make our way down the hall of shame as Celeste asks about every single family photo.

"That's my grandpa. He was a prisoner of war at the end of WWII in Europe. Struck up a friendship with a German nurse who gave him a camera to keep safe when the allies marched on Germany. They got separated. He searched for her for five years and finally found her in France. They had a torrid letter writing affair, before she joined him in the US. Got married. Had some kids. Lived happily ever after, or as close as two real life humans can."

Celeste has that adorable scrunch between her eyebrows again. "No way. That sounds like the plot to the novel I'm reading."

I clear my throat. "Oh?"

"Yeah, it's a historical romance one of my clients gave me: Captive Hearts." She holds her hand to the side of her mouth and whispers like she's telling an illicit secret, "It's kind of spicy."

I should tell her. I should give her the benefit of the doubt and tell her that it's me— I wrote that book. But what if she gets squirmy at the idea of a guy writing books enjoyed mostly by women? Emotional, smutty, uplifting tales of history and courage with a guarantee of a happily ever after? Will she pull away? Think I'm too sensitive? Judge me for not having a "real" job? A "manly" job?

All it takes for a job to be manly is to be done by a man, but my dad didn't agree with that.

My courage fails me, and I deflect. "You're reading about old people having sex?" I ask with mock horror.

"No!" she gasps, then recalibrates. "Well, I guess. They're

young twenty-somethings in the book. Frida thought I needed...
I don't know, to lighten up, I guess."

"So she gave you a book about World War two? Dark chick.
I dig it."

"It's got a lot of hope for a war book." Celeste grins at me,
sending my pulse pounding in my chest. "And those old people
were surprisingly kinky in the bedroom."

"Scandalous."

"I know. What happened to your grandparents?"

"Are you asking about their sex lives? Because I don't—"

"No! No, just their safe-for-work life events."

"They moved out here, and Gramps became an aerospace
engineer. Grandma stayed home raising babies and beating all
the other ladies at gin rummy. She was a shark."

"You sound like you were close to them." She reaches up to
touch the picture of my grandparents at their sixtieth wedding
anniversary.

"Grandma made a German chocolate cake, and Gramps
played the accordion as she danced around his chair. I'd idolized
him as a kid. He was a real-life hero."

"Really?"

"But he was also a complicated man. He had untreated
PTSD, like many veterans. He was supportive if you were going
along with what he wanted."

And writing books containing scenes of healthy, consensual
sex was apparently very disappointing to him. Even though I'm
proud of my books and what I've accomplished, I don't tell
people about Trudy Belle. If someone I loved and admired
could be so judgmental about it, I don't need the whole town
gossiping behind my back. I don't need people asking if my sex
scenes are inspired by real life (nope) or if I want to hear their
juicy stories (of course).

They've got enough ammunition on me already.

18

CELESTE

HAYDEN'S FAMILY IS NOTHING like Brett's or my own. I can practically see the love sparkling in the air around them as they tease each other and laugh. His sisters are merciless. Hayden gives as good as he gets, and the brother-in-law fits in seamlessly. How does he do it? I feel like an interloper into some magic tv sitcom. The kind of family I always wished for when I was a kid growing up in a tension-filled house. I wanted to give my kids this gift—unconditional love and acceptance, a warm home with open hearts and open doors that would always be a safe space for them to return to.

I failed with Brett.

Molly is somehow doing it on her own. She's much braver than I was. But she has the family support I never did. I like Hayden's oldest sister. She's about my age and much blunter than I've ever dreamed of being. I like it. I get the sense that she's fought for the privilege to speak her own mind, and what you see is what you get. She's not apologizing.

I want to be like that. Being nice never got me anywhere.

Kirsten and her wife are less in the thick of it, but Hayden said Kirsten is a therapist and doesn't ever say mean shit even in jest. Lara is quiet, like me. She gives me a tentative, but warm smile as she hands me a glass of lemonade. "It's a lot to walk into, huh?"

"Is it that obvious I don't belong here?" The lemonade is perfectly sweetened with a hint of mint.

"Not at all," Lara says. "I was completely overwhelmed when I first met them too. Honestly, I still get overstimulated when the whole pack is together like this."

"Pack?"

"They're like a wolf pack," She tucks a braid behind her ear. "I'm a big reader. Some families are vampires, you know?"

God, do I. I nod and take a sip.

"This one is one of the good ones. Protective, playful, and all about the pups."

"You're lucky to have them," I say diplomatically, then change the subject before she starts asking questions about my relationship with Hayden and my future in this pack. I see the heat in his eyes when he looks at me, but I'm scared. I'm taking it one day at a time. I want a partner who desires my body, but more importantly, I want a partner who loves my soul with all its bruised and broken bits. That's probably too much to ask of a younger guy with options. "Do you play pickleball too?"

Lara shakes her head. "Roller Derby. Hayden hasn't convinced me to try pickleball. Ball moves too fast."

"You'll shoot your eye out!" Kirsten quips.

"Haven't convinced you *yet*, Lara," Hayden says, coming up to stand close to my side. He doesn't put his arm around me, but I can feel the heat of his body wafting off him. He smells like fresh cut grass and summer rain. "But I bet you try it once and fall in love."

"Now where have I heard that before?" Lara exchanges an affectionate look with Kirsten, and I feel like I'm intruding on something special. I want that. Those shared inside jokes, those shared memories.

Samantha and Aaron join us, and Aaron slaps Hayden on the back with a wicked gleam in his eye. "Did Hay-Hay here bet you the same thing, Celeste? He's had a run of bad luck on his wagers lately."

Beside me, Hayden stiffens.

Samantha laughs, but it seems to be in good fun. "Remember that time Molly bet you that you wouldn't eat a toad?"

"I was ten," Hayden says.

"Oh! Remember that time Kirsten bet him he couldn't win the yodeling competition in Leavenworth? He yodeled the alphabet backward and won."

"And he looked so cute in his lederhosen."

"Or the time he bet he could start a viral dance trend, and Addy said he could only use moves inspired by kitchen appliances?"

"The Senior Center still loves that dance."

"Remember the time he ran the Salmon Bay Half Marathon wearing two different shoes?"

"What about the bet he made that he could 'make the kazoo great again' and join the Sea Lion Lodge All-Star Band?"

Aaron chuckles. "These Holstroms are cheeky. You gotta watch them, Celeste. Hayden tried to bet me that he could outrace me with him running and me paddle boarding."

"He would have won if the flock of geese hadn't blocked the trail." Sam bats her husband playfully on the shoulder. "I'm pretty sure you bribed them with popcorn to trip him up. I had to take him to the wedding looking like David Crosby. You should have seen the looks we got."

"I still think you should have kept the 'stache," Addy says. "It was epic. 'Staches are in now, anyway."

"It was skibidi!" Elias shouts, at the same time Aaron says, "I bet it itched."

Time slows as everyone talks over each other. My stomach lurches, like the cement trucks that roll down Salmon Bay Avenue. What they're saying makes sense, but not to me. What are they saying?

Hayden grew out a mustache on a dare to go to a wedding.

Those cement trucks dump at my feet and I'm sinking as the world keeps moving around me. I turn my head slowly to see Hayden. He returns my gaze, thick eyebrows furrowed. Did he know?

"Lander liked the tux, right?"

"And he wore those old sunglasses of dad's all night, even inside."

"Like the great philosopher TayTay says, 'Play stupid games, win stupid prizes.'"

"Where are the pictures, Sam? Did you wear something to match?"

"Of course not. I wasn't dumb enough to make that bet. Aaron didn't want to go to a work function. He thinks Lander's annoying."

"Lander *is* annoying."

I stumble back. My ears are ringing, and the cacophony blurs until I can't hear individual words, only the thumping of my heart. How could I be so stupid? How could I be so gullible and naïve? Hayden was porn 'stache guy? Hayden pretended we hadn't met? Hayden had his tongue between my thighs, my juices coating his stupid mustache?

"Celeste—wait!"

I see Hayden's face in front of me, but it's blurry through the tears I refuse to shed.

"Wait. What's wrong—?"

I choke on a laugh.

"You recognized me, right? What part of that conversation was a surprise?"

"No." My legs zombie walk out of there, back around the stupidly beautiful haunted house, and stumble through the iron gate. My skin feels clammy. I think I'm going to throw up.

"Celeste!" Hayden's right behind me, but I can't look at him. If I look at him, I'll burst into tears. "Shit! You knew it was me, right? I thought you just didn't want to talk about it. I thought I was following your lead—"

I head to my car, remembering too late that Hayden drove me here. I could walk home, but it's at least three miles. I slam my fist on the top of the car and pain shoots up my arm.

"Celeste—I'm sorry. I really thought you remembered—"

"Why?" I whisper.

"Why, what? I kept waiting for—"

I spin on my heel and press my back against the car. Hayden's face is white, and he tugs on his hair with both hands. "Why? Why me? You didn't even know me then. Is this some stupid game to you? A bet, huh? Let's set up the middle-aged divorcee for a good laugh? Did Brett ask you to—"

"No! No." He cages me in with his arms on either side of the car, not touching me, but preventing me from fleeing. "Please. I didn't know who you were. I was there as a favor to my sister. I've never met Brett, and I wish I didn't know Lander."

"You're friends with L-Lander?" I don't know why that feels worse. She can have my ex-husband, and good riddance. But the thought of her with Hayden makes my chest clench.

"I'm not, sweetheart. I'm not friends with any of them. I didn't mean to lead you on in costume. It seemed like you were into it, and I was trying to play it cool. That closet was the hottest scene of my life—"

"Scene? Did you...did you film us?" Big saltwater tears are dripping down my chin now.

"No! God, no, Celeste. I would never!" He cradles my face with his big hands and wipes beneath my eyes with his thumbs. "Please, I had no ill intentions. I was in heaven, and then you ran. I thought I'd done something wrong, and that I'd never see you again. I never imagined you'd walk back into my life and not recognize me."

"You could have said something."

"In front of everyone playing pickleball? Should I have said, hey, baby, remember how I ate you out in a closet at your ex-husband's wedding?"

I sniff. He could have said something less obvious.

"I thought we were on the same page! You were the one who left that night. I wasn't going to bring it up if you were ashamed. I just wanted a second chance with you!"

"With me?" I search his eyes for any hint that he's lying. He's saying everything right, but I've been burned before.

His forehead rests against mine. "Of course with you. Always you. You're right, I shouldn't have assumed. But if I brought it up, would you have run again? You seem like a runner. By the time we started actually playing together one-on-one, it was too awkward to mention. You seemed to actually like me, the real me."

I sniff again and lick the tears off my lips. I don't know what to think. I still feel betrayed.

Hayden kisses the top of my head. His lips are warm and soft as a summer's day, and I want so much to curl up in his arms and forget everything that's made me so afraid to trust. But he broke that. I don't think I can go forward from here. I put my hands on his chest and push. He steps back, more because he's acquiescing than because I could actually move him with any force.

"Ask me now." His voice is gruff. "Ask me anything. I'll answer truthfully."

"I dare you to tell me the truth, the whole truth—is that how it works?"

"No. No games. What do you want to know?"

"Do you do that often? Hook up with random girls in storage closets?"

"God, no. You were the first." He chuckles, but it sounds hollow.

I wipe my eyes. God, what is this, perimenopause? I never cried in front of Brett. I was stone cold sober.

"Please. I never meant to hurt you. I swear it."

"I hear what you're saying." I take a deep breath and curl my hands into fists. "But I need some space to sort out my feelings. I'm so embarrassed now. I don't know how I can look your family in the face ever again."

"I didn't—"

"Listen!" I would never talk to Brett like that, but I know deep in my bones that Hayden is nothing like my ex. "I need to go. I need to sort myself out. Please."

His Adam's apple bobs in his throat. "Yeah, okay." He clutches the back of his neck instead of reaching for me. "I'm sorry. I really am, Celeste. I never meant to hurt you."

"But you did."

His head drops like a sunflower in the fall, drooping toward the earth. "Yeah, I get it. Here, take my car. I'll have one of my sisters drop me off later to pick it up."

"I can call a cab."

"Let me do this for you. Please." He looks so lost, but I can't forgive him right now. I need to sort out my feelings. It hurts too much, but I recognize this isn't all on Hayden. My baggage has baggage. I just feel so blindsided. I need space to breathe.

I take the keys offered and slip into the driver's seat. Hayden stands on the sidewalk with his hands tucked into his pockets, his broad shoulders slumped. I hate leaving him like this, but I'm so used to being gaslit, I don't know what's real anymore. Did he really think I knew? Or is he just twisting reality until I believe his version of events?

Conflict ties me up in knots, trained from birth to be the peacekeeper. It was easier to let Brett bowl me right over, like a blade of grass in a thunderstorm; I never risked standing tall, never wanted to call down a lightning strike, and I can't live like that again. I'd rather be alone.

Marissa answers on the second ring. "Hello?"

"Marissa, can I come over?"

"Oh, babe. Get on over here. I'll get out the ice cream."

19

CELESTE

Days pass with churning acidity in my stomach. I'm counting the nicks in my house's trim, not the hours since I learned the hottest hookup of my life was my pickleball coach.

Was he really just my coach? My doubles partner? My date? Because we did go on dates that had nothing to do with pickleball.

And I liked them.

I liked *him*.

Miel Bagels is busy, but the memory of Hayden sitting across from me while I worked on the crossword last week is all I can see. For once, the clues aren't drowning out my self-doubt. I stare at the piece of paper like it contains all the answers to the universe. The theme is "Physical Activity", and all I can think about is playing pickleball with Hayden. Rethinking every interaction in a new light. Ruminating on every word he used. Every conversation. Every time he introduced me to someone on the court, did they know how clueless I was?

17-Across: Trouble that Leaves You Breathless.

I've felt like I can't take a full breath since I learned about Mustachio's real identity. My chest aches with embarrassment.

Five letters. SHAME? That's what I feel right now when I

think about how I missed all the signs. I don't know. I'll try 1-Down and see if it gives me the first letter of 17-Across.

1-Down: "Very good—Agreed!" Four letters.

Hissing in between my teeth, I force myself to focus. You know what was very good? That orgasm in the broom closet. I've ruminated on that late at night, half convinced I imagined the whole thing. Is *Trouble that leaves you breathless*, REGRET? No, that's six letters. I regret running out on him instead of getting his number.

Would I have had the lady balls to call him? No, but if he had my number, I would have picked up. I think.

Maybe it's not too late.

Next to me, Ginny and Armando are trying to out-insult each other on a weird breakfast date. They waved to me when I sat down and made small talk, but it felt genuine. Not just people who know me as Celeste-the-mom or Celeste-Brett's-wife. Celeste, the whole person. The camaraderie of the pickleball court is spreading out into Salmon Bay, and I don't want to lose it.

Does this new community hinge on my relationship with Hayden? Or have I just replaced my other hats with Celeste-Hayden's-doubles-partner?

Marissa finally arrives for our meeting and hobbles over to my table. The barista, Henrí, helpfully carries her bagel and coffee. He sets it on the table, sees me working on the crossword, and gives me a hesitant smile. Does he know I hooked up in a closet with his buddy? Were they laughing about it together as he filled my rainbow bagel order?

"You good?" he asks. I nod, and he lets us have our space.

"You look like someone killed your dog," Marissa says, before she mainlines half her cardamom latte in one go. She's an overachiever like that.

"I just feel so embarrassed," I admit.

"Girl, I didn't recognize him either. Don't be so hard on yourself. That 'Stache was epic."

"I thought he was actually interested in *me*, and—"

"Stop right there. What makes you think he isn't interested in you? He's volunteered to coach you in pickleball, for free, took you on at least three dates, and brought you to meet his family. No offense, babe, but that's a lot of work for someone not interested."

I look away, to the next table where Armando and Ginny have stopped arguing and are not very subtly listening in on our conversation.

Armando's lips curve in a wry smile. "You finish that puzzle yet?"

"Max does the New York Times crossword every day," Ginny informs us. "He says the Miel puzzles are too easy."

"But the subtext is killer," Armando points out. He twirls the edge of his mustache. "I like to think Lord Lexicon is watching us, like some dark puppet master, as we dance for his amusement."

"Do you think it's a Bellemare?" Ginny asks.

We all turn to look at Henrí right as he drops a baker's peel of bagels on the ground. There's a short brunette at the counter in front of him. She's reading something on her phone, not aware of the baker at all.

"That's a no," Armando says dismissively.

"Didn't he play football in high school?" Ginny asks. "He's got butterfingers."

"Guess he peaked at eighteen," he says.

"Takes one to know one," she shoots back.

"At least I'm attracting dick, not driving it away."

Marissa cuts in smoothly. "I always thought it was the youngest, Margo, who made the crosswords. She's smart. Isn't she studying to be a doctor?"

Do I really want to know who Lord Lexicon is? I tune them all out as I try to get my emotions sorted. Being impulsive and making assumptions is what got me into this mess. I just don't know how to face him now. Was I a joke to him?

7-Down: Unbearable yearning. Four letters.

Marissa leans in and drops her voice. "Hun, I know Brett-the-small-dick gaslit you all the time, but this is different."

"How? I feel like I'm walking around with a big sign that says 'Gullible'. I've been afraid to let anyone in, but the one time I do, he pretends he doesn't know me? That he hasn't had his tongue up my lady bits?"

"Tell. Me. More," she begs.

I flatten my lips together and write in ACHE for 7-down. That means 18-Across starts with SH, TH, or CH.

*18-Across: *Errors abound with balls at this spot (in baseball)*

Spots in baseball—Outfield? Infield? One of the bases? Home, first, second, th— oh. Third. THIRDBASE. I write it in.

"Okay, fine." Marissa whines. "He's an asshole. Is that what you want me to say? Did he brag to all the pickleballers that he made you come in a supply closet? Has he said anything insulting? Has he tried to get in your pants again?"

"Whose side are you on?"

"Yours, always. And I know it hurts. I know. But what are you really afraid of? What's the worst that could happen?"

"What if I can't differentiate between charming and sincere anymore? What if I'm giving off doormat vibes?" I huff out a breath and force myself to clear my mind of clutter.

There's no room for anxiety when I'm concentrating on finding an eight-letter solution to 30-Across: *Cleans up, as with a ball next to a hole (in golf).* My dad plays golf, because it's a rich person's game, and he's all about projecting an upper crust image. Even if our family was never well-off. Should he pay for my piano lessons or his tee time fees? No question in his mind which was worth his money. I've always come second to other people's plans.

Marissa sets down her cup. "Is that the only thing bothering you? Or is this feeling so overwhelming because it's one of many burdens you're carrying?" She eyes me up and down, and I can feel her annoyingly perceptive BFF-vision strip away the mask I'm wearing. "You ready for this weekend? You've got the real estate exam and the qualifying match. Which one is bothering you?"

"Both?" I say as I write TAPSITIN in the margin before writing it into the crossword. "What if I fail?"

"What if you succeed?"

29-Down: Easy-breezy term for athletics. Ten letters.

Ball game? Team exercise? Physical Exercise? Sports contest? Jock...game...player?

Jock contest...is eleven letters.

Sports jock?

SPORTS BALL! I write it in.

*49-Across: *Athlete possibly subject to illegal touching (in football)*

Hayden's touch should be illegal. Even though I'm mad, I can't lie to myself and say I didn't like his hands on me. His hands were magical. His tongue, mind-altering.

Okay, football player involved in illegal touching. Eight letters. Is this a person's name? A real case that made the news, or a standard position on the field? I don't know anything about football. Brett was a fan, but I was usually in the kitchen making wings and fried cheese sticks while he watched a game.

"You've got that tight crease between your brows. If you can't get over your bruised ego to ask Hayden for a little de-stressing help, you can pour all that angst into the game. You're going to crush Warren for me, right?"

"But—"

"Ceecee, babe. You need to defend my honor. You can't let that asshole win." She leans across the table to see what I've got so far. "Why does it say Celeste?"

"What? Where?"

"There." She points to the clues and drags her finger down the first letter of each one:

MAPETITECHERIECELESTEPLEAS-

ESAYYESLETSLEVELUPOURDOUBLESGAME-
WITHTHISDIAGONALTEXT

Ma petite cherie Celeste please say yes let's level up our doubles game with this diagonal text.

There's a weird buzzing in my ears. Sometimes the puzzle creator pokes fun at the people of Salmon Bay, but it's never this pointed. They don't call people out by name. "It's not necessarily me. I'm not the only Celeste."

"Do you know another Celeste in Salmon Bay?"

Another Celeste who is playing a doubles game? What are the odds that it's not me? A phantom hand grips my gut and squeezes. Lord Lexicon is someone I know in real life?

34-Across: Luau fish option. Three letters.

That could be a couple of things. Poi. Lei. Eel. Ahi. I'll have to look at a corresponding down answer.

21-Down: Slangy start of some encouragement.

Sweet, awesome, go get 'em, way to go, you got this, yay, nice job, boo-yah...but it's only four letters. Cool? Epic? Good? Nothing is clicking. What does Hayden say when he's encouraging me?

Atta girl.

I squirm in my chair as I write in ATTA. That makes 34-Across: AHI.

41-Across: Traditional romance novel ending. Three letters.

Oh, I got this, even if I've only read one romance novel. I should ask Frida if she has any more suggestions. I like the promise that no matter what crap the characters go through, I'm guaranteed a happily ever after. HEA. If only real life could be as easy.

"Can I get you anything else?" Henrí's deep voice snaps me out of the zone.

I blink up at him. "Henrí, if I guessed the identity of Lord Lexicon, would you tell me?"

"He wrote this one for you." Henrí taps the crossword paper.

Shit.

Even Marissa is distracted by this new revelation. She eyes the gentle giant speculatively. Good. Her laser glare should be turned on someone else for once.

I turn back to the crossword with renewed determination. But there it is, French: *Ma petite cherie. My little darling.* It can't be, Hayden. Right?

"*Voulez-vous coucher avec moi?*" Marissa says in broken, gawd-awful high school French.

Henrí splutters, and his cheeks burn apple red. The poor guy doesn't know how to handle Racy-Rissa. "*Mon cœur est occupé.*" Spinning on his heel, he retreats.

"Oh, my gosh, isn't he adorable?" Marissa mutters. "Who do you think he's pining for?"

"He's a little young."

"Psht! He's the same age as your boy-toy."

"I don't have a boy-anything. No, you know what? Better wipe the drool off before you go home to Drew."

"Not for me, you doofus. Drew's lucky I'm addicted to his peanut butter pancakes."

"Is that what the kids are calling it these days?"

She laughs. "We're invested in this now, girl."

I'm too busy filling in the answers that make up the diagonal. Across. Down. Anything I can answer easily. My brain is shouting the answer, but my heart won't listen. I need proof.

47-Down: Documents demanding confidentiality: Abbr.

I'm pretty sure the answer is NDAS, the opposite of what Mustachio and I should have had. We should have talked. Names. Sexual health. Birth control. We should have discussed so many things before we did anything naked. I know better.

OMG.

"How's it going, Sherlock?" Marissa asks.

"I don't know if I'm excited or terrified."

"Nerd."

"Says the woman who Marie Kondo'd her underwear drawer."

"I told you that in confidence."

"As your bestie, I reserve the right to pull it out for emotional blackmail any time I want."

"Fair."

Marissa is silent for a while, and I'm lost to the void when I notice she's been pulled into a discussion with Armando and Ginny, who have drawn their chairs closer and are all staring over my shoulder.

A three-letter answer to *31-Down: "Wowww...that feels good"*.

Seriously, I'm going to die of mortification before I finish this.

He wrote this for me. *Me!* Maybe the message won't even be positive. If it's Hayden, he wrote this before we had our fight, or whatever we're calling it. Lord Lexicon turns in the puzzles on Fridays.

I glance up when a shadow falls across my paper, and I look up to see the brunette who was flustering Henrí is Hayden's oldest sister, Molly. I swallow down my embarrassment, but feel my cheeks flame anyway. Even if she hadn't known what Hayden and I had gotten up to in the supply closet, I ran from her family get-together without saying goodbye.

"Working on the new one, eh?" she asks. Her smile is relaxed, not at all like she's wondering about the crazy woman who ran crying out of her family home last week. She's got a bagel and cream cheese in one hand and a bowl of Lebanese lentil soup in the other. Maybe she doesn't know what happened? I like her, though I've noticed she seems to have a little raincloud hovering over her head when she's not directly talking to someone. Being a caretaker to her mother and a single mom to two tween boys is a lot of stress and responsibility. I don't know what happened to the father—either hers or the boys'—but I get the sense their absence is part of that shadow.

Does Hayden have his own shadows lurking beneath that sunny exterior? Does he feel pressure to step in and make people laugh to offset some of that burden? He never struck me as cruel. Maybe he really thought I knew?

Molly raises her eyebrow, and I realize I've been staring at her instead of answering.

"You know who made this, don't you?"

She takes a bite of her bagel as she chews on her answer. Finally, she swallows. "Would it affect your enjoyment of the crossword if I did?"

My skin heats as I search her face.

"I wouldn't want to take that away from you," she says. "My grandpa used to do those crosswords religiously." She's matter of fact, as if turmoil isn't bruising my insides like a tennis ball volley. "He'd take us to the bagel shop every Sunday after church to get the newest edition hot off the press." She licks the cream cheese off her finger. "The new crossword author values his privacy, but if he's got something to tell you, he's not going to be subtle about it. Why don't you finish and see what you find?"

Hot and cold, shivering and sweating, I turn back to the puzzle to try to distract myself from thoughts of Hayden's lean abs as he pulled up his shirt to wipe his brow. Hayden's easy smile. Hayden's jokes. He wouldn't lead me on to be unkind. I know this. I need to believe it.

"The original crossword guy was secretary of the Sea Lions Club and a big mover and shaker in Salmon Bay before he passed. He's the one who started the theme of slipping bits of gossip and local trivia into the crosswords. Gramps always claimed it kept his mind sharp, but we knew he was really in it for shade."

"What did your grandpa think of the new guy?" Did he know the identity of Lord Lexicon? Was he proud of his grandson's cleverness?

The shadow passes over Molly's face again, like a wisp of

cloud blowing across the sun. "Sometimes people have personality changes late in life, you know? Gramps lost his filter after a couple strokes. He didn't like change, even though the new creator did his best to make it even better than the old one. The subtext is clever now, rather than mean." She shrugs. "Just like Gramps used to be."

The buzzing in my belly ramps up. "And if I guess right, would you tell me?"

She mimes zipping her lips and throwing the key over her shoulder. "I was sworn to secrecy."

Marissa butts in, leaning forward on both elbows and whispering loud enough that the neighboring table stops arguing to listen in. "What's up with you and the big guy?"

She tilts her head in the direction of the register, and we turn together to stare, finding Henrí watching our table with a dreamy expression. Caught, he quickly turns away and runs right into his mother, who's holding the pitcher of water she's just refilled. Little Mama Bellemare squeals as the water sloshes over the rim and soaks her. Henrí's ears burn bright red, and he starts muttering, "*Desolé, Maman!*" as he tries to mop her up with beverage napkins.

The three of us turn back to our table, biting our lips to keep from laughing and making the moment more embarrassing for the big guy.

"So?" Marissa prods.

"No clue," Molly says.

"He was staring over here."

"Probably watching Celeste figure out the message," Molly says. "I was worried when you disappeared from the barbecue, Celeste. I hope it wasn't something we did. We can be a lot."

"You all were lovely."

Molly taps the crossword in front of me. "Finish this, okay? My brother has a big, sensitive heart underneath the jokester. He'd never do anything to intentionally hurt you. He's one of the good ones."

Goosebumps on my arms.

My little darling, Celeste.

"Can I trust him?" I ask her, but Molly just gives me a lopsided smile.

"Being brave doesn't mean you don't feel fear. It means you're afraid but you do the hard thing anyway. I hope you forgive him for whatever he did wrong. He's my little brother— I love him, but I know he can be dense sometimes. Give him another chance."

Marissa puts her hand over mine. "At least through the tournament, right? You're not going to let that guy who hurt me win. I'm counting on you."

I guess that's fair.

"I'm going to get out of here," Molly says, "before I put my foot in my mouth, and little bro puts sugar in my salt shaker again." She gathers up her purse and purchases. "Hope to see you at the house again, Celeste. We can hit a ball around together, if you like. I'll let you trounce me."

"I'd like that."

Molly waves and leaves, and Marissa and I both cast surreptitious glances back at Henrí. He pauses drying out his mama to watch Molly's ass sashay out the door.

"Unrequited love." Marissa rubs her hands together like a cartoon villain. "And she's totally oblivious."

I turn back to the crossword feeling like I'm on a high dive staring at the drop below. Do I want definitive proof of Lord Lexicon's identity? Do I want to see the man behind the curtain? Or would I rather keep the mystery alive? Can I keep lying to myself about everything?

My feelings are already complicated. There's no point denying that Hayden and I have chemistry. Everything he's shown me so far, except lying by omission, has shown a kind, caring, clever, steadfast man. If I give in to my fear, what was the point of obtaining my freedom?

"Maybe we should give her a hint," Marissa muses, still

hung up on Henri-Molly drama. "I can't take the sad puppy dog eyes."

"Leave the poor guy alone, Rissa. She's probably trying to let him down easy. It would be cruel to crush her little brother's best friend's squishy heart."

Am I crushing her little brother's squishy heart?

Not everyone is manipulative like my ex.

"What should we call them—Hen-lly? Mol-rí?"

I let Marissa spitball plans, only half listening while I fill in the gaps of the crossword.

My doubles partner wants to level up our relationship with the answer to what the diagonal spells out.

DINKSTHENDRINKS

I barely hear Marissa over the ringing in my ears.

"—If you're moving on from lusting after the pickleball coach and Molly's hot little brother, should we set up those online dating profiles for you?"

"Marissa—"

"Or are you ready to stop hiding and have an open conversation with him about how you feel?"

"Marissa! Look at this."

Ma petite cherie, Celeste. Please say, yes. Let's level up our doubles game with this diagonal text: Dinks then drinks.

I hide my face in my hands so she can't see all the emotions playing out across my face.

"Girl," Marissa sucks in a hard breath through her teeth. "Is Lord Lexicon really Hayden? If it's not a *hell, no*, you owe it to yourself to go talk it out with him. I know he hurt your feelings, but not everyone is like your evil ex. Give him the opportunity to come clean. Give him a second chance. Don't let your fear of getting hurt again hold you back from a good thing."

I groan. I'll never be able to do these crosswords again without thinking about Hayden's mustache tickling my thighs. Can I get over my embarrassment? Lord Lexicon is outing himself to the whole town to ask me out for drinks. If he submitted this on Friday before I found out about Mustachio, it backs up his claim that he thought I knew. He's not lying to me on purpose. Can I give him another chance? What do I stand to lose if I don't forgive him?

"Or we can go back to iEros," Marissa says. "Find a new stranger on the internet. Keep searching every lily pad until you find your prince. The second one will be easier, and the third, until you're a dating savant."

"I definitely don't have time for that. The job comes first."

"Does it? As your boss, I commend your diligence. As your bestie, I think your priorities need adjustment. But maybe you'll meet someone through work, like I did. Some enchanted showing, a tall dark stranger could come waltzing in, asking about the knob and tube and new plumbing...waxing poetic about good bones and a strong foundation—"

"Not going there."

"I won't say I haven't played matchmaker for clients before—"

"Just stop!"

Sometimes having a best friend is the worst.

Physical Activities
by Lord Lexicon

Miel Bagels - *Sweeten your day the Montréal way*

ACROSS

1 Minor celebs
6 Agreement
10 Price tag disclaimer
14 Expensive pillow fill
15 They're in the rights business, in brief?
16 In check, with "up"
17 Trouble that leaves you breathless
18 *Errors abound with balls at this spot (in baseball)

DOWN

1 "Very good – Agreed!"
2 Exercise alternative that sucks?
3 License fig.
4 Usually one who's it
5 Prague people movers
6 One is often on the back
7 Unbearable yearning
8 Routes going right to the top
9 Disorder

ACROSS

20 Cry before "No hands!"
22 Heroine of Jane Austen
23 Extra-small cat call
24 Round initial fig.
25 "Injured playing peekaboo? Go to the ICU", et al.
27 Eurasian UN member, once
30 *Cleans up, as with a ball next to a hole (in golf)
33 Easter Bunny bounce
34 Luau fish option
35 Encouraging expression
38 Some woodwinds
41 Traditional romance novel ending, for short
43 Establish
44 Promiscuous woman, once
46 "Larry King Live" broadcaster
48 Evian, par exemple
49 *Athlete possibly subject to illegal touching (in football)
51 Story lines
52 Espadrille linings
54 Start of MGM's motto
56 Angry crowd
57 You'll see Moscato here
59 Yodeling country by l'Italie
63 Exploit the rules... and a hint for 18-,30-, and 49-Across
66 Stock
67 Late co-founder of Reader's Digest, ___ Wallace
68 Entertaining entanglement
69 Thin-stemmed mushroom
70 Squawk
71 Length of a bridge
72 Erudite figures

DOWN

10 Officer radio alert, briefly
11 Underwater terror
12 Blown-up region?
13 Leftover dishes, often
19 Edmond ___, the fictional Count of Monte Cristo
21 Slangy start of some encouragement
26 Greenhouse pest
27 Apprehensive comment
28 Mentsuyu go-with
29 Easy-breezy term for athletics
31 "Wowww...that feels good"
32 It's something to say
36 Taco topper, slangily
37 Haydn number
39 Theatrical 2025 film from Pixar
40 "Happy to hear it!"
42 Imaginary Taylor, of clothes
45 Series of video games that has sold 200+ million copies
47 Documents demanding confidentiality: Abbr.
50 It's just over a foot?
51 Airline based in Seoul
52 Get at
53 "Oh really?"
55 Nitwits
58 Ancient Mayan site Chichen ___
60 Lock lips, in London
61 Teriyaki tipple, theoretically
62 Every class at Yale
64 Xanthan gum goes in it, slangily
65 Tokyo bread

20

HAYDEN

I SLAM ANOTHER PICKLEBALL against the concrete, and it breaks. I've got to stop ruminating about all the ways I should have brought up our past sooner. All the ways she could have taken that admission. All the ways I could have fucked up. I was afraid of her turning away, so of course I did the one thing guaranteed to make her leave me—I lied by omission.

I didn't mean to though. I really thought she knew. What's she going to think when she finds out about Lord Lexicon? Is this going to pile on the mistaken identity? Rub dirt in the wound?

It's embarrassing that she didn't recognize me. Even though I had her little moans in my head on repeat, her scent embedded in my tastebuds, the memory of her soft skin beneath the loops and whirls of my fingertips, to her, I was forgettable.

My dad sure drove that point home when he left. We are forgettable. Replaceable. Not important enough to stay for.

I rub my hands down my face and try to find my chill. I gotta go for a run and get the endorphins to drive out this sick feeling in my stomach.

"You okay, Hay?" Addy calls out. My youngest sister is thirty-two and a serial dater, classic daddy-issues type as Kirsten points out. Her hair is half shaved and half long, which she wears in a bunch of braids with sparkly ribbons. She's a free spirit, but reliable, and she decided to stay with mom for the weekend to keep her company—freeing me up to have my "little meltdown" as she called it.

Usually, she lives in Seattle, where she says she's more likely to meet a guy she didn't go to high school with. She's discerning, and her one true furry love has even higher standards. If Billie-Jean doesn't like you, you don't get a second chance.

"I'm fine."

"Little brother, you can't bullshit a bullshitter."

"I messed up."

"So apologize."

"There's more I'm keeping from her."

"Why?"

"Why? Why! Did you see how she ran when she found out that we'd met before? That's the second time she's run away. I'm definitely not telling her now. I've worked too hard to rebuild my brand and launch a new pen name. There's no way I'm gonna risk my career again if she's not sticking around when things get tough. Look what happened with Jordyn. I can't repeat that. I won't."

"Not everyone is like Jordyn."

"All it takes is one." I rub my face, trying to keep down the bile that fiasco brings up. I'd worked so hard for my dream, only to have it ripped apart by trolls and performative lemmings online. Jordyn posted my real identity. She didn't even mean to start something, but it got out of control.

"I only met Celeste once, but she's nothing like Jordyn. That witch was desperate for attention to patch up her low self-esteem. She should have talked to a therapist, not TikTok." Addy wraps her arms around me and squeezes like I'm still the little brother who cried for six months straight when dad left.

"And you should have listened to Billy-Jean; she's a great judge of character, and she never liked your ex."

I sigh. "Maybe you should bring your ferret on all my first dates to sniff out the good ones for me."

"You've got the biggest heart, little brother. You'll find someone who loves you for your whole, squishy, sensitive self, just like we love you, farts and all."

"Thanks, Adds." I rest my head on top of hers and wonder where I went wrong with my life. I want everything to wrap up neatly like it does in a book, and real life never does. Dad desperately wanted a boy, but he got four girls before he finally got his wish, and then he got me. Never tough enough. Never aggressive enough. Didn't like football or contact sports. Didn't want to play shoot 'em up games or go hunting.

Must be gay, I heard him grumbling to mom one night after he thought I was in bed asleep.

I'm attracted to women—generous curves, soft skin, full lips. I'm just not an asshole.

Not usually.

"How do I make this better?" I ask Addy. "I really like her, and I want another chance, but now I'm terrified to let her in."

Addy pulls back to look up at me. "Give her time to sort her feelings, then reach out and ask for what you want. Do you want to play pickleball with her? Do you want to date her? Do you want forever with her? Think carefully. She's just as afraid as you are—you've both been burned. We're all looking for a partner who will listen to us, really see past the flesh sack to who we are on the inside."

"That was beautiful, Casanova."

"Thanks." She slugs me on the arm, and the girl hits hard. "I bet you she'll let you know by the end of the week."

"What do I get if you're wrong?"

"You should care more about what you'll get if I'm right, Sherlock. Start drafting what you're gonna say."

So I go back to doing what I do best—spinning straw into

gold and angst into happily ever afters. I pour all my feelings into my manuscript and stay up for forty-eight hours on coffee and regrets. Addy leaves food outside the door of my carriage house, and nobody disrupts my flow. Occasionally I tune back into the bird song out my window, the happy squeals of the kids playing catch with the neighbor's dog, the distant barking of sea lions at the marina.

No clue what day it is, or how bad I smell, when someone knocks on my door and breaks into my manic haze. I stumble down the stairs to tell them to fuck off, but when I drag open the door, I'm slammed with a vision straight from my naughty daydreams.

Celeste is standing there in one of her cute little tennis dresses. The half zipper is down, showing off her cleavage. Her curls are twisted partially away from her face, but the rest of it hangs down past her shoulders. Her toned thighs are on display beneath the tiny white skirt that I'd like to flip up, even knowing there are shorts beneath.

She's biting her lip as she waits for me to say something, and I know I started the weekend drafting this speech before I got lost down the rabbit hole of writing my next book, but I can't remember a single thing I wanted to say.

"Hey," I say, showcasing what Publisher's Weekly called *snappy dialogue with a dash of wry wit.*

"Hey."

"You...you want to come in?"

She gives me a slow once over and raises her eyebrows. "Are you sick?"

"What? No." I surreptitiously smell my armpit, but it's a lost cause. I can't smell myself anymore, which means it's past time for a shower. "I'm not sick; I was working. Here, let me clean up real fast, then we can...talk?"

Please be here to talk. Please be here to give me a third chance. I deserve that, right? She wouldn't show up in that hot as hell getup to rub it in my face that I'll never have a hope in hell of running my hands up her smooth thighs again. She's not cruel.

She nods, and I lead her into the woodshop and up the stairs to the door of my apartment. I explain that the woodshop was my grandpa's passion project. He collected decorative woods when people around the neighborhood would cut down their maples, walnuts, and oaks, then dry the wood and hoard them for projects—mostly side tables and shelves.

"This was his mancave where he'd go to escape the female-energy in the house. He had two daughters, my mom and my aunt Cindy."

She runs her fingers over the whorls in a piece of honey locust that's been drying since the mid-eighties. "It's beautiful. Did he teach you what he knew?"

"I know how to wield a power tool, but I learned more in stage crew class in high school than from gramps. He had soul of an artist—hoarding supplies for that magical *someday* when he'd have time for all his ideas."

"Sounds like a remarkable guy." She stops to inspect a wooden shelf with holes for lining up pickleball paddles that Russell was making for the courts at Salmon Bay Park.

I would have cleaned up if I knew I'd have company. I take the stairs at a near run with the hope of tidying up before she makes it in the front door. "I'm not usually a slob, I promise. I just got in the zone, and the whole weekend passed by like that." I snap my fingers, wishing I could magic away the mess that easily.

She inspects my apartment as I hurry around trying to clean everything up at once. "It's fine. I'm used to living with teenage boys."

"I'm definitely not a teen," I growl. "But I'll admit I get a little lazy when I'm working."

"Writing?" she asks hesitantly. "What are you working on?"

My gut clenches. Can I trust her with this? I can't afford to lose what I've built. Starting over the first time was devastating.

And she's proven she's a runner—I don't think every woman is going to do what Jordyn did, but I need a little more stability before I can take that chance. "Just some editing." Technically correct, but I'm well aware that she's going to assume I'm editing someone else's words.

She sits down on the edge of the couch and blasts me with those beguiling eyes, and the words get stuck in my larynx. "Please sit. We need to talk."

I sit on a green tufted armchair opposite her. The coffee table is between us—a no man's land in the middle of the battlefield. I can't tell from her face if she's about to tell me to fuck off or spread her legs and let me earn myself back into her good graces. Now is not the time to tell her I'm a love expert as long as the relationships are entirely fictional.

"I was really hurt and embarrassed that we'd hooked up and you never told me who you were."

"I'm sorry."

"I didn't recognize you."

"I get that now."

She holds up her hand to cut me off. "But I also have to admit that I regretted running the first time. I was embarrassed and out of my depth. You made me feel things, and I'd been numb for so long. I was terrified. It wasn't you. It was a me problem. You were lovely."

"Thank you." I'm holding my breath, waiting for the other shoe to drop.

"After I calmed down with a lot of Cherry García—"

"Good choice."

"Thank you. As I was saying, after I calmed and slept on it, I realized that I still wanted you. I was upset because I was mad at myself for rushing out of there and not getting your number. I didn't know who you came with, and I could hardly ask Lander for her guest's personal info."

"Side note—Lander would totally give you everyone's deets. She thinks privacy is dead."

"Okay, well she probably would get in trouble with Brett for helping me find the hot guy I hooked up with at my ex's wedding."

I clench my jaw. "Define trouble."

She kneads her hands together and looks off to the side. "Let's say, he isn't the calmest person to live with."

Death is too good for the bastard. I should write a scathing epitaph and tarnish his name in immortal literary prose. "You have my number now."

"Yeah, but I wanted porn 'stache guy's number. I didn't know you were the same person."

I choke out a laugh. "Charmed, I'm sure."

"If the shoe fits."

"Speaking of that, Cinderella, I really, *really* wanted to get your number after the wedding, but I also didn't want to approach bridezilla for reasons. I'm sorry I didn't say anything when we met again. It seemed too good to be true, and I didn't want to jinx it."

"I appreciate being able to talk to you without you flying off the handle."

I'd appreciate not being lumped into the same asshat category as her ex and every other toxic man-child who can't regulate his emotions. Not sure why the bar is so low.

She unclenches her hands and rubs them on her skirt. I can almost see the V of her thighs beneath the pleat from this angle. I pick up a throw pillow and hug it in my lap.

"So, do over?" She holds her hand out to me. Her fingers are long. The ring finger on her left hand is indented at the base. She must have worn a ring for a long time.

"Do over," I agree and take her hand in mine. She's grown calluses on her palm from the pickleball paddle, and it makes me feel warm to imagine her practicing her swing.

"So." She settles back against the couch cushions, looking a lot more relaxed than when she got here. "The qualifier is this weekend. What are we going to do now?"

I turn you over the back of that couch and make bad pickleball puns for the next hour.

"You still up for it?" I ask.

"Marissa won't let me quit."

"Atta girl. Let me jump in the shower, then we can run some drills. That work for you?"

"Yes, milord."

My face flames. "I guess you solved the puzzle."

"You guess right." Her pretty plump lips press together to keep back a smile. "Why didn't you tell me?"

"I guess I didn't want to ruin crosswords for you? Learning how the sausage gets made usually turns me off of sausage."

"Makes sense. I guess I'll tell you my answer is yes."

I hold my breath, afraid to hope.

"Yes, I'll get drinks after dinks."

I let it out in a quick burst of air. "Thank god. I guess I was assuming we've been going on romantic dates, but given our failure to communicate, I want to put it all out there for you in triplicate. Celeste—will you do me the honor of going on a romantic date with me?"

She giggles. "Yes, Hayden. After you shower."

"But of course." I jump in the shower to return to humanity and leave Celeste giggling over the names in my plant collection.

I hop out, dry myself, and brush my teeth twice, in case someone might get up close and personal. May the odds be ever in my favor.

"Why is this one named Humperdink?" she asks when I emerge, still damp, in a pair of grey sweatpants, a wicking tee shirt, and my Time for Pickleball hoodie.

"Humper-dink? I couldn't refuse the Princess Bride x Pickleball reference."

"Clever. Your crosswords are clever too. I've always admired them. Admired you."

"I try to put some humor in." I run my fingers through my

wet hair. "When I was a kid, I learned to use humor to deflect. It's come in useful even after I stopped being picked on."

"You must be pretty smart."

"Smart enough to get you to give me a third chance, so, yeah."

Her smile is sweet and soft. "Maybe I'm a pushover."

Absolutely not. My long strides eat up the distance between us. I wrap her in my arms, and she sinks her weight against me. "You're strong and brave and refreshingly real, sweetheart. Why do you think I can't stay away from you? I'm desperate for you to give me the time of day. I wanted so badly for you to play pickleball, just so that I could get another chance to talk to you."

She hides her face against my sweatshirt.

"None of that. Let's hit the ball on the half court in the driveway. That okay with you? I'm not quite ready to share you with the world."

"You've got a court?"

"Not full sized, just a paved rectangle, but it works for practice." I show her the half court I used from my younger basketball days, the backboard and net weathered but holding on. I've spray painted court lines for pickleball. Rackets and balls fall out when I open the shed doors. Badminton, croquet, racquetball, tennis, softball, lacrosse—we're ready to outfit our own rec league. I grab paddles and s pickleball and we get set up.

Her thighs look heavenly in that little flippy tennis skirt. I need a distraction if I'm going to stand a chance in this game. "At the risk of bringing up the fraught past too soon, want to make a wager?"

She snorts. "I'm wary but interested. What did you have in mind?"

"I bet I can make the next two points. I win, I get a boon. You win, lady's choice."

"Pretty open-ended, don't you think?"

"Parameters? Fine. I get to kiss you, above the waist, clothes on, no voyeurism."

She pauses before the next serve and wipes her brow. I love how the little curls at the edge of her hairline curl up like little octopi tendrils. "And if I win, you get to kiss me, below the waist, clothes off, still no voyeurism, it's not my kink."

I miss the ball she serves my way. Complete swing and a puff of air. "Damn it, sweetheart. I can't play with a hard on."

"I bet you can't last this whole game without a hard on." She cuts me off at the knees. I'm dead.

"The spirit is willing, but the flesh is weak."

"Chicken, Unca Hay-Hay?"

I chuckle. "Not you too. Fine, but two can play at that game." I dig out my foulest memories to soak in while I race to the ball. My elbow is tender from a weekend of nonstop typing. I should learn to dictate, but I process my thoughts more slowly. I didn't even speak until I was three—mom says my sisters were too busy talking for me.

The next thing I know, Celeste has crossed around the net and stormed up into my personal space. She clutches my shirt and drags me down to her. God, I love this side of her. Like a little ocelot—fangs and claws, but so cute. I'm going to enjoy cuddling up with this one. I can't wait until she feels safe and secure in our den.

"You're hard," she purrs as she rubs my cock over the sweats.

"I'm a young man, and you're a beautiful woman. Not a sin. Not a crime."

Her lips press against mine, and I taste cinnamon and coffee, a hint of chicory. I try to go slow, but I've been dreaming about this moment for a month. I lick the line of her lips, and she opens for me beautifully, like a Queen of the Night cactus, blooming beneath the moon for a single night. I wrap my arms around her and clutch her to me like I can keep her from fading away with the morning sun. She makes a little mew of pleasure in the back of her throat and tentatively licks my tongue with hers. I can't help my growl in response. She's warm and soft and for this moment, all mine.

I won't scare her off this time. She's giving me another chance—third time's a charm and all that. I'm going to take it and make this so good for her, she forgets all the good-for-nothing assholes who came before me. *Go slow, go slow.* But she presses up on her tiptoes to meet my mouth with equal fervor, lips and tongue, teeth and taste. I've completely forgotten where we are, who we are, wrapped up in this moment with this woman I've dreamed of.

"Get a room!" The yell out the window of the big house has us both startling.

She drops back to her heels and buries her face against my chest with a moan of frustration. "Oh, God."

I keep my arms firmly around her, locking her to me. My heart is beating in my throat with the thought that she'll run again.

"Mom! Ethan's bothering them like you said not to!"

"You narc!"

I hear Molly telling the boys off before she shoos them away from the window and slams it shut. She drops the blinds for good measure, but not before giving me a wink and a smug smile.

Family. Ugh.

"What must your family think of me now?" Celeste's voice is muffled in my shirt.

"I think they're going to get coal in their stockings." I stare at the window like I can pulverize them with my laser eyes. "Don't worry about it. Molly's getting back at me for all the times I spied on her and her boyfriends as a kid. She's got a long memory and a stone heart."

Celeste pulls away and looks up at me. Her beautiful big eyes are crinkled at the corners in a smile, and my chest feels like fireflies are dancing inside. "But why? Why are you interested in me? I'm so much older than you."

I scoff. "You're Molly's age. Sure, she was an insufferable know-it-all when we were kids, but now we're good friends. I'm not some young stud sewing my wild oats. I'm twenty-nine. I'm a fully grown adult male who knows my own mind, and I want you."

"But there's such a stigma..." She trails off and chews her lower lip.

"Who cares? Guys have always been into older women. You just weren't old when you were younger."

She laughs and buries her face in my shirt again, her skin bright pink to the delicate curve of her ears.

"Look, you can either decide to give it a go, or not. We're not going to change society's opinion. I spent my childhood trying to conform to my father's ideal of masculinity, and it was a betrayal of my true self. I was miserable, overweight, socially anxious as fuck. It wasn't until my gym teacher, who was also the track coach, took me under his wing that I got to see a healthier male role model. He taught us boys that real men express our emotions, are self-aware, care for ourselves and our community, and treat all people with dignity and kindness."

"That's why you coach track for your nephews' team?"

"Yup. I'm giving back the gift that I was given in Coach Johnson. If I can change one kid's trajectory for the better, I know my time on earth was worth it."

"That's beautiful, Hayden."

I wink at her. "Now if only I could get my nephews to stop being little shits when I'm trying to seduce my girl, I could die happy."

She laughs, and it lights up her whole face. "Oh, Lumiere, you're always so dramatic."

She wants to play. My chest feels too tight. I sink into the character I pulled out on a whim back at the wedding and try to remember more of the French Henrí taught me. "*Vous êtes si belle, je pourrais vous regarder éternellement.*"

"For a candlestick, you say such lovely things!"

"Only for you, *ma chérie*." I sweep her into my arms, which is less smooth in real life than in the movies, but I'll do it a hundred times if it keeps making her giggle like this. She's not light, and I'm not in the habit of carrying grown-ups around, but I've been lifting weights with Sam on the off chance that someday I could use this move. Smooth, like butter. Celeste doesn't seem to mind my dorkiness. She's perfect for me.

I carry her to the carriage house, and we have a very inelegant shuffle where I almost drop her trying to open the door. "This always seems easy when the hero does it in the movies."

She pats my chest. "Real life problems."

"Indeed." I have to put her down to open it, and she waltzes through, shaking her cute round ass and taunting me with that short, short skirt. "I think I hurt my back. You're going to have to walk up the stairs yourself."

Turning to look over her shoulder, she catches my eyes glued to her butt and gives me a wicked grin. "Is that so? Lead the way, handsome."

"Oh, no. I've got to go behind you so I can catch you if you fall. Wouldn't want to be responsible for anyone getting injured on my property. Insurance reasons." She knows I'm joking, because I still can't lift my eyes off the smooth skin visible under the bouncing pleat. If I were in a book, I'd be drooling, but as it is I have to swallow. I force myself to lift my eyes to her face before I do something stupid, like bury my tongue between those plump cheeks.

By the time we get to the top of the stairs, my cock is throbbing in my sweats. I open the door, and she squeezes past me in a burst of white orchid shampoo. She hesitates once we're inside, her playfulness sliding away as her insecurities rise.

"We don't have to do anything you don't feel comfortable

with," I assure her. "We could watch a movie and cuddle. Or... or talk. Do you want some tea? I can make tea." I pass by her and go to the kitchen cabinets, searching for something to offer. "Ginger, Egyptian mint—that's got some green tea in it— jasmine, Assam. I might have some English biscuits in here too." I'm too busy trying to head off her running before she even gets the idea in her head, that I completely miss what she's doing behind me.

She stops me with one word. "Hayden."

I freeze at the sensuality pouring through my name from her lips. Slowly, holding my breath, I turn.

Celeste is standing in the middle of my living room, and her gaze is on me, a force field that I couldn't escape even if I wanted to. Not dropping her gaze, she holds the zipper of her dress and pulls down, *slowly, slowly,* revealing creamy full cleavage squeezed up by a sports bra. My mouth waters. Forget English biscuits. I need to put my mouth on those. The zipper stops right above her bellybutton. She trails her fingertips up her chest, over her breasts, to the collar of the dress. I've never been so jealous of another person's hands before. I want to knock her hands away and be the one to pull that dress off her and expose all her beautiful curves to the sunlight. But I can't move. She's got me trapped like a black widow, and I'm going to die a very, very happy man.

Her fingertips find the inside of her collar as she pinches the fabric and slowly drags it down her shoulders. *Slow, slow.* I'm frozen in the headlights of the approaching train. Fear and wonder. How did I get here? Is this my beautiful life? And when the dress slips down to pool at her feet, leaving her in a sports bra and black lace panties, I fall to my knees.

21

CELESTE

THE UNABASHED APPRECIATION on Hayden's face when I slip off my dress is enough to make me forget my anxieties about my softer, squishier mid-life body and embrace the heat of the moment. I'm not eighteen anymore. White lines like old claw marks stretch across my wider hips. My fuller breasts swing as I step free of the puddle of fabric of my tennis dress. I don't think Hayden minds their new, voluptuous shape, if the reverence on his face is anything to go by.

He's on his knees like a penitent, and it makes me feel powerful. Wanted. Worshiped. Maybe I am. Maybe I have power in this new shape. I certainly have more self-respect than I ever did at eighteen. That's power. Loving myself enough to leave. Loving myself enough to risk my fragile ego for this. I pull the sports bra up and over my head, and Hayden makes a noise that sounds growly and wild.

"You are so gorgeous." His voice has deepened. It sends shivers over my skin and down low across my belly. I squeeze my thighs together against the ache. What now? Brett always took control in the bedroom. It took all my courage to get this far. If Hayden rejects me now, mostly naked in the middle of his apartment in the middle of the day, I don't think I'll ever be able to live it down.

He scoots forward on his knees until his face is pressed right against my belly, and his big hands clamp down on the backs of my thighs. He's lower than me, putting me in the power position, and I'm grateful that he knows this is hard for me without me saying it out loud.

He rubs his nose from my belly button to the elastic edge of my panties and makes a growly noise in the back of his throat. "You smell so good, Celeste. I can't wait to taste you."

"Are you sure?"

He pulls back and looks up at me, one eyebrow climbing. Can I let myself be vulnerable again? I need to, if I want to move forward, but there's a lifetime of doubt trapping me in cobwebs. "You don't have to tell me if you don't want to, but let me guess, he-who-must-not-be-named made you feel ashamed about oral."

I break eye contact. It's too much. I nod.

"You tell me if anything doesn't feel good, and you let me worry about what feels good to me, okay? I want to do this. I'm dying to do this. I get off on getting you off, okay? So get out of that pretty little head of yours and just feel."

I bite my lip and nod down at him.

"Say it."

"Yes. I'm...going to let you do...whatever you want."

His eyelids slam shut and his shoulders tense. "Goddamn it. You have no idea, babe, how hot that is." His breath is deep and shuddering. I'm frozen, worried I've messed this up somehow, but he opens his eyes again and takes my hands from where I was clenching them together. He places my hands on top of his head and gently squeezes, instructing me to clutch his hair. His intention calms, grounds me. "But what I meant was, tell me you understand that I'm going to stop as soon as you tell me something doesn't feel good. You're not going to go along with anything to please me, because what pleases me is making you feel like rainbows are sparkling outta your pretty pussy. I want your unfiltered honesty, Celeste."

I swallow. "I'll try."

"Attagirl. Use your words, but if you can't, I want you to pull my hair. Direct me. Play me like a marionette. I'm your dirty little toy, babe. Move me around and grind your pretty pussy into my face."

Oh. My. God. My legs feel like jelly, but Hayden braces me against his strong shoulders as he nuzzles his face between my thighs.

He pulls back and stares up at me. His eyes sparkle, eyelids are heavy with lust. "Let's get more comfortable, okay?"

At my nod, he sweeps me up like a storybook damsel and carries me down the hall into his bedroom. It's decorated in shades of grey and green with a pop of bright pink from a throw pillow. Just like in the living room, plants are everywhere. I don't get a good look at them before he's laying me down gently on his plush grey bedspread and taking off my panties with his teeth. They get stuck around my hipbones, around my knees, at my ankles. By the time he gives up, we're both laughing so hard my whole voluminous body trembles like Jello.

"That move always sounds suave in books. I need to practice." His eyes devour every inch of me, and he makes a low, pained growl in his throat.

I've never felt so powerful.

He spreads my thighs with his big hands, and I feel a flush of embarrassment burn across my skin. His gaze flicks up to mine, and he licks his lips. "You know how gorgeous you are? On my bed, legs spread for me?" He cups the straining tent in his pants. "I've never been so hard. You're wrecking me, *ma petite chou*. Let me show you how much I love the way you taste."

He starts at my toes and kisses each one while he massages the arch of my foot.

"You have a foot fetish I should know about?"

"Only for these feet." He kisses the arch and trails his tongue up the inside of my calf, pausing to lave the sensitive skin on the back of my knee. I squirm as he tickles the other leg too. He squeezes and kneads the muscles in my thighs. His strong thumbs dig into my IT band, releasing the tension. "Put your fingers in my hair. Direct me, *ma petite chou*."

I run my fingernails along his scalp and a shiver runs down his spine. He makes a breathy, involuntary moan that lets me know how true his words are. He really wants to do this. I guess I should let him, right?

He's teasing me, and the massage feels so good, but the anticipation is driving me to madness. Wrapping his curls around my fingers, I gently pull him up toward my core. He chuckles against my skin, breath warm and feathery. "Feisty little wench, aren't you?"

"Only for you."

"Good." His smile makes my toes curl. When he finally lowers his face to where I need it, the first lick of his tongue sends my back arching. My desperate moan fills the air.

I let all the worries fade away as Hayden strums me higher. I can't help riding his face, yanking the silky strands of his hair, and the growl he makes tells me that he likes that as much as I do.

I lightly scrape his scalp as he works, and his approving hum vibrates through me and twists the building tension in my body. He winds me tighter and tighter, until the world dissolves into one long muscle spasm, over and over. He tends me through it, not stopping until I push away his head. I'm too sensitive.

What is this feeling I've been missing all these years? The tension flows out like the tide, peace flows in. Languid and hazy like sun on the morning dew.

Boneless. An earthquake couldn't shake me from this bed. I feel Hayden shift beside me and the mattress depress as he scoots in close. He drags me to his hot chest, and I fall asleep wrapped in his safe, warm embrace.

When midnight rolls around, my eyelids flutter open to find the heat is Hayden wrapped around me from behind. He's lightly snoring in my ear, but I don't mind. His skin burns through me, igniting warmth in my core and waking me up better than coffee. I push back against him, and his body comes awake, hard and ready for round two. I'm in the mood. I'm relaxed. And for the first time in a long time, I feel totally comfortable with my partner and asking for what I want.

Even if I'm not sure what I need, Hayden is more than eager to play around until we uncover it, together.

22

HAYDEN

LATE SPRING ON THE SHORES of Puget Sound smells of petrichor and the salty sea. I'm running along the boardwalk by the marina, about five miles into my run, when I notice two younger guys are pacing me. I speed up, and they follow, slow down, they do that too.

Finally, we hit the dunes at the end of the asphalt, and I stop to catch my breath. On the water, the wind fills the sails of a school of little, white, two-person sailboats. Seagulls circle loudly overhead. The bark of sea lions echoes down the beach.

I wipe my forehead with the hem of my tee shirt and turn to face my shadows. Last time I saw them, they were standing stiffly in their tuxes at the wedding. They're more relaxed in running clothes, but still gangly, with the hint of baby fat in their cheeks. College aged, I think. The shorter one has a mop of curly brown hair the same color as Celeste's, and the taller one has the roman nose of her ex.

They pause about ten feet away and communicate silently with each other. I wait them out. I can guess what they're here to say, but I'm going to enjoy watching them squirm. I start stretching as I stare them down.

Finally, the shorter one steps forward. He's about six foot two and his shoulders are wider than mine, but I've got ten years of experience on him. "What's up?"

"'Sup."

I nod, wondering how long this is going to take. They're both puffing out their chests like we're about to throw down on the sidewalk outside the Sugar Shack. I never connected with the chest thumping, head butting ritual that my dad thought boys were born with.

Am I expected to prove my worth to mate their mother in a dominance battle like wolves? Are we arranging pistols at dawn?

I check my watch and glance between the two. Which one is Brody and which one is Ryder? If I want to have Celeste in my life, I know these guys are going to be a big part of it too, but if it comes to blows, I bet it ends in a draw.

Celeste wouldn't like it if I hurt her babies. I hope she'd be similarly alarmed if they hurt me.

"Listen, man," the curly top says, lifting his chin, "my mom likes you, but she's in a vulnerable place."

I nod and watch the other kid sidle up to my right side. I turn to keep them both in my peripheral vision.

"She's very important to us," the nose says. "We don't want to see her get hurt."

"O-kay. And which one of you is which?"

They exchange a startled glance. "I'm Brody," says curly top.

"Ryder," says the nose.

"Hayden." I offer up my hand to shake, and Brody takes it in a firm grip. "Your mom is a strong, independent woman who knows her own mind. I'm sure she'd appreciate knowing you have her best interests at heart, even if she can stand up for herself."

"Sometimes," Ryder grumbles.

I shake his hand next, and he tries to break my fingers. "You got something you want to get off your chest, friend? Cuz your mom likes what I can do with these fingers." I pull out of his vice grip and wiggle said fingers at him just to mess with him.

Brody looks a little green and Ryder snarls.

I smirk. "Just playing with you. You want to protect your mom—I get it. I respect that."

"She deserves better than a quick hookup in a storage closet," Brody says.

Ouch.

"She needs stability," Ryder adds in a tone that says he doesn't think that someone is me.

"Someone reliable. Someone who's got her best interests at heart."

I clear my throat and give him a lopsided smile. "How about passion? How about spontaneity? How about someone who will push her out of her comfort zone and help her experience life outside the ticky-tacky box? I don't think your mom wants a less-volatile Brett, boys. I think she needs a different model entirely."

The boys exchange another loaded look. I guess I'm not what they expected, but this isn't my first time coaching teen boys. I've been where they are, and I know the best place for people is not letting them hide themselves away in a safe, predictable existence.

If Coach Johnson had let me be all those years ago, I would never have had the courage to invest or write a book or learn new skills. I'd have probably ended up in basic training like my dad wanted. I'd have let some drill sergeant "make a man out of me" and closed myself off from my emotions.

"Okay, so you're giving me The Talk, I get it. I have a mom and four sisters. I've been where you are. But I still have six miles to go. Let's see what you got." I start jogging back toward the tunnel under the train track that winds along the shore.

They fall into step behind me, and I pick up the pace. We

leave the beach behind and exit through the short tunnel lined with mosaics and graffiti of sea life. As we burst out on the other side to the cobblestones that lead sharply uphill, I put on a burst of speed.

Eat my dust, kiddos.

Pretty soon we're sprinting up the steep street that switchbacks down the bluff, and I'm pushing off the ball of my foot to leap the stairs. This is where I'll lose them.

The first part isn't so bad, but after the dog park where I usually stop to stretch and ogle cute puppies, the next set of stairs is a glute burn up a mountain. Ryder and Brody fall behind, but not as bad as Aaron did when I first challenged him to this long loop course.

And it's not like we're on opposing sides. We both want what's best for Celeste—for her to be happy and healthy and fulfilled to her fullest potential.

We just might disagree on the path to get there.

I'm biased, of course.

I've climbed the stairs twice a week for years and quickly leave the boys panting behind me. "You need to do more squats!" I yell over my shoulder.

I hear Brody groan and Ryder chuckle before I'm leaping the last few steps to the top of the bluff. Evergreen trees block the view of Puget Sound here, except for a narrow tunnel through the branches to the sparkling grey-blue water. Never ceases to strike me how beautiful home is. I might not be as traveled as Celeste, but I know what's important. I got it all right here, now that she's in the picture.

I'm chuckling to myself and stretching my quads when Brody bounds up after me, cursing and holding the stitch in his side.

"That was badass, bro," he says admiringly. "You ever time yourself on that?"

"That was nothing. My stamina is excellent."

Brody's smile slides off his face. He looks like he's gonna

shoot lightning bolts from his eyes and burn me to death. Ryder comes panting up the stairs next. He wipes the sweat from his brow and gives me an approving nod.

"Here's the thing," I step closer to the boys and put hands on their shoulders. "I'm not going anywhere. If you actually want to help your mother, you'd put yourself to work helping her fix that house."

Ryder's brow furrows. "She never said she needed help. She never asked—"

"She's a strong, independent woman who is used to doing everything alone." I give them both my best stern coach glare. "She needs workmen, and if you've got time to stalk her boyfriend on a run, you certainly have time to go lend a hand to paint or carry or move shit. Whatever she needs done, she could use your help. The sooner she gets that house patched up and sold, the sooner she can get her career off the ground. She'll have financial independence. She can make her own choices about whom she does or doesn't date. Capeesh?"

"You think you know her, huh? Did she ask you for help?" Brody asks. "She sure as shit didn't ask us."

"We know her better than you—" Ryder cuts in.

I raise an eyebrow and stare them down. Just like puppies.

Ryder scrubs a hand down his face. "I guess I never asked if she needed a hand."

"But—" Brody objects with a growl. He's still in that awkward stage where he feels like he's supposed to have it all figured out, but his brain hasn't finished snapping all his circuits yet. He'll get there.

"A man doesn't wait around to be asked to help. That puts the onus back on her to dictate and micromanage, which puts more on her plate. We don't want to add to her mental load, do we?"

The boys share a look, but I can see I've hooked them.

"No, boys, we don't," I tell them. "We look around to see what's gotta be done, and we get 'er done. Got it?"

Brody kicks a rock with his shoe. "Got it."

"Good." I release them and step back. "Now who's gonna race me back to the start?"

The slow downhill portion of the course is the easiest, and they keep pace.

I still win.

23

CELESTE

THE SPRING RAIN LET UP in the early hours of the morning, letting the sun start to dry up the mess of water on the pickleball court just in time for the qualifying matches. Today teams that want to compete in the summer pickleball tournament have the chance to be placed in a ranked bracket. The ones who lose will be put in a separate unranked pool, and the winner of the second chance bracket will compete against the winners of the ranked bracket in the finals.

Nerves swim in my belly, but also a calm acceptance that the anticipation is almost over. Hayden is helping clean up, using a giant squeegee to move the water to the farthest court. The rain last night knocked down a mess of twigs and leaves, and Russell, his older friend with the khaki pants and red shoes, is using the push broom to sweep up. It's still pretty damp. Not sure how the pickleball will bounce on wet asphalt, but I know I need to learn if I have any hope of winning this tournament.

Summer is the best time to play pickleball in the Pacific Northwest for obvious reasons, but beggars can't be choosers. I have to learn to play in whatever weather the good lord gives me.

Hayden spots me and the smile on his face is warmer than my spring fleece jacket. I remember his tongue in me, his hands on me, his touch and taste and smell. The sounds he made as he came. I'm sure my face says it all—it's hard to put back up the mask now that Hayden has seen me without it.

He sets the squeegee aside and jogs over. "Hey, Beautiful. You ready to crush the competition?"

"Yes?" I wipe my palms on my tennis skirt and try to count my breaths.

"Attagirl." He jogs to the bench to pick up his paddle. "Let's warm up before everyone realizes the rain's over and the court gets mobbed."

I follow him like a lost little duck to the driest court, and we start dinking the ball across the net.

"Soft hands," he says low. "Good."

That throaty whisper sounds like he means so much more. *Just like that, sweetheart. Take it, babe. Your soft hands feel so good. Let me make you come again. And again.*

My heartbeat is thrumming like a hummingbird in my throat. I hit the ball too hard, and it pops up to give Hayden a perfect slam shot, but he doesn't take it.

He catches it in the air and the corner of his mouth lifts in a lopsided grin. "Got your head in the game, partner?"

My cheeks are on fire. "I'm trying."

He winks. The air between us zaps with awareness, electric and thick.

The courts are starting to fill with hopeful pickleballers who don't mind a little adverse weather. More men than women, but there are a couple old ladies who can really slam the ball. One in particular stands out—she's several inches shorter than me, in a purple sweatshirt and a helmet of close-cropped white hair. Hard to believe she's a shark on the court, but I've seen her play, and it's inspiring. Life goals, for sure. I want to be her when I'm seventy-five. Strong enough to still do the activities that bring me joy. Fierce enough to face off with bigger, bulkier humans decades younger than me.

Hayden notices who I'm watching. "Watch out for Anh; she's one of the top players in the area."

"You think we have a chance?"

"I know it. We got this, babe."

His faith in me is like putting on Wonder Woman's armbands. I could do anything. Be anything. Achieve anything if I work hard enough at it. Hayden never cuts me down to feel better about himself—he'd sooner cut out his own spleen. Maybe it's the coach in him, or maybe it's the four sisters. Maybe it's because he was bullied as a kid and knows how to do the opposite.

The line is long, but Fran hands out biscochitos and the high school librarian, Ms. D, offers everyone lemonade. Competing teams are signed in and given a number. Dr. Fisher and the AP Statistics teacher, Dr. Otterson, bring out a hand turned bingo cage full of colorful numbered balls, and they start matching teams up randomly for the first set.

Unfortunately, the odds are not in our favor for our first match. We get Anh and her partner Larry. I'm sweating before we even start playing.

Just then I hear someone call out, "*Fan ja*! Get it, *Gumma*!" and I'd know that voice anywhere. I scan the crowd and there she is in all her fabulous style—Frida, wearing a jean jacket over a neon pink midriff top and white cutoff shorts that take a big set of ovaries to wear. A stylish wrap holds her hair back from her face, and her giant sunglasses are Hollywood gold. She's waving madly with long white-painted nails and a big smile.

"Fan club?" Hayden asks.

"She came. I didn't think she'd make it." But butterflies take flight in my sternum. My mother never showed up for my school performances, but here is Frida, the swearing, smoking Scandinavian fairy godmother that I never knew I needed.

Hayden puts his hand on my lower back and gives me a little nudge. "Go say hi. Larry is still putting on his court shoes."

"Only if you come too."

Hayden grins. "Is that wise?"

"Gird your loins," I joke. He follows me to the bleachers that have been set up for spectators, staying a step behind my shoulder as if he's afraid of the little old spitfire grinning in front of us. "Frida! So glad to see you."

"I would not miss dis for anyting. Introduce me to dis tall glass of water."

I pull Hayden forward and give him a little push. "Frida, may I present my pickleball coach, Hayden Holstrom. Hayden, this is my friend Frida."

Frida clutches Hayden's offered hand, and I'm suddenly worried that she's not going to give him back. "You were not joking. He is verra handsome."

Hayden glances at me with a twinkle in his eye. "My reputation precedes me."

Frida scoffs. "Humble too. Dis is gud. Fine choice, girl. Now you go back dere and win dis ting. I have prospects to talk to." She drops Hayden's hand and flutters her fingers at us, before turning to her neighbors on the bleachers and striking up a conversation. Does she even know those people? Does it matter? I want to be like her when I grow up.

Returning to the court, Larry and Ahn are waiting for us. Larry is an older gentleman with a wiry white plume of cotton for hair and racquetball glasses. He's not quick on his feet, but he sure can hit the ball.

"Try to put it in the far corner," Hayden whispers to me as we switch places for the next serve. "His backhand is weak, and he can't get in position."

I serve. I'm learning Hayden's style of play, and he's picking up on mine. We're less like two buffalos awkwardly butting against each other on the centerline and more like dancers weaving back and forth. Half the time I hold back instead of toeing up to the kitchen, because part of my brain is still playing tennis. My confidence is growing with every point I score. Hayden applauds every good hit I make with an *atta girl*. He notices every little thing, which is thrilling and scary. I've never had someone's undivided attention. It's a heady feeling.

Ahn is, unfortunately, a very good player and more than makes up for Larry's tendency to hit the ball out of bounds. It's a close game, but when Larry manages to surprise me with a curved shot to my backhand, we lose.

"Chin up," Hayden says as he rubs my back and shoulders. "Best of three make the ranked division. We're not out yet."

Between matches, we watch other teams, and Hayden gives me a feel for what to be ready for if we're called to play against any of these teams. Harold, the guy who busks with his accordion outside the grocery store, is teamed with Piper, who is playing in a black skater dress and black lace choker. Her long black nails and black lipstick look more at home at a goth poetry reading than a pickleball tournament, but if living in Salmon Bay has taught me anything, it's that it takes all kinds.

Friendly faces wave from every side, even though I've only been a part of this pickleball community for a month or two. I've got more people saying hi to me than I ever had, people I see at the post office and the hardware store, people stopping me on the street and striking up a conversation at the gym. Not just people—*neighbors*.

And Hayden's family too. Aaron shows up with his two adorable little girls to watch Unca Hay-Hay kill it on the court. His sister Addy stops by with his mom, for moral support. His best friend, the reticent giant Henrí and a younger sister I haven't met yet—Margo—stop by with the Miel parents to cheer for their middle sister Amalie. Even my boys make a surprise appearance, showing up with flowers of all things and giving Hayden some kind of secretive boy message in looks and grunts.

"How do you know my boys?" I ask once they've left us to watch from the sidelines.

"They're important to you, sweetheart. We're destined to be best buds."

I flush and glance back at them. My sweet boys. What do they know?

"You should bring them to the next family barbecue."

"Your family barbecue? Oh, I don't know—"

"Celeste." He waits for me to meet his gaze, serious for once. "Are you embarrassed of me?"

"No! Of course not—"

"Perfect. Then you won't have any problem introducing the most important people in your life to the most important people in my life. Right?"

"It seems fast," I hedge. What if they have a problem with me being with someone so much younger than me? What if it doesn't work out?

"You think they don't date? Come on. This isn't some fling for me, Celeste. I really like you."

His words send butterflies through my belly, even though I know this. He likes me. I like him. I can't let my fear keep me from something good. "I like you too, Hayden."

He gives me that boyish grin that makes me weak in the knees and wraps one arm around my waist to guide me to our next match. "That's what I like to hear, beautiful."

Maybe my fear of getting hurt is keeping me from good things. I blamed Scandinavian reticence for the freeze—that's what people told me when I first moved to Salmon Bay, at least — but maybe it was just me? Maybe Salmon Bay isn't the problem. Maybe I was hesitant to get close to anyone, to let anyone in, because we moved so often. Why make friends when I couldn't keep them?

But I don't have to leave this time. I could choose to stay.

Put down roots deep into the fertile soil, nurtured by these *neighbors*, and this funny, handsome doubles partner of mine.

When I see Warren and his friends riding up on electric green scooters like a geriatric motorcycle gang, I lift my chin. I'm not going to let bullies chase me from this court. This tournament is mine.

24

HAYDEN

THE COURTS ARE AT CAPACITY with teams looking to rank in the Sea Lion Lodge's first annual pickleball qualifier, but I'm proud of how well Celeste is handling the pressure. Tough break drawing Ahn in the first round, but Celeste took the loss in stride.

Principal Larsson, on behalf of the Sea Lion Club, and Dr. Fisher, for Parks and Rec, are in attendance. They're officially in charge, but Marjorie Mead and Tia Fran are doing most of the work checking in teams and orchestrating the who plays whom. Dr. M—who insists I call her Marjorie since I haven't been in her class for years—was the most hellacious English teacher ever to darken the halls at Salmon Bay High. I'm still terrified of her, even though she's morphed into a sweet older lady with a volunteering problem. Every time I see her—at the library, the grocery store, the local coffee shop...perils of a small town—I want to tell her about Trudy Belle. The words sit heavy on my tongue—*who's got grade A ideas, C/D writing now, Dr. M?*—but I swallow them down. She's one of those literary snobs with a stick up her ass about romantic fiction. As a teacher, would she still be proud that one of her students is a published author? Or would the look in her eye when she finds out my genre be as crushing as getting that first comment on my first essay in her class?

That fear of judgement is hard to shake even when I've got the glowing New York Times book review to counter it. Add in my dad and my grandpa and my ex-girlfriend, and it's no wonder I'm hesitant to spill my guts. I'm going to tell Celeste. I am. I just have to figure out the right way to word it. If she knew she was my muse, would she freak?

A sour feeling stirs in my gut at the prospect. This thing is still so new, and I like her a lot.

Four of the eight pickleball courts are reserved for qualifying matches, while the other half is open play. Paddle stacks line both sides of the court. As we wait for our next placement match, Celeste and I watch the current round of hopeful teams next to a friendly, drooling, Saint Bernard mix named TopDog. His person, Jersey, is playing Ahn. TopDog's head swings back and forth following the ping of the ball. Ahn is making Jersey work for it. He should know better than to face her after she overheard him talking smack about how easy it would be to slay an old lady. That old lady is going to mop the court with him.

His dog is nice though. I introduce Celeste, who kneels and gives TopDog some good scritches. "Who's a good boy? Who's a good boy?"

I'm not a jealous guy, but he's pushing it by casting those big sad, heart-eyes at my girl. "I didn't realize a dog is the perfect wing man."

Celeste laughs. "He's a handsome boy, isn't he? You should get one."

"Plant dad. I would, but so many in my harem are toxic to animals."

She raises an eyebrow. "You could get rid of some plants?"

I gasp in mock horror. "I won't tell Seymour you said that, and he won't try to eat you in your sleep."

She shakes her head, but she's smiling, not pulling away.

She's forgiven me, but I still have one secret to figure out how to share. Not right now though, when the last one is still so fresh.

I bring her over to meet the other furry regulars at the pickleball court. Anh brings her two corgis, Fred and Ginger, who pant after every ball but know better than to chase them. Russell brings his terrier, Russell Junior, who's so old he probably couldn't chase a ball if he wanted to. He's usually drooling on the sidelines half asleep while people step over him to place their paddles in a stack. Even now, he's inching forward from where Russell put him down under the bench. He's got about a foot before he'll hit his target—the waiting stacks of paddles—where he'll spend the rest of the day nipping at anyone who tries to jump the line. Good dog.

I'm talking through plays and strategies, when the king of the court approaches. Warren is wearing high waisted khakis and a shirt that says, "Less talk, more dink". His hairs are slicked back, and he's wearing a gold chain around his neck with a pickleball charm on it. He surveys the paddle line with a critical eye; I think he'd straighten the stacks, but Russell Junior gives him the stink eye, and he wisely keeps his distance.

Seeing us, he swaggers over. "Hayden, just the man I wanted to see. What's this I hear about you talking to the Superintendent about tennis courts?"

Fault. I spare a glance at Celeste, who is watching me curiously. I clear my suddenly dry throat. "Nothing big, Warren. Just checking in with where he stands on supporting the sport."

Warren crosses his arms and looks back at Celeste. I can see his dislike plainly on his face, as if she's responsible for trying to take his kingdom away.

Eyes on me, bro. "Look, we're up now. Gotta hustle or Bob will try to snatch our court."

Bob's eyeing the paddle line like no one will notice if he quietly moves his stack ahead. He's searching for anyone to claim the next stack, and if we don't hop up like our asses are on fire, he's going to scoop us.

"You're never going to win," Warren persists. "But you'll alienate a lot of people if you turn your back on us. We fought hard for these courts."

"Why don't we let the tournament decide it? We win, you share the courts. You win, we'll share the courts. Everyone wins."

Warren harrumphs. "You're too green to remember when Parks and Rec let the Tennis Foundation choose to resurface only the tennis courts and leave the pickleball courts cracked and broken. They didn't want to play nice with us. You think we should just roll over?"

I think he might have bribed Dr. Fisher over to the pickleball side in order to get his little fiefdom, but I still think we should share. "I know you fought hard, Warren. We all appreciate what you've done to get the sport recognition and court space. Now if you'll excuse us."

With my hands gently on her shoulders, I turn Celeste toward Amalie, my friend Henrí's younger sister, who is holding up our paddles and waiting for our set of four to show up and claim our court. I hope Celeste will grab ours before we have to get into it with Bob.

"You think this poacher has what it takes?" Warren calls after us. "Or is your plan to have her sit and look pretty while you defend the whole court?"

Celeste's shoulders stiffen beneath my hands. I shut my eyes and take another deep breath through my nose. How did I not notice how patronizing Warren is? It's like now that I'm seeing the world through Celeste's eyes, I'm picking up on so many more micro aggressions that I was blind to. And it's not like I was totally oblivious—four sisters, remember? It's just that now I take it personally. I want to protect Celeste from every asshole who ever made her feel less-than.

I look around the courts and count how many more men

there are than women. Has this place that was so welcoming to me been less than welcoming to anyone with a uterus?

"Naw, man," I tell Warren. "Let's let the match speak for itself."

Celeste and I grab our paddles and get ready to play our next qualifying match. I bump fists with Max and turn to give Amalie a hug, when Warren taps Max on the shoulder. He whispers in Max's ear, and Max's mouth tightens. Next thing I know, he shrugs and strolls off the court. Warren's smile doesn't reach his eyes as he takes his place next to Amalie. She eyes her new partner, brown eyes extra wide behind her coke-bottle glasses, lips pressed tightly together.

"You can't switch out team members," I tell Warren. "Registration already happened."

"You sure about that?" Warren's face is much too pleasant right now. I want to hit him with a Nasty Nelson.

"Since he's married to one of the women doing the registration, you think he cares about the rules?" Celeste whispers to me.

"Should we let this slide?"

She nods. Okay then. I guess we're doing this thing. I feel a little bad drawing Amalie into our little war. She's a newer player, and she's always been a little socially awkward. We start dinking across the net to each other to warm up, slow and easy to wake up the brain-hand connection. Celeste has made huge strides to pull back on her bangers, and she easily kisses the ball across the net and stays out of the kitchen. My little gherkin is all grown up.

Warren starts putting top spin into his dinks, making them land harder at Celeste's feet but she's unperturbed. She returns the ball to Amalie, including her in the play when I only want to make it difficult on Warren, and Warren only wants to trick Celeste. Amalie is innocent in all this.

Warren catches the ball. "Enough dinking around. Let's play."

He moves into position but doesn't wait for anyone else to indicate we're ready before he serves—fast, low, and right at Celeste. She's directly across from him, so his serve isn't going diagonally like it should, but she can't get out of the way fast enough and it smacks her in the chest.

"One-zero, serving two," he chuckles.

"What?" Celeste turns those big caramel eyes to me as she rubs the new bruise on her chest. "How is that his point? He's supposed to serve it to you."

"Interference, doll face," Warren calls as he changes places with Amalie. "If you're just going to watch, go sit in the bleachers."

I give her an apologetic wince. "It's called a Nasty Nelson. If he can hit his opponent on a serve, he gets a point."

"But I didn't know that!" She scowls at Warren. "That's a stupid rule. Now I've got a bruise."

"If you can't stand the heat, get outta the kitchen." Warren winds up and serves again, this time diagonally to Celeste.

She lets it bounce and returns it down the middle, where Warren crowds his partner out and sends it back toward Celeste with enough top spin to whip cream. She misjudges the mad bounce and sends the ball right into the net.

"Sorry," she mutters to me as Warren and his partner tap paddles and switch places.

"Don't be. We got this."

"Three—Oh, two," Warren says as he serves back to me. I don't miss the opportunity to smack it to his feet on his backhand, so he's forced to stumble backwards. He manages the return by the skin of his teeth, then I hit it to the far back corner, and he misses. "That was out!" he shouts.

"No," Celeste calls. "That was in."

Warren puts his hands on his waist and gives her a disappointed look that just withers her. "I know you're new at this, but the person closest to the ball calls it, and I say it was out."

Celeste flattens her lips together but doesn't argue when I give her a tiny nod. The play moves on from there. Warren is not playing to lose, but I'm not going to win by bending the rules to suit me. That's not in the spirit of the game. Amalie and Celeste have a good volley, before Celeste puts it down the middle and both Amalie and Warren reach for it, slamming their paddles into each other. The ball sails past.

"Shit!" Warren swears. "Get out of my way!"

I don't usually enforce this rule, but since Warren is being a dink, I'm going to throw the rulebook at him. "Penalty for swearing on the court."

"I didn't," Warren says.

"We all heard you." I look to Amalie, who gives Warren some side-eye before she nods in agreement. "Loud enough to lose a point."

"We're not allowed to swear?" Celeste catches the ball that a waiting player tosses back.

"Not according to the rule book. Why do you think I've trained myself to say Fault, Dink-head, and Pickled?"

She snorts. "I guess I thought you don't swear because you hang out with kids so much."

"Heck, no. Those gremlins have a way worse vocabulary than I do."

"Noted." Celeste reports the score and serves a beautiful low arc that hits right in the back, close to the centerline, and I get chills.

"Babe, it's so hot how you slid that right between their legs."

Her lips quirk but she keeps her eyes on the ball. So hot.

The score is ten to ten. Warren is doing less trash talking and more poaching into Amalie's territory right at the kitchen line. Amalie hangs back; she's visibly intimidated by Warren's aggressive play.

"What do you say to a wager, buddy?" Warren asks as he tries to catch his breath before the next serve.

My competitive spirit is riding me hard, but when I glance at Celeste, she avoids my gaze. Is she still sore about the betting game that led to our wedding exploits? It's not like I was trying to trick her. I scratch the back of my neck. Warren's face is blotchy. His nostrils flare.

Will he call me a chicken if I don't accept? Do I care? I guess at twenty-nine I should unpack this need to prove myself. I don't have to accept every bet thrown at me. It's a game, I've told myself for years. But is there more to my need to win?

"I win," Warren says, "and you forget about meeting with Fisher."

And there's the metaphorical drop shot; Warren is putting me in my place.

"And if I win?" I ask.

He shrugs. "I'll talk to Fisher on your behalf."

Celeste's spine is straight. Don't think she knows what I was planning to talk to Fisher about—I wanted to surprise her—but someone spilled the beans, and now Warren is marshaling against it. *Eyes on the prize, Holstrom.* I run my gaze over my petit chou, her juicy curves, her soft skin, her blushing cheeks and riotous curls.

Why doesn't she realize how beautiful she is? She's blinding.

"I don't think so, Warren," I say slowly. "Not this time."

Warren's lips curve down. "No?"

"No. Stop stalling." I give Celeste a peck on the cheek. "Come on, Little Cabbage—let's get our heads in the game." As I take my place kitty-corner to Warren, the noise of the crowd fades out. Nothing touches me in the zone. I'm one with the ball. One with the Force. My grip is sure on my lightsaber as I stare down my pickleball father figure.

But Warren is mad that he can't get me to take his bait. The score is ten-ten, but we have to win by two. He hits all his shots to Celeste—the weaker player. He serves before she's ready, and the score climbs to eleven-ten.

He muscles into Amalie's side so that he can hit all the balls, spinning them to places a new player wouldn't expect. Celeste hustles, but it's not enough. There's nothing I can do to stop the wreckage. The ball doesn't come to my side at all, as they climb to twelve-ten.

The loss hits me right in the sternum. I almost look down to see if I have a purple circle with whiffle-shaped holes in my chest. Warren is smirking at me as he strolls forward and holds out his paddle to tap like we do after every game. Amalie's not sure if she should feel happy for the win or guilty, but as she stares intently at Warren's paddle, burning it into her memory, I'm pretty sure she's going to avoid his stack from here on out. He doesn't like to lose.

Who does?

"Sorry, Hayden," Celeste says softly. She's biting her lip again. I reach over and tug it gently out from between her teeth, then lower my head and kiss it better. Everything fades away as our lips touch. Her taste is addictive. Her smell goes right to my head, turning on my pleasure receptors. Warren clears his throat loudly, but I enjoy her taste for longer before I break away. She's gazing up at me with those big eyes unfocused, pupils dilated. I'd like to cage her in against the fence and kiss my way out of this crushing disappointment.

"Not your fault, buttercup."

"But Marissa will skin me alive."

"All hope is not lost. We're still in the unranked division. There's still time for us to practice and climb to the top." I lean down to kiss her, but she shies away.

"People will talk."

"I didn't think you were hiding me away like a dirty secret."

"I'm not!"

"Fuck what other people think. You're hot and sweet, and I'm lucky to be the guy to sweep you off your feet." I scoop her under the knees and back in a bridal carry as she laughs.

"Sportsmanship, Holstrom?" Warren growls. "Or are you too butthurt to tap?"

Ignoring him, I stare into Celeste's chocolate eyes and rub our noses together. "Pick your battles, amirite?" I carry her to the net, put her gently on her feet with one arm wrapped protectively around her waist, and hold out my paddle to tap Warren and Amalie's. "Good game. Good game." Celeste follows my lead with her paddle. Amalie looks between us like we're the best game on the court, her eyes sparkling.

"Can't bring a knife to a gun fight," Warren says. "Just give up. Tennis isn't coming back." He looks Celeste up and down. "Better luck next time, *Williams.*"

We yield the court to the next match and join the waiting players on the sidelines. "Is he calling me Williams because I play tennis? Like Serena Williams?"

"I think so."

"She's a badass, so I'll take it." Celeste shrugs. "I hate that guy. And the feeling is mutual."

"I've never seen him pick on someone like this. I'm sorry. I don't know what flew up his butt."

She wraps her arms around herself. "Maybe there's something about me that attracts bullies."

"Fuck, no." I pull her into my arms and wrap her tightly. "No, babe. You put that thought right in the trash and light it on fire. You're strong and smart and kind, and there is nothing that makes this your fault. Nothing, you hear me?"

She shrugs against my chest.

"What would you tell your kids if someone was picking on them?"

"Of course I'd tell them it wasn't them—"

"Then why would you tell yourself any different?"

"I don't know. Just feels different, I guess." She sighs and snuggles in closer. I love the feeling of her in my arms. I could get addicted to this.

"I was bullied as a kid," I admit. Most of my classmates who've stayed in Salmon Bay remember only too well. It's immortalized in every yearbook. "I was fat, nerdy, socially anxious. I had acne, thick glasses, and low self-esteem. Do you think I deserved to be bullied? That it was my fault?"

"Oh, Hayden! Of course not."

"Coach took me under his wing and got me running. I grew into myself, and suddenly all the girls who'd never give me the time of day before wanted to date me. But inside, I was the same person no one tried to get to know. I still watch Star Wars, play D&D, and read Manga. I'm still more comfortable staying home to read than peopling. I'm still me, no matter what my body or bank account look like. And I've never wanted to be with anyone who wouldn't take me as I am."

"You shouldn't have to!" She's looking up at me through her lashes, and she cups my cheek with her hand. "We all want someone to love us exactly as we are; but we're not all lucky enough to find that person."

"That's what family is for."

"I guess." She drops her hand, and I realize that I don't know much about her family background. This subject is probably best visited in a more private location, with cookies.

"I get it. My dad wanted a son that fit a different mold, but you can't win them all. The rest of my family is great, and I've got enough to share."

"Your sisters seem pretty great."

"Just wait until you really get to know them," I mock whine. "We're out of the rankings, but we can still play for our starting spot in the unranked division. You up for another round?"

"Yeah, okay." We sidestep Russell Junior to put our paddles in the stack with the handles to the side and find a place near Fred and Ginger to lean against the fence while we wait. Celeste squats down to give the corgis some love. "I feel bad I let him get to me."

"Don't worry about it. He's feeling territorial. I think he might pee around the courts next."

Celeste snorts. We both watch Warren in the crowd regale his followers with some pickleball brag. "You think we still have a chance?"

I can't help myself. I pull her against my chest and tuck her head beneath my chin. "Sure do. That's the great thing about pickleball—every game has a chance to flip. And besides, everyone will be rooting for us."

"Because we're the underdog?"

"That's right. Everyone loves an underdog." Celeste has made me realize how bro-ey pickleball can be when people abandon the spirit of the game. Salmon Bay should support dedicated spaces for multiple different types of athleticism and play. It was kind of a long shot convincing Dr. Fisher to put aside courts for tennis, especially after how hard the pickleball community rallied to get our sport space in the first place, but it's not right to erase tennis courts just because we have bigger numbers.

Warren might not realize it, but he's thrown down the gauntlet. I'm more invested than ever in convincing Dr. Fisher to set aside a couple courts for exclusive tennis play, but Warren's shown me that I have to think strategically. Dr. Fisher and Warren are both members of the Sea Lion Club, and that's the room where it happens in Salmon Bay. I can't get in there and be one of them, but I know plenty of people with influence and a toe in the door. I've got an audience who expects gossip threaded in their crosswords and a sister who works for the Salmon Bay Tribune. I wonder how much it would take to convince people to write letters on my behalf? It's easy to ignore one guy. It's harder to ignore half the town.

I'd tell Celeste my germinating plan, but I don't want to get her hopes up in case I fail. I also know she won't want to call attention to herself from a mob of pickleball players coming for her with their paddles raised because she dared to claim a court for tennis. Warren will stir the pot when he finds out. I need to shield Celeste from more bullying. She's got enough on her plate.

There will be casualties, but not my woman. This is war.

25

CELESTE

I RECOGNIZE SAMANTHA when I walk into the personal training room the next morning and breathe a sigh of relief. Her smile is easy and welcoming. The twinkle in her eye is a little unnerving, but I doubt she'll give me the third degree about my relationship with her little brother while we're at her place of employment.

I hope not at least.

"Welcome!" She envelops me in a strong hug that almost knocks me over. She's wearing gold sweatbands on her arms and a wicking tee shirt that reads *Women of Wonder*. Her highlighted hair is pulled back in two French braids, and she's bouncing on her zero-heel sneakers like she can't wait to get started. That, or she drank six cups of coffee.

"Thanks?" I look around at the other women my age who have shown up for the Midlife Muscle class. It's a range—sporty soccer mom types and professionals who look like they exchanged their power suit for athleisure for the lunch hour. I wish Marissa could have come, but even if she wasn't injured, she's on twin duty today as Drew walks through a job site.

"Don't worry, it'll be fun."

"I'm ready," I tell her with more enthusiasm than I feel. I've never lifted weights in my life. Brett always said the weight room was the jock's mancave. My space was the yoga studio.

Samantha doesn't have time for stragglers—she starts at twelve on the dot with a rousing jog around the block. When we get back, she has us foam roll our IT bands, glutes, and lats. Most of the participants seem like they've done the routine before, but Sam is very encouraging and patient with us beginners.

"Our culture views midlife as the end, but what if we reframed it as a beginning? We've shed the inexperienced, naïve maiden and become the sage, sophisticated mother. Our hard-won wisdom is our biggest strength, and to share that with the world we need to embrace all the power of the divine feminine." Sam strolls down the line of women lifting kettlebells and takes time out of her lecture to adjust forms and fix stances. "Lift your caldron with your core power—that's right, ladies, engage those abdominal muscles. Breathe out and feel your torso squeezing, then hold those muscles as you rise from your squat. Yes, good job, Molly. Celeste, let's switch out for a heavier kettle bell."

I'm better at this than I thought I'd be, but kettle bells and sandbags don't feel that different from lifting grocery bags or squealing children.

"Remember, ladies, that we lose muscle mass after forty. Keep your goals foremost in your mind as you squeeze your pelvic floor and push into the ground with your feet. That's right. We are actively working to protect ourselves from joint injury, and to improve our balance and coordination. We are a force to be reckoned with. Feel your power. Feel your strength blazing from your uterus."

I'm not sure I got this side of Sam's personality at the family BBQ. I'm impressed by how many people show up for this class twice a week. If I didn't already know Sam and want to make a good impression, I might be too intimidated to come a second time.

After class though, I can feel my muscles trembling, and I know I got a better workout than I have in a long time. It's not only physical—it's mental too. I do feel strong, maybe not quite like Wonder Woman, but lifting weights with a bunch of other women at my stage in life does connect us in a sisterhood of sorts. A camaraderie of women who choose to show up for ourselves and our health. Women who are embracing our scars as merit badges instead of something to be embarrassed about.

"Good work today, Celeste," Sam says. She hands me a towel and tells me to wipe down my mat.

"Thanks," I drop to my knees and spray the yoga mat that's streaked with my sweat. "You got the girl power pep talk down."

Sam smirks. "My dad's mom was a Rosie the Riveter at Boeing during WWII. I come by it naturally."

I stand and roll the mat up. "I guess that explains why Hayden is so well adjusted?"

Sam's smile falls. "Actually, our dad was pretty hard on him as a kid. Hayden persevered despite dad's outdated gender ideas. His track coach gets most of the credit for giving him a different role model."

"Got it. My role models weren't too great either."

"Rough childhood?"

"My parents were wrapped up in their own drama. No time for a kid, unless it was using me as a chess piece in their endless bickering."

Sam nods and puts her hand on my arm. "You're here now. You're showing up to do the work. That's what matters. We all have learned behaviors we're working to reprogram. Be gentle with yourself and channel that rage into that kettlebell."

"Is it rage? I feel like it's grief. Grief for the childhood I wish I had but didn't. Grief for the marriage I couldn't save."

"Women are trained to suppress our rage, Celeste, and that is worth grieving."

She leaves me with that thought as she filters through the

class, checking in with the woman who couldn't lift the bell on her left side because of an old injury; the woman who broke down during the final pose when Sam told us to love ourselves; the woman who has been here every class for years and could easily teach it herself, but is here to give up the burden of every micro decision every day, letting Sam call the shots, order the reps, push her past her perceived limits. I don't know everyone's story, but I can imagine—it's in the shared understanding when our gazes meet. *I, too, am a woman. I, too, hold up half the sky. I, too, am tired and angry and beautiful exactly as I am.*

I leave the class feeling invigorated, until I'm in the locker room in nothing but a towel, and who sidles up but Lander, naked as a jaybird, with her small perky boobs and completely hairless skin.

"Oh, my god, Celeste," she says with a breathy voice that I'm trying not to hate on principle. "You won't believe what Brett asked me to do yesterday."

She's leaning in, and I brace my core in anticipation of the verbal punch I feel coming. Why do I live in a small town again? The chandeliers on the ceiling and industrial chic vibe are so not me. I'd find another gym, but I just discovered Sam's class, and I shouldn't let this girl chase me away. I don't want Brett back.

"What?" I ask hesitatingly.

"His laundry." She laughs as if this is the most ridiculous thing anyone has ever asked her to do. "Can you imagine?"

Brett doesn't know how to do laundry. He never bothered to learn, and why would he? He made the money, so I did everything else. It didn't matter that he had convinced me to drop out of school and strongly dissuaded me from even thinking about getting a job outside the house. He wasn't going to start helping with chores or childcare or dinner, so who would do all that crap if I was in an office somewhere?

I'm not sure how he convinced Lander to marry him without her seeing what a complete slob he is. He wants a mommy, not a life partner. Should I have let her know the truth before they said their vows? It's not my place, right? But the familiar guilt sours my gut.

"What did you tell him?" I ask, since Lander is hanging around like she wants to gossip or vent or something. Like we're friends. Even if she wasn't married to my ex-husband, I don't think we'd have much in common.

"Of course, I said he should do it himself!" She starts towel drying her hair, her boobs swaying with the movement and she doesn't care. "How did you have him for so long and he doesn't know how to take care of himself? You must be a saint waiting on him like that. I've got more important things to do. I don't even do my own laundry. If he wants someone to do his, he can hire that shit out. The laundromat even does pick-up and delivery now."

As if Brett would ever have let me pay for someone else to do the laundry. He didn't even like me spending money on new towels and bedsheets.

How is this my problem to fix? It's not my fault he doesn't cook or clean. It wasn't my job to raise him.

Lander doesn't seem in a hurry to leave, so I start dressing awkwardly under the towel so I can escape instead. I'm pulling on my underwear as she chatters on about Brett this and Brett that. *Stand up for yourself,* Sam would say if she was here. I half want her to walk into the locker room and tell Lander to STFU, but I know I need to fight my own battles. This is where I set my boundaries, and if I don't do it now, it'll be all that much harder in the future.

I pull up my leggings and give Lander my back so she's not staring straight at my larger, less perky boobs. Hayden seems to like them. He told me so more than once. I fasten my bra and slip a large, paint-stained tee shirt over my head. It's not the outfit I'd like to be wearing to face down my ex's new wife—I'd rather be armored in Spanx, Jones Road, and Chanel no 5—but Sam's words play in my head. *I love myself as I am.*

"Lander." I look her in the eye. She's not mean, more clueless, but I still don't want to be in a position where I'm her safe space to vent about Brett. "Sorry to hear the honeymoon phase is over. Brett is...to be honest, we were eighteen and nineteen when we got together. I'm sure you're in a better life stage to make cohabitation work."

"Wow. You were babies."

I nod. I felt old at the time. Getting married felt like a real grown-up thing to do. Neither of us had ever lived independently, and I wouldn't know a boundary if it hit me in the face. We didn't set out to fall into unhealthy coping patterns, but neither of our parents had modeled a better way. "There are some good marriage counselors that could help you work things out, but I'm the last person to give you advice."

"But you've known him the longest."

"And it didn't work out. Good luck with that."

She pulls back. "Oh. I guess Brett was right."

Her tone drips with displeasure, and I steel myself for conflict. "Oh?"

"Yeah," she drops her volume. "You can be a little bit of a bitch."

Right. I can feel the blood drop from my face, a strange ringing in my ears starting as the feelings I used to have on the regular rear their ugly heads. I thought I'd moved on, but maybe I suppressed all this rage?

Sam, Goddess that she is, shows up exactly when I need her. "Everything alright here?"

"Samantha!" Lander squeals with none of the animosity she just unloaded. "Do you know Celeste? She's my—"

"Yeah, of course!" Samantha pulls me into side hug that takes me off guard, but she turns a blinding smile on Lander when she drops the bomb. "Celeste is my brother's girlfriend. My future sister-in-law."

26

HAYDEN

I'm waiting outside the club for Celeste with a double shot cardamon mocha from her favorite bakery and a saffron bun, when Lander storms out of the front door. She startles when she sees me but drops the bitchy face and gives me a tight smile.

"Hayden."

"Lander." I don't say more because we've never been close. Her friend circle and mine have intertwined over the years—the dating pool in Salmon Bay is small—but her social media obsession is a big turn off. Her friend group is cookie-cutter, snap-happy, drama magnets. No depth. The only reason I went to her wedding was because Aaron didn't want to do it, and I lost that stupid bet.

My author pen names don't have an online presence other than a website. My work speaks for itself, and I've been lucky that my publisher markets the hell out of my books. I'll never put myself in a position to get harassed online again, no matter how many more books I could sell with that notoriety. It isn't worth it.

Lander isn't scared off by my less than enthusiastic greeting. She must want something. "Your sister spilled the beans." She gets up close and I can see every scraggly fake lash that claws out from her eyes like spider legs.

"...about?"

Her lower lip pouts out. "When did you start dating my husband's sloppy seconds?"

I clench my jaw. Gloves off then, got it. I might avoid drama, but that doesn't mean I let anyone push around me or the people I care about. "Sounds like you're married to my girlfriend's sloppy seconds. Not sure what the problem is."

Her nostrils flare. "Just a girlfriend, huh? There's no problem as long as I get what's owed me. I'm not going to let a mama's boy like you mooch off my new husband via some cougar."

"Your opinion means less than nothing to me, Lander, especially when you refer to Celeste like that. But to set the record straight, I have a job, and it's not a gigolo. I do just fine for myself, and I live with my mom to take care of her, not the other way around. I'm not sure what you feel like you're entitled to, but after twenty years, Celeste is entitled to half of everything their household owns, including retirement savings. She's not mooching. That's her money. You and I have no part in it."

Lander rolls her eyes. "Brett should've gotten a prenup the first time around. She didn't even work all that time."

I'm taking deep breaths through my nose and thinking about how the joy of giving Celeste this latte will be better than the joy from throwing it in Lander's stupid face. My front row seat to my sisters having kids has left me under no illusions that being a mom is anything less than a lot of hard work. Rewarding work, but intense and unyielding, nonetheless.

Celeste exits the gym at that moment, followed by Sam, and I feel like the sun breaking through the clouds after a hailstorm.

"Hayden?" Celeste asks, hesitant, and I hate that seeing my mad face makes her nervous, but we can fix that. It will just take time. She kneads her hands together. "Everything okay?"

I let my smile say everything I feel for her and hope she gets it. My sister's glee burns along my skin, hotter even than normal, but I don't mind. Everyone should know how I feel about this woman. She's beautiful, inside and out. "I got you something."

The compostable lid spills a few drops when I thrust it into her hand, but I love the way her wary eyes light up. Has no one ever brought her coffee before? Lander is an idiot, and she married a bigger idiot. This sweet woman deserves the world.

"What'd you bring me, little brother?" Sam asks as she throws her arm across my shoulders and pinches me in the side.

"Nothing but my sparkling personality," I snap back. I shrug off her arm and she laughs. She's enjoying seeing me squirm a little too much. I guess this is payback for all the times I teased her about her past boyfriends.

"Must be love," Sam says.

"Sure is." Celeste's eyebrows shoot up, but she keeps her eyes downcast on the blue ceramic planter next to Magnus Fitness front door that's bursting with yellow zinnias and trailing white lobelia. Her skin turns pink from her neck on up. It's adorable.

Sam, evilest sister, gives a wicked little giggle. "I knew it!"

"Your girlfriend was just telling me how you met at my wedding." Lander's tone is sour, but her words fill me with a fizzy pop-rocks feeling in my chest.

I want to shout *girlfriend* to the whole town. Take out a billboard. "We did. Thanks for the assist."

"I didn't know you were there." Lander crosses her arms.

"I had a memorable time." I watch Celeste suck her bottom lip between her front teeth and feel my blood rush south. "How's the coffee, love?"

She peeks up at me through her lashes. "Good. Thank you."

"Brett bought me a bag of Raven's Rendezvous Dark Roast yesterday," Lander announces. "It's delicious. Have you tried it yet?"

Celeste's mouth tightens before she gives Lander a sad smile. "I have. I've got to get to work. Have a nice day, Lander."

My chest puffs up when she links her arm with mine and all but tows me down the sidewalk. She smells like fresh soap and the white orchid shampoo from Magnus Fitness. Her cheeks are flushed, and her wet curls are drying in the spring sunshine.

My *girlfriend*.

It has a nice ring to it.

My sister gives me a wink, then distracts Lander with some work-related question. She's a saint. I should offer to babysit this weekend so she and Aaron can go out.

"You okay?" I ask when we get to the end of the street. "And don't say 'fine'."

She squeezes my arm. "Brett bought that coffee for himself —it's his favorite. He expects Lander to make a pot in the morning, if the past is anything to go by. But she wanted too badly to show that Brett is caring for her." Celeste shrugs helplessly. "Who am I to disabuse her of that notion? She married him."

"I'm sorry you had to live with a partner who didn't value you for so long, but I'm not sorry you're free now for me to take care of, *girlfriend*."

She chuckles shyly. "Your sister threw that out there—"

"I like it."

"Are you sure? It's not too fast?"

"Hell, no. I was just going at your pace."

"Really? That's sweet. I'd like that—officially dating, I mean. Just as long as you know I can take care of myself."

That warm, sparkling feeling spreads in my chest. "I know it, babe, and it's hella sexy watching you get shit done. But you don't have to do it all alone. I like caring for you. It makes me feel good to make you feel good. This latte? Selfish on my part. I wanted to buy your smile to light up my day."

She snorts. "Your lines are sweet enough to give me cavities."

"Is it working?"

She looks up into my eyes and I feel my heart trip in my breast. "Yeah. Yeah, Hayden. It's working."

"Good." I give in to the need that's been driving me since she walked out the door of Magnus Fitness and taste her lips. Coffee and cardamon and the sweet flavor that is Celeste. "Delicious."

Her lips quirk. "I don't know. I think I need a second sample."

I oblige. We're making out like two teens on a downtown corner for all of Salmon Bay to see. Someone honks and catcalls out their car window, but Celeste keeps kissing me and our smiles tangle with our tongues. This is what I've been missing. The romance, the comfort of being with a person who sees your crooked parts and likes you anyway.

The next week passes in a blur. I'm writing a new book, a small-town contemporary romance, and the words are shooting like fireworks out of my fingers. Celeste is pretty busy between fixing up her house and studying for her real estate exam, but whenever she can carve out an hour or two, we practice pickleball.

She's getting a lot better. I'm falling a lot harder.

If it seems too good to be true, it's because it is.

27

CELESTE

I'VE GOT THE TOILET REMOVED from the wall and am snaking the ever-loving life out of that pipe when someone comes slamming through the front door. I startle, but that just makes me realize how comfortable I've gotten without Brett in the house anymore. I used to live in constant freeze waiting for him to explode like a geyser of boiling steam. A wave of negative energy blows through the open door with him. His demanding, gruff voice calling my name like I'm a dog to come to heel is a soundtrack I haven't missed. Not at all. I used to be so afraid of what I would do on my own if I gave up the house and the provider, but the truth is: anything I want.

"Celeste! Where are you? Are you ignoring me?" Brett huffs and stomps his feet on the old porcelain tile floor, bits of dirt smearing on the new grout I applied last week.

I count backwards from ten in my head.

"Celeste?"

I pull the snake out and watch the water empty. "How can I help you, Brett?"

"You can help by responding back to my messages, for one. I thought you were getting this dump ready to sell? Or have you been too busy trolling iEros to do any work?"

The new toilet is still wrapped in plastic, and the old, cracked one is sitting next to my boot. The floor and walls have been re-grouted, by me. The walls painted a soft eggshell blue. I exchanged the light fixtures at the Salmon Bay Reuse store for a more attractive, modern shape, and I figured out how to install them myself from YouTube. After three plumbers who tried to mansplain what I needed, I found a female plumber in an apprentice program who talked to me like I'm a competent homeowner. She had her professional mentor sign off on the work, but I didn't have to deal with him. I'd hire her again in a heartbeat.

Not doing any work? I want to laugh in Brett's face, but I've had years of biting my tongue so as not to set him off. I choose to turn the other cheek, because escalation is always worse.

Still, it's harder to let him roll right over me when I've had a taste of freedom. Hayden's ego isn't too fragile to handle disagreement. He actually wants to know my real thoughts and opinions. If he thinks I'm agreeing with him to placate him, he calls me out.

I stand tall and put my hands on my hips. What would Sam do in this situation? She wouldn't let her ex-husband push her around, that's for sure. "What I do with my free time is no longer your concern. Is there a specific item you needed to address?"

He crosses his arms. I used to love the strong breadth of his shoulders, the square cut of his jaw. He's aging like Pierce Brosnan, but inside he's still Peter Pan. Wendy has led several generations of young girls astray.

"Lander said you're bothering her at work."

"Bothering her? She approached me."

Brett draws himself up and takes a step toward me. "We're not together anymore Celeste. I know it's hard for you to watch me move on when you're still stuck, but you can't harass my new wife where she works. You should find a new gym."

I resist the urge to step back and let him gain ground. I'm not a violent person, but what would it be like to punch him in his self-centered face? "I've belonged to Magnus Fitness for years, just like you. You and I met the trainers for the first time together at the new member orientation. I'm not going to stop going to the gym just because you've decided to move on with one of them."

"It's not appropriate, Celeste."

"Appropriate? Was it appropriate for you to be flirting with gym girls when we were still married? Is it appropriate for you to storm in here without being invited and order me around? We're not married anymore, Brett—I don't answer to you. I'm working my ass off to get this place fixed up after you refused to do any maintenance for years! When I sell this place after all the sweat equity I've been putting in, I still have to give you half. Go bother someone who cares, so the grown-ups can work."

His face goes dark, sending my pulse racing. I pushed him too far. I never talk to him like this. He puffs out his chest, the silverback ready to defend his ego, and my heart rate skyrockets. "You're a real piece of work, you know that? As if I'm the one making a public spectacle of myself sucking tongue with much younger partners. What kind of role model is that for Ryder and Brody? Do you want it to get back to them that their mother is a—"

"Do not finish that sentence. You don't get to tell me what to do with my body. Lander and Hayden are the same age—"

His laugh is ugly, and it makes my eyes water. "Right. What would a young fit guy want with you? You're not young and hot anymore, Celeste. Get real. You're a washed-up, middle-aged divorcee, and he's probably only with you because he knows you're desperate. You're easy. Too bad you're also a frigid—"

"Get out."

"Really, he lives with his mom and spends all his time fleecing retirees at the public rec center. I'm sure the other old chicks like the attention, but are you so lonely and desperate that you can't see the truth? He's a user. He's probably looking for a sugar mama, and I'm not giving him a penny of my house profits. This is mine. Are you that naïve that you think he could actually be interested in you?"

I talk over him. "Which is it? Am I using him or is he using me? You seem to have your stories crossed. It's none of your business what I do or who I do it with. And you have no reason to be in this house—"

"I still own half—"

"You will get your half when I sell it. That was the deal. So get out of my way. I have a lot to do and no time for your bullshit. Not anymore."

He rears back. "You didn't use to be so crass. What does your boy-toy think of your dirty mouth?"

I put all my anger for Brett and my attraction to Hayden into my smile, letting him see beyond my peacekeeper, placating mask for the first time in years. "My boyfriend loves my dirty mouth." And I smack my lips and push past a shocked Brett. I hate to cede ground to him, but the strategic move is to disengage from the battle so I can win the longer war. I grab my keys off the table and slam the front door behind me, not before shouting, "Lock up when you leave!"

That asshole better not still be here when I get back.

28

HAYDEN

"Where are you taking me?" Celeste asks as I help her step onto the small boat in the marina. The rocky coastline stretches north to Canada, and to the south the land curves around to a large headland that used to be a military fort but is now a huge city park. We'll take a picnic there another day, to the lighthouse that warns ships off the point.

"You don't want me to ruin the surprise, do you?"

She bites her lower lip but smiles, and there's real excitement wafting off her. How long has it been since someone planned a fun day out for her? She's been caring for her nest so long, she's forgotten she has wings.

I thought about blindfolding her so this date could be a real surprise but getting on and off a boat blind is a recipe for disaster, so I pocket the silk tie to use for later. Celeste is in a pretty little teal jumpsuit that shows off her curves nicely, until she covers up with the ugly orange life jacket. When she buckles the strap, the tight jacket pushes up her generous cleavage. It's going to take all my willpower to wait until after dinner to get my hands on her. The wind blows her curls away from her face and stings her cheeks a cherry blossom pink.

Being on the water is thrilling, but nothing like finally

getting Celeste on a date where we won't be surrounded by people we know. Jørgen Park is far enough from Salmon Bay, that I'll finally get her all to myself. We motor around the bend and enter the outer canal, passing beneath the iconic iron railroad bridge that's on every Salmon Bay poster.

"I've never gone through the water this way," Celeste says. "It's a completely different view of town."

"Like a postcard of Norway, yeah? Or at least how I imagine it. The Scandinavian immigrants felt right at home in these little fjords. Fishing and timber, just like back home. The sea is in our blood." I point out important landmarks that are interesting to see from the water side. We pass Fisherman's Terminal, where the boats are moored overnight and the docks where they get patched up in the off season, and motor beneath the bridge that connects Salmon Bay to the South. "How long have you lived here?"

"Four years. We moved when Brody was going into his senior year of high school. He was so mad to leave his friends behind."

"What about you? You have to leave much behind?"

She shrugs. "Nothing too irreplaceable. I've left a small trail of friends across the world, chasing after Brett." She tucks her curls behind her ears and stares off into the distance. "In hindsight, I think Brett preferred it that way. The fewer friends I had, the more he had my attention all to himself."

"I can't imagine, Celeste. I've lived in Salmon Bay all my life. My friends are mostly here too. Same bat time, same bat channel."

She nods. "It's a nice place."

Nice? Her lack of roots is disturbing, even beyond my anger on her behalf at her ex. What if she up and leaves Salmon Bay just as easily? Her kids aren't here, and I imagine she'd like nothing more than to leave Brett and Lander and all their bullshit behind her. I guess I'll have to make her fall in love with Salmon Bay too. First Pickleball, then the town, then, if I'm lucky, me. By that point she'll be too involved to get weirded out by a man writing sexy "bodice rippers," right?

My grandfather's words come back to me. *I throw them right in the trash.* Gramps had always been so supportive of everyone and everything before that. It was like my hero stabbed me in the gut, and the wound was still festering. If I were brave, I'd come clean to Celeste right now, but that fear is potent, poisoning hope for the future.

As we wind our way through the serpentine bay, Celeste tells me about the places she's lived. Naples, Seoul, Munich, Virginia. Adventures along the way. I'm not just spinning out her memories because my author brain is taking notes for future stories—I'm hooked on her every word. What did it taste like? What did it smell like? What parts does she miss? What parts made her homesick? She's far more worldly and traveled than I'll ever be. I've lived a thousand lives, but only in books.

Maybe someday we could travel together.

"Where's your favorite place you've visited?" she asks me as I point out our destination in distance.

"Honestly? Backpacking in the Alpine Lakes Wilderness with my friend Whittaker. Most beautiful place on earth."

"Really?" She smiles. "How do you know if you've never been to every place on earth?"

"Easy. It feels like home."

"Hard to top that, I guess. I've always wanted to find a place to feel like home. Where would you go if you could travel anywhere?"

"Somewhere in Scandinavia, probably. I want to see if it really feels like Salmon Bay. My ancestors were from Sweden."

"Yeah?"

"And castles. I want to see a real castle. Oh! And tour the WWII battlefields where my gramps fought. Lots of places, really."

"How come you haven't gone yet?"

I shrug. "Felt bad leaving my mom. She needs care, and I

never wanted her to feel abandoned. My dad leaving really did a number on everyone."

"Even you?"

"Especially me." I guide us around a floating dock where a fat male sea lion is sunning himself, not a care in the world. On the surface, I've got that same vibe; laid back, a joke for everything. Shade seems to slide right off me. But it's hard to share the squishy inside parts when I was abandoned by the guy who was supposed to be there forever.

"Can't your sisters help with your mom if you wanted to go on vacation?"

"Yeah, of course. But Molly and Sam have kids, and Addy and Kirsten were in school for a long time. I just never felt a driving need to leave, you know? I got everything I need right here—mountains, ocean, family. Traveling by myself seems lonely."

"I get it. I've lived a lot of places but didn't get the chance to explore much. It was always navy housing and taking care of kids. Someday I'd like to vacation travel." She wrinkles her cute nose and stares off at the horizon, where the Olympic Mountains rise majestically into a crystal blue sky. "But not by myself."

"Maybe we can go together."

She bites her lip and turns back to me. Her attention is like a drug. "Yeah? I'd like that."

"Good." I lean forward and press a kiss to her lips. I can't get enough. "The best part, I hear, is coming back home."

She looks away, toward the land where the rocky shoreline melts into cliffs. A juvenile bald eagle flies overhead, hunting for fish. "I'm envious of your attachment to this place. I've always been an outsider. Always drawing close to the fire but not allowed in the circle of warmth."

My poor sweet chou-chou. "Doesn't have to be that way. You get to choose your family. It's not always the people you're born to. I'll lend you mine."

Her lips quirk up. "Sam, at least, seems to have already adopted me. Do four sisters even let you have your own pick?"

"Good thing Sam and I have good taste."

"So, where's this mystery destination? Somewhere in one of these hangers?" She points to the former Naval base-turned public activity center that is Jørgen Park. Right on the water, the nearest building is a center for wooden boat building, paddle club, and youth sailing lessons. Farther away from the docks are indoor soccer arenas, a massive rock-climbing gym, and a curling club. Art studios take up the smaller hangers, and the artist collective puts on open houses once a month with cider tasting and hands-on craft sessions.

I draw up to the public docks and help Celeste step onto shore. Our life jackets get thrown back in the boat, and I pull her lush body to me, happy not to have bulky foam and orange nylon between us anymore. "Ready for this?"

"You still haven't told me what we're doing."

"Have you been to Jørgen Park?"

"I don't think so. Maybe I drove my boys here for an activity? I don't remember."

"You've been missing out, but I'm glad I get to pop your cherry."

She snorts.

Releasing her, I pull out the silk tie and snap it for flare. Her eyes widen, lips part in surprise, and I hope some anticipation. "You trust me, don't you?"

"Should I?"

"I promise you'll like it."

She bites her plump lower lip. "Tie me up then."

God, that's hot. I slip the blindfold over her eyes and tie it just tight enough to stay on. I wrap one arm around her and take her other hand to guide her. "Slow and steady, beautiful." Giddy anticipation thrums in my gut. I'm not nervous, except maybe at getting my ass kicked and looking like a fool, but I hope the pleasure on her face will be worth it. She deserves everything she's dreamed of.

We stumble awkwardly over some cracked pavement, but we're laughing by the time I draw her into the Eliason Tennis Center. I sign us in to the court I reserved and take her into the hanger where five full size tennis courts gleam under industrial lighting. Her head cocks as she listens to the softer sound of balls bouncing off rackets and floors. Not the *pop* of the pickleball.

"Do I hear tennis?"

I can't help taking her lips with mine as I slide the blindfold off. She leans into the kiss and gives a little squeal when she sees the courts stretching to either side. "Where are we? Are we actually playing tennis?"

"Yeah, sweetheart. We've got the court for two hours. Show me what you got."

Turns out hitting a tennis ball with a big ol' racket is a crap ton harder on my elbow than pickleball is. We're both dragging by the time we're done, but we're laughing too. Celeste has shown me all her tricks, giving it to me as good as I dished out when I introduced her to pickleball.

"Not sure tennis is the sport for me, but if I get to play it with you, I'll gladly suffer through."

She gives my arm a playful swat. "You did well. Don't let tennis's superior strengths chase you away from playing a real sport."

"Pickleball is a sport."

"Is it in the Olympics? No? Not a sport."

"Not yet." I lead her back to the boat and show her the picnic lunch I brought. We dine on salmon dip and rye crackers, grilled peach and farro salad with goat cheese, and a fine bottle of non-alcoholic champagne that Sam recommended. The sun glints off the water of Puget Sound, and I'm pretty sure I couldn't have planned a more perfect day if I tried.

By the time the sun is setting over the Olympic Mountains,

I've got my perfect woman in my carriage house with her hands braced against the windowsill as I drop to my knees behind her and pry her jumpsuit off her perfect ass. The pink light clinging to the clouds looks like cotton candy, and the last ray of daylight makes Celeste's Rubenesque body look like a watercolor painting.

"Don't move your hands, sweetheart."

"Or else what?" She pushes her ass back and my mouth waters.

I run my big hands over her smooth skin and squeeze gently. "Or else I'll have to get creative with my pickleball paddle."

"You wouldn't."

"*Mais, oui, ma chérie. Je possède ce cul.*"

"What does that mean?" She laughs and glances back at me from underneath her eyelashes. So coquettish. I love this side of her, playful and light. She needs more lightness.

"It means I'm going to do whatever it takes to bring this gorgeous body to ultimate pleasure, so hold on, *mon coeur.*" I slide my hands down her thighs and push apart her legs to expose her, glistening and slick with arousal. "My little cabbage likes being bossed around, do you?"

"In the bedroom, maybe. It's hard to shut off my brain, you know?"

"Leave it to me. You're to hang on that windowsill and let me eat out this pretty pussy. I've been dying to taste you."

Her arm muscles flex as she tightens her grip on the window, and she sinks into the bent over pose like every wet dream come to life. Fuck, she's got a beautiful ass. I clamp my hands on her thighs and take my first taste of her—salty and sweet and fucking luscious. She's dripping on my tongue and her legs are shaking with every lick. We're both moaning.

As she comes down, chest heaving, I stand, sweep her boneless body into my arms, and carry her to the big bed. Her luscious skin is so smooth as I pet her gently, easing her. I can't get enough. She's blissed out as I take her the first time, but I hold myself back. Go slow. Keep eye contact steady so she knows I'm here with her. I see her. Hear her. Taste her. Feel her clench around me as she comes again.

Celeste. My beautiful goddess.

When she falls asleep, I stay awake and watch her for a long time. This is the way I want to remember her, soft and sated and covered in my scent.

The problem with my current manuscript seems laughingly obvious now. Unable to sleep, I gently lay her head down on my pillow and tuck her in. My muse snuggles into the sheets with a smile playing across her lips. I hate to get up, but the ideas lighting my synapses aren't gonna let me sleep until I get them down on paper. Celeste is in every fiber of my heroine, and the hero's love for her is nothing short of autobiographical. I pull on some boxers and a V-neck cardigan, sit down at my desk, and open up my laptop.

29

CELESTE

I DREAM OF HAYDEN going down on me and wake up to warm flannel sheets tangled around my limbs. Light filters through the curtains, but it's still early. Hayden is bent over his computer and his hair is sticking up every which way. He's wearing the dorkiest grandpa sweater, but he's paired it with only his tight black boxer-briefs that show off the toned muscles in his long legs, and I have to wipe the drool off the corner of my mouth.

Images of last night make me blush, but it's a happy feeling. Champagne bubbles in my chest. Tingling warmth pooling in my core. I wonder how he feels about a repeat.

"Did you sleep?" I ask, and my voice is sleep roughened and sexy as hell.

He glances over and smirks. "Babe, you have no idea how sexy you look splayed out in my bed." He types something, then shuts his laptop and stands, stretching so that the sweater rides up and I can see the cut V of his adonis belt. He catches my eye and stalks forward, slowly unbuttoning the cardigan like he's giving me a strip tease. I remember how he bossed me around last night, and how safe I felt putting my body in his hands. I love how he's not afraid to be playful too. He doesn't need to be dominant and domineering, but he's got no problem taking the reins so I don't get tangled up in my own head either.

He's swaying his hips as he slowly drops the sweater from his shoulders and then he's on the bed and caging me in with his big body above me. His eyes are a little bloodshot, but he still looks yummy enough to eat. "Did you sleep well, *ma chérie?*"

"Yeah. Where did you go?"

"Right here, watching you."

"Like a stalker?"

"The best kind. Composing odes to your beauty, serenaded by your dulcet snores."

"I don't snore!" I push him playfully, and he groans and rolls to the side, scooping me up against his chest.

"My mistake. Those were the sounds of his majesty, *la bête*, from his tower above your *chambre*, my lady."

"What were you doing instead of sleeping?"

"The markets open at six thirty, Pacific time. Work waits for no man."

"Do you still help little old ladies invest their funds?"

"Not directly, but sometimes I give investment talks down at the senior center. Grandma never managed any money herself, besides using it to buy groceries and clothes, until Gramps died. She'd probably have put all her savings in a pillowcase under her mattress if I hadn't convinced her otherwise. There are a lot of older women who were in trad marriages like that, and they've never had access to their own funds. They were taught it was rude to talk about money, so they don't for help. I like to pay it back, you know? Give a talk once a year and direct people to more resources."

Brett hadn't wanted me to ask about money either. He made it, so he spent it as he liked. I don't want to bring up my ex when I'm in bed wrapped so warmly in Hayden's embrace though, so I just listen. "How did you learn?"

"Trial and error, mostly. I'd taken an intro to investing class in college, and I was keen to try my hand at what seemed like wicked magic." He lets out a self-depreciating chuckle. "It was rough going at the start, but once I lost some of my grandma's money, I was hell bent on earning it back. Eventually I learned from my mistakes and got her investment portfolio steadily earning. She started bragging about me to her friends, and next thing I knew, her bridge club all wanted to hire me to help them too."

God, and I was the asshole who thought he might be swindling old ladies out of their cash at first.

"A lot of the work is reading the economic reports and setting up the computer to make the trades. Gives me a lot of time for extracurricular activities."

"Playing pickleball? I thought that was your religion."

"Nope." He rolls us so that he's on top again, this time pressing me into the mattress with his pelvis wedged firmly between my thighs. The hard ridge of his morning wood slots right against my labia, separated only by the thin cotton of his boxers. "My religion is worshiping this goddess body."

He dips his head and takes my lips, even though I haven't brushed my teeth yet. I try to turn my head, and he chuckles and moves his questing tongue down my jaw to suck my earlobe between his teeth. He bites down gently, and my clit spasms. All the while his hips are slowly rubbing against mine.

The friction is delicious. He's ratcheting me higher and higher, and I clutch his sculpted ass and pull my core tighter against him. I'm chasing that high that he brought me to last night, a high I didn't even know was possible.

I always figured there was something a little bit broken about my body, but I guess I just didn't have a partner who cared about my pleasure. This guy is super smart and super sweet and super sexy, and much too young for me.

"I can almost feel your brain pulling you away, sweetheart. What's wrong?"

"Nothing."

"Uh huh. You're fine, are you?"

I sigh and shut my eyes, cursing my insecurities for getting in the way again. "Why don't you let me return the favor?"

He kisses my eyelids and the tip of my nose. "You want to? Or you feel obligated to?"

I feel exposed. It wasn't a task I enjoyed with my ex, but everything is different with Hayden. I'm different. "I *want* to pleasure you."

"I live to serve my muse."

"You call me the silliest things."

Growling playfully, he scoots down and slips the sheet off my chest, exposing my pebbled nipples to the air. I want to run my fingers through his crazy hair and hold him to my breast, so I do. He rubs his head up into my hand like a cat asking for pets, making me giggle.

"You are so beautiful. My body is yours to play with, *mon amour*. Direct me." He sucks my nipple into his mouth, and I arch into it. His fingers dig into my hips. "Ground rules, first. What is your one job?"

"To...ah!...hold on to the windowsill?"

"To *feel* what I'm doing to you. You're not going to get up in your head about what you should do or what you should feel. You're going to stay in your body and do what feels good. Capeech?"

"But I want to make you feel good too."

"Believe me, I do. You touch me anywhere, I feel fucking fantastic."

Feeling emboldened, I tug on his hair until he raises his head and meets my eyes. "Roll over, baby. Show me the goods."

The spark in his eyes spreads across his face like a wave, drawing his smile and making him move. One moment he's on top of me; the next, he's star-fished in bed with his proud dick pointing toward his belly button. He's got a very nice package, and I lick my lips as I imagine fitting it in my mouth. The tip, at least. His body is beautiful—lean muscle and a dusting of hair over golden skin.

I have a brief moment of concern that he shouldn't want to be with me—he could have anyone—but I shove it ruthlessly back down. There's no place for self-doubt and should-be's. He told me just to do what feels good. I can follow that direction.

Maintaining eye contact, I rise up and straddle his thighs. His gaze dips down to where I'm open and on display, and the hunger on his face starts an answering heat in my low belly. I actually want to take him in my mouth and draw out his moans, so I do, wrapping my fingers firmly around the base of his shaft and licking the mushroom tip. His groans are like gold stars telling me I'm earning an A in Physical Education. His taste is a little salty on my tongue as I take him into my mouth.

His moans ratchet my own arousal higher. I grind against the hard muscle of his thigh, trying to relieve the ache, and he moves one of his hands to rub my clit while I take him to the back of my throat.

For the first time in my life, I have all the power during sex. He's turning to putty in my hands, and I like it. I love it. The pulse of his smooth length along my tongue. The heat of him, and the way he can't help but move his hips. He's coming undone; I'm undoing him.

"Celeste—stop, I'm going to—"

"You can come in my mouth."

"I want to come in your pussy. Can I do that, beautiful? Please?"

Who am I to deny a request like that? I let him flip me and revel in the feeling of all his hot, hard body pressed against my softer curves into the mattress. The texture of his chest hair against my smooth skin. The knowledge that even on the bottom, I've got the power to ask for what I want, and he'll listen.

He takes a condom out of his bedside table before he adjusts my hips and slides in, murmuring complements and nonsense in equal measure. He rests his weight on his forearms and pistons home, and my eyes roll back in my head.

"You feel too good, beautiful, the way you're strangling my dick. Fault, your pussy is heaven. I'm not going to last long."

My chest is tight. What if this is all a dream? What if I let myself fall for him and it doesn't work out? What if this is just a game for him—a hot young guy with an older, lonely divorcee?

"I can see you spiraling, naughty girl. What's your one job?"

I moan as he hits a particularly sensitive spot inside of me. "To...feel...good."

"Damn straight. Accept my offering as your due like the goddess you are. Goddesses demand to be worshiped. They don't get on their knees for their penitents. They make us work to earn their pleasure. Do you understand, Celeste?"

Wow. Maybe? "Yes?"

He's not happy with my halfhearted agreement, and he bites me. The next moment, he's soothing the bite with his tongue.

Ouch. "Whaat? That's..."

"Hot?"

"I-I don't know."

"Filthy?"

I scrunch up my nose while I try to put it all into words. How do I know what I really like if I've never toed any boundaries? Sex used to be the same old routine...wham, bam, roll over and start snoring. No experimentation to find what lights up my body—always assuming there was something wrong with me if I never saw stars. Do I want to be manhandled? Dominated? Or does that bring up too much baggage? I don't even know. "It was aggressive? And...and...smutty? Fifty Shades of Gray-ish?"

His whole-body stills. "Not into trashy books?"

"Not really."

For a long moment, neither of us breathes. What did I say?

Am I too boring for him? Now I'm sure I've done something wrong, but after that lecture, I don't want to ask.

He rolls off me and puts his forearm over his eyes.

"I didn't mean for you to stop," I whisper. "I was just surprised. It felt...interesting. I mean, I like your mouth on me... Say something, Hayden. What did I do?"

"Don't worry about it. We should probably get up and start the day."

My stomach turns over. This is how it was with Brett, though a million times worse. I'd say something and he'd get mad or shut me out. I'd freeze and fawn and be afraid to put a hair out of place.

Do I apologize? Do I say I liked it? I didn't get a chance to make up my mind! Does he hate how vanilla my experience is?

He rolls to the side and puts his legs on the floor, his back to me. I sit up too, with the sheet clutched around my torso like a shield. Everything was so good, but I ruined it, didn't I?

Please talk to me, I beg him. But the words won't pass my lips. Maybe he needs time to calm down. Maybe I do.

"Are you studying today?" he asks me as he stands and digs in his dresser drawer for some jeans. I watch him pull them on, the taut muscles in his back flexing with the movement.

All of Brett's bullshit comes back to me—why would Hayden be with someone like me?—but I push it away. I'm responsible for the ideas I let filter through my brain. I'm not my thoughts, but I can choose which to hold on to and which to observe but release. I have to actively fight against the poison Brett spewed about my new relationship, just like I had to fight against the poison he tried to feed me about being a real estate agent.

I'm going to prove to him that I can do it myself. I'm going to prove to myself that I don't need him to take care of me. I don't need Hayden either. I choose Hayden, that's a different story.

"Yeah," I say. "I'm going to study. Test is next weekend. Are we going to practice this week?"

He runs his hands through his hair, and it sticks up even more. "Sure. If you want."

If I want? I swallow the bile that rises in my throat and remind myself that I am fine. I am fine on my own. "I've got a lot of prep to do on the house. As soon as I get my license, I have to put it on the market. Brett's breathing down my neck wanting his half the money."

Hayden tugs a shirt over his head. It's dark purple and says, "Careful, I'll put you in my novel." Does he write? I want to ask him, but his expression is closed off. I feel like we've taken a big step back from yesterday. Can we have a do-over?

"I'm training with Sam this week," I say as I stand with the sheet wrapped around me and find my jumpsuit on the living room floor. I have to decide between pulling back on my wet panties and going without. I'm grimacing down at them when Hayden suddenly looms over me, smelling of clean laundry and orchids. He plucks the panties out of my hand and brings them to his nose, taking a deep inhale and making a low growl in the back of his throat. My face burns as he smirks and stuffs them in his pocket. "Are you stealing my underwear?"

"Too filthy for you?"

I frown. "L-like some trophy of conquest?"

His nostrils flare. "No good?"

Do people really do that outside books? I guess Hayden does. I'm not sure how I feel about the possessive angle. Maybe it's too much after being sidelined in my own life for so long? Or is it something I feel like I'm supposed to say no to? Like with the biting, I feel like I'm out of my depth.

Maybe he senses my hesitation, because he steps up to me and stares down at my face, searching for something. "You make me half feral. There's nothing for you to feel embarrassed about. You're what I want, Celeste. What you have to decide is if you feel the same way about me. I'm not a fixer upper. I'm not airing all my dirty laundry, either, but I've opened up to you more than I've ever opened up to anyone before. I've been hurt in the past too, but I'm doing my damnedest not to let it define me. I'm not going to pretend to be someone else. Not for anyone."

"You...you think I want to change you? You're too good to be true."

"I assure you, I'm not." He tucks a curl behind my ear and the touch of his skin sends sparks down my sensitive nerve endings. "I like you, Celeste, just the way you are. I've been the kid who got picked on for not liking the right things. Dressing up in pink, sparkles, and feather boas with my sisters. Playing dolls with Addy and baking with Kirsten. Singing along to NSYNC with Molly."

"Who made you feel bad for playing with your sisters?"

"My dad. He wanted a son. Thought he'd play football and raise a little mini-me. He wanted me to like fast cars and rock 'n' roll and grunting one syllable answers. I don't know. He had this idea of what a son should be, and I wasn't it."

"I'm sorry. Brett had similar ideas for our boys, but we didn't have girl toys or clothes because no sisters."

"I might have given my sisters hell like any little brother worth his salt, but I looked up to them. I wanted to be like them. Wanted their attention, their love, more than I wanted my dad's. Even as I kid, I could see that my dad's love came with conditions. My therapist says I have trust issues because of it. I'm hesitant to share the deepest core of who I am until I can trust people won't leave me for it."

"I would never." I take his big hands in mine, grounding him. Guess the easy going, funny guy is more of a mask than I thought. "So, what happened?"

"When I got to be a teen, I got into DnD, reading, and video games. Still not interested in being the star quarterback my father dreamed of. So I learned how to disarm people before they could criticize me for my interests or appearance."

"Appearance?"

"You saw the pictures. I was a fat kid, and once I sprouted up and got into running, suddenly girls who wouldn't give me the time of day thought I was hot...but they still wanted the cool jock, not the nerdy nice guy. I was done trying to fit inside the box other people drew for me a long time ago."

"I would never try to fit someone else inside a box, especially when I've just escaped my own."

His hazel eyes peer into mine, searching for my truth. My breathing hitches.

"I mean," I lick my lips and give him a tenuous smile, "you can get inside my box anytime. I quite enjoyed it."

My joke breaks the tension, and Hayden's handsome face relaxes into the teasing smirk I know and love. "That's my word nerd. I might need another peek at this box. See if it's a good fit."

"The best fit."

He hums deep in his throat, and warm arousal flashes low in my belly. He walks me backward with gentle pressure on my hands until the backs of my knees hit the mattress. I like how he takes control without pressuring me. I like how he checks in, making sure I'm with him every step.

"Remember your job," he murmurs low.

"Stay in the present."

"With me. Eyes right here. Who's taking care of you?"

"You are."

"Say it."

"Hayden."

"That's right. I love the way my name sounds on your swollen, sinful lips. Makes me want to do bad things to them. Makes me want to wrap your hair around my fist while you swallow me down."

I lick said lips, feeling flushed and needy. I never felt like this before Hayden. Blow jobs were a necessary chore to keeping Brett calm, just another people-pleasing, hyper-vigilant tool in my arsenal for keeping control of the situation.

But with Hayden, I *want* to please him this way. I want to make him come undone, not because I think he's going to get mad if I don't, but because I want to watch his eyes roll back in his head and his lips part in an *Oh* as I take him down my throat.

Hayden's breathing hitches. His tongue darts out to wet his lips. "Yeah. Okay. You sure?"

Always checking in. He makes me feel valued with his attention. He cares if I want to do this or not, and that makes all the difference.

"Please, sir," I say with a sultry scratch to my voice that I didn't think I was capable of making. "I want to, Hayden."

He nods. I think I've robbed him of words. Pleasure spools in my belly. I'm in charge, and I'm going to make him feel as valued as he makes me feel. I'm going to show him that I like him exactly as he is, and I like him quite a lot.

Sinking into the mattress, I pull him by the waistband of his sweats to stand between my thighs, then drag them down over his sculpted ass. His cock springs out, erect and free. I lick my lips as I stare at the purple tip and smile when it bucks beneath my gaze.

I run my fingernails lightly over his skin, and Hayden groans. "You're a tease, woman."

"Just enjoying myself. Good things come to those who wait." I take his fisted hands before putting them on my head, urging him to wrap his fingers in my hair as he promised.

"Jaysus."

I look back up at him, taking in his dilated pupils, his parted lips, as I very slowly run my tongue up the underside of his shaft. "Eyes on me, baby."

"Minx."

"Be a good boy and hold still."

Hayden's face breaks into a wide, delighted grin. "Oh my god. You are perfect."

Taking his tip into my mouth, I taste the salt of his precum and hum my appreciation. Every little movement makes Hayden's muscles dance as he tries to stay still. It's heady, this ability to wreck him with pleasure. I've never felt so powerful. So playful during sex. I wring every noise I can out of him, collecting his moans and muttered curses close to my chest to take out later and examine, like ornaments on the holiday, each one shining with remembered joy.

By the time I take him to the back of my throat, his thighs are shaking. His hands are fisting my hair, and he can't help but thrust a little. I hum and slurp and keep collecting little acorns of joy, feeling the heat pooling between my thighs in mirrored pleasure, until he finishes with a shout.

I swallow, then clean him up with my tongue, and he collapses beside me on the bed. Curling his arms around my torso, he pulls me into his arms. I rest my head on his chest and listen to the thunderous beat of his heart beneath my ear.

"Fuck. You're amazing." He murmurs sweet nothings to me while he catches his breath. He runs his fingers through my hair, petting me like a cat. I think I like this best. The connection and intimacy after the act. Neither of us are in control or in charge; we're two opposite charged magnets clinging to each other.

30

CELESTE

I'M TOO BUSY STUDYING and finishing up the house and driving clients to retirement homes to see Hayden the next week, but he's barely responding to my texts, like he's fallen in a deep dark hole and isn't coming back out. I'm trying really hard not to take it personally. He's been so honest since the whole Mustachio incident. He wouldn't ghost me now, would he?

I stop by Magnus Fitness during my lunch break and try to find out from Samantha if he's still alive. She's in the middle of racking the kettlebells and doesn't seem too worried about her brother.

"Hayden? He's pits deep in a new project. Don't know when he'll resurface. Don't worry about him. Molly drops off snacks at his door."

"Writing something?"

"Yeah." She doesn't elaborate.

I should ask Hayden more about his job, not give his sister the third degree. She has me run agility drills until sweat drenches my back and forehead, and I'm panting when I exit the personal training studio and run right into the last person I want to see here.

Brett steadies me when I practically bounce off his chest and chastises me for my clumsiness. "You stink," he says. "Better get cleaned up before you meet your pool boy."

"What do you want, Brett?"

"I need the money from the house, Celeste. I've been patient over the last year, but Lander and I need to liquidate to have the down payment for something bigger and better. Real estate in this town is a joke. You people are scammers."

I'm not even a licensed agent yet, but he manages to insult me anyway. "I'm working on it. There've been a few setbacks with the remodel."

"I need it now, Celeste. Unless you want to renegotiate?"

"Good things come to those who wait, Brett."

"Good things come to those who buckle down and get it done. If you stopped fucking around and actually worked on the damn house, you'd have sold it by now."

"Right. Well, I better get back to it. Have a...a day." It takes every ounce of strength I have to give him my back and keep my spine straight as I head toward the changing room.

"No idea why you thought you could survive in the real world without me," he calls after me. "You had it easy sitting around the house and painting your nails all those years. You're not cut out for hard work."

Yeah, like doing all the cooking, cleaning, and childcare for twenty years was a walk in the park. I bite my tongue and let his barbs bounce right off. Seeing Hayden in action has given me a role model of sorts. Haters gonna hate, right? I'm not responsible for his emotional regulation. Good luck, Lander. They're in a very expensive apartment overlooking the canal, and he's probably blowing through his savings for it. He tried hard to keep me from getting half of everything in the divorce.

He doesn't keep yelling at me down the hallway, thank goodness. Berate me in private, yes. In public, he's a picture of charming, friendly, stand-up, good-old-boy. He doesn't want to tarnish his reputation.

Lighter footsteps follow me down the hall, and the next

thing I know Sam has her arm around my waist in a side hug. "You're strong, girl. Way to put him in his place."

"Really?"

"Really. Saying nothing to a bully is often the strongest way to fight back."

"He really is a bully, isn't he."

"The bullies closest to us are the worst ones. My brother was able to laugh away the kids in school, but our dad's offhanded comments always drew blood. You have a lot in common."

I give her some side eye. "Is this part of your 'future-sister-in-law' campaign?"

"Damn straight." Sam laughs and squeezes me. "I like you. You make my brother happy. Unlike Molly's disaster of a relationship, I see no red flags here. Let's lock you down."

I breathe out a laugh. "Raging ex-husband isn't a red flag?"

"Not at all. He's an ex, isn't he? You cut that ball and chain, and you're moving on up. Good on you. You did the hard, brave, thing, and you're ready to shine. You deserve all the happiness in the world."

My eyes prickle with emotion. "Thanks, Sam."

"Now go dig that brother of mine out of his writing cave and make him show you how good it could be. I'm rooting for you two."

"I don't want to bother him if he's too busy..."

"Nah." Sam playfully swats my arm. "Everyone knows orgasms make you more productive. Go get some."

You rarely get to choose the family you marry into, but Hayden was right when he said he had a good one. If things don't work out between us, do I have to give up Sam too? Suddenly it feels like I have more to lose.

On the way to the Holstrom House, I check in on Marissa —my one friend, ride-or-die who'll like me even if my romantic relationship sours. I've been too nervous to have this conversation, worried that she'll pull away, but talking to Sam made me realize that I need to make sure Rissa and I are solid. I love that I've gotten to meet so many people through Hayden, but I also need a friend who's just mine, who's not invested in Hayden and I working out.

"Celeste!" Rissa crows when she sees me. She's lounging in an Adirondack chair on her wrap around front porch with her ankle raised.

"Don't get up," I tell her when she looks like she's going to push herself off the chaise.

"Not you too. Drew has been waiting on me hand and foot, so I keep off this stupid ankle, but I hate feeling like an invalid."

"And you'll be back to your boss bitch self sooner because of it. Trust the process."

She takes off her reading glasses, which she pretends she doesn't need, and gives me a once over. "You look tired. How's everything going?"

"No rest for the wicked." I sit on the wicker porch swing and push gently with my feet on the railing.

"You feel ready for the exam this weekend? You're going to ace it."

"Don't jinx me." I tell her about my run in with Brett.

She's suitably enraged on my behalf. "The day he's not an asshole will be news. Stop stalling. Tell me what happened with your new batteries-not-included-boyfriend."

"He's pretty great, but we're still figuring each other out, you know? And I've got all this baggage—"

"Don't bullshit a bullshitter. Everyone has baggage. And you cut yours free."

I shrug and look away. Marissa's office windows look out on a pretty little rose garden with a gazebo. Red, pink, and yellow blossoms are unfurling, reaching toward the sun, ignorant of their own thorns. Do the thorns keep them safe or hold them back? "I guess I'm afraid."

Marissa leans toward me. "Who isn't frightened? If you're not a little bit scared, you're not pushing yourself enough. You deserve so much, Celeste. You deserve to be happy. You deserve to be loved for who you are, not what you do for someone else. I don't care if it's that mustachioed Mario or someone else—you will find a person worthy of you. I believe it."

"You were a lot more realistic before you met Drew."

"I was a glass half-empty kinda girl and you know it. Meeting Drew has convinced me that I was wrong to swear off love. I just hadn't met him yet. Don't waste any time thinking about what might have been. You know what you want, girlfriend. You need nothing less than a person who'll adore you."

I give her a crooked smile. "Thanks, Rissa. You're a good friend."

"I'm a great friend, and an even better boss. Now tell me what's really on your mind. We're friends, Ceecee. You can tell me anything."

"I'm not sure sales is for me."

"You're going to do fine!"

"No, I..." I take a deep breath. "I didn't want to upset you, because I've really, really appreciated everything you've done for me."

"Cee, no. We're friends. If you quit right now, we're still going to be friends."

"I'm not quitting! I just was thinking...what if I worked on Drew's side of the business?"

"House flipping? I thought you hated working on your house."

"No, I like the creative part of it. I just don't have enough hands. What if we expanded the services we offered? What if we found a team of female plumbers and electricians and technicians and offered more home repair services to our clients? Some of them don't even want to move. What if we could make it easier for them to stay in their houses?"

Marissa sits back in her chair and regards me with a flat look. "We're a real estate company."

"But I don't want to be part of pushing people to move when they don't want to. It feels like I'm part of the problem."

"Is this about Frida?"

"Partly, yeah. But I also know what it's like to be a lone woman trying to get male technicians to take me seriously. There's a real need for home services that caters to older female clients—building those relationships, Rissa. Eventually they'll sell and need a real estate agent, but they can be clients for years earlier if we expand our services."

She taps her nails on the desk. I've been thinking a lot about this idea that Hayden put into words for me, but I never would have been brave enough to suggest it if I hadn't learned to advocate for myself with this home renovation. To push back against Brett's decrees. To be brave enough to build community with Hayden's pickleball players. To understand what Frida wants—what *I* want—control over our own lives and decisions.

"Okay, babe. I can see this is important to you. Why don't you start drafting a proposal? No rush. You're still going to need your license and to get that showpiece project off the ground."

The tension leaves my shoulders. I owe her so much. I couldn't bear the thought of disappointing her. "Thanks, Rissa."

"I'm sending you home for the rest of the week to study and fix up that big project and hopefully get railed into the ground by your boy toy. Don't come back until you've got all three crossed off your list."

I give her a crooked grin. "I might need a fairy godmother to finish the house in time. How about one out of three?"

"No deal." Marissa steeples her fingers and gives me her best boss-bitch stare down. "Where there's a will, there's a way. Do it." She points toward the door. "Now get."

31

CELESTE

I'M COVERED IN PAINT, drywall tape, and desperation when the doorbell rings. Not Brett again. Please, not him. I'm not going to finish this project if I sleep at all this week. The test is tomorrow, and I'm listening to an audio study guide while I put the finishing touches on the cabinets. I'm supposed to stage the house after the pickleball tournament, and, assuming I pass the test, list it the next weekend.

I need a miracle.

The doorbell rings again. I put my head in my hands and try not to burst into tears. I can do this. I can do this by myself, and I'll feel so much better in two weeks. Everything I've worked so hard for will be worth it. I can do this.

"I'm coming!" Striding out of the kitchen and toward the front door, I glance out the window to see a small crowd on my doorstep. What the heck? I open to find Hayden. He's in a one-piece, navy, workman jumpsuit that shouldn't look so sexy, and he's holding a bucket of paintbrushes, which is also sexy, because I asked for a miracle, and he showed up. How is this possible? "Hayden?"

"Here to work, boss," he gives me that smirk that curls my toes and a salute. "Can we come in?" Behind him are Brody and

Ryder, his sisters and their spouses, and a bunch of people I recognize from the pickleball court. Some are strangers that look like young college jocks who must be friends of my boys.

"I...I don't know what to say."

"Just tell us where you want us," Hayden says as he steps up to me and plants a kiss on my lips, claiming me in front of my boys, his family, and all their friends. I stand there like a guppy as the audience erupts into cheers and catcalls. When he pulls away, leaving me breathless and horny, he tucks a curl behind my ear and gives me the sweetest smile I've ever seen. "We're all yours, Ladybird. Let's bang this project out so we can get back to the good stuff."

I stand back and let them in, this crew, this community I didn't know I had available to ask for help. I've been so used to doing things quietly by myself. Apparently, changing my behavior patterns is harder than changing my address.

It shouldn't be such a surprise at how fast it is to get through projects once I have a team. I flit from place to place, supervising and directing, and the crew gets things done. It's strange but invigorating to be the one in charge. Instead of a house of horrors of half-finished ideas, I'm watching my vision come to life before my eyes. Half the team gets started painting the walls in soft coral and mint green and pearl. The floors are buffed, the cobwebs banished, the windows scrubbed so clean I'm worried birds will try to fly through them.

The college boys clean out the gutters and spread the mulch while listening to a sportsball game on the radio and trash talking each other. Hayden's friend Russell replaces the lightbulbs and fixes the leaky faucet in the bathroom. Kirsten and Lara iron all the curtains and rehang them. Aaron pulls out all my appliances and cleans behind them before setting them back up. Samantha climbs on the roof and sweeps the moss off the shingles while Brody and Ryder hover like worried puppies beneath her in case she falls.

Henrí shows up with bagels and coffee for the whole crew,

and I almost start to cry. What even is this? It never occurred to me to ask for help.

Molly is planting flowers in the front garden with Elias and Ethan, when Brett's Ford Ranger Raptor pulls into the driveway and the man himself gets out. Lander exits the passenger door and stands there looking around the newly spiffed up yard and painted house with what can only be called avaricious gleam. Brett scowls at her before pulling on his charming persona like a coat he's worn right through.

Oh, no. Not here. Not now. What will Hayden think? What will his family think?

"What does he want?" Hayden asks from over my shoulder where I'm peeking through the window like a storm's approaching.

"When he showed up before, he said they've been having trouble finding a house in this market, and he wants to live in this one now that I've polished it up."

"He's been showing up while you've been working here alone to harass you?"

Besides Marissa, I can't remember the last time someone was outraged on my behalf for the shit Brett's pulled. I turn to Hayden, wrap my arms around his neck, and pull him down for a long kiss, hoping he can taste my thank you on my lips. "You're my hero, you know that?"

He licks his lips. "I'll never turn down your kisses, but I'm pretty sure you know how to slay your own dragons. I'm happy to be back up. Your trusty steed, perhaps?"

"My sword and shield?" I wink at him and love the way his eyes widen, then crinkle at the corners.

"I'll be your sword anytime, *ma chou*." He kisses me again, long and slow and full of promise.

I hear Brett stomp through the door and scoff when he catches sight of us, but Hayden isn't in a hurry. He's still kissing me like we have all the time in the world, like it's a lazy Sunday afternoon with not a thing to do but explore each other. His hands smooth slowly down my back to cup my ass and pull me against him.

"Wow. You'd never know this was the same house!" Lander says, and even though I'm not her biggest fan, her compliment and obvious enthusiasm for all my hard work sends happy moths fluttering in my belly. "Brett! Look at the new lights!"

He grumbles something and then comes our way, slowing as he realizes we're not about to stop to suit his timeline. I can feel Hayden smile against my mouth. His tongue licks up one side and down the other, lazily exploring, tasting of mint gum over coffee. He's growing hard against my soft lower belly.

Brett clears his throat.

Hayden takes his sweet time raising his head, but he doesn't let go of my ass. He meets Brett's thundercloud gaze and holds it. Hayden usually gives off laid back, golden retriever vibes, but right now he seems ready to bite back. I'm not afraid though— he'd never use his power to grind other people under his heel. He leads by example, encourages, and sacrifices his own time to help others achieve their dreams.

I feel safe in his arms. Safe, and undeniably turned on.

"Celeste," Brett barks. "Come here."

Hayden's hold on me tightens. "Brett, to what do we owe this intrusion?"

Brett blinks at Hayden. I don't think anyone's ever stood up to him before. A muscle ticks in his jaw, and it immediately sends my adrenaline pulsing. I know that look. The pressure will build until he explodes with shit everywhere.

Lander steps in and puts her hand on Brett's chest. "GI Joe, babe. Why didn't you tell me how much better it looks? This is totally livable now. Mid-century is so hot. Look at this alcove and picture window! I could do reels from here. We could hire an interior designer and live here until we find something better."

I'm grinding my teeth with every backhanded compliment. Part of me is pissed at her audacity. If only Brett had let me put money into repair and restoration when we lived here, it could have looked this good all the time. She can't waltz in here and take over. This is my project. My baby.

Brett opens and closes his mouth like a codfish and then sneers at the painted walls and fixtures and restored hardwoods. "We agreed to keep costs to a minimum, Celeste. Who are all these laborers you've hired to do this shit? You told me we'd get more out of the house by fixing it before selling it, but you're lighting good money on fire."

Lander leans into him and bats her fake eyelashes, and I almost swallow my tongue as his rising anger ebbs like a red tide under her magic pull. What the hell? Is that something I could have done all those years to deescalate the beast? Is there something wrong with me that I didn't know how to stand up to him? Is she really better, prettier, more—

Hayden puts his long fingers on the side of my jaw and tilts my head away from the dumpster fire and up at his face. He must see my spiral, because he doesn't hesitate to lower his lips to mine. It's not a quick peck. It's a claiming. His tongue licks mine with strong, firm strokes. He smells like paint and a male who's been pleasantly sweating. Tangling his fingers in my ponytail, he tugs gently to pull my attention like I'm a fish and he's the hook. He's dragging me up from the depths, opening my senses to his siren's song, keeping me grounded.

That's right; I don't need Brett and his bullshit. I've escaped and I've built something I'm proud of all on my own. No, not alone—with the real friends I've made along the way who lift me up instead of grinding me down to feel better about themselves.

When the kiss ends, I'm flustered enough that I don't realize the growling noise behind me is coming from Brett until Hayden's gaze goes over my shoulder and he smirks. "We're working here, bruiser. You want to continue this convo surrounded by Salmon Bay's finest, or find a better time and place?"

"Or pitch in, dad." Ryder says, stepping forward with Brody at his side. "Mom's done a ton, and this place looks great, but if you wanted it sold already, you could help."

"Boys—"

"Ryder is right, dad," Brody says. "I don't like the way you're talking to her."

I turn in Hayden's arms to find my ex furiously grinding his jaw, face beet red. The vein in his neck that I've been trained to monitor pulses dangerously.

"That's rich, turning our kids against me," Brett growls.

"You did that all on your own." Hayden's arms are solid and warm around me, anchoring me. I'm not alone facing off against Brett's wrath for once.

"Just wait, pool boy. You're going to wish you'd thrown this one back." Turning on his heel, Brett storms out of the house, with a worried Lander hurrying after him.

Ouch. Once, a comment like that would have gutted me, but with Hayden's arms around me, strong and steady, I can't find two shits to give. Hayden has never once made me feel less than. His scent calms my nervous system. His warmth heats the chill from my bones.

He presses a kiss to the top of my head before whispering in my ear, "My little angelfish, I'd swim the whole ocean to find you."

"I can't even be mad when you're here with me." I turn in his arms and greedily take another kiss from his lips. "I'm so lucky to have found you."

I hear giggles and some kids start singing, "Unca Hay-Hay and Celeste sitting in a tree, K-I-S-S-I-N-G...."

"Mommy! Is Unca Hay-Hay having a baby?"

Cue parental shushing.

I blush and hide my face against Hayden's chest. The vibration of his laugher rumbles against my skin, and I know that this place in his arms is the only place I want to be.

32

HAYDEN

CELESTE'S BUFFOON OF AN EX didn't stick around to watch me kiss her silly. He was too dumb to treat this beautiful woman like the queen she is, but his loss is my gain. I'm addicted to making her smile, and those rainbows are getting more frequent the more she drops her walls around me.

Celeste's face when I showed up with half the pickleball court and my family in tow almost brought me down. Has no one ever done anything nice for her before? Even when I was picked on as a kid, I always had family to come home to. Celeste has been alone. The least I can do is show her what real community is—all its guts and all its glory—weird and imperfect, but impossible to live without.

Even if sometimes I'd like to fit them all with muzzles and send them into space. Especially when it's Russell flirting with my girl just to get under my skin, or my sister making not-subtle-at-all innuendo that they should all leave me and Celeste alone so we can "have some privacy". Privacy to stop painting and instead slam Celeste up against the wall, stamping her sexy ass all over the fresh paint for a risqué new-age wallpaper? I don't think so. I shudder at the thought of combing dried latex paint out of my pubes.

Celeste is running around supervising everyone and kicking ass. She's got that quiet confidence that'd make a great coach—the softer, lift you up kind, not the drop and give me twenty that my own coach was. She's going from person to person telling them what a good job they're doing like we're all a bunch of puppies learning to piss outside.

I can't wait for her to finish the circuit to tell me what a good boy I am.

I'm a goner.

"You're a goner," my sister says unhelpfully.

"Get it Uncle Hayden!" Elias crows, and my sister cuffs him lightly on the back of the head. "Hey! Auntie Sam said the same thing!"

"Slander," Sam says as she joins us on the back patio. Aaron's finishing up the yard work, and the place is coming together. "Hay-Hay, you should take your girl out to celebrate. Maybe chowder at the Salmon House and sunset at the beach?"

I give her a flat look, because after all this brouhaha, I'm gonna need a nap.

Don't get me wrong, I have vivid daydreams of some stimulation I'm definitely up for after this, but it's not going to be my best work. My back is killing me from wielding a paintbrush.

"How'd you get rid of the ex?" Molly asks. She took one look at Brett and her hands balled into fists, ready to throw down for my girl. That's what family's for.

"Threw him off a parapet," I deadpan.

"Why can Uncle Hay-Hay joke about murdering people, but I can't?" Elias whines.

"Because I gave up trying to teach my little brother manners a long time ago, but I still have hope for you. Come on, let's get home and get washed up. Pizza night." The boys cheer, and Molly gives me a peck on the cheek before herding her little buffalos toward her car.

Sam gives me a side hug as we watch Aaron wipe his brow

and roll up the extension cord for the mower. "I love watching that man sweat."

"TMI, big sister."

"Uh-huh." She nudges me in the side and points out Celeste, who's coming around the house with twinkling eyes and a smudge of grease across her nose. "Go get 'em, tiger." She gives me a high-five and sashays down the front steps to meet her hubby halfway. They're annoyingly in love. Grandma told them to never stop dating in her speech at their wedding, and they took that to heart.

Celeste has paint all through her hair—blue streaks give her a bit of a punk air—and she looks exhausted, but happy. I'm watching her hips sway. Wondering how I got this beautiful girl to go out with me. Wondering how the fuck I'm going to come clean about my nefarious activities and whether she'll be super weirded out by a man who reads and writes romance. Her ex is the alphahole of alphaholes. She was obviously into the kind of guy my dad wanted me to be—big, in charge, takes no prisoners, makes no apologies kind of guy. Is she still attracted to that? I'm not a pushover, but I'm not keen on setting myself up for rejection either.

I should tell her. "Celeste—"

Before I can think what to say, Brody and Ryder join us. Celeste hugs them with the strength of a mama bear, even though they're both taller than her. I like that look on her face —the pride and love pour off her. Her boys can do no wrong.

My mom feels the same about me, but not enough to shield me from some of my father's worse comments.

"Thanks for coming, lovies," Celeste says as she hugs Ryder. "I hope you're not missing schoolwork for this."

"Mom, we want to help," Ryder tells her. "We didn't know you needed an extra hand. Sorry for letting you down."

"Yeah, we had to be told by that guy," Brody says. "We're not little kids anymore, ma. You don't have to hide shi—stuff from us. We can take it."

Celeste looks at me with surprise. "Hayden told you I needed help?"

Brody gives me a bro nod. "Yeah. He's cool."

Her cheeks color, probably wondering what else I told them about our relationship. Somethings don't need to be spelled out, little mama.

"About your father—"

Ryder wraps her in a bear hug. "Mom, we've been neutral parties for far too long."

"Yeah, mom," Brody says. "You know what they teach us about bullying in third grade? Bystanders who do nothing are part of the problem."

"I don't want to be responsible for ruining your relationship with your dad."

"You aren't responsible." Brody wraps his arms around his brother and mom in a big group hug that I'm tempted to join. One of these days. "He's screwing it up all on his own."

"We're adults, mom," Ryder says. "You don't have to hide the way he treats you to spare our feelings. You shouldn't have to hide abuse like that at all."

"Thank you, sweeties." The tears are audible in Celeste's voice. "Thank you for helping me. It means so much."

"Love you." The boys give her an extra squeeze and shuffle off before the waterworks start, because they're both tough grown men who haven't had a healthy emotionally balanced male role model yet. That's going to change.

I'm there to dry her tears. If I have my way, I'll be a permanent fixture holding her up and helping her shine.

Clean-up is fast with a whole team of helpful neighbors—no singing appliances needed—but saying goodbye and thank you to everyone who came out takes an hour. Afterward, I offer to take her out on that picnic, but she agrees that going home sounds better. I love how she says "home" like she belongs there. She does.

We pick up clam chowder and raspberry milkshakes at the

Salmon House. "It's not Carnegie's, but it hits the spot," I say as we recline on my couch and turn on the latest Almost Live! local comedy sketch show.

Good thing we've both seen it before, because as soon as we finish chowing down on chowder, I turn Celeste into my dessert.

Summer Sports Event
by Lord Lexicon

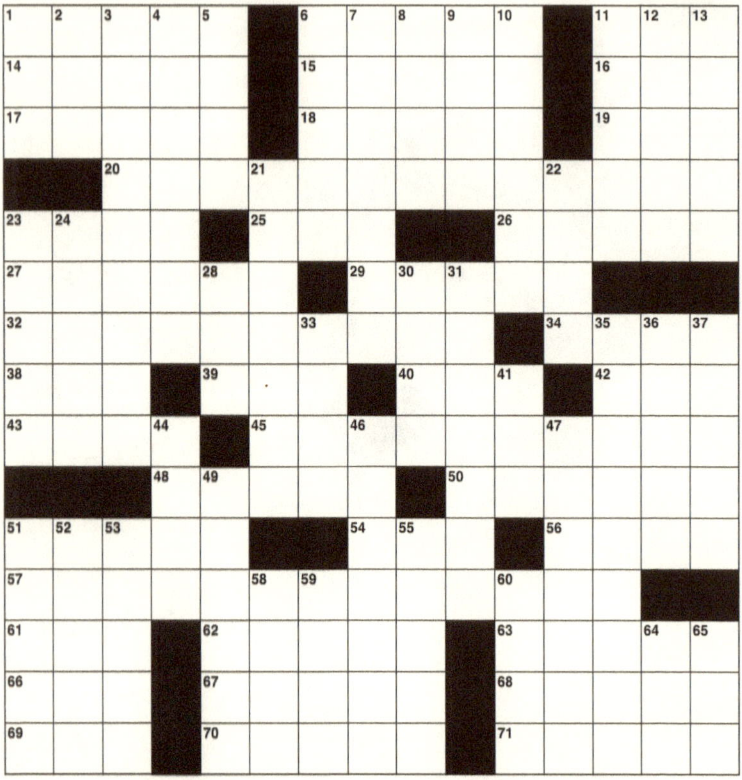

Miel Bagels - *Sweeten your day the Montréal way*

ACROSS

1 Pertaining to Robert Francis Prevost
6 Get steamy
11 Hat of Disney's Aladdin
14 Sherlock's teenage sister
15 "Dancing With the Stars" winner Ohno
16 Mendes or Longoria
17 Sauce with one consonant
18 Disposable lunch box?
19 Lasso on Apple TV

DOWN

1 Item that kept a fairy tale princess up all night
2 Singer DiFranco
3 Hairstyle boosted by Lucille Ball
4 "Do this one thing for me"
5 Write : written :: lie : ____
6 Model on 400+ romance novel covers
7 Where you'll find a slow boat to China

ACROSS

20 Dillydallying, and what's happening at the Sea Lion Club this summer
23 Gaucho's cattle-catcher
25 1, 2, 3, 4, and more: Abbr.
26 Vigorous
27 Common baby shower gift
29 Awards won by Caitlin Clark and Simone Biles
32 With 45-Across, the Sea Lion Club sports event of the summer
34 Salmon Bay, for one
38 Spot to get help for a hide-and-seek injury, briefly
39 Canon letters?
40 OPEC member
42 Leader of China until 1976
43 Head, to Henri
45 See 32-Across
48 Fudged
50 Fur wraps
51 Chocolate essential
54 Boozehound
56 Kiss from a señorita
57 "I won't settle!", and an invitation to the Sea Lion Club this summer
61 Arranged introduction?
62 Ermine, by another name
63 Pool noodles and penne
66 Trouble
67 ___ nous ("between you and me")
68 Site to remember?
69 "New" prefix
70 Distributed cards
71 Wetland wader

DOWN

8 It's hammered
9 Beauty products brand
10 Badly
11 Womb lodger
12 Big book signing, e.g.
13 Slang for an attractive and confident man
21 Show deference for
22 Depose
23 Frenetic children's toy from Hasbro
24 In cold storage
28 They, in Calais
30 Drunken mumble
31 Has an expectation that one will
33 Penciled facial feature
35 Breakfast buffet station
36 Opposite of waxes
37 "False!"
41 Polish off Polish pierogi, say
44 Internet auctioneer
46 Disentangle
47 Tyranny of the majority?
49 Released, quaintly
51 House network
52 Eagle's nest
53 Green with five Grammy Awards
55 Eight-piece band
58 Magazine that's "A Different Read on Life"
59 Teensy-weensy bit
60 Canyonlands National Park locale
64 Genre for "I Miss You"
65 "Junior" to "Senior"

33

HAYDEN

THE SEA LION LODGE'S first annual Pickleball Tournament falls the weekend before the Milk Carton Regatta, the first event of the Salmon Bay SummerFest. The festival celebrates all things Salmon Bay and was dreamed up after WWII to build community for returning veterans and to showcase our maritime history. Just about every business in town is a sponsor. Festival highlights include a lutefisk eating contest; a Milk Carton Regatta featuring paper mâche Viking cows and Elvis Impersonators; a boat flotilla led by the Mead & Marauders on their amphibious ship, *The Knotty-Lass*; and music concerts at the marina ranging from Axel jamming on the nyckelharpa to Priest mixing tracks of Swedish House Mafia. My favorite, as a runner, is the Twilight Marathon that's slowly being taken over by vampire costumes and body glitter.

"The Lodge ladies have been busy decorating," I tell Celeste when I open the passenger door for her after picking her up bright and early for the tournament. She's wearing another flirty little tennis dress, and I'd rather bring her right back home and explore what's under that skirt than stay and play pickleball.

She puts her slender hand in mine, and I help her out of the car, right into my chest. I kiss the tip of her nose. She's so beautiful with the summer sun picking up strands of auburn and grey in her brunette curls. "I loved the new crossword puzzle, Lord Lexicon."

"Thank you, love." Her approval fills my chest with glowing warmth. I thought it was clever. Tying the crosswords to events in Salmon Bay have made the puzzles something of a local sensation, and the Pickleball Tournament is an obvious choice.

"You're very witty." She takes a deep breath. "Are we doing this thing?"

"You ready?"

"I think so?"

I give her another quick peck for luck and lead her to the Lake Dribble courts, where Tia Francesca is manning a registration table with some fellow Sea-Gulls, the spouses of Sea Lion Lodge members who get shit done behind the scenes. Officially a "decorating committee," but I'm pretty sure the Lodge gets nothing done without their project management. They've tied helium balloons all around the court fences and woven colorful ribbons through the chain links. The banner is seventy percent local business sponsors and thirty percent tournament title, but they've made the official name so long that the letters barely fit on the vinyl.

"Registration?" Tia asks. "Please show Marjorie your driver's license to verify your age and give Ruth your pickleball rating. Remember, this is a mixed doubles tournament for charity—we want evenly matched teams, not superstars. Vasa Goods is donating ten dollars for every point scored to the Sea Lion Charitable Foundation, so do your best to have high scoring games!"

Ruth scribbles down our ratings and calculates the average while Tia holds out her tin of cookies. "Have a biscochito, niño. You need to keep up your energy."

"Thanks, Tia. Who is Warren playing with?"

"Amalie refused, so he bribed her sister to do it. She's raising money for children who need heart transplants. Be nice to her. Good luck out there and remember eleven points to nine raises more money than Eleven-zero. Happy dinking!"

I look around for Henrí and find him hovering anxiously over his littlest sister Margo, the cardiovascular surgery resident who hasn't needed his helicoptering in years. Her new heart works fine. She pats his chest with fondness. Maybe he should get a kid. Or a dog.

We make our way over to say hi and scope out how Margo is feeling. I didn't know she played pickleball. There are extra dogs on the court today, as everyone is prepping for a long day of sweat and spectatorship. Celeste immediately gets distracted by the drooling love fest and her nerves melt away. Good. I'd take her into the squat brick bathrooms behind the courts and de-stress her another way, but I doubt my shy woman is into the thrill of getting caught. If I'd realized getting a dog would be such a draw, I'd have adopted one years ago.

"Margo! Good to see you," I give her a hug. Since Henrí's like a brother to me, his little sisters are like mine too. I point that out only when I want to annoy him. He doesn't want my sisters like that. At least one of them.

Margo and Celeste get talking about racket sports and brain health while I give Henrí a hard time about not joining the tournament himself. He's an athlete, but he feels too big and awkward on the pickleball court with a little paddle in his giant paw. He's sticking to *real* paddling, as he calls it, on the Dragon Boat team for the Norselander Club.

Everyone is warming up. Some teams are stretching, some bouncing balls on their paddle, still others catching up with old friends.

"You should have got matching track suits," Margo tells Celeste as I point out the teams who've gone all out. Everything from tee-shirts tie-dyed using wiffle balls to green jumpsuits with pickle-printed fabric to elaborate costumes that will most likely impede their ability to play.

She giggles at the sight of Bob and his friend, also named Bob, wearing red and white striped Where's Waldo shirts and stocking caps. A couple teams are dressed all in green with green skull caps that make them look vaguely like pickles.

Russell catches my eye and joins us. "Beautiful day for a match, eh?"

"Sure is."

"You're looking spiffy." He nods to me and Celeste, which makes me look down and realize that we're color coordinated entirely unintentionally. Oh, no. We're one of *those* couples. Celeste keeps giving TopDog scritches as she smirks at me. She doesn't seem to mind how corny we look.

As the day goes on, I make the rounds and introduce Celeste to everyone I know who's ever played tennis before this. I plant the seed of making space for both sports. Celeste knows a lot more pickleball regulars than she did when she first showed up at the courts, and when she's drawn into conversation with a group of ladies who pitched in the day we helped her fix her house up, I'm able to slip away to reconnect with the former tennis players and suggest a letter writing campaign to the superintendent.

We're in the unranked division, after our failure at the qualifier, so we separate to the far courts to see if we can crush the competition. The winner of the unranked division goes on to play in the final four bracket against ranked teams.

Our first game is against the diminutive Shirley and her fourth husband, Judge, a giant of a man with a bald head covered in tattoos and a neatly trimmed goatee. Shirley is five foot nothing with a short pixie cut and giant gold hoop earrings. She can't stop talking about how pickleball peaked in the 70s, and she has a different paddle for every type of weather. While we set up, she regales Celeste with the superiority of her Dominator3000, which has a triangle cut out between the handle and the face of the paddle to make it more aerodynamic.

Every time it's her turn to serve, she raises her finger to test the wind direction and speed, and changes out her paddle for a new one.

"I bought the first composite paddle in 1984, you know, and I've got it framed over my fireplace." Shirley serves a fast, low ball to Celeste, who returns it down the middle. Both Shirley and Judge go for it but pull back at the last minute, so they don't crash. The ball sails through the gap between them, bounces, and goes out.

I slap Celeste lightly on the ass and tell her, "Atta girl." She still smiles so sweetly at compliments, her cheeks blooming with embarrassment. Someday, she'll accept them as her due.

Judge has long arms and a wide reach, but he's slow to move his feet. Shirley is short, but fast. Together they keep us on our toes until Celeste hits the game-winning shot, a lob to the far edge of the court that falls right behind Shirley.

"Good game, hot shot," I tell her and plant a kiss on her lips.

We all tap handles, and Shirley starts telling Judge about how he should have used a different paddle if he wanted to win. The big man smiles down fondly at his wife and ushers her from the court.

Our second game is against Ginny and her newest fling, Severin, who seems to have been selected for his good looks, not his pickleball skills. Even I can admit he's nice to watch as he runs and reaches across the court, muscles rippling, tight ass flexing. Max is leaning against the fence with his arms crossed and a scowl on his face, while Armando hovers by the net with a dreamy look. Drama is thick in the air—and it makes it hard *not* to pickle them eleven to zero.

I'm trying to win points for the fundraiser; I swear.

Ginny bursts into big soggy tears and laps up the attention when Severin rushes in to kiss her better. Armando steps forward to rub her back and make soothing noises in her ear, so that she's pressed between the two of them, and I can practically see the steam coming out of Max's ears.

"I almost feel left out," Celeste jokes.

"I've got a waffle welt from that last one," I tell her. "You want to kiss it better?"

She leans in and puts her lips gently on my shoulder. "How's that?"

"Better. And here?" I touch the edge of my jaw. She smirks and presses a kiss to my clean-shaven skin.

"How about here?" she whispers against my lips.

"Yeah, definitely hurting here too." I love the way she tastes as she gives me a too-short peck and pulls away with a giggle. I hardly want to become a fodder for gossip like Ginny, Max, and Armando, but I wish Celeste would claim me more forcefully in front of an audience.

We get a break for thirty minutes to hydrate and listen to Salmon Bay Radio's live updates on the tournament, with commercial breaks by Vasa Goods—they're *var så goda!*—and the Sea Lion Lodge. The SBR host is a high schooler named Cody from the amateur broadcasting club who I used to coach. We catch up while the Vasa Goods representative is gushing about the Sea Lion Lodge's fresh seafood dinner options.

Turns out Celeste knows Cody too.

"Hey, Mrs. Knowles," the kid says. "Is Brody here?"

"He's getting coffee with his brother," she tells him. "Is this a summer internship for you?"

"Yeah, I want to be a sportscaster, and it looks good on my college application. Not all of us can be star athletes."

I nudge Cody's shoulder with my own. The kid has grown since he was on my team, but he's never going to reach six feet. "You found a way to follow your passion, Codes. That's awesome. I'm proud of you."

"Thanks, Coach." Cody checks the time and excuses himself to start his show after the break.

"You're good with people," Celeste says.

"I wasn't always," I admit. "Kids and old people are easier to talk to than people my own age."

"Old people, like me?"

"Woman, you're only hard to talk to because you're so far out of my league, I'm intimidated."

She scoffs, and I wrap her with one arm and pull her into my body so that I can bury my nose in her coconut scented hair.

"You're beautiful all sweaty and red faced like this. I can't wait to get you home to get you all sweaty and red faced in private."

"You're such a tease."

"Only for you." I kiss her temple and guide her to our next match with my hand on her lower back. She's getting more comfortable with PDA. I want to shout to the world that she's my partner on and off the court, but I need to tell her about my secret writing life. What if she freaks? What if her vindictive ex finds out and does the same thing Jordyn did? I can't go through that again.

The day flies by as team after team falls to our excellent synergy. We balance each other out—Celeste coming in with the hard bangers and my well-placed dinks. We've come a long way.

Our next game is against Harold the accordion player and his friend Andrea who plays the box dulcimer. They're wearing matching green berets and suspenders over green shorts. Their yellow shirts say, "All-Star Dinks", and they have smears of green face paint under their eyes to cut down the glare.

"I feel under dressed," Celeste murmurs to me as we set up.

Molly roshambo'd the other Salmon Bay Tribune photographer for this assignment, and she's on the scene capturing the costumes and competition. Probably good that Celeste and I didn't dress up, because neither of us wants to be front page news.

On the court next to us, Warren is grinning ear to ear as he decimates the competition despite Margo's best efforts to make a high-scoring game. Marjorie is keeping track of the wins in each bracket on a large white board on the side of the court.

We're both moving up in our divisions. We could face off in the final.

Harold serves to my forehand, and I return it with a powerful drive down the middle. Andrea scoops the ball and lobs it to Celeste's side of the court with a grunt. Celeste bats it down with all the energy of a tennis serve. The ball slams into the ground an inch from Harold's foot, but he's able to get his paddle on it with a wonky dink that starts a dinking battle at the kitchen. I slide the ball down the sideline like a hot knife gliding through butter for the win.

"You made that look easy," Celeste tells me as we get water and take a breather.

"Practice." I give her a sweaty hug, and she giggles and pulls away.

"You look hot doing it. I've got something else you can practice when we get back home."

I raise a playful eyebrow. "Do I need practice?"

"Ten thousand hours, I think."

"For proficiency."

"Exactly."

"I'm only too happy to test that theory," I tell her with a slap on her ass.

By the time the final four bracket games starts, we're dragging, but we've made it. Cody is shouting into the microphone about our underdog status, and the audience is buzzing with anticipation. Music is playing and the sidelines are full of retirees and hipsters sitting in camp chairs drinking Rainier Beer and Rain City Kombucha. The head of the Salmon Bay PTA has wheeled a fair-sized popcorn maker to the park and is selling bags to raise money for new unicycles. My family is all here watching, as well as Henrí, his parents, and some of my other high school friends. Frida is gossiping with the Sea-Gulls and ogling the players. Brody and Ryder fetch their mom electrolyte drinks and keep her cool with a spray fan.

The community really came out for this event.

And then there were two: Warren and Margo versus Celeste and me.

Warren approaches the net with his arms raised like a boxing champion. His white teeth could blind a guy. He's at the top of the world. "Holstrom," he purrs. "It was always going to come down to this."

"Time to unleash the fury, Warren." I shake his hand, and he tries to crush mine in his grip.

"The Dink Dynamos are about to Dino-smash you," he says. "Say *auf wiedersehen*, Wimbledon."

34

CELESTE

WARREN LOOKS PERFECTLY SERIOUS, but his partner Margo covers her laugh with her hands. The audience is too boisterous to hear his smack talk. I wish Cody was standing closer with his mic. From the stands, Marissa waves a pompom, and Drew gives me a thumbs up. I can't believe we made it this far. If we lose now, I won't be able to look my friend in the eye.

Hayden and I retreat to half court to conference.

"We got this, Ladybird." Hayden puts his big hands on my shoulders and massages my tense muscles. "You're doing great. Don't let him get in your head."

"Wimbledon?" I laugh.

"Goodbye, fair well, auf wiedersehen, adieu," he sings playfully.

"To him, to him, and every bully out there." My change in the lyrics is off key, but Hayden's grin is worth the cringe of embarrassment.

"That's the spirit, love."

The Park Superintendent calls us back to the net for the coin toss, and Margo calls heads for the win. They get to serve first. We shake hands. Warren is practically foaming at the mouth at the chance to put us in our place. Margo rolls her eyes behind her partner's back, and I give her a return smile.

"You ready?" Hayden asks, pulling me in for a quick good luck kiss. "This game is ours."

"You want to learn tennis next?"

"If you're offering lessons, Ladybird, I'd learn to handstand and play the tuba."

I snort. "We'd have to level up for that."

"Let's get this match in the bag, then we can plan for our next shot."

Hayden said he'd never played Margo before—she goes to med school over in Seattle and seems pretty new to the game— but she serves like a professional, straight, low, and fast. I return it, and the ball is volleyed back and forth until Warren hits it with so much top spin that it sails by my paddle and bounces out of the court.

Warren chortles. "That's how you do it! Take notes!"

Margo serves to Hayden this time, and he hits it back deep. She lets it bounce and returns it to my side of the court. I accidentally pop it up, and Warren slams it to the far back side of the court for a point.

"Sorry," I tell Hayden.

He takes me by the shoulders and kisses the sorry out of me. "What'd I say about sorry, sweetheart? You ready to buy me that drink?"

How does he always know what to say to make me relax?

"That's right. You got this. Say it, babe."

"I got this. We got this."

"That's right, partner."

Warren doesn't stop trash talking, and it rattles me enough to miss a few. The pressure is fierce with half of Salmon Bay and all our friends and family watching. I can't let the bully win. My palms are sweating.

The Dink Dynos pull ahead five to zero.

"Brush it off," Hayden tells me. "Eyes on me, babe. One dink at a time, okay? We've practiced for this."

"I know." I drink some water and try to get my head back in the game. I return Margo's next serve to the back line, and she unbalances.

Hayden gets ready for the pop up and jumps over the kitchen to stand outside the court boundary, where he hits her ball out of the air and slams it down at her feet. It's a move I've only seen in videos online—and it looks even cooler in real life.

Margo can't recover and the ball moves to our serve.

Warren's face gets red. He points one meaty finger at Hayden. "Fault! Your paddle crossed the net!"

Hayden holds his hands up. "I made contact with the ball while it was still on my side. Only my follow through went over."

"Bull-snot. Your foot was on the line."

Dr. Fisher throws the ball back to me and tells Warren that the play was good.

Hayden smirks at a scowling Warren and gets in position to serve. The play moves back and forth, and we earn three more points before the serve comes to me. I hit a short angled serve just past the no volley zone at the sideline, forcing Margo to run forward and stretch to reach the ball in time. Her return has little power, and I'm able to lob it back in the hole where Margo used to be.

Warren lunges onto Margo's side of the court to cover, but he's too late.

One to five, my serve. Hayden and I tap our paddles as we switch places, then I serve on the opposite diagonal to Warren, who's ready for me. He sends it back, starting a rapid-fire exchange. Margo intercepts a low return, initiating a dinking battle near the net, and I move to the kitchen to hit those light, perfectly placed shots that are nothing like tennis.

"Crushing it, babe," Hayden tells me after I score a point.

"You're not so bad yourself, hot stuff."

His grin is everything.

We even the score, five to five, even though Warren is only hitting to me, the weaker player. He's aggressive, but I'm holding my own for the most part. Still, it's been a long day of play, and my muscles are getting tired. When Margo misses a drop shot, Warren starts pushing her over to cover more of her side of the court. Teamwork is not the name of his game. He reminds me of Brett in so many ways—here for the glory but refusing to acknowledge his partner's contribution.

If he had to choose, Hayden would pick me over winning.

The serve goes back to the Dink Dynamos and before I know it, we're neck and neck, ten to eleven. We have to win by two. This could go long. The audience is here for it though, even though the sun is descending over the horizon. Fisher calls a ten-minute break, and Hayden's oldest sister, Molly, brings us snacks.

"You doing okay?" she asks.

"Tired, but good." I wipe my forehead with a towel and accept some power jellybeans gratefully.

"Better give up now, Wimbledon," Warren calls from the other side of the court. "Wouldn't want to twist your ankle like your friend. Quit while you're ahead."

My sweet boys were on their way to talk to me and overhear Warren's comment. They both stiffen and turn to step threateningly toward the older man.

"Dude. Are you threatening our mom?" Brody growls.

"Good sportsmanship is important, man," Ryder tells him. "What kind of model are you showing the kids?"

"Think of the children!"

Warren backs off with a flustered sneer as Hayden pulls me against his chest to kiss the top of my head. "You have nothing to worry about, Ladybird. I'll hold him down while you whack him with the paddle if you want."

"That'd get me some great photos," Molly quips. "Tell me

before you start beating people so I can send my impressionable tween boys home, mkay?"

"Maybe you could publish only bad photos of him," I suggest. "Get a couple with food stuck in his teeth, or toilet paper hanging off his shoe."

"I like the way you think." Molly gives me a grin. "Keep this one, Unca Hay-Hay."

"Like you have a say in it. I'm still trying to convince her to give me a chance."

"She's here, isn't she?"

"Bribed her with prizes." He wraps his arm around me and gives me a squeeze, even though we're both sweaty. "I'm terrified that once this tournament is over, she'll drop me like a hot potato."

"I'd never!" I laugh and hit him playfully on the shoulder, but there's a flash of vulnerability in his eyes that sobers me. "I've gotten used to your face. Would be a shame to have to start over with a stranger I meet on the internet."

"That's right, convenient, I am."

He needs to know that we've moved past that. This is something real. Boyfriend, not just pickleball partner. I push myself onto my toes to plant a kiss on his lips, trying to tell him without words that I'm claiming him in front of half the town—there's no going back. "Besides, you promised to let me teach you tennis."

"I did, didn't I?" Hayden runs his hands down my arms, and I love the feel of his warm, calloused fingertips raising goosebumps on my skin.

Dr. Fisher calls us back to the game, and we get our second wind. I'm focusing so hard on the ball, Warren's jeers don't even register. We tie it up and pull ahead to twelve-eleven, only to lose the next point. A month ago, Warren's agitation would have sent me into fight or flight. I would have stepped back, quieted down, offered soothing words—anything to diffuse the anger he's radiating. But now I'm more pissed at how he's crowding out Margo to take most of the court. Teamwork is trusting your partner to have your back.

I aim for the hole he's left open on the far side of the court.

"Excellent placement," Hayden tells me as he catches the ball that's tossed back and hands it to me for the serve. He brushes his fingers against mine and trails them up my arm to my shoulder. "I wish we could get outta here and go back to my place, but I won't earn my dessert until we wipe that smug look off Warren's face."

I bite my lip and look up at him through my lashes. "Me too."

"Let's slay this dragon for every princess who ever got locked in a tower, and then you can show me what a good boy I've been."

"The best." Feeling warm in more ways than one, I take a calming breath and wipe the sweat from my brow. *Focus, Celeste. You can do this.*

I hit a soft lob just on the other side of the kitchen line. Margo runs for it and hits it back to my side. We all rush the kitchen line as the rest of the world disappears. Nothing exists but the *pok-pok-pok* of a rapid volley.

I hit a perfectly placed shot that lands right on the baseline.

"That was out!" Warren yells, but he's forgotten how closely the audience is watching this match, and they start booing.

"You blind?" Addy calls, and spectators roar their agreement.

"I'm closest to the ball. It's my call!" he growls. "Margo?"

But Margo is not going to be bullied into cheating to win. She shakes her head, and Warren scowls.

"Fine. Your point. Happy?"

"Very." Hayden gives me a pat on the ass as we switch places.

This is it. I lock eyes with Warren as I stand tall and call out the score. "Thirteen-twelve, serving two."

The audience collectively holds its breath as I drive the serve low and hard and just inside the line. It's a beautiful shot, and Warren has been so wedded to the center line and crowding his partner that he's out of position.

He can't get his paddle on the ball.

And that's game.

We did it.

Fourteen-twelve for the win. I can't believe it. I'm frozen, staring across the net as Hayden starts whooping and hollering.

He scoops me into his arms. "You did it! You were amazing! So hot. So beautiful."

My eyes start watering. "Oh, my god. We did it." I grab his face in my hands, shaking, searching his face for confirmation. "We did it?"

"We did it, beautiful. Today the court, tomorrow the world. My Celeste is on fire!"

The audience pours onto the court and sweeps us up. Family and friends and everyone we've ever played with wants to shake our hands. Hayden's firm grip anchor's me to earth, and I keep hold of his arm so I don't float off into space. I did it. I defeated the dragon. No more letting myself be pushed down by bullies. No one can tell me what to do anymore.

"Good teamwork, sweetheart. You crushed it." He kisses me full on the mouth, and I sink into it even as the crowd is screaming and the flashes of cameras go off on the sidelines.

Hayden twirls me around before setting me down and twining our fingers together. My cheeks hurt from grinning. All my soreness has melted away. I feel like I could run the Twilight Marathon. Climb Mount Rainier. Sail around Deception Point with a wing and a prayer. Frida was right—I can kick ass and take names if I put my mind to it. I am a wonder woman.

"Good game," Margo says as she holds out her paddle to tap.

"Good game, Margo," Hayden says. "Warren."

I make eye contact with Warren. "Good sportsmanship for the win."

Warren grunts, taps his paddle grudgingly, and strides off toward his wife to drown his sorrows in biscochitos.

The sidelines are full of fans. All Hayden's sisters, Marissa and her family, every new court friend I've made over the last few weeks—they're all here and all cheering for us. We're paraded and photographed and congratulated for what feels like hours.

Rissa makes sure to give me an extra squeeze as she tells me how good it felt to watch me stick it to The Man on her behalf. "I knew you'd do me proud, Ceecee. You crush everything you put your mind to."

"Thanks, Rissa. This was a lot of fun."

"Kinda glad I got injured, are you?" She waggles her eyebrows at Hayden, who's glistening with sweat and grinning ear to ear, then winks at me. "Worked out."

"It did."

"Told you so."

"You did."

"That's what friends are for."

"Thank you, Rissa, for pushing me out of my comfort zone."

"Any time, babe. Now go celebrate with that fine batteries-not-included-boyfriend. You deserve an orgasm or ten."

I laugh and watch Drew grab her ass as she hobbles back toward the car. Those kids.

It feels like hours before Hayden manages to disentangle us from the hullabaloo. The light is almost gone. The radio station and sponsors are packing up.

We find Dr. Fisher before we leave, even though he's deep in heated conversation with Warren. The tired smile he gives us makes my stomach clench. "Congratulations, Celeste. Hayden. We raised a lot of money for the fund today."

"We're looking forward to using the new court," I tell him.

Dr. Fisher and Warren exchange a glance.

"Can we talk about this later?" Dr. Fisher asks. "The Sea

Lion Lodge is managing awards and prizes, as the court is on their property. Warren will get back to you once all the paperwork is triple checked."

"I sure will." Warren's smile doesn't reach his eyes. "You have a good night now."

"Warren?"

"Yes, Hayden?"

"I'll be expecting your call tomorrow."

"You'll be certain to have it." Warren salutes, but he's not making me feel warm and fuzzy about my winning.

"You think something's wrong?" I ask Hayden as we watch the two men walk off toward the parking lot.

"No, babe. We'll figure it out. Everything is going to be okay. I promised you a tennis court. I'm a man of my word."

"We won it together, partner."

"That we did, and I've never seen anything hotter in my life."

"Really?" I raise an eyebrow at his naughty smirk that never fails to melt my insides.

"Maybe I need a refresher."

"Maybe I need a celebration."

"Maybe I'm feeling a little hungry for dessert." He tugs me into his arms and wraps me in his warm embrace. Even though it's July, the evenings have a bit of a chill in the air. I love the firm grasp of his strength around me, the warm male scent of him. I tilt my head up for a kiss, and he meets me halfway. My worries about the court dissolve in the soft, sweet press of his lips. He's right—it will work itself out. And if I had to choose between a court and this man kissing me like it's his dream job, I'd pick the man.

He's sweet and funny, and he makes me feel safe.

"Take me home, Hayden," I murmur against his lips.

I can feel his grin beneath my mouth. He tugs my bottom lip between his teeth, sending an answering tug in my core.

"Come-on, *ma chère mademoiselle*. Your carriage awaits."

Hayden takes me back to his carriage house and everything feels new, like I haven't seen the big birch tree swaying over the gingerbread trim or the weathervane over the cupola stuck at north. It's like a cozy storybook villa in the dark. I'm not worried about impressing anyone—I impressed myself today, and I'm high on self-confidence for what feels like the first time in my life.

"What's going on in that pretty head of yours, *ma belle*?" Hayden asks as he carries me bridal style through the door, peppering kissing along my neck.

"Thinking of all the new goals I want to make. I set a ridiculous goal and made it. I could do anything. Maybe I should run the Salmon Bay Half Marathon? Or take up curling? I know! Synchronized Swimming. Do you think I should try out for the Aqua Follies at Lake Dibble? I feel young, like I still have my whole life in front of me and I can do anything."

Hayden laughs against my hair. "You can do anything. You're fierce."

"Thank you."

"But what would actually bring you joy, *mon amour*? Not what would give you bragging points. The practice should be as joyful as the winning."

I sigh as he drops me on the bed and starts undressing me. "Killjoy."

"I have some things I need to practice that will give me very much joy."

"Really?"

"Practice makes perfect." He spreads my legs and pulls me down to the end of the bed, where he kneels between my thighs and presses open mouth kisses up the seam between my pelvis and leg.

I giggle and squirm away from his mouth, but his strong hands keep my thighs clamped firmly down. He looks up at me through his long thick lashes and shakes his head slowly. "Tsk. Tsk. Be good and hold still, ladybird."

"What if I don't want to be good?" I whisper. I've been a good girl all my life. Dotted every I. Crossed every T. Made myself smaller so other people wouldn't be offended by my presence. Swallowed down my objections, my hopes and fears.

"You can be anything you want," Hayden says, voice deep and gravely, "as long as you're mine."

"I belong to myself."

His smile softens. "Always, *ma chère*. You can be strong and independent and still be my woman. You own me, body and soul."

I think I love you, I want to say, but the cautious part of me still says *wait, wait, wait*.

His kiss to my bare skin sets fire to my core, and he doesn't let up until the room is spinning above me and my vocal cords strain with my cry of pleasure.

35

HAYDEN

CELESTE SLEEPS DEEPLY with her head pillowed on my chest, a soft snore escaping from her parted lips. I can't stop smiling at this gorgeous woman in my arms. She'd cocooned herself so tightly when I met her, and over the last few months, she's ripped her way out, piece by piece, and emerged more beautiful than ever into the brilliant light. A fierce little fighter.

I'm worried about Dr. Fisher and Warren, but that's a tomorrow problem. I wouldn't have suspected anything, except now that I'm looking at the world through Celeste's eyes, it didn't look like they were cooking up anything good. Paranoid? Maybe, but I can see how the good old boys club isn't operating a level playing field. Warren resents Celeste, and he's not going to lie down and let her win.

I don't want to leave this cozy nest, but when she sloughs off the covers in her sleep and rolls out of my arms, her skin glistening and rosy, I take the opportunity to get out of bed, take a piss, and sit down at my laptop to crank out some long overdue emails. I've been making a list of every pickleball player I know who is also associated with tennis. Some of them used to play. Some of them have spouses or kids who play. Some of them are exactly the sort of rebellious souls that I know would support an underdog story.

I crack my knuckles and get writing, putting every trick I know into crafting the perfect tale that will tug at heartstrings and win advocates to our cause.

The faintest light of dawn splits the sky like dewy spider silk around four am, and Celeste turns over and bats her beautiful lashes open. Her hair is a riot of curls across my pillow. The sheet is wrapped around those generous curves that would make Rubens weep. I wish I had a camera to capture this perfect vision to fall asleep to every night.

Maybe I'll get lucky, and she'll let me have her in my bed every night. I feel like we're headed that direction. She's lowered her walls and softened her guarded heart toward me. Will she run when she finds out my last secret? She doesn't seem anything like Jordyn, but all it takes is one careless word on social media, and my pen name is ruined. Jordyn didn't set out to destroy my budding career. Her passive-aggressive post about a man writing in a space that's historically been by-women, for-women, was all it took. Blood in the water. The sharks couldn't resist.

"Hayden?" *My Celeste.* If I could spin her morning voice into cotton candy and swallow it down, drink up that rasp that makes my dick hard, taste her honey on my lips, I would.

"But soft, what light through yonder window breaks?" I murmur to her as I climb back in bed, untangling her from the sheet long enough to replace it with my body. I wrap my arms around her and pull her softness against my hardness. She melts right against me with a breathy moan. This woman. I want to keep her like this forever.

"Where'd you go?"

"When the muse speaks, I listen."

"Crossword clues?"

"A puzzle of sorts. But hush now. Go back to sleep, beautiful."

She bites my nipple playfully, and I growl. "What if I'm not tired?"

"Minx."

Her hands are callused from holding paddles and paintbrushes. She runs them down my sides, and I love that my woman has these badges of courage on her skin. She wraps her arms around my waist and takes a firm grip of my ass, grinding us together.

I roll her beneath me and pull the sheet up over our heads like a tent. There's not enough light to see her face, but I can hear her giggle, and it sends my heart flipping in my chest. Her laughter is the most beautiful sound in the world. "Ooo la la, *ma chére*, you are playing with fire."

"But I want to polish your candlestick, *mon amour*!" she says in a fake high voice. Silly. Playful. The real Celeste unburdened by all that sadness she had tangled around her when we first met.

I love this version. I love every version, but this is the real her. Beneath the scars and the armor. This Celeste fits me perfectly. "You tease. Let me show you how it's done, *hon hon hon*!"

She's already wet when I trail my fingers along her slit, and I gather up all that moisture to rub around her clit. She's mewling and begging me to let her come by the time I slide into her wet heat, and the combination of my dick filling her up and pressure on her clit has her squeezing around me in record time. I keep thrusting through her orgasm, milking it as long as I can, before I lift her knees to her chest and slide deeper.

Finding the perfect angle, I hit a place inside that makes her eyes roll back and she moans out my name like a prayer.

Fuck. I pull out and flip her over, raising her hips to my mouth and licking into her swollen folds from behind. I let my body calm down while I wind her up, until she's wriggling her luscious ass against my face with the need to come again.

"Hayden, please!"

"You ever play here?" I ask as I run a knuckle soaked in her own arousal over the rosebud of her ass.

She squirms away. "Nu-uh."

"Do you trust me?"

Her body stills as she debates her answer, and I hate that we're not as far along as I wished we were, but I know we'll get there. Her body and her brain are fighting her past learned responses, but I can wait. I can wait as long as it takes for her to get there.

After a long moment, where I keep my hands steady on her hips, giving her support without pushing her any direction, she lets out a deep breath. "Yes. I trust you."

So hot, sweetheart.

"I won't let you down," I promise.

Kneeling behind her, I spread her legs wide and sheath myself back in her body, her inner muscles clenching around me like a warm embrace. I force myself to slow, every thrust is sure and hard, every withdraw languid as her inner muscles try to hold me back. I lube up my thumb with spit and gently circle her rosebud, letting her get used to those lovely new nerve endings lighting up. The stigma around anal is another barrier to pleasure, and I am more than happy to show Celeste everything about it even if we have to go at a glacial speed.

With my other hand, I wrap around her hip from the front so I can apply pressure to her clit with my middle two fingers, and her moans crescendo as I pick up the pace.

"You like that, don't you? You're my good, dirty girl, aren't you?"

"Hayden—I..."

"What do you need, love? I'll give you anything you want."

She pants. "Any..anything?"

I can see the gears turning in her head. Cheeky little thing. "Your heart's desire. Name it."

"A..a dog?"

I laugh. "Absolutely, a dog. A big, fluffy, slobbery mutt, the ugliest one we can find and name him..."

"Pickles."

"Perfect. Pickles is exactly right. You're perfect, babe." Her hips come back against me, and I swear I've found the secret to Nirvana.

"What about...*ughnf*...your plants?"

"Sweetheart, I'd give away every last plant if you asked me to."

"But...your babies—"

I swat her ass, and she gives a little squeal. "If it's important to you," I punctuate each word with a thrust, "it's important to me."

"You. I only need you."

She's panting, sweaty and beautiful. Her big breasts sway with our rocking hips, and I wish I had brought her up to hands and knees so I could get a better view.

"Oh, god, Hayden!" She pushes back against me, taking me deep, and her inner muscles start to convulse.

My vision goes white and my brain fuzzes out in perfect, empty, bliss. It's never been this good.

When we collapse into the mattress, I roll her on top and clutch her to me, both of us sweaty and sticky and smelling like a good time. Our breathing is ragged. Our hearts race each other, galloping wild ponies across the painted desert. There's no one in sight, no end in sight, no place I'd rather be than right here with this woman.

Why is it so easy to come up with make believe stories but hard to put into words what I really feel? *It's the possibility of rejection, dumbass.* If she doesn't like my dirty talk, no biggie. If she doesn't like the real me, my hopes and dreams, my fears and failings, that's gonna hurt a lot more.

"Celeste?" I whisper.

She's half asleep and can only manage a soft hum of acknowledgement.

"I love you."

The quiet snore is all the response I get, but for now, I'll keep it tucked close to my heart.

I love you, Celeste. Sweet dreams, beautiful.

36

CELESTE

THE SALTY BRINE OF PUGET SOUND wafts through the open window, teasing me awake. I stretch, lazily, my body deliciously sore. I flex my toes and feel the day-after burn in my thighs and calves from pounding the pavement yesterday. The muscles of my right shoulder whine at me, but my elbow is quieter than it usually is after a tennis match. Huh. Maybe I should treat myself and book a massage. I rarely spend money on myself—frivolous, Brett would call it—but I worked hard, and I deserve it. Hayden's been rubbing off on me. I want to seek out things that make me happy. To be motivated by joy, not guilt.

The sound of the shower running tells me where Hayden is. I roll over and find a sticky note in the indent on his pillow. *Gone running. XO.* A warm glow spreads through my chest. Hugs and kisses. Hayden's running shoes are sitting by the door, like he just toed them off, and I roll my eyes at the energy he has. I'm usually the one getting up early to pack lunches and get work done, but here I am sleeping indulgently after a sinfully good late night getting railed by a hot younger man.

What is happening to me?

I don't know, but I like it.

Hayden's laptop is open on the desk next to the bed, and it dings with an incoming email. Which reminds me to check my work messages to see if anyone has scheduled a home tour. I grab a tee shirt of Hayden's off the floor and pull it on, before sitting gingerly on his tufted rolling chair. Oh my god, last night. His dirty talk and finger in my ass. I had no idea I'd find that so hot. It came out of nowhere, and I liked it. A lot.

I can't believe I wasted so many years thinking it was me who was the problem in the bedroom.

It ain't me, babe. I needed a man who can find my clit and knows what to do with it.

Hayden is the real deal. Too good to be true.

Shaking my head and trying not to obsessively replay what I remember from last night, I click out of the screen saver on his laptop. His email is open. I don't mean to spy, but something catches my eye that has me opening the message with slow, halting hesitation.

Hayden—Loved the new closet sex scene! You've captured the forbidden energy of Maddox and Celia's affair. The possessive drive Maddox has protecting her from her ex-husband and whisking her off to the broom closet to rip off her pants, I really believe it now. You've found what was missing—their chemistry is smoking! Can't wait to read the other rewrites with this new feeling of passion. Keep up the good work! – Susan, Senior Acquiring Editor, Heyer Press.

Closet sex scene? What the hell?

It takes a long moment to compute. My stomach feels like I'm perched on the edge of a cliff, looking down at the waves eating away at the base. Hayden wouldn't share our personal lives, even with assumed names. Would he? Rewrites? Heyer Press is the New York Publishing house that specializes in all things romance, which I know only after looking up Trudy Belle when I finished the book Frida gave me.

My fingers move over the track pad without conscious thought, and I find a word document open and waiting, a novel by the look of it. The header reads HOLSTROM / HOLLAND / UNRAVELED.

WTF?

I find myself typing BROOM CLOSET in the search bar and skip to the scene where Maddox and Celia are hiding in said closet. It's almost a surprise to read what happened three months ago. Almost, but not quite, because a little part of me was always waiting for this. If something seems too good to be true, it usually is.

Hayden wrote about our hookup in great detail. Maddox goes down on Celia in the closet before she runs out on him, with almost the same choreography that we had. Did he plan it this way? Was he acting out something he already wrote, or did he write this after our little tryst?

He said he did editing. Some ghost writing. Is he ghost writing for this author, or is this his original work? But he wouldn't put *us* into the story, right? He can't be using me as a muse to write sex scenes, right?

I do a search on his computer and find more word documents that look like fiction manuscripts, including one by Trudy Belle that I've never heard of. I don't know what to do with this information. Could Hayden be the real author behind Trudy Belle, award winning historical romance author? And what about this other author listed, Bella Holland?

I look up her website, and just like on Trudy Belle's site, there's no photo of a real person. Trudy's got a whimsical illustration of a pinup-style girl with a typewriter. Bella only has a logo with her initials in a heart. She's a best-selling contemporary romance author and has no social media presence. There's nothing online about who she really is.

Has Hayden been lying to me? Is he using our sex life as material for his books? Why wouldn't he tell me something like that? Why would he share intimate details of our lives with anyone?

I think I'm going to throw up. My hands shake as I scan through the document, looking for more tell-alls about our lives together.

I can't be with someone who's lying to me, even if it's by omission. How can I trust him when he's spilling private details into his manuscript for publication? Is he laughing at me with all his friends behind my back? Me, the sad cougar so desperate for love that I'll believe anything?

Every bad thing Brett has ever said about me comes raging back. I'm naïve. Too gullible. Too soft. Too timid. I'm too much. Too little. Never enough to earn the love that everyone else seems to find unconditionally.

Fat tears are stinging my cheeks as the screen blurs in front of me. I wipe them away and search through his email with less hesitation. What else will I find?

It's almost a relief to see an email from the Sea Lion Lodge about our tournament prize, but I brace myself anyway. The universe has a way of heaping shit on top of shit, and I've been here before. I shouldn't have let down my guard.

The email is from Warren and dated last night. It's been opened, so I know Hayden read it. He never mentioned it. We were supposed to be a team.

The Sea Lion Lodge is proud to announce the winners of the first annual Salmon Bay SummerFest Pickleball Tournament! Thank you for your participation, and we look forward to welcoming you onto the new pickleball courts at our lodge. After the initial exclusive use by our tournament winners, the court will be open to all club members on a first come, first serve basis. (Please note, to maximize capacity of the courts, play is restricted to pickleball use only. No tennis playing will be allowed.)

I'm not sure which is more disheartening—that Hayden would write about our sexcapades or that he wouldn't tell me that the Sea Lion Lodge had changed the tournament win to be pickleball only. My whole body feels numb. This was all one big mistake.

The sound of the shower turning off is deafening. The bathroom door opens, but I don't turn. I can't look at him.

"Good morning, beautiful."

I wish I'd never met you.

"I...what?"

I guess I said that out loud. It's been a long time since I let fly the words screaming in my head, but I don't owe Hayden anything but the truth. "Do you write porn for women?"

"I...no. Romance. I write romance novels. There's a difference."

"Do you ghost write them? Who is Trudy Belle? Bella Holland?"

He clears his throat. "Both are me. Pen names for anonymity, obviously, but I was going to tell you—"

"When? When the book detailing our sex life comes out?"

"What? No—"

"No?" I turn to him and let him see the devastation in my eyes. "Will I hear about my closet sluttiness in the grocery store aisle as all the old ladies gossip about their favorite passages from the book?"

"No, baby, no—" He rushes toward me, but I put up both hands.

"Don't touch me. Don't baby me. Do you laugh with your friends over how gullible I am?"

He links his hands behind his head so that he doesn't reach for me. "I never told anyone about—"

"Don't lie to me!" I hiss. "When were you going to tell me? When the book was published? When I get the new copy from a client at work and read about my sexual escapades in print?"

"It's not like that—"

"You didn't write about our hookup at Brett's wedding?"

"I mean, yes, but that was the day after, before I knew you. I thought I'd never see you again."

"But you did! And you didn't say anything! You let me believe we'd never met, until someone else spilled the beans, leaving me a laughingstock in front of your whole family. Then your friends had a good laugh that I was obsessed with the crossword that you wrote. Now this! Is this all I am to you? A big joke?"

"No, no! Listen—"

"Don't lie to me! Was anything about us real? I saw the email, Hayden. The Sea Lion Club changed the fine print and won't let me play tennis on the new court. Were you going to tell me? What was the point of building me up if you just planned to tear me back down?"

He grabs handfuls of his hair and tugs. "How can you accuse me of setting you up like that? You know me, Celeste. Better than anyone outside my family. What could possibly make you think so low of me?"

"That email, Hayden. Not telling me about your real job, Hayden. Using our sex life for your amusement, Hayden!" I stand and face him.

"I was going to tell you about the Sea Lion Club being jerks this morning. Unfortunately, Dr. Fisher is a member of the club, and Warren wrangled the members to make the change. It's not fair, but I'm not sure what we can do about it. I wasn't trying to keep it from you; I didn't want to disappoint you."

"But you did. You kept so much from me. I trusted you. I actually—god, I've been such an idiot. Why would someone like you be with someone like me?" My laugh is half sob.

"No, sweetheart, it's not like that—"

"Yeah? Well, I'm done. I'm done being the butt of people's jokes. I'm done being put last, like I have no feelings, like I don't matter—"

"You matter to me!" Hayden sinks to his knees in front of me, but I don't let him touch me.

"I spent twenty years making myself small to fit the box someone else drew for me, and I promised myself I never would put myself in a vulnerable position like that again. I won't listen to you spin some tale about this and let you smooth it over because gullible little Celeste will believe anything. No more. I'm standing up for myself. You won't publish this."

"It was an old draft. Once I saw you again, I was never going to use that scene."

"But it's in this manuscript! Your editor wrote you back about it!"

"What? No, no that's a mistake. I must have sent the wrong draft—"

"How convenient," I spit out. My anger and hurt are roaring in my ears so loudly I can't hear myself sob.

Hayden stands to his full six foot two and stares down at me stonily. "Trust goes both ways. I've hung my heart on my sleeve since the first moment I met you. Everything about our relationship has been real—realer than anything I've ever had."

"You keep lying to me."

"I'm not lying! Omission, maybe, but I've been hurt too, okay? I've been trying to figure out the right way to tell you. I care—"

I scoff.

Swearing, he spins away from me and stomps toward the window, only to turn back, heart in his eyes. "I'm sorry I wasn't upfront with you, but I've also been burned before."

I scoff. "Of course. Make it about you."

"I'm not—"

"You used me! You exploited my feelings!"

"Show me one time I maliciously abused your trust." He comes back toward me, frustration vibrating in every inch of his body. "I didn't mean for Susan to read that scene—"

"I don't believe you." It takes every ounce of strength to

stand up to him, when he's so tall, glaring down at me with that hurt puppy dog look. I'm the injured party. I won't let him gaslight me.

Giving him my back, I find my clothes on the floor where they dropped last night and pull them on, stuff my shoes on my feet without socks, and snatch my purse from beside the door.

"Where are you going, Cinderella?"

"Away from you. I deserve to be with someone who respects me."

"I do!" he shouts, pacing away to the window and back again. "I do. I respect the hell out of you, Celeste. Don't do this. Don't run away from what we have. I was scared, all right? I'm sorry. I like you, so much, and I couldn't bear the thought of you looking at me differently if I told you—"

"Me?"

"You called them trashy books, okay? Writing is like spilling my guts all over the blank page for the whole world to see—and getting rejected for what I write is eviscerating. It's hard to get bad reviews, but they're just one stranger's opinion. I care about your opinion, okay? You matter to me. I care so much I was too afraid to tell you."

His loud voice, his emotional energy—it's all putting my nervous system in freeze or flight. I have to get out of here. I know he's nothing like Brett, but a lifetime of hypervigilance has taught my body to treat any conflict like an exploding bomb —I have to get out.

His eyes are red as he watches me from across the room, arms folded and muscles bunched with tension. "You won't even stay to fight for us?"

"I have to go."

The noise he makes is cold, a bite to it, like the wind off a glacier.

I shake my head. I'm doing the right thing by standing up for myself. I won't be gullible for pretty lies. I can't.

"I've seen you fight for what's important to you, Celeste.

You fought when Marissa got injured and you set out to kick Warren's ass. You fought to get your house ready and on the market despite setbacks. Despite bullying from your ex. I know I did wrong but fight with me. Yell at me. Don't just abandon what we have when the going gets rough. You're strong enough to work through this with me. We're both scared."

"I can't."

He chokes out a laugh, steps back and sweeps an arm toward the front door. "Fine. Don't let me keep you from the ball."

A sharp pain clenches in my left breast. My hands are shaking so hard, it takes me three tries to unlock the door and open it.

I don't look back.

37

HAYDEN

BLINDING DISAPPOINTMENT HOLDS MY TONGUE. I think I'm going to throw up. I'm eighteen again, and mom is too sick to work, and dad walks out because he can't handle the stress. The girls are all out of the house, and I'm technically an adult, so he's done his time. He's going to take his midlife crisis and ride off into the sunset. I'm not enough for him to stay.

I'm twenty-three again and desperate to show Gramps the book I wrote about him to show off how all those years of dreaming and DnD have turned into my dream career, only to have Gramps spit on my accomplishment because it wasn't highbrow enough.

I'm twenty-five again and gutted as my girlfriend's video exposing my romance writing to the world goes viral. The trolls online didn't bother to even read my book—they ripped the story and my personal character apart with no compunction. Unsurprisingly, Jordyn left too.

Now, I'm twenty-nine, and Celeste doesn't even give me the benefit of the doubt. She's got her own misplaced stereotypes about me, and she's not interested in hearing my side of the story.

Lying to her? I told her I was a writer; I just didn't say what type. Sure, I've been pouring this newfound passion into my characters' interactions, but all fiction is inspired by real life. Love is universal. I never tried to manipulate her or talk down to her. Why is she looking for ways to compare me to that ass of an ex-husband?

Yes, it was shitty for the Sea Lion Lodge to change their rules for the new court they built, but they reserve the right in the fine print. I suspected Warren would get involved when he was being so hostile to Celeste, which is why I tried to come up with a backup plan. Did I tell Celeste about it? No. I wanted to fix it for her without adding more stress to her plate.

I wanted to be loved for me for once. She's just proved my fears were valid. She got the full scoop and ran out of there like her tail was on fire.

I rake my hands through my hair and swear loudly. I kick a chair, bruise my toe, and realize that the whole he-man thing was always a stupid way of blowing off steam, so even though I already went for a run, I lace up my sneakers and head out.

Running for miles along the shoreline puts the burn in my body and clears my head. The sting of salt air in my eyes only makes me tear up a little.

I'm tired of chasing her. Why am I so easy to leave? I'm done pining after someone who is too afraid to meet me halfway. Celeste won't take the risk, and I can't keep waiting for her to up and disappear when things get tough.

The barking of the sea lions that have taken over the docks down at the marina sounds too much like harsh laughter.

Later, when I'm spent and shaking from miles of asphalt, I drag myself out to Priest's brewery and pull myself onto a bar stool. Priest and I overlapped on the Salmon Bay High track team when coach first took me under his wing, and since we've both stuck around town, we've become better friends.

"'sup, Hayden?" he fist-bumps and leans against the polished mahogany bar. "Don't usually see you this early."

"Rough night," I say. "Gimme your booziest beer, please."

Priest is a big guy. He's got the whole lumberjack vibe going with his uniform of flannel shirts over his six-foot seven frame, big bushy beard and blond manbun. He leans into the muscled, grizzly bear act to keep customers and rowdy tourists in line, and the Sea Lion Lodge is always trying to get him to join their Viking Marauders, if only because he's terrifying. He's not known for his warm, fuzzy personality, and he doesn't hesitate to tell it like he sees it, especially right now, at eleven am on a Monday morning.

"No."

I grip the edge of the bar. "No?"

"No."

"Is this a drinking establishment or not?"

"Not for you."

"What the hell, man?"

Priest shakes his head and turns his back to me. He grabs a pint glass and fills it with water from the sink, then sets it down firmly in front of me. "That'll be five cents."

"For water?"

"For psychiatric help. The doctor is in." He points to the Peanuts cartoon taped to the mirror behind the bar, where Lucy gives Charlie life advice, then crosses his arms and levels his full growly bear glare at me.

"If I wanted psychiatric help, I'd ask Kirsten."

"If you need a sex therapist, I doubt you'd ask your sister."

I thin my lips. Most people don't know Kirsten's specialty. But he's got a point. I chug half the glass of water.

"Better?" Priest asks.

"Yeah."

"So what's wrong? Town's all a-buzz about your big win. Problems in paradise already?"

I study the paintings behind the bar. His sister Liv makes them, and she's quite talented, but she came home from art school in New York with a baby and no degree. I doubt even Priest has pried the story from her lips, even though he takes the whole town's confessions. That could have been me—well, not the baby, but giving up on my dream—if I'd let my dad or gramps or my ex and her online followers' opinion get to me. And then what? Would I be as jaded as Celeste after twenty years of doing what other people told me to do? Of living the life someone else envisioned for me, would I be too afraid to take a risk on something that felt so right?

Bottoms up, I drink the rest of the water and set it down on the counter. "Do you read fiction, Priest?"

He grunts. "Birdie is partial to books about dragons eating tacos. Read that one 'bout a thousand times."

My fingers turn white on the bar. "What about love stories?"

"Like Titanic?"

"With a happy ending."

"I always thought Rose coulda scooted over and made room for Jack on that door."

"Yeah?"

"Yeah. Would a been a better movie." Priest's lips curve. "Life's sad enough without killing off the good guys."

I wonder if Celeste would move over to make room on the door for me. Seems like the answer is no.

38

CELESTE

LIFE GOES ON. The sun still rises, and I'm still here. I still get up, get dressed, drink my tiny cup of instant coffee, even though it tastes like the muck dragged home on the bottom of my kid's cleats after a soccer game. I miss the fancy coffee maker at Hayden's. I miss his weird plant collection, even Seymour. I miss his soft mattress and the rain forest smell of his room. I even miss his sweaty post-workout tee-shirts and the cloud of Old Spice.

If I thought Frida would start mothering me over the puffy eyes and tear tracks down my face, I would have been wrong. She takes one look at me and pulls out a cigarette, even in full view of her daughter-in-law, who's standing on the porch with her hands on her hips and a mouth pinched like a schoolmarm.

Frida lets me stew in my pity party while we drive in silence over the bridge. The Olympic mountains are beautifully lit up today behind the iconic Salmon Bay railroad trestle. Half the boats in Fisherman's Terminal are out at sea already.

When we finally pull up in front of the next retirement home, Frida is watching me out of the corner of her eye as my nose runs like a toddler's in the winter. I'm ugly crying, silently, like I used to do when I was married. No one can hear my anguish. But no one is here to judge me for it either, no one but Frida, and she's not big on caring what other people think.

I feel like I'm right back where I started, living with a big bruise where my heart should be. Terrified of stepping out of my safe little closet. He's nothing like Brett. I know that. But reading about our sex life—having some stranger read about it—made me feel so exposed and vulnerable. Why wouldn't he tell me he's a romance writer? Why didn't he trust me with his secrets? He seemed so genuine and open with me, but he abused my trust.

"Are we going in?" Frida asks.

"Just a minute." I grab a tissue out of the door pocket and blow my nose. What a mess. I should have called in sick today.

"You have a little..." Frida motions to the corner of her lip to indicate I've got something on my face, and I quickly try to dab it. "A little heartbreak hanging right dere. Wipe that shit off and get moving."

I stop trying to rub nonexistent smut off my mouth and stare at her. Here I thought we were friends.

"Don't look at me like that, *lille en*. You are showing your weakness. Da wolves will come circling."

"Sorry to disappoint."

She tries to say something, but her lungs squeeze like a punctured tire, and she starts hacking. It works to break me out of my misery. I grab her a tissue and a bottle of water that I keep in a cooler in the backseat for clients. She keeps coughing, until I'm pumped full of adrenaline and all out of tears. Should I take her to the hospital? Call 911? Do I remember CPR? What do I do?

The thought of Frida dying is enough to snap me out of my pity party. She's right. I can't give up while I've got my health. I've got this body, soft and worn in like a favorite tee, but all my parts are in working order, not shiny, but reliable. Strong.

Frida's lungs clear, and she wipes the tears from her wrinkled eyes. "Cheesecake?"

"Huh?" I wipe my eyes again and try to get a grip. "Are you okay? Should I take you to Urgent Care? I don't think we can go to—"

"Pssssst!" She waves my concern away. "I'm fine."

"But you were coughing—"

"Dats noting. Now. Are we eating cheesecake?"

I take a deep breath in through my nose and let it out through my teeth. "This place is known for gelato, I think."

She tuts. "Start de car."

I've got no idea what her plan is, but her head is lying back on the headrest, her eyes closed. She doesn't look like she's up for touring a retirement home today, and frankly, I'm not either. I start the car, my heart rate still high. "Are you sure I shouldn't take you to the hospital?"

"Fook no. We're going to de brewery."

"I don't think that's—"

"I might die. You wouldn't refuse a dying woman's last request, would you?"

Probably should refuse, but I'm feeling reckless today. The itch to flee crawls beneath my skin. I want to be in one of those sail boats leaving the harbor. Following the wind westward. Leaving the safety of the shallows, of the marina and protective breakwaters, I follow her directions and drive us back into the heart of downtown Salmon Bay, to Station no 18.

When I pull into a parking spot, Frida finally cracks an eyelid open and confirms that I followed her "last request".

"Good girl," she says, and hops out of the car with a spring in her step that belies her age.

I shouldn't be doing this. With my heart sinking, I follow her in. It's early, but there are always patrons at the town's best loved brew joint. Priest stands behind the bar cutting limes.

Frida climbs onto a barstool and smacks her hands down on the bar. "Dis is de place, *ja*? Two lagers, *tack*."

More cautiously, I sit next to her and study the chalkboard behind Priest's head. He gives us a nod, but he's about as emotional as the brick wall behind him. "Do you have anything non-alcoholic?" I ask.

"No," Frida inhales. "We are nursing your broken heart, not feeding babies."

"I don't drink," I tell her.

Her face says it all, but Priest hands her a beer, then fills a pint glass with a fuzzy amber drink and sets it in front of me.

"Your usual," he grumbles, low.

I thank him. When he shuffles off to wait on some other table, Frida pounces. She drags the whole story out of me, though I keep Hayden's secret, and honestly, I feel like the little kid with his finger in the dike. She pulls one brick, and it all comes flowing out. Hayden and his secrets. Brett and his demands. My trust issues. My insecurities. How can I tell if someone is lying to me when I've spent the last twenty years being gaslit and manipulated? Living in fear of getting in trouble? Fawning to stay safe?

Frida listens to it all and snorts. Not sure what I was expecting, but a little sympathy? Compassion maybe? She studies me with those weathered grey eyes and tsks. "So, kiss and tell. You are embarrassed."

"That's not... well, yes. I know it's a little thing for you, but—"

She makes a rude noise in the back of her throat. "I heard a lot of 'poor me.' And I say, '*Det bästa stället att hitta en hjälpande hand är i slutet av din egen arm.*'"

"What does that mean?"

"De best place to find a helping hand is at the end of your arm. You have trouble trusting. He has trouble trusting. You have been hurt. He has been hurt. Who hasn't? We are all ugly little salmon trying to find our way back to de stream we came from, only to fuck and die. You know what is sad? Losing out on precious time because you can't get your head out of your ass."

I want to tell her Hayden's secret, but I can't. I'm not

vindictive. I don't want to hurt him. I bite my lip and let the sting of pain ground me. I guess I could have gone to Marissa if I wanted someone to rub my back. She'd have sided with me even if I claimed the world was flat. Frida is not afraid to call me on my bullshit.

"You know why I was eager to give my heart to that charlatan? I'm not lonely and senile like my son and his good-for-noting wife believe. Nej. I gave him my time because he filled it with joy."

"The guy who scammed you? Don't you regret that?"

She shakes her head as she studies the bottom of her glass. "Regret, *lille en*, is de albatross we choose to wear around our necks. We can take off dat damned bird any time we want. We can never buy more time. Tings are replaceable. Joy is de nectar of the gods, *ja*? Dat man waltzed into my life and lit up my world for de months we were together. When he waltzed back out of it, he took the money, but he can't take away de joy. Dat belongs to me."

"Shouldn't we learn from our mistakes? Work hard to not repeat the same patterns?"

"Pfft. We live with our choices. Life is full of hellos and goodbyes." She finishes her beer and raps her knuckles on the table for Priest to serve her another. The big bartender ambles over, and I drop my gaze because I don't want to see pity on his face.

"Ginger beer not to your liking?" he asks. His deep baritone and giant frame have always intimidated me.

I clear my throat. "I haven't even tasted it yet." I take a big sip and my eyes water at the strength of it. I manage to swallow and start coughing.

"Dat'll put hair on your chest," Frida cackles.

"Liv says it's good for what ails you," he says quietly. "But I think a good sleep and a good conversation iron out most things." He points to the cartoon taped to the mirror behind the bar. "That'll be five cents."

I can't help a watery chuckle. It reminds me so much of Hayden, how he'd always use humor to put me at ease. I miss him already.

Priest walks away and Frida puts a heavy hand on my shoulder. "De biggest regret of my life was walking away from de..." she pauses, "person who lit up my life like de *Norrsken*, de nort'ern lights."

"The man who—"

"*Nej, lille en. Nej.* Long ago, when I was young and dumb and still too caring of what my family tought. Long ago I met a beautiful soul who made de sun come out from behind de clouds. I said tings I regret. I left."

"Hayden's been lying to me. That's a red flag—"

Frida grasps my arm, her bony fingers digging into my soft bicep. "I left the best ting to ever happen to me, because I was afraid." She leans into me, her voice filled with urgency.

"But lying, Frida. My ex-husband led me on all the time, telling me whatever he wanted to manipulate me. I can't get involved with someone who would do that."

"And did dis boy lie to you to manipulate you? Or was he protecting his feelings? Have you been upfront with him airing all your dirty laundry, *ja*? Have you stripped yourself bare to show your heart too?"

I bite my lip. I guess she has a point.

"You are afraid. But you have to understand his motivation. We all lie—to protect our tender hearts, to protect our egos, to protect our family from hurt. We lie to ourselves most of all."

"I am afraid. I'm afraid of falling for someone who will gaslight me. Someone who won't be honest with me, and I won't know until it's too late to untangle myself. What if I fall for him and he hurts me?"

"It is too late, *lille en*." She sits back and downs the rest of her beer. She stares at herself in the mirror behind the bar, and her eyes are suspiciously glassy. "You see dat old woman dere?

She is a liar. A fraud. She hurt de ones closest to her. You tink she is deserving of forgiveness?"

This time I'm the one reaching out to take her hand. "Of course, Frida."

Frida swallows. "I had love once. She was the light of my life. She was worth risking everything for, but I let fear win. Now, I would give up everything for one more day with her."

39

HAYDEN

It's been a long week of sulking, and I can't outrun this churning in my gut. I got the right manuscript—without the closet scene, much to my editor's disappointment—sent off. I turned in another crossword and it comes across only slightly angry and disillusioned—okay, I lied. The theme is, "Thus with a kiss I die," and the answers are full of the worst love stories of all time. Doomed relationships and unrequited passions from Shakespeare to Hollywood. I pulled in Helen and Paris, Juliet and Romeo, Jacob and Bella, Jack and Rose. The secret message cost me a night of rumination, because what should I say?

Better to have loved and lost than never loved at all? No.

Love all, trust few? Better.

Please, Celeste, I'm sorry I wasn't ready to tell you all my secrets, but please give me another chance? Almost made it in, but self-preservation won out.

Even Henrí was hesitant to publish it in case customers swarmed the shop asking what was wrong. I pointed out a swarm of customers would be good for business, and he relented.

Mama Leah was another story. She made me eat my weight in lentil soup and spill all my problems.

But I'm still frustrated. This is the first time I've been back to the pickleball court since the tournament. I couldn't bring myself to face the ghost of Celeste in those cute short tennis skirts and her sugar-sweet smile.

The pickleball cracks against the pavement, and I swear. My nerves feel raw, exposed. She knows my secrets and rejected me —what happens if I come out to everyone, and then I can't go out in public without whispers following me around? The grocery store, the gym, the pickleball court—will I have to leave town? My whole life is here, and it feels like shitting where I sleep to let so much of myself be up for public consumption. I'm a long way from that fat awkward kid in middle and high school, but bullying leaves a mark.

Russell runs his tongue over his teeth but doesn't chide me for my swearing. He takes another ball out of his pocket and serves. I return it with all the force of my anger at myself. I got so twisted up over a woman, I forgot to protect my heart.

The court is full of fair-weather pickleballers, and I kind of hate that the sport I love has gotten so popular. When I break another ball, Russell holds up his hands and says he's done.

"Who pissed in your coffee this morning?" he asks as I pick up the cracked ball and toss it in the ball-waste bin. "Wanna talk about it?"

"Not really."

"This have anything to do with a girl?"

"She rejected me. Is that what you want to hear? She found out I write romance, and she freaked and left."

Russell gives me a long flat look that would make his dog proud.

"Fine." I run my hands through my hair. Sweat drips down my neck, but the adrenaline coursing through me feels like I've just downed five shots of espresso. "She found a scene I wrote back when I thought I'd never see her again, and she thought I'd published our dirty laundry."

"Did you?"

"No!"

"Then what's the problem?"

"She says I'm lying to her and broke her trust."

"Well? Did you? Or did you evade and give her the same packaged answer you give most people about your career?"

"I was going to tell her!"

"Ah."

We both put our paddles in a stack and lean against the chain link fence to wait our turn. Some might say it's a beautiful day for some ball, but I feel like thunderclouds are following directly over my head.

"So," Russell says. "Might not be the writing but the lying that she finds fault with."

"Maybe. But it's not like she gave me the benefit of the doubt. She read the scene I'd written and ran out of there like she discovered I'm a serial killer. Like, doesn't she know me better after all these weeks? Have I raised any red flags? Have I ever treated her like her ex did?"

"I dunno. Did you?"

"No. I mean, he tore down her self-esteem and lied to her all the time. I'm nothing like him."

"But you did lie to her."

"By omission."

"Maybe you can grovel and ask for another chance. Come clean and try again."

I cross my arms over my chest. "Why should I ask for forgiveness? I didn't do anything."

"Sometimes it's not about being right. You've got to meet her in the middle, and she's human and scared. You're human and scared. That's real life, Hayden, not a book. You can't write her dialogue for her and push her around like a character. Real life is messy, and it doesn't have a happy ending—we're all dying slowly, every day. The question is, what are you going to do while you're still alive? Let the girl get away? Keep protecting yourself so hard you never let anyone get close?"

"I don't do that. I've got lots of friends."

"Kid, you keep making jokes to deflect away from yourself. How many of these people actually know the real you?"

"That's cold, Russ."

He nods to the court in front of us, where a couple of brand newbies are fumbling around with the ball. "It's easy to be warm and welcoming when you approach from a place of experience. You'd walk right up and befriend those guys. Put them at ease. Get their life story. It's easy to make them feel easy, because you're confident in your skills. But what about when you're approaching something new? When you're coming from a place of vulnerability? Can you open up to that girl and trust her with the parts of you that aren't practiced and shiny? The dark parts? The broken pieces?"

"You know what happened with Jordyn almost ended my career."

"Sure. That's why I stay off social media. Relationships aren't about two perfect people finding perfect bliss every day. They're messy. Complicated. You've got to wake up every day and choose to be with that messy, imperfect person, over and over, day after day. Some days you aren't going to want to. You're not going to feel like doing the work. You got to do it anyway. Choose to stay together despite the world trying to rip you apart. Sure, maybe that means sometimes groveling when you didn't do anything wrong. The little things aren't worth bitching about. You're trying to win the long game."

"Did you win the long game, Russ?"

"I tried my damnedest. Sometimes that's not enough." He shrugs. "If I had another chance, I wouldn't waste it breaking pickleballs with you."

I consider Russell. He and his wife divorced before I was born, and I guess I never pictured him pining for anyone. I never asked.

He turns toward me and grips my shoulder. "Time heals all

wounds, kiddo, but time is in short supply. Don't wait too long." He pats me and strides off to check on Russell Junior.

My feelings push tightly against my chest. The chickadees are singing. The squirrels chitter at each other from tree to tree. The happy squeals of children fly from the nearby playground. The warm summer day isn't humid yet, but a perfect seventy-five degrees. By all accounts, this should be a perfect day, but without Celeste, the black hole inside me won't let me enjoy it.

Jordyn really did a number on me, piling on pre-existing scars. But if I really thought it would work out with Celeste, I should have given her the benefit of the doubt, right? It never feels like the right time for sharing my deepest insecurities. I thought I loved her, but I didn't trust her with my truth.

40

CELESTE

"Thanks for being here, sweet peas." Brody and Ryder set the fruit and cookie plates down on the counter and step back. I follow their gazes around the kitchen, taking in the new bright white cabinets and cork floor. I wipe my sweaty hands on my black slacks.

"It looks great, mom," Ryder says. "You have nothing to worry about."

"Just nervous for my first listing," I tell him. Being strong in front of my kids is so ingrained, I can almost pretend I'm not nauseated with the thought of talking to a parade of strangers today. Maybe no one will show?

"Mom, where's Hayden?" Brody asks.

I rub a speck of dust off the counter.

"Mom?"

"He's not coming."

"Why? I thought he was cool," Ryder says. "He helped with all this. Why wouldn't he show up for your big day?"

I cross my arms. "We didn't work out."

Brody and Ryder exchange a look, that secret communication of close siblings. Does Hayden have that with his sisters? I'm so glad my boys have that bond, but it's slightly annoying when they use it to talk about me.

"What happened? He seemed to really like you, mom." Brody nudges me with his shoulder.

"I'm not really in a relationship place right now, boys."

"That's stupid, mom. You don't get to choose when the universe drops a good thing in your lap."

"Yeah," Ryder piles on. "You always told us to trust our gut. Have you talked it out? I thought he made you happy. You seemed more relaxed. You smiled and shi-stuff."

"You can do it all on your own," Brody says, "but that doesn't mean you have to. You deserve nice things."

"Did he hurt you? Because if he did, I'll—" Ryder raises his fists.

I quickly cover them with my palms, horrified that he would even think Hayden could do something that bad. "Ryder! No. I'm a big girl. You don't have to worry about me."

"But we do, mom. We want you to be happy, and you seemed good together."

"Don't throw away a good thing because you think you don't deserve it." Brody hugs me from the side, and I lean into him. My sweet baby.

"I'm fine, sweethearts. I'm good." I'm lying but I don't have the energy for this right now. "The open house is about to start."

"Love you, mom." Brody kisses the top of my head, just like I used to do to him a lifetime ago. When did he get so tall? My eyes start to feel itchy; too many big emotions all at once.

If Hayden were here, he would have cracked a joke to get me out of my head. Thinking of him now just makes my chest ache.

"Celeste!" Marissa limps in the front door, somehow still looking like a real estate queen despite the walking boot, and I feel my shoulders ease a hair.

I've been helping her at open houses, even though my shyness has been a hurdle to overcome. This shouldn't feel so terrifying but being in charge and having people look at this giant project that I designed and managed myself makes me feel exposed. Will they like the light green I painted the dining room? Will they approve of the sputnik chandelier or the modern globe sconces in the living room? I kept the midcentury vibe but updated everything I could for modern families.

Should I have kept the bubblegum pink bathroom with the tub right beneath the window looking out on the street? Because someone, somewhere, might have a secret Barbie fetish and have fallen in love with that bathroom I've hated, and I screwed it up by tearing everything out and putting in subdued white subway tile and grey quartz counters.

"Relax," Marissa says as she hobbles into the kitchen. She's paired a sunny yellow blouse and slacks with her walking boot. Her hair is in some fancy updo that takes her five minutes but would probably take me an hour. "The house looks great. If I didn't know better, I'd say this house was flipped by a professional designer."

"Yeah, mom," Brody says as he hugs me from behind and rests his chin on the top of my head. "This place is sick. You should have gone to architecture school or something."

Ryder swats him on the back of the head, and Brody lets go to wrestle his brother. They may be taller than me, but they still remind me of baby buffalos most days. At least now I don't hear any tattling or complaining. Brody gets Ryder in a headlock as Ryder squeezes him around the waist.

"Boys, you mess up your mother's hard work and you'll be spending the rest of your summer break scoping sewer pipe for me," Marissa tells them.

I laugh at their affronted squawks. Having them here means so much to me. I tour the house one last time before the open house starts and try to see it all through a stranger's eyes, instead of through my perfectionism. It does look nice. Every room is painted and staged. Every broken electrical outlet and switch cover has been replaced. Every ding in the drywall has been patched. Every scrape on the old oak floor has been buffed and waxed until it shines.

I would never have been able to get this all done without Hayden setting up that work party. Until then, I thought I was all alone. He showed up without me asking. He pitched in because he knew I needed it. He gathered the community behind me that I'd been too blind to acknowledge having. He might not have given me all his secrets, x-rays and medical records, favorite colors and flavors, but we've only known each other for a few months. It's felt like much longer. We clicked, and that scared me most of all. How can I trust my intuition? It felt too good to be true, and he's right, I've been waiting for a sign, any sign, to end it and run away.

Not because Hayden is waving any red flags, but because I'm scared out of my mind. I've fallen for him so fast and so hard, and I'm terrified he'll realize what a mess I am and back out. What happens when he gets bored of me? What happens when he decides I'm not enough?

Brett and I were in love, until we weren't. I was scared to leave, even though I knew it was the right thing to do. This time I'm scared to stay.

Neighbors start showing up at the house as soon as visiting hours open. It's always the people who live right next door or across the street, curiosity driving them to finally see inside and what we've done with the place. I know them all. They're not looking to buy; they want all the gossip, but that gossip will spread across town and hopefully someone actually in the market for a new home will hear and come on by.

The rooms quickly fill up in a way they never did when we lived here, neighbors laughing and catching up. Admiring the upgrades, they point out similar floor plans and how they could use some of my changes to spruce up their own houses. Brody and Ryder head out when it gets too crowded, each giving me a squeeze on their way out the door.

Once I get chatting, it's surprisingly easy to keep the

conversation going. I'm not selling so much as answering questions about the house's history and my design choices. My creative project is a success, and it's not difficult to relax when the compliments keep coming.

The open house is supposed to close at four, but the block party keeps jamming until the last person leaves at five. My feet ache. My cheeks hurt from smiling so much. My head is fuzzy from nonstop being "on." All I can think about is how nice it would be to go back to Hayden's place with the crisp sea breeze, the plants crowding every windowsill, and the moonlight streaming through. Most of all, how nice it would be to let him wrap his arms around me and just be. No talking, but we wouldn't need to. I don't have to talk for Hayden to understand me. He's so easy to be with.

He feels safe, at least he did until I read what he'd written about us.

A little part of me hoped I would see him at this open house, but it would be awkward, wouldn't it? None of his sisters came either. I must be on the shit list, and I can't even blame them. I keep running from him and returning. Fleeing. Crawling back. I'm the one who's giving him whiplash.

I'm the one being like Brett—keeping Hayden on his toes wondering what my true feelings and intentions are. I don't even know.

"Great job today," Marissa says with a side hug. She's pulled herself off the couch where she's been sitting with her boot up. Anytime someone comes to her with questions, she directs them to "the woman in charge." That'd be me. After three plus hours, it isn't quite as scary.

"Thanks." I take a deep breath and give her a crooked smile. "Hopefully someone wants it enough to bid." Tuesday is the bid deadline, which is a tight turnaround, but pretty typical in this market. Salmon Bay is close enough to Seattle to be a bedroom community, and the new ferry connecting the downtown core means that our real estate prices have skyrocketed. Goodbye sleepy little fishing village.

"I've had at least five agents indicate intent to bid." Marissa hands me a small stack of business cards. "You did an amazing job on the house. You should be so proud of yourself."

"Thanks, Rissa. It was stressful, but I enjoyed parts of the design process. I liked being my own boss and bringing my ideas to life."

"Babe, you project-managed the shit out of this one."

Two months ago I would have laughed in her face at the thought of me being in charge of a company. Me, managing a team of people. Brett had worn me down so much I didn't even realize how I was still making myself small to fit the box he put me in.

Hayden saw past that. He inspired me to get outside my comfort zone, and he was right—winning that tournament gave me a shot of self-confidence that I hadn't realized how much I needed. "Have you thought anymore about my idea?"

"You mean expanding the home renovation side? Of course I have. I'd miss you working with me, but I'm not going to hold you back from doing something that puts that light in your eyes. You're more alive talking about your design ideas for this project than I've ever seen you talk about another house. You can't fake that passion."

"So that's a yes?"

"Hell yes."

I start cleaning up with a big smile on my face, tossing the empty cups and napkins, and straightening the throw pillows. "I want to help clients like Frida stay in their homes longer, if that's what they want, or to fix up their homes to sell for the best value. I'd feel like I was making a difference, you know?"

Marissa puts a hand on my shoulder to stop me with my mad cleaning. "Girl, you're going to rock this new role. I'm so proud of the growth you've shown, really taking the bull by the horns. Even in the last three months, you've come out of your shell. I hope that whatever that boy did to get on your bad side, there's room for him to grovel his way back into your good graces. You seemed happy together."

I nod. I don't have words for all my complicated thoughts. This week has been good for me to see how much I've been missing without Hayden in my life. He saw me. He sees me. He's not perfect, but neither am I.

Marissa ruffles my hair. "My little do-gooder. You could provide low-cost, no-bullshit home repairs for people on fixed incomes. Bet all your networking on the court would translate to a big client base."

"About that, the Sea Lion Lodge reneged on the court prize. They announced it's only for pickleball."

"Fuckers." Marissa scowls, then grins. "Good thing you like pickleball."

"You're not mad?"

"Babe, I was game to play tennis with you, still am, but we can always make a reservation at a less busy time and not let anyone bully us off the court. Until Dr. Fisher changes the rules so that the Parks and Rec courts can only be used for pickleball, we can still use them for tennis."

My shoulders relax. I didn't realize how nervous I was to tell Marissa that we wouldn't have the exclusive tennis court we planned for. Is this the same reservation Hayden had about telling me the news? I guess so. I might have been too hasty to yell at him...it's just that there have been multiple instances where he wasn't completely truthful with me. Relationships have to be built on trust.

"Or we could just play pickleball," Marissa suggests. "Drew's game, as long as it isn't against that asshole who maimed me."

"We can do both." I imagine playing doubles with Marissa and Drew, and me and Hayden. It's happy. Joyful. The kind of life I want to reach out with both hands and grab hold of.

We both hear the chimes as the front door opens, and I have

a moment to think how much I don't miss the squeak of the hinges anymore, before someone is stomping through.

"I'm so sorry," I call out as I make my way out of the kitchen to the entryway, "but the open house is—" I break off when I see it's Brett.

"Celeste," he says. His eyes are a little bloodshot.

I tense. A couple months ago, I would have bent over backward to appease the charging moose. But I don't have to be that woman anymore. I deserve better. Owning the space, I plant my feet and lift my chin. "The open house is closed, Brett. Please leave."

"You talked to Lander?"

"No...?"

"She said she left you a message. Made you an offer. Coulda avoided this whole waste of time, but you are so stubborn."

"Excuse me?" I pull out my phone to check my messages, and there is one from an unknown number from a few days ago. I check the transcript. Sure enough, it's Lander saying she'll take the house. "You can't take the house, Brett. I've worked my butt off fixing it up."

"If only you had done all this shit when we actually lived here, we could have had something nice instead of a dump. Isn't that your job? Taking care of the house? I never realized it could look so good."

I tighten my fists against my thighs. "You always said no when I brought up fixing things. You didn't want to spend the money."

"Where'd you get the money for this now? Huh? You don't think I believe you paid for this stuff yourself? Did that rich boy take the washed-up MILF as his little project and funnel you some funds to keep you busy?"

"Stop. You don't get to storm in here and insult me or make demands."

"I still own half—"

"No. You don't. The contract gave me control for eighteen

months to make improvements and sell it, and I'll still give you your half minus the investments and my real estate commission."

He steps closer, using his bulk to intimidate me like he always has. "That wasn't the agreement."

"You are free to read the fine print. You can still read, can't you? Or are your aging eyes giving you trouble?"

His eyes widen.

"Now if you've changed your mind on this 'shit hole'"—I air quote— "then you and Lander are free to put in an offer Tuesday by eight pm along with everyone else. Marissa will strike the names so that I can evaluate the best offer without any bias, if you don't trust me to give your offer equal merit."

He snorts and puts his hands on his hips, ready to lash into me again.

"Now I have the right to not get harassed in my place of work. If you have anything else to say to me, you can pass along the message through my lawyer. This has to stop. Now."

"What do you—"

"No, Brett." I hold firm, though my whole body is shaking with the effort. "You are not going to push me around anymore. I don't have to listen to your verbal abuse. I will call the cops."

"I bet Ryder and Brody will have something to say about that—"

"Our sons are not part of this. I'm done hiding behind what's best for them. They're grown men. They will understand. Or they won't. But it doesn't matter. I matter, my feelings and safety matter. You will talk to me civilly or not at all. For now, talk to the lawyer. You want the house? Make a good offer. There's no loyalty discount."

He scoffs, but I turn and make a strategic retreat to the kitchen. "You can't do this to me, Celeste. Lander wants this house. I'm going to give it to her."

"Talk to my lawyer."

Marissa claps me on the shoulder as I pass her into the

kitchen, and she blocks Brett from following me. Hobbling, she ushers my gaping ex-husband to the front door. She even hands him her business card, in case his agent wants to call and set up an appointment next time.

"What do I tell my wife?" he growls loudly as Marissa hurries him outside.

"Your wife, your problem." Marissa shuts the door firmly behind him.

I rest my head against the quartz counter and let it cool some of the angry flush in my face. Deep breath in, deep breath out. I can't believe I stood up to him. I can't believe I didn't melt beneath the fury of his gaze, like I have so many times before.

I want to tell Hayden. He'd understand how hard it was, and he'd be so proud of me. I want to sink into his embrace and be. He accepts me with all my failings and faults. I'm the one who didn't trust him enough. And Frida is right—I can't let my fear keep me trapped anymore. Not from letting Brett still rule my life. Not from accepting the hope of a new love with the man who makes me feel beautiful and respected.

Confidence has always been ephemeral to me, but over the last few months, I've found enough to stand up to my bully. I can take a leap of faith that Hayden wasn't lying out of malice, right? But how to ask for another chance? He's right—it isn't fair to him to constantly be chasing me and waiting for me to run again.

41

HAYDEN

MIEL BAGELS IS BUZZING with the usual Monday morning crowd. My sisters sit around me for our weekly breakfast hang, but I have no idea what they're talking about. I can't take my eyes off the beautiful woman in the corner who is hunched over her laptop with her lip caught between her teeth. Her hair is pulled back in a tight ponytail, but a few curls have escaped to dance playfully around her face. There's a crease between her brows as she concentrates on the screen, and I want to kiss it away. Does she look more tired than usual? Has she been lying awake thinking about me like I've been thinking about her?

Someone kicks my chair, and I jolt.

"Earth to Captain Obvious," Sam snarks.

Addy nudges me in the side, and I scowl at her. "You should probably close your mouth and wipe that drool off your lip, bro."

"Try talking to her?" Kirsten is always the voice of reason, but I can't.

"Yeah, little bro. Staring is just creepy." Addy takes a sip of her latte, and I use that moment to elbow her back, making her splutter. She gives me the evil eye, but I'm immune.

"Celeste voted with her feet," I tell the peanut gallery. "I can't sit around waiting for someone to reject me over and over."

"Don't you think she's as scared as you are?" Kirsten asks in her best therapist voice. She leans on the table toward me. "Relationships take—"

"Yeah, yeah. Save your lecture. We've all got it memorized."

Her pout lets me know she doesn't appreciate being cut off, but I'm not in the mood for them all to pile on. Feels like I'd never seen her in Salmon Bay until a few months ago, and now I see her everywhere. The grocery store. The coffee shop. The library. She's a phantom I can't escape. Seeing her rips the band aid off every time.

"You need to blow off some anger. Try a real sport, like Derby," Addy starts.

"Weightlifting," Sam says.

Molly removes my hand from where I've been griping the table and squeezes it. "We love you exactly as you are, baby brother. I wish you'd let everyone else see the creative, sensitive soul you are inside. Everyone else would love you as much as we do."

"And anyone who doesn't can fuck right off." Addy flexes her bicep right in my face to show me how a roller derby girl solves her problems. Maybe if dad had been a bit less gender biased, he could have embraced his youngest daughter's violent streak. The mean little thing would have made a great tackle.

I watch as Henrí brings a mug over to Celeste's table, pulls out a chair, and sits down opposite her. The smile that lights up her face on seeing him sends a stab of pain through my gut. She used to gift that smile to me.

"Wow, growling," Sam says. "I never thought you had it in you."

Addy throws her arm around my shoulders. "You want me to beat him up for you? I could take him."

"Addy, he's six five and weighs two fifty. He could take you down with his pinkie."

"I may be little, but I'm fierce."

"Saucy tickle-brained squarer."

"Lily-liver'd boy."

"Canker-blossom."

"Hey, you wanna be a giddy goose and let your best friend sweep in and steal your girl out from under you, be my guest." Letting me go, Addy sits back in her chair and crosses her arms, satisfied that she got the last word.

She's not wrong, as much as it pains me. I am being cowardly. I'm tired of putting myself out there and not being enough.

I think Kirsten is going to step in to soothe things over, but she surprises all of us by laying down the gauntlet. "I bet you a batch of white chocolate chip macadamia nut cookies that you can't go over there and find out what they're talking about."

We all stare at my least drama-prone sister, before moving our collective gaze to the table where Henrí and Celeste have their heads together. Addy might not be able to take him, but maybe if we teamed up together? Between Sam and Addy, they've got enough muscle to get a good hold on at least one limb.

"Even if we hadn't broken up, she's free to talk to whomever she wants." I just can't bear to watch her chat so easily with my best friend. My brain knows he's taken, but my heart is such a rotting piece of fruit that it can't help stuttering over the idea of the two of them together.

"You look like someone kicked your dog," Sam says. "Go over there and talk to her."

"Molly should do it," I say.

"What? Why me?" Molly squeaks.

The part of me that wants to see the world burn wants to mess with Henrí and tell Molly everything. If I'm gonna be miserable, everyone else should be too. But the hopeless romantic in me can't throw Henrí and his Olympic-sized torch under the proverbial bus. It's not his fault my love life caught fire like a western forest in the summer.

"To hell with it." I stand and adjust my sweatpants. "Kirsten, I want two batches. One Snickerdoodle."

"Done."

"And cardamom braid from the bakery."

"Don't push your luck."

"Fine." The first step feels like my sneaker is full of cement. The second is weighed down with rocks. The third, only gum stuck to the sole, holding me back. Finally I'm weaving between tables, until I can hear their conversation.

"You sure about this?" Henrí asks.

"Yes. I can't keep going on like this," Celeste tells him. "I have to make a stand. It's my life, you know? And I've been letting other people dictate it for far too long."

Something cold squeezes in my belly. I never pushed her to do something she wasn't comfortable with, did I? Sure, I nudged her out of her comfort zone. Took her in a closet at her ex's wedding, which I'm sure got back to her family and friends and kids. Convinced her to play pickleball instead of what she wanted, tennis. Was she going along with me to please me?

My hands fist at the idea that she didn't want any of what we had. Would I even know if she was faking it or really wanted it? I thought it was real, but if everything we felt was real, then why was it so easy for her to run from?

I'm not enough for her. She can't trust me. We both have our baggage. Giving up and ghosting is the easy way out. It's modern love's MO, and I get it now.

I thought Celeste was different.

I've been letting my imagination get away from me, like gramps always accused me of. Painting shapes in the clouds when everyone knows they're only water vapor.

I run my hands through my hair and tug at the roots, the pain grounding me in the present. At that moment, Celeste notices me. How could she not have seen me? Am I that insignificant to her? My whole body has been tracking her from the moment she walked in.

You draw me, you hard-hearted adamant.

Did she complete last week's crossword yet? Did she read between the lines and see the Shakespeare words for what they were—my pain, my frustration at being found lacking yet again? How can I call myself a writer when I need to use a dead man's words to express what I really feel?

Celeste slams her laptop closed. Her cheeks blaze red. What is she hiding?

Henrí leans back in his chair and the big dopey smile on his face says he's enjoying my discomfort way too much. "Dude. What's up?"

"Molly needs a top up on her coffee."

He stands up so fast the chair falls over. "*Merde.*" He fumbles getting the chair righted, then smooths his hair down self-consciously, staring over at my sister's table like the fool he is. "Be right back." His departure is so fast, he leaves a phantom plume of smoke in his wake.

I take his chair and sit. For a long moment, all I can do is stare at the face that launched a thousand beats of my heart. I feel like Menelaus pining for Helen across the Aegean. Word play is my jam, but my tongue is tied in gorgon knots.

"Hi, Hayden," she says softly.

Why did I come over here again? I should have told her sooner, but she rejected me just like I was afraid of. I just want to be close to my sunlight. Celeste. She's so beautiful. Staying away is too painful to bear.

When I don't say anything, she licks her lips. I follow the movement. "Let me guess, your sisters made a bet?"

"Yeah." She wants the truth? I'll give it to her, even if it makes the shadows veil her face and her eyes drop to her closed laptop.

"I see."

"Do you?"

She glances up, then shuts her eyes and shakes her head. "I'm trying to be brave, Hayden, but I've got so much to work through. Did you know I had my open house this weekend?"

"Yeah. How'd it go? I know you were nervous." I actually parked down the block and watched neighbor after neighbor trek in and out of her showpiece project. I couldn't show my face, of course, but I needed to know it was well attended. She deserves every success.

"It went well." She tucks a lock of hair behind her ear and glances up at me through her lashes. "I channeled you, and small talk came easy."

One side of my mouth lifts. "Charming, but shallow."

"No!" She grabs my hand from its grip on the table and squeezes it with both of hers. "No, Hayden. You are anything but shallow."

"The more you run when you see my messy middle, the less I trust that I can open up to you."

"I know. I know, and I'm sorry."

"I didn't lie to manipulate you. I wasn't going to publish those chapters. You can choose to believe me or not, but I can't keep putting myself out there and getting turned down. I don't want to always walk on eggshells thinking you're going to run when things get hard."

"Why didn't you tell me you write romance novels for a living? You made it seem like you write anything else."

I run my fingers through my hair and make myself tell her the truth. "We've both got trust issues. After my first book came out, my girlfriend at the time made a post that went viral about her boyfriend pretending to be a woman to write romance. People who'd never read the book started piling on. They said all sorts of bullshit—from not qualified to write authentic female characters because I don't have a vagina to glorifying World War II because the love story was between an American POW and a German nurse. The plot is based on a true story.

You've read it—is there anything in that book that in any way indicates support of Germany?"

She shakes her head. Her eyes are wide and glossy.

"Yeah, no. But I got actual death threats. My publisher canceled the sequel, even though the book was critically acclaimed. And for what? Fifteen minutes later, the mob was on to a new target, leaving my career and hopes and dreams in smoldering ruin. It took me years to dare to write romance again, but it's what I love. I'm good at it. Readers write me and tell me that my books got them through really hard times."

"I had no idea, Hayden. I'm so sorry."

"You know what? I'm not ashamed of my work, and I'm not ashamed of hiding my real life behind a pen name. A lot of people won't pick up a romance book written by a dude. I'd rather have my books out there spreading joy than fame and fortune."

"A little fortune might be nice. Think of all the pickleball courts you could resurface."

I laugh out a breath. "Think of all the dog rescues I could support."

Her smile is genuine but wobbly.

It takes every ounce of my self-control to not pull her into my arms right there, but she has to make the choice. I can't make it for her. I stand. "I wish you could see the strong, courageous, creative woman I see. I love you, Celeste, but I also know you need to learn to love yourself before you can believe that."

"Hayden—"

I pause, waiting for I don't know what. A promise? A reciprocation? I put my heart out there for everyone to see, and she's too scared to catch it. "Take care of yourself, Ladybird." Turning, I walk away with even heavier steps than I arrived with. My sisters watch me with long faces as I gather my crap and nod my goodbyes. I can't be here anymore. I need a break from Salmon Bay and the memories of Celeste that haunt these streets.

Maybe my dad was right, I'm too sensitive. Maybe my gramps was right, I'm too idealistic. Maybe my editor is right, and I need to get the hell out of this town and see the world so I can write about my own adventures. I bet Molly can take care of Mom now that the boys are older. She hardly needs me to babysit, and it's not like we don't have three other sisters to help shoulder the load.

Right now, I need to give myself space and time. Deep in my soul, I know Celeste will always be the one that got away. She's that sweeping emotion that I was looking for, the grand affair that poets write about, but turns out, I don't want the up and down and drama of a mad affair. That's not sustainable. I want slow mornings doing crosswords over coffee. Walks along the beach together holding hands, not talking if that's what we feel like, with the warm silence of two people who don't need to fill the space with words. I want to cook for her as we laugh about our days, to cuddle on the couch and watch Downton Abbey or Bridgerton, to fall asleep wrapped in each other's arms after I've plowed her into the mattress.

Not a flashy love, but a lasting love.

Not a sprint, but a marathon.

I want so much more, but I know one thing: I love myself enough to hold this boundary. Celeste needs to decide for herself if she can take a chance on us. I can't do this rollercoaster anymore.

42

CELESTE

I'M KNEE DEEP IN OFFER LETTERS when I get a call from Dr. Fisher. His name, followed by a caller ID for the Salmon Bay Department of Parks and Rec, flashes on my screen. I rub the bridge of my nose to stop the tension headache that's building. What now? Is he going to tell me that he's changing the public court rules to be pickleball only?

I answer. "Celeste speaking."

"This is Dr. Fisher from the Salmon Bay Parks and Rec." We make small talk, until he tells me something that has my breath catch in my throat, and a sob leak out.

"Thank you, sir. I'm so appreciative."

"Your boyfriend did a good job advocating for it. Thank him, not me."

"I will." I hang up, still feeling awash in regret for the way I killed our relationship before it could hurt me more. He didn't tell me about this plan either. Why? I could have helped. It's so sweet, better than roses or chocolate. Hayden was working on this long before we knew the outcome of the tournament. For me. He doesn't even play tennis, so it was all for me.

Not ten minutes pass before I've got another phone call. Carolinda Lykke, the Grand Marshal of the Syttende Mai

Parade and Commissioner of the Salmon Bay SummerFest, calls to ask me about my new business venture. At first I think Marissa must have pitched her on the idea, but she sets me straight.

"I got your name from my dear friend's grandson, Hayden Holstrom. Such a sweet boy. He's very keen on your plan, and to be honest, I see a need. Salmon Bay is aging, dear. We need more services that connect our community, and not just a festival or parade. Not window dressing. We need something that meets people where they are—old people, young people— and draws them together. I'm an idea woman, myself, but I need a project manager. I need someone to get the houses in shape."

"I'm interested," I tell her.

"I like the cut of your gib, girl." And she proceeds to tell me her plan to connect aging residents with college students or young twenty-somethings to live together. The residents get companionship and help around the house—allowing them to stay in their homes longer and providing social connection. The young adults get mentorship and free housing in a difficult market. The model has been successful in Japan, and she wants to bring it to Salmon Bay. My business would focus on home improvements to make them ADA compliant and easier to care for. I'd assemble a team of reliable, female technicians, plumbers, and carpenters to work with residents.

I immediately think of Frida and tell Carolinda about her. She could be our first case study. So much hope fills my chest, I think it's going to come bursting out of me in dazzling color.

Hayden did this. He believed in me from the beginning.

I don't know whether to laugh or cry, but I know I messed up, and I need to beg him for another chance. *Don't give up on me*, I need to beg him. *I'm scared, but I'm willing to take the risk now. I want to make this work. You're worth it. I'm worth it.*

I just have to figure out the perfect grand gesture to tell him, and the whole town, that I'm all in.

43

HAYDEN

My suitcase weights as much as one of my nieces, but I couldn't decide which books I might need on my trip. Am I going to do the research for the new project my editor approved? Or am I going to hide away in the cabin rereading *The Time Traveler's Wife* and crying into my Cherry Garcia? If I don't bring the reference books, I'm going to itch to pour over them while I'm away. If I lug them all the way out to Kalaloch, I might not read them, but I can use them for weight training.

I hired Molly's boys to plant-sit for me while I'm gone. They were only too happy to fleece their uncle for all I'm worth. Molly promised to check in on my babies to make sure the boys are doing their job, and I left detailed instructions for feeding Seymour. Hope August isn't too smokey from wildfires this summer, because I'm not coming back until time has superglued the crack in my left ventricle back together.

Pausing outside Miel Bagels, I have to clear the clog in my throat. I'll still be able to make crosswords from Kalaloch, but the internet out there is almost non-existent. Henrí said they'd figure something out if I can't make one a week. It almost sounded like he had some interest from a new crossword maker, but that can't be right.

I'm going to miss this place.

Henrí is kneading dough in the open kitchen area when I enter. He nods to me and begins dusting flour off his hands. "You sure you have to go?"

"Gotta go lick my wounds," I tell him. "I'll be back before cross-country practice starts."

He nods and comes around the counter to wrap me in his bear hug. Despite being a former high school football star, he's never been afraid of showing his feelings. Unlike me, I guess. I'm happy to show anything calm and confident, but I protect the soft squishy bits. Who doesn't? Especially when the people who are supposed to love me for who I am reject those parts.

"I've got the new crossword," I tell him as I set down my messenger bag and start to get it out. "Hot off the press."

"I didn't think you'd be able to get it done."

"You're counting on me, yeah? I wouldn't miss it."

Henrí rubs the back of his neck and looks over at the wall, where the weekly crossword has been blown up, printed out, and slapped up. Takes me a moment, but slowly I realize I haven't seen this crossword before.

"What's this?"

Henrí takes a few steps toward it. "This week's crossword."

"But I haven't turned it in yet. I've got it right here—"

He casts me a disappointed look. "You're not the only one who can make a crossword."

I scoff. I'm being replaced? "But I'm the best."

"Didn't say you weren't, but you might want to try this one. See what the competition brings to the table."

"What's this about, Henrí? You're getting rid of me?"

"No, dude." He comes back to me and tries to suffocate me again. "But you've had a lot going on. Just try this one, okay? I'll get you a latte. The cabin isn't going anywhere."

I grumble, but acquiesce, because people are starting to notice and my eyes itch suspiciously. Must be the flour in the air. I'm headed to Whittaker's family cabin; I use it sometimes when I'm on deadline and need to get away from the distractions of the city. Definitely need a distraction right now.

Following Henrí to a table in the back, I notice that quite a few of the patrons are already working on the interloper's crossword. I'm so easily replaced.

"Don't go anywhere," Henrí tells me as he slaps the paper on my table with a grin.

There's a weird prickling at the back of my neck—Spidey senses tingling. I pull a number two pencil out of my bag and study the clues in front of me. It's not too hard—which might be why so many people in the café are actually working on it. The clues are a little clunky, like this puzzle maker is new to creating, but a crossword always sucks me in. My competitive streak is too hard to ignore.

This one has an extra message. Five answers have their letters circled in the grid, and I'm curious enough to skip the first few clues until I get to one of these.

15-Across: "Star Wars" Actor. Six letters long.

Henrí interrupts with two lattes. He folds himself into the chair across from me, which makes it look doll sized, and stares at me while I work.

"What?" I ask.

"Nothing."

"You're acting real sus."

"No, I'm not."

I raise an eyebrow at him.

"Really. I'm watching the master work." He's almost vibrating in his seat.

I turn back to the crossword and the circled answer. Could be HAMILL, FISHER, NEESON, RIDLEY, or more. Even my name, HAYDEN, for the actor who played young Anakin Skywalker.

That prickle on the back of my neck spreads down my spine. "Who clued this?"

He zips his lips.

I need to check the first letter, so I look at *1-Down: "Black Panther" role*, five letters. SHURI? That would make 1-Across start with H. Hamill? Hayden. The cafe noise fades away as every atom of my being alines to solving this puzzle. Do I really want to know what it says?

It's too late, isn't it?

25-Across: Expression of regret. Seven letters.

I regret hurting Celeste's feelings, even unintentionally. Regret making her feel less-than, when she's everything.

43-Across: Relationship milestone declaration.

I swallow down the ghost of the words that already left my tongue. Doesn't matter if I never say them again. The heart wants what the heart wants. How are words to compete?

"Are you gonna do all of them, or skip to the good parts?" Henrí asks.

"Should I finish this later? I should. I should get on the road before traffic gets bad." My heart is thumping a mile a minute, and it feels like everyone in the coffee shop is watching me. My heartache is a billboard for everyone to laugh at. Exactly what I've avoided for so long by keeping my identity a secret. I make to stand and Henrí thumps his big paw down on my shoulder to stop me.

"You're not leaving until you solve that," he growls.

"Woah, dude. Who turned you on Beast Mode?"

He lets go of me and crosses his beefy arms over his chest. "You can thank me later."

"What if I prefer to cut my gizzard out in private?"

"Stop being a drama queen and finish the damn puzzle."

"I'll tell Molly—"

"Molly will whoop your ass if you don't finish that right this second. The whole town is invested in this now. You can't shove the genie back into the bottle."

My knees melt under me, and I sit. I'll come back to the rest of the clues. Lady Lovelorn's plea is too obviously meant for me, and I'd be a fool to ignore it.

55-Across: "Absolutely!". Seven letters.

The crossword comes to life before my brain can compute what I'm seeing.

HAYDEN

IMSORRY

ILOVEYOU

FORSURE

BEMINE

A wash of cold, then heat, travels down my body and into my toes. I spear Henrí with my eyes. He's grinning like a loon. "Celeste wrote this."

He nods.

"Everyone in town will know now."

He sets his elbow on the table and rests his chin in his hand, batting his eyelashes like he's a Disney princess.

"Did you put her up to this?"

"Hell, no. This was all her idea. She approached me." He pulls an envelope out of his apron pocket and slides it across the table.

Holding my breath, I open it up and pull out the note paper decorated with watercolor monstera.

Lake Dibble, court #1.

I lick my lips. My throat is tight. My shy girl is putting everything out there for the whole town to see. She's *sorry*. She *loves* me.

SHE LOVES ME.

"Well?" Henrí thumps his big hand on the table. "What are you waiting for? Go get your girl."

I don't need to be told twice. With shaking legs, I rise and move toward the door. Dimly I realize that people are staring. Pointing. Clapping.

"Go get her, Hayden!"

"Atta boy!"

"So sweet!"

My feet move faster, imaginary wings giving me the speed of

Mercury as I find my way down the street to the courts at Lake Dibble. There are signs lining the pathway, each with an arrow and a crossword-type clue on it. I don't stop to solve every one of them, but the ones that register are all about the number two —second chances. She doesn't need to ask me twice.

Just as I reach the gate to the court, music turns on: Fools Rush In by Elvis. Inside, there's a crowd. My sisters are there. My mom. Nieces and nephews. Neighbors. All our Pickleball friends. Even Warren. They all cheer when I step through the gate, but I only have eyes for the woman standing in the middle, holding a pickleball paddle and a ball.

"Hayden Holstrom," she calls. She's wearing a cute new tennis dress in light pink. Her creamy thighs are thick, and I want to pry them open and wrap them around my head. Her hand flexes around the paddle handle, sending indecent thoughts through my brain of her hand fisted around something else. This woman. "I challenge you to a match. Winner gets a prize of their choosing."

"Is that right?"

"You bet your cute butt it is."

My lips kick up at the corners. "A bet. You know I can't turn down a bet."

"Don't be a chicken, Hay-Hay. Cluck, cluck!"

"Bring it, sweetheart." I accept my paddle from Molly, who must have let herself into my apartment to pick it up on the way here. I'm surprised my sisters didn't spill the beans. How long has Celeste been planning this?

"Zero-Zero, Love" Celeste says as she readies to serve. "There is no love in pickleball, but I found you." She hits the ball over the net, but her words make my reaction slow. I fumble the ball, and she scores. She grins at me. "Goody. I can't wait for my prize."

"What are you going to ask for if you win?"

"Everything."

I raise my eyebrows. "No pressure."

"One-Zero."

This time I return the serve, and she parries it back. Do I want to win? Or am I more curious about what "everything" means to her? The audience is rapt. Warren starts telling me to show up, and his wife tells him to sit down. My sisters cheer Celeste on and trash talk me. Figures.

"You've been practicing," I say, when I finally get control of the ball and set up for my serve.

"Turns out I have a good thing going," she tells me. "I'm going to hold on to it and show up every day." Her chocolate eyes flash at me, and I know she's talking about more than the game.

"Not going to let trying something new scare you off?"

"Naw. I'm done being afraid. There's no way back to that person I was before Brett, Tennis or no. I wouldn't want to be her even if I could."

"I happen to be very fond of this version of you."

"Yeah?"

I give her a faint smile. "You're pretty perfect for me. I wouldn't change you one bit."

"You're pretty perfect for me too, Hayden." Celeste moves toward the kitchen, where we dink the ball back and forth. "Too perfect, but I'm done holding myself back because I don't think I deserve good things. I'm ready to seize what brings me joy."

"Is that right?"

"Yeah, cute butt. And you're it."

I let the next ball go, giving away a point for my beautiful opponent. "Oops."

She shakes her head as the audience cat calls. "You don't have to go easy on me. I'm tough enough to beat you at your own game."

"Never doubted it for a minute. You're fierce."

She gets the ball and suddenly all her focus is on scoring. She's a shark. I try hitting to her backhand; she slices it back to the opposite corner. I try landing it at her feet; she scoops the ball and returns it to the far corner of my side of the court. Perfect placement.

"You're not holding back anymore," I say after I stop to collect a ball she put past me.

"No, I'm fighting for what I want. This isn't a game. This is life or death."

The bruised organ in my chest is flipping, but I'm still wary that all of me isn't what she wants. The real me, with all the awkward bits. All the parts that don't fit the narrative of dominant, emotionally reticent, red-blooded American manhood. All the parts of me that don't fit the stereotypical characteristics that my dad and grandpa value, but I don't.

I'm not going to pretend to be something I'm not. I'm going to continue to model the character traits I want my nephews to embrace—all the sensitive, creative, kind, nerdy, and imaginative parts.

I catch the ball midair, the need to speak overwhelming my need to win the bet. "Celeste." I approach the net, stepping right in the kitchen. "I need to know you're not going to run away again. My heart can't take it. If I let you in, I need to know you're not easy to scare off."

"I won't, Hayden. You didn't scare me. I scared myself, because I knew from the start it would be so easy to fall for you. I wasn't sure I could stand up for myself, be myself, without falling into all the bad patterns of my past. You never made me feel small, but my first response is still to fawn."

"I need you to give me the benefit of the doubt. I was trying to find a good time to tell you everything, but I didn't want to overwhelm you. I was trying not to scare you off."

She rests her hand over mine where I've placed it on the net. Her fingers squeeze gently. "I'm so sorry. You deserve to be loved unconditionally, and I do. I love you. I love the way you name all your plants and treat them like people. I love the way you make living playful, fun. The silliness and the banter, the courage to try new things and not take life so seriously. I love the way you take care of your family and the way you're so involved with your nieces and nephews. I love the way you pull people together to build community bonds; you're so accepting and encouraging."

"And sexy as fuck?"

She laughs, and that sound is like a jump start to my poor abused heart.

"Even the first time I saw you, when that hideous giant mustache blocked your handsome face, I was attracted to you. Your soul shines brightly, Hayden. I was in a dark place, and you broke through the clouds like my own personal ray of sunshine."

"I thought you were going to say like an alien tractor beam."

She grins, full and wide, all bright white teeth and laugh lines around her beautiful caramel eyes.

Our friends and family surrounding us start yelling suggestions.

"Finish the game!"

"Kiss her already!"

"Get a room!"

I'm not above taking good advice when I hear it. Reaching across the net, I pick her up and pull her into my arms. I plant a big claiming kiss on her lips, and the crowd goes wild. Her arms come around me and squeeze, letting me know she's exactly where she wants to be.

"My brave woman," I say huskily. "You hate attention, but here you are declaring your heart in front of a crowd."

"I needed to show you I mean business."

I chuckle. "I believe it, boss girl. But what would you have done if I hadn't stopped by the café before heading out of town? What if I hadn't let Henrí convince me to finish that imposter's crossword? What if—?"

She shuts me up with another kiss before pulling back. "I

knew you wouldn't let Henrí down when he was expecting your next crossword, and I knew you wouldn't be able to turn down a dare. You're loyal to a fault and charmingly competitive. I love that about you. I know you, Hayden. I see you."

"You're saying I'm predictable, huh?"

"Predictably rational in your behavior. Predictably loyal to your friends and family. Predictably able to make even grumpy middle-aged ladies laugh with your off-the-wall and unpredictable humor."

"Grumpy? You?" I shake my head even as I feather kisses along her eyelids and down her nose. "Not my Celeste. You're just a little shy. That's not the same thing at all."

"You'd know, Lord Lexicon."

"That's right. I would. Don't doubt me, gorgeous. I know what I'm talking about."

Her smile is all the sunshine I need.

"You want to finish this match?"

She shakes her head. "I already won. I have everything I want right here."

My nose prickles as emotion rises up like the tide. This woman. My woman. "Let's go home then, babe, and I'll show you how much I like playing doubles with you."

"You wanna dink?"

I laugh, and it makes the tears spill over. I have to blink hard to hold them back. "Yeah, babe. If that's part of your definition of everything, I definitely want to do that."

"*Mais, oui*, my handsome candlestick."

I set her down and check in to make sure dismissing the audience is okay with her. "You didn't have any other surprises to spring on our unsuspecting friends?"

She winks at me. "Not this time, handsome." She turns to our community and clears her throat. "Thank you for helping me show the sweetest, smartest, kindest man I've ever met how much I want to be his doubles partner in every part of my life."

The crowd is laughing and cheering. My sisters wipe away

happy tears, all except Addy who smirks at me. *Goodbye freedom*, she mouths.

I touch two fingers to my forehead in a salute. *Farewell, spinster.*

She rolls her eyes.

Pulling Celeste into my chest, because I can't stand not to be touching her now that I know she's mine, I raise my voice. "I am so grateful you all showed up today. I look forward to beating some of you next week back here on the court, or, if you're family, catching up sometime next year—"

Ethan hollers, "Does this mean you're finally moving out of your mom's garage?" and Molly pats him on the back to peals of laughter.

"No, dearest nephew. Get ready to run laps at six thirty, Monday morning." He pouts good-naturedly. "But I'm going to take the weekend and whisk away my beautiful partner to finish this match without an audience."

More catcalls and whistles meet this pronouncement, and we are pushed off the court to a flurry of pickleballs. Everyone in the crowd had one tucked away, and they throw them in the air like rice. I laugh and cover Celeste's head.

"Guess that idea sounded better in my head," she says sheepishly as we dodge balls raining down, the *tuk-tuk-tuk* loud against the asphalt.

"Good thing we don't play tennis," I say.

She playfully whacks me on the arm. "You should be so lucky."

"Or bowling."

The short drive to my house is agony. We can't stop touching, kissing, holding tight to what we almost lost. She can't go back after announcing to the whole town and all our friends and family that she loves me. Or, at least, she can't go back and still live in Salmon Bay. This is a big commitment.

"You announced to the whole town that you're mine."

"Yup." She squeezes my hand.

There are butterflies in my stomach. I always thought that was a tired metaphor, but it's so apt. "You can't take that back."

"I'm not going to. You make me happy, Hayden. You make me feel so lucky to be alive. I can't let fear keep us apart anymore. I don't care if you're too hot and too young and too good for me. I want you, and as long as you'll have me, I'm going to take you."

"Goddamnit. Don't say crap about yourself like that. I'm going to spend the rest of forever proving to you how gorgeous, sexy, smart, and amazing you are. You're who I want, Celeste. Not anyone else.

"Then take me."

We get to my apartment, and I do just that. Quick and demanding gives way to slow and steady, showing her how good it can be. How good it will be now that we're not hiding anymore.

A Declaration
by Lady Lovelorn

 **Miel Bagels** - *Sweeten your day the Montréal way*

ACROSS

1 Sounds heard at La Tomatina, the world's biggest food fight
7 Slightly open
11 "Eat, Pray, Love" setting
15 "Star Wars" actor
16 It's a long story, really
17 It might spell doom
18 Like leftover contents of the lost-and-found bin

DOWN

1 "Black Panther" role
2 First airline to fly worldwide
3 Ancient Greek instruments
4 Ending to block or char
5 Gumshoe, quaintly
6 68-Down show: Abbr.
7 Laos locale
8 Door frame
9 Era
10 Walkie-talkie

ACROSS

20 Inclination
21 Carly ___ Jepsen, singer-songwriter
22 Catch
23 "Oh yeah? Just watch me!"
25 Expression of regret
29 Typical shoe insert
30 Last name for 14.7% of South Korea
31 "This American Life" broadcaster
33 Cat calls
37 Butt hurt, say?
41 Couples
42 MAX television
43 Relationship milestone declaration
45 ___-Manuel Miranda, playwright
46 Quarrel
48 Future and Common, e.g.
50 Pants
51 Allows
52 Stage scenery and props
53 Promises
55 "Absolutely!"
59 "Red Rocks" city in Arizona
62 Prohibit
64 UK healthcare system
65 Leave out intentionally
66 Making it onto the Billboard charts, say
71 Buggy spot?
72 Answering machine sound
73 Valentine's Day sentiment
74 Requests
75 Hurricane centers
76 88% of bronze

DOWN

11 Drink sometimes served with cheese foam
12 Word of affirmation
13 Middle of a bull's eye?
14 Enthusiastic about
19 At all
24 Apple device, e.g.
26 Elderly
27 Has faith in
28 Stagger
29 Norse goddess of love
31 Tennis player Djokovic
32 Gets ready, briefly
34 Van Gogh medium
35 Court order
36 W-2 IDs
37 See 62-Down
38 Magical beginning
39 Pointers, e.g.
40 Palindromic billionaire
44 More or less
47 Reddit "likes"
49 TGIF bit
54 Squander
55 TGIF bit
56 Square
57 Cologne is right next to it
58 Perfume compound
59 California pop
60 Flightless birds
61 Soft shot in pickleball
62 See 37-Down
63 Mars, in Greece
67 Demure, and possibly mindful
68 6-Down network
69 Logical opener?
70 Axe booster, for short

44

EPILOGUE: CELESTE

ONE YEAR LATER.

"HONEY, HAVE YOU SEEN MY MEASURING TAPE?"

"You don't need tape, darling. It's ten inches and hard as steel," Hayden calls back from the bedroom. "Come back here and let me show you."

I roll my eyes. "We're stopping by the new project on the way back from pickleball. I need that measuring tape to start planning out the new design. Raina is going to meet us there to discuss plumbing."

"Is she bringing the kid?"

"You want to hold her baby so the boss ladies can talk?"

"I know my place is eye candy and holding a baby increases my rizz."

I laugh and shake my head. I finally gave up my apartment when the lease expired, but I had been effectively living with Hayden since I announced to all and sundry my intentions. I've shown up. I've faced down my fears. I've given Hayden the benefit of the doubt, because he's nothing like my ex. He's the sweetest guy I've ever met, and though we haven't made it official in the eyes of God and the government yet, our relationship is as serious as it gets.

We even adopted a baby together—a fourteen-pound mutt from the Salmon Bay Animal shelter that was in serious need of a forever home. We're it. Pickles is like his namesake—a Frankenstein of different breeds mixed together into an insanely joyful puddle of fluff. Addy moved back to town, opened a small business, and adopted all the toxic plants to decorate her new store. We still have quite a few, including Seymour, but none that could hurt our pup.

A year ago, I couldn't imagine what happy would look like.

Now, I couldn't imagine a different path where I didn't wake up every day next to a smiling, handsome, creative man who makes me feel like a goddess.

He's encouraged me on my new business venture, and I've already hired a small team of craftspeople. Our business is split between helping Marissa's elderly clients update their homes for sale and renovating homes for aging in place with Carolinda's Lykke Foundation. Carolinda's program has some complicated Scandinavian name, but people are already referring to it as "Rent-A-Granny". They've placed a dozen young twenty-somethings in homes with older Salmon Bay residents, and the program is making waves. Molly took pictures for a big spread in Sunrise Magazine that was reprinted in newspapers in Minneapolis and Stockholm. The Swedish consulate in Seattle even reached out to Carolinda about bringing young exchange students from Sweden to live in Salmon Bay while they study at the UW.

I love my new job. I'm putting good into the world. I get to be my own boss and make my own schedule. I'm flexing my creative muscle and working with my hands—and I'm damn good at it.

I take a glass from the cabinet and pour myself some water from the filter on the fridge. The stainless-steel front is covered with wedding and baby announcements from all the friends we've made playing pickleball, but my favorites are the postcards from Frida. She thought she would get a young guy to move in with her, but then she met a Silver Daddy on the pickleball court and took off with him on an around-the-world sailboat tour. At every port, she sends me another snapshot of her life. I'm so happy for her.

"Babe," Hayden calls. "Come back to bed."

"You've already been up and run six miles," I point out. "You could have stayed in bed cuddling."

"What would be the point of that? I know you love these cheese grater abs."

"I love you, no matter what you look like,

He huffs good-naturedly and sashays out of the bedroom in only his tight, wool boxer briefs that cling to his cute ass and hard bulge. "Looking for this?" He holds up the tape measure and grins wickedly at me. "It's gonna cost you."

"Is that right?"

"Yeah, babe. I need a taste before my boss lady goes out to kick ass and take names."

"Have you been good?"

"Very."

Setting down my glass of water, I drop my hip and saunter toward him, only too happy to give into this playfulness that Hayden brings to everything he does. I spent decades without play, and now I can't get enough. "Drop to your knees," I order.

He is quick to grin. We don't have labels for what we like, because they're limiting. Instead, we take turns leading the role play. Sometimes Hayden likes me to be the boss lady. Sometimes I like him to tie me up. Whatever we do, it's full of joy and lightheartedness that was missing from my experience.

"Yes, ma'am," he says as he drops to the floor. I step out of reach of his long arms, and he pouts.

"Feisty already, are we?"

"Am I on the naughty list?"

"Crawl to me."

He is too happy to oblige and grabs my hips when he can reach. "Let me make it up to you, Queenie. Let me taste this fine pussy and come on my tongue."

I giggle. "I've got work."

"I'll be fast." He tugs me closer by the waistband until he can bury his face against my mound. His hot breath sends shivers over my skin. "Time me."

I laugh but dutifully check my watch. "My illicit candlestick has turned into a stuffy grandfather clock."

"Yeah? Well, I can still wind your chain, little missy." He swats me on the ass, and I shriek a laugh as he catches me behind the knees and sweeps me off my feet onto the floor, catching my weight so that I fall gently on the rug. I'm laughing too hard at his affronted face, as he pulls up my shirt and puts a big old raspberry on my belly.

A year ago, I would have been totally self-conscious about attention to my midsection, but Hayden has made no secret how much he loves every soft, squishy part of me. He loves me, exactly as I am.

Pickles loves it when we roughhouse like this, and she barks happily while jumping around and over us.

"Get a dog, she said. It'll be well trained, she said." Hayden kisses down my belly and pulls my leggings down with his teeth until my pussy is exposed. "Can't cuddle a plant, she said, but at least Seymour never tried to interrupt sexy time."

I swat his head playfully. "You love Pickles."

"That's a good boy," Hayden coos at the dog. He's absolutely in love with our fur-baby. He takes him running every morning and throws balls at the park with him every afternoon. Pickles joins us at the Pickleball courts, where he's made friends with TopDog and Fred and Ginger.

"Now be a good boy and scram while mommy and daddy play doctor."

"You're going to scar him for life."

"Too late." Hayden dives in between my thighs, and as

predicted, he makes it fast and furious and fantastic. He knows my body like his own and can make me come faster than I can myself.

"I love you," I say, when we lay breathless and panting on the floor, the dog having finally given up and curled beneath a nearby chair to send moony eyes at us.

"I love you to the moon and back," Hayden says. "You go get 'em, boss lady. I've got a spicy scene to write." He's been churning out pages and his editor loves every word of them. Turns out being in love is great inspiration for a romance writer. Last week he hit a best seller list, and we celebrated with a whale watching tour around Puget Sound, followed by a very thorough canoodling in the long dune grass by the beach.

"Is Colonel Mustard going to seduce Miss Scarlet in the Conservatory with the Candlestick?" I ask him.

"You know it, babe." He plants a kiss on my lips, and I stretch like a cat in the sun.

"You're perfect."

"Only for you. You make me believe in magic. Now go do your thing, then come home and let's finish this discussion."

"Yes, please."

I know I'm the happiest woman in the world.

———

ACKNOWLEDGMENTS

THANK YOU, DEAREST READER, for reading LOVE AND PICKLEBALL! If you enjoyed this book, please share a review online. It really helps indie authors! Please tell your friends and ask your local library to stock the print and ebooks—word of mouth is the best way to get more stories like this coming. Merci beaucoup!

Deeply grateful to my friend Scott for creating all the crosswords for this book, for pickleball ideas and blocking, and for formatting and design help! I can't thank you enough. This book wouldn't be the same without your hours of work. I appreciate you!

Thanks to Joy Adare and Anna Richland for keeping me on track and holding my hand as I got back into writing after a long break. Thanks to my wonderful editor Susan for coaching me through these labor pains. It's a better book because of you!

Huge appreciation for my family for making this possible, for reading many drafts (especially my mom!), and cheering me on—I couldn't do it without you! Love you forever. Xoxo

ABOUT THE AUTHOR

KIRA BRADY is an award-winning author of paranormal and contemporary romance. Her debut, HEARTS OF DARKNESS, was named one of the Best Books of Summer 2012 by Publishers Weekly, which called it, "Dazzling...thrilling... irresistible."

Kira grew up in a small Scandinavian town on the shores of Puget Sound, where she fell in love with cardamon braid and Kringle. LOVE AND PICKLEBALL is the first book in the Salmon Bay series, interconnected, sweetly-spicy, humorous, sport romances set in a cozy, Scandinavian town in the Pacific Northwest.

When not writing, Kira loves reading, hiking, pottery, knitting, learning to play pickleball, and spending time with her family. She loves hearing from readers!

Let's connect:

- Website: kirabrady.com
- Newsletter: subscribepage.io/kirabrady
- Social Media: kirabrady.com/links

CROSSWORD ANSWER KEYS

Mature Professions

Lord Lexicon

ACROSS

1 What a baker has?
10 Singer-songwriter Bareilles
14 Bulletins
16 Greek god of love
17 What a mailman has?
18 Gremlins and Hornets of automotive history
19 Really old letters?
20 In jeopardy
22 Wise old goat in "Animal Farm"
25 Words before "coming" or "so good"
26 Egret cousin
27 What a grocer has?
30 Website where you'll see stars
31 Style
32 Many crossword clues... and a hint to 1-,17-,27-,41-,54-, and 63-Across
39 Billionaire with a book club
40 Duchamp's art movement
41 What a diver has?
45 Piquant
46 Novel
47 Dr. Jekyll's counterpart
49 Traditional handmade toy
52 Lingus beginning
53 Stick in the mud, say
54 What a farmer has?
60 Member
61 "Why didn't I think of that?!"
62 Mexican dough?
63 What a butcher has?

DOWN

1 Jibber-jabber
2 Dictator Amin portrayed by Forest Whitaker
3 Mean number: Abbr.
4 Spoonful
5 LAX carry-on container
6 Bowling in Bergamo
7 "Family Matters" nerd
8 "The Marvels" director DaCosta
9 Sonic creator
10 Northwest airport named for two nearby cities
11 Fleet of warships
12 "Dick Clark's New Year's ___ Eve"
13 Strengths
15 Stand-up routine
21 Soft luster
22 It's out of office
23 Pakistan's official language
24 Stark in "Game of Thrones"
26 Tucked away
27 Grannies
28 Narrow strip of land: Abbr.
29 Brain disease for many ex-NFL players: Abbr.
31 Word
33 "Ha ha, yeah right", in a text
34 Clean Air Act govt. org.
35 Critical WWII event
36 Shoe part above the sole
37 Barely triumph over
38 "So, here's a thought..."
41 Stretch
42 "Seinfeld" role
43 River in the Middle East
44 Give up ownership of
45 Beat the wheat, in a way
47 First lady before Jackie
48 Romulus' twin
50 "Come on!" in online shorthand
51 Shakespearean "happily"
55 Vacay, initially
56 DMV-provided ID
57 Vehicular prefix to meter
58 IBM competitor
59 Hefty Cinch ending

Grid answers:

G	I	A	N	T	B	U	N	S	■	S	A	R	A
A	D	V	I	S	O	R	I	E	S	■	E	R	O	S
B	I	G	P	A	C	K	A	G	E	■	A	M	C	S
■	■	■	B	C	E	■	A	T	S	T	A	K	E
■	■	M	U	R	I	E	L	■	H	A	D	I	T
H	E	R	O	N	■	N	I	C	E	C	A	N	S
I	M	D	B	■	T	A	S	T	E	■
D	O	U	B	L	E	E	N	T	E	N	D	R	E	S
■	O	P	R	A	H	■	D	A	D	A
W	E	T	C	L	A	M	S	■	T	A	N	G	Y
A	L	I	E	N	■	M	R	H	Y	D	E
R	A	G	D	O	L	L	■	A	E	R
M	I	R	E	■	F	I	R	M	M	E	L	O	N	S
U	N	I	T	■	G	E	N	I	U	S	I	D	E	A
P	E	S	O	■	F	R	E	S	H	C	O	C	K

Love Is a Game for Two

Lord Lexicon

ACROSS

1 Def predecessor
4 Winding
11 One millionth of a gram: Abbr.
14 Words before a fresh start
17 Words for bending the rules
18 "Smol" yowl
19 Trouble
20 Objects once burned for loved ones, briefly
21 Big hotel waiter?
22 49-Across skill
24 Actress Thurman
27 Brand with a butterfly logo
29 Legal org. founded in 1878
30 "Let's settle this!"
32 Bedazzle
33 Nip
34 Concisely
35 Dorm supervisors: Abbr.
36 Senior worries, briefly
38 Happy-hour seat
39 Bed buildup
40 First class, briefly?
41 Lustful
42 Cut
43 TV spot seller
45 Post-WWII treaty grp.
46 Stark in "Game of Thrones"
47 Like one just out of the shower
49 22-Across expert
50 Time for a booty call?
54 Roman magistrate
58 Words to start a relationship
60 Words to end a tennis match
61 Parched
62 Savvy
63 "How Do I Love Thee?", for example

DOWN

1 Inedible type of candy
2 Enterprise entrance
3 Baker's mixture
4 "ttyl" response
5 Confess, with up
6 "Yeah, there's a noise"
7 LPGA golfer Thompson
8 Affirmative additions
9 Bill devoted to science
10 Lincoln's party, in brief
11 Robin Hood's lady love
12 Pedestrian paths
13 Lead-in to X, Y, or Z
15 Morning moisture
16 Global time standard: Abbr.
21 Himalayan retreat?
22 One on a beat
23 Scam with a fake email
25 Ecstasy, slangily
26 Even one
28 Arizona competitor
31 Actress Birch of "Ghost World"
37 Sharply criticized
39 Atlas page for the United States
44 Sly looks
46 Blarney
48 Yarns
49 Weather away
50 Rapper in the press for dating Kylie Jenner
51 Feathery type of frost
52 Widely read Persian poet
53 Love of one's life
54 Inks
55 Latin jazz bandleader Puente
56 One time only
57 Former NPR host Diane
59 Loo

Grid solution:

1	2	3		4	5	6	7	8	9	10		11	12	13
A	B	C		C	O	I	L	I	N	G		M	C	G
R	E	A	D	Y	W	H	E	N	Y	O	U	A	R	E
M	A	K	E	A	N	E	X	C	E	P	T	I	O	N
	M	E	W		A	I	L		C	D	S			
C	A	B		C	P	R		U	M	A		M	S	N
A	B	A		O	H	I	T	S	O	N		A	W	E
T	O	T		P	I	T	H	I	L	Y		R	A	S
S	A	T	S		S	T	O	O	L		S	I	L	T
P	R	E	K		H	O	R	N	Y		T	A	K	E
A	D	R	E	P		O	A	S		S	A	N	S	A
			W	E	T				E	M	T			
T	H	R	E	E	A	M		P	R	A	E	T	O	R
Y	O	U	R	P	L	A	C	E	O	R	M	I	N	E
G	A	M	E	S	E	T	A	N	D	M	A	T	C	H
A	R	I	D		S	E	N	S	E		P	O	E	M

Physical Activities

Lord Lexicon

ACROSS

1 Minor celebs
6 Agreement
10 Price tag disclaimer
14 Expensive pillow fill
15 They're in the rights business, in brief?
16 In check, with "up"
17 Trouble that leaves you breathless
18 *Errors abound with balls at this spot (in baseball)
20 Cry before "No hands!"
22 Heroine of Jane Austen
23 Extra-small cat call
24 Round initial fig.
25 "Injured playing peekaboo? Go to the ICU", et al.
27 Eurasian UN member, once
30 *Cleans up, as with a ball next to a hole (in golf)
33 Easter Bunny bounce
34 Luau fish option
35 Encouraging expression
38 Some woodwinds
41 Traditional romance novel ending, for short
43 Establish
44 Promiscuous woman, once
46 "Larry King Live" broadcaster
48 Evian, par exemple
49 *Athlete possibly subject to illegal touching (in football)
51 Story lines
52 Espadrille linings
54 Start of MGM's motto
56 Angry crowd
57 You'll see Moscato here
59 Yodeling country by l'Italie
63 Exploit the rules... and a hint for 18-,30-, and 49-Across
66 Stock
67 Late co-founder of Reader's Digest, ___ Wallace
68 Entertaining entanglement
69 Thin-stemmed mushroom
70 Squawk
71 Length of a bridge
72 Erudite figures

DOWN

1 "Very good - Agreed!"
2 Exercise alternative that sucks?
3 License fig.
4 Usually one who's it
5 Prague people movers
6 One is often on the back
7 Unbearable yearning
8 Routes going right to the top
9 Disorder
10 Officer radio alert, briefly
11 Underwater terror
12 Blown-up region?
13 Leftover dishes, often
19 Edmond ___, the fictional Count of Monte Cristo
21 Slangy start of some encouragement
26 Greenhouse pest
27 Apprehensive comment
28 Mentsuyu go-with
29 Easy-breezy term for athletics
31 "Wowww...that feels good"
32 It's something to say
36 Taco topper, slangily
37 Haydn number
39 Theatrical 2025 film from Pixar
40 "Happy to hear it!"
42 Imaginary Taylor, of clothes
45 Series of video games that has sold 200+ million copies
47 Documents demanding confidentiality: Abbr.
50 It's just over a foot?
51 Airline based in Seoul
52 Get at
53 "Oh really?"
55 Nitwits
58 Ancient Mayan site Chichen ___
60 Lock lips, in London
61 Teriyaki tipple, theoretically
62 Every class at Yale
64 Xanthan gum goes in it, slangily
65 Tokyo bread

Solution Grid

D	L	I	S	T		P	A	C	T		A	S	I	S
E	I	D	E	R		A	C	L	U		P	E	N	T
A	P	N	E	A		T	H	I	R	D	B	A	S	E
L	O	O	K	M	A		E	M	M	A		M	E	W
		E	S	T		B	O	N	M	O	T	S		
U	S	S	R		T	A	P	S	I	T	I	N		
H	O	P		A	H	I		L	E	T	S	G	O	
O	B	O	E	S		H	E	A		S	E	T	U	P
H	A	R	L	O	T		C	N	N		E	A	U	
	T	I	G	H	T	E	N	D		A	R	C	S	
I	N	S	O	L	E	S		A	R	S				
M	O	B		A	S	T	I		S	U	I	S	S	E
P	L	A	Y	D	I	R	T	Y		B	A	N	A	L
L	I	L	A		M	A	Z	E		E	N	O	K	I
Y	E	L	P		S	P	A	N		S	A	G	E	S

Summer Sports Event

Lord Lexicon

ACROSS

1 Pertaining to Robert Francis Prevost
6 Get steamy
11 Hat of Disney's Aladdin
14 Sherlock's teenage sister
15 "Dancing With the Stars" winner Ohno
16 Mendes or Longoria
17 Sauce with one consonant
18 Disposable lunch box?
19 Lasso on Apple TV
20 Dillydallying, and what's happening at the Sea Lion Club this summer
23 Gaucho's cattle-catcher
25 1, 2, 3, 4, and more: Abbr.
26 Vigorous
27 Common baby shower gift
29 Awards won by Caitlin Clark and Simone Biles
32 With 45-Across, the Sea Lion Club sports event of the summer
34 Salmon Bay, for one
38 Spot to get help for a hide-and-seek injury, briefly
39 Canon letters?
40 OPEC member
42 Leader of China until 1976
43 Head, to Henri
45 See 32-Across
48 Fudged
50 Fur wraps
51 Chocolate essential
54 Boozehound
56 Kiss from a señorita
57 "I won't settle!", and an invitation to the Sea Lion Club this summer
61 Arranged introduction?
62 Ermine, by another name
63 Pool noodles and penne
66 Trouble
67 ___ nous ("between you and me")
68 Site to remember?
69 "New" prefix
70 Distributed cards
71 Wetland wader

DOWN

1 Item that kept a fairy tale princess up all night
2 Singer DiFranco
3 Hairstyle boosted by Lucille Ball
4 "Do this one thing for me"
5 Write : written :: lie : ___
6 Model on 400+ romance novel covers
7 Where you'll find a slow boat to China
8 It's hammered
9 Beauty products brand
10 Badly
11 Womb lodger
12 Big book signing, e.g.
13 Slang for an attractive and confident man
21 Show deference for
22 Depose
23 Frenetic children's toy from Hasbro
24 In cold storage
28 They, in Calais
30 Drunken mumble
31 Has an expectation that one will
33 Penciled facial feature
35 Breakfast buffet station
36 Opposite of waxes
37 "False!"
41 Polish off Polish pierogi, say
44 Internet auctioneer
46 Disentangle
47 Tyranny of the majority?
49 Released, quaintly
51 House network
52 Eagle's nest
53 Green with five Grammy Awards
55 Eight-piece band
58 Magazine that's "A Different Read on Life"
59 Teensy-weensy bit
60 Canyonlands National Park locale
64 Genre for "I Miss You"
65 "Junior" to "Senior"

P	A	P	A	L		F	O	G	U	P		F	E	Z
E	N	O	L	A		A	P	O	L	O		E	V	A
A	I	O	L	I		B	E	N	T	O		T	E	D
		D	I	N	K	I	N	G	A	R	O	U	N	D
B	O	L	A		N	O	S			L	U	S	T	Y
O	N	E	S	I	E		E	S	P	Y	S			
P	I	C	K	L	E	B	A	L	L		T	O	W	N
I	C	U		S	L	R		U	A	E		M	A	O
T	E	T	E		T	O	U	R	N	A	M	E	N	T
			B	L	O	W	N		S	T	O	L	E	S
C	A	C	A	O			S	O	T		B	E	S	O
S	E	E	Y	O	U	I	N	C	O	U	R	T		
P	R	E		S	T	O	A	T		T	U	B	E	S
A	I	L		E	N	T	R	E		A	L	A	M	O
N	E	O		D	E	A	L	T		H	E	R	O	N

A Declaration

Lady Lovelorn

The completed grid (letters):

S	P	L	A	T	S		A	J	A	R		B	A	L	I
H	A	Y	D	E	N		S	A	G	A		O	M	E	N
U	N	R	E	C	L	A	I	M	E	D		B	E	N	T
R	A	E			N	A	B		I	C	A	N	S	O	
I	M	S	O	R	R	Y		F	O	O	T				
		L	E	E		N	P	R		M	E	O	W	S	
S	A	D	D	L	E	S	O	R	E		P	A	I	R	S
H	B	O		I	L	O	V	E	Y	O	U		L	I	N
A	R	G	U	E		R	A	P	A	R	T	I	S	T	S
G	A	S	P	S		O	K	S		S	E	T			
		V	O	W	S			F	O	R	S	U	R	E	
S	E	D	O	N	A		B	A	R			N	H	S	
O	M	I	T		S	C	O	R	I	N	G	A	H	I	T
D	U	N	E		T	O	N	E		B	E	M	I	N	E
A	S	K	S		E	Y	E	S		C	O	P	P	E	R

ACROSS

1 Sounds heard at La Tomatina, the world's biggest food fight
7 Slightly open
11 "Eat, Pray, Love" setting
15 "Star Wars" actor
16 It's a long story, really
17 It might spell doom
18 Like leftover contents of the lost-and-found bin
20 Inclination
21 Carly ___ Jepsen, singer-songwriter
22 Catch
23 "Oh yeah? Just watch me!"
25 Expression of regret
29 Typical shoe insert
30 Last name for 14.7% of South Korea
31 "This American Life" broadcaster
33 Cat calls
37 Butt hurt, say?
41 Couples
42 MAX television
43 Relationship milestone declaration
45 ___-Manuel Miranda, playwright
46 Quarrel
48 Future and Common, e.g.
50 Pants
51 Allows
52 Stage scenery and props
53 Promises
55 "Absolutely!"
59 "Red Rocks" city in Arizona
62 Prohibit
64 UK healthcare system
65 Leave out intentionally
66 Making it onto the Billboard charts, say
71 Buggy spot?
72 Answering machine sound
73 Valentine's Day sentiment
74 Requests
75 Hurricane centers
76 88% of bronze

DOWN

1 "Black Panther" role
2 First airline to fly worldwide
3 Ancient Greek instruments
4 Ending to block or char
5 Gumshoe, quaintly
6 68-Down show: Abbr.
7 Laos locale
8 Door frame
9 Era
10 Walkie-talkie
11 Drink sometimes served with cheese foam
12 Word of affirmation
13 Middle of a bull's eye?
14 Enthusiastic about
19 At all
24 Apple device, e.g.
26 Elderly
27 Has faith in
28 Stagger
29 Norse goddess of love
31 Tennis player Djokovic
32 Gets ready, briefly
34 Van Gogh medium
35 Court order
36 W-2 IDs
37 See 62-Down
38 Magical beginning
39 Pointers, e.g.
40 Palindromic billionaire
44 More or less
47 Reddit "likes"
49 TGIF bit
54 Squander
55 TGIF bit
56 Square
57 Cologne is right next to it
58 Perfume compound
59 California pop
60 Flightless birds
61 Soft shot in pickleball
62 See 37-Down
63 Mars, in Greece
67 Demure, and possibly mindful
68 6-Down network
69 Logical opener?
70 Axe booster, for short

www.ingramcontent.com/pod-product-compliance
Lightning Source LLC
Chambersburg PA
CBHW030221120726
47903CB00005B/1319